BELONGS to S.MEJIAS

Steve's book

110648317

THE
LONESOME
GODS

THE LONESOME GODS

LOUIS L'AMOUR

BANTAM BOOKS
TORONTO · NEW YORK · LONDON · SYDNEY

To the Applebaum boys,
Stuart and Irwyn

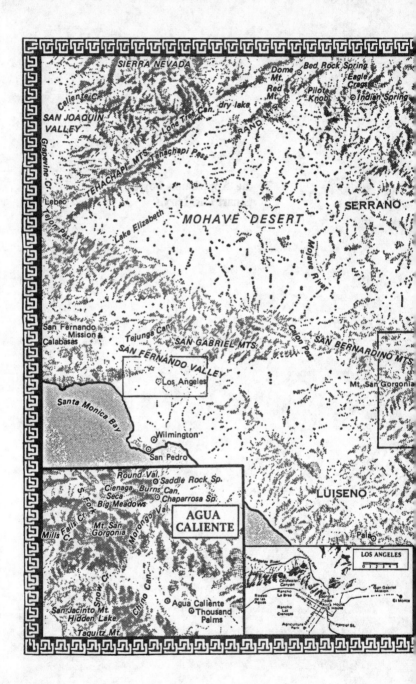

Map by William & Alan McKnight

THE
LONESOME
GODS

1

I sat very still, as befitted a small boy among strangers, staring wide-eyed into a world I did not know.

I was six years old and my father was dying.

Only last year I had lost my mother. She died longing for that far-off, lovely California where she was born, and of which she never tired of talking.

"Warm and sunny," people said when speaking of California, but I knew it as a place where fear lived.

Now we were going there. We were crossing the desert to face that fear, and I was afraid.

My father sat close beside me trying to sleep, but torn occasionally by violent spells of coughing that caused the other passengers to turn their heads, some in pity, some in irritation.

Our wagon, drawn by six half-wild mustangs, plunged into the night, rocking and rumbling over a dim track that only the driver seemed to see. Ours was a desperate venture, a lone wagon with two outriders attempting the crossing from Santa Fe to California.

Lying awake in the darkness, I remembered what people in Santa Fe had said. "It's a crazy idea! One wagon? Even if they can slip by the Apaches, the Yumas will be waiting at the crossing of the Colorado."

"Remember what happened to that last outfit? The Yumas agreed to ferry them across the river, but when they had half of them on the far side, the Yumas just took off with all their goods and stock. Left 'em to die in the desert, with nothing."

"Only they didn't die. Not all of them."

"I'll say one thing. If anybody could take a wagon through alone, it would be Doug Farley."

"Maybe. But he's only one man. As for me, I'll just wait until spring and go through with a wagon train."

When I told my father what they had said, he nodded. "We have to go now, son. I cannot wait." He hesitated, then continued. "Some folks would think me wrong to tell you of this, but you must be prepared.

"I cannot wait until spring, Johannes. The doctors say I haven't that much time. They say I am going to die. You will have to grow up without me, and growing up is never easy. People only talk about how wonderful youth is when they have forgotten how hard it was."

We had gone together to see the wagon. Doug Farley had built it for the purpose, and the planks were not only tightly fitted but caulked so it would float if need be. The side walls were lined with a double thickness of buffalo hide to add more protection from bullets.

Eight people could ride in the wagon in some comfort, but on this trip there would be but six, including me, and I wasn't very large. Each man and woman was required to have a rifle in good condition and at least two hundred rounds of ammunition. Each was required to demonstrate that he or she knew how to load and fire his or her weapon.

"We will travel by night," Farley warned us, "wherever possible. No loud talking, no noise. No shooting unless we are fired upon."

"What about hunting?" The question was asked by a thick-necked, powerful man in a black suit. His name was Fletcher. He had a square, brutal face with small eyes. I did not like him.

"There will be no hunting," Farley answered. "We have supplies enough, so there will be no need. A shot would only attract the trouble we're trying to avoid."

"You've been over this trail?"

"Five times, and I've scouted it just for this trip. Every stopping place is chosen now, and I've selected alternatives if something goes wrong."

"How'd it go before?"

"The first time was with a party of mountain men. We had one hell of a fight—five men killed, and we lost all our furs."

"The other times?"

"The army survey party was strong and we had no trouble except for losing some mules and one man who just wandered off and was lost.

"Another time, with a wagon train, we got through to Los Angeles, losing only two wagons and some stock."

"Los Angeles? What's that?"

"It's a little cow town about twenty miles from the sea. Used to be an Injun village. That's the place we're heading for."

"What's this here trip goin' to cost?"

"Three hundred dollars each. Cash on the barrel head."

"That's a lot of money."

"Take it or leave it. If you wait until spring, you can go through for half that. Maybe less. I am taking people who wish to go through *now*." He paused. "We leave at daybreak."

"How about my son?" my father asked.

Farley glanced at me. His eyes lingered for a moment. "He's small. He can go for one hundred dollars."

"That's not fair!" Fletcher was irritable. "You asked for people who could handle guns. That boy certainly can't."

My father turned slowly to look at Fletcher. "As to that, my friend, we shall see. In the meantime, I believe I can shoot well enough for both of us."

"What the hell does that mean?"

Father glanced over at Farley. "Mr. Farley? I am Zachary Verne."

Doug Farley lit his cigar and dropped the twig back into the fire. "That's good enough for me."

"But—"

Farley ignored the interruption. "He goes," he said, and walked away.

My father dropped a hand to my shoulder. "Let's get our gear together, son."

As they walked away, I heard the heavyset man, Fletcher, protesting to the others. "Now, what does all that mean? He just says his name and Farley's ready to take him on. The way he coughs, he won't last the trip!"

"Whoever he is," someone said, "Farley knew him."

At our room my father told me to wait and he went in to pick up our few things. I sat on the bench shivering, thinking of that fierce old man who awaited me in Los Angeles. He had hated my father, and when my father and mother fled across the desert, he pursued them, hoping, it was said, to kill them both.

Nor dared I tell my father how frightened I was. He did not know of the times I overheard my parents talking when it was believed I was asleep. "After all," I had heard my father say, "he is the boy's grandfather. How could he hate his grandson?" And then he added, a note of desperation in his voice, "There is nobody else, Connie, nobody at all."

Once my father had been tall and strong; now he was pale and shrunken from illness of the lungs and now he grieved for the wife he had loved and the son he would never see grow to manhood.

A dozen times, seeking some way out, they had repeated almost the same conversation. "Zack," my mother would say, "what else can you do? There is nobody else."

Then suddenly one night, only shortly before my mother's death, my father had suddenly burst out, "There's that other thing, Connie! If only I'd had sense enough to keep my mouth shut! He would never have known that I knew!"

"You were angry, Zack. You didn't think."

"I was angry, but that is no excuse. I was angry for Felipe. He would have told no one, but he was killed. Murdered.

"How could a man fall off a cliff he had walked and ridden a hundred times, in dark and daylight, in storm and wind? The night was moonlit, the trail was clear, and Felipe was a careful man. No, it was murder, it had to be murder."

"I know my father is a hard man, but—"

"He is a proud man, Connie. Pride of name and pride of family are an obsession with him. Of course, he isn't the only one. Most of the old Spanish families are that way. The difference is that in California some of the first settlers were simply soldiers or mule drivers, and those who came later did not wish to be associated with them.

"In your father's world a gentleman did not work with his hands, and a gentleman was always a man on horseback. In my world men who worked with their hands, men who could *do*, were the most respected. When I met you I was an able-bodied seaman, even though my father was a ship's captain, and that was what I intended to be.

"In his world a man like me never spoke to a man like him unless addressed, and then only with hat in hand and head bowed. To make it even worse, I was an Anglo and a Protestant. I don't know how I had the courage to speak to you."

My mother's voice was low, but I heard her say, "I wanted you to. You were very handsome. My mother thought so, too."

"Then three of your father's vaqueros came to me and said if I ever spoke to you again, they would horsewhip me."

"I heard of that."

"I told them they were fine men, handsome men, it would be a pity for them to die so young."

"I heard it, Zachary, I heard them talking of it. We women, we cannot speak much, but we can listen, and there was very little we did not hear. They admired you for it. I remember one of them saying, 'He is a man, that one!' "

There was silence; then my father asked, in a much lower tone, "Connie? Did Felipe *know*?"

"I . . . I believe so. What other reason . . . ? I mean, he was a fine old man. He had been with us forever, it seemed."

"But why *that* night? What happened?"

There was no answer, and lying in the darkness and listening, eyes wide with wonder, I knew there would be no more talking. Whenever that subject came up, conversation ended. My mother would talk no more.

What dreadful secret could there be that so frightened my mother? What was it my grandfather feared to have known?

The wagon went westward in the morning, driving over a hard-packed trail, simply one wagon alone, that might be going anywhere. Only when we neared the lava beds did we begin traveling by night.

After that there were usually no more campfires at night, and those by day were brief, for cooking and coffee. By day the horses grazed and the men slept, always in carefully selected places where they were hidden from observation. One of the outriders was forever on guard. I came to know them both.

Jacob Finney was a man of medium height, a man who never seemed to smile, but with a droll sense of humor. He was a slim, wiry man, part Cherokee, and from northern Georgia. "Been huntin' my own meat since I was frog-high," he told me. "I was nigh onto seventeen before I et meat I didn't shoot myself."

He was twenty, he said, but he seemed older. "Pa, he up an' died, leavin' the place to Amby an' me. Amby was fixin' to marry, an' that place wouldn't support the both of us, so I taken out."

He paused. "Amby's wife was a Natchez woman. You know about them? They was a dif'rent kind of Injun. Worshiped the sun. They got theirselves into a friction with the French from Loosiana and those Frenchmen wiped 'em out. Well, almost.

"Them that got away, some came into our mountains, an' Amby, he taken up with one. She was a rare kind of woman, tall and mighty handsome. She'd been one of their top folks, one of the Suns, as they called them. Amby, of course, he's a fine-lookin' man. Tall, strong, and better educated in his books than me. I taken to the deep woods and far country, he taken to readin', talkin', and the like.

"Well, seein' them together, it looked like I was the odd number, so I told 'em to hold a plot in the buryin' ground and I taken off west.

"Had me some Injun fights then, one led by a man name of Karnes where twenty-odd of us stood off more'n two hundred Injuns. We gave 'em what-for, we did."

The other outrider, Kelso, was an older, quieter man, a man with dark red hair streaked with gray. He'd made two trips over the Santa Fe Trail as a teamster and was veteran of two or three fights with the Kiowa and Comanche.

Steadily we moved westward, keeping off the skyline but using the high, wide-open country of a night when it was possible. Before daybreak we'd be holed up in one of those hideouts Farley had scouted long before. There we would sleep, read, play cards, or wonder the hot days through, waiting for the blessed coolness of the night.

Inside the wagon we talked little, and Papa least of all. Papa was a sociable man most of the time, but on this trip he kept to himself. Maybe it was his illness, but maybe it was something else, something that worried him more and more as he drew closer to California.

Jacob Finney rode up beside me one day when we were walking to ease the horses. We'd been on the trail no more than an hour, and it was coming on to moonlight.

"Want a ride, son? You can he'p me look for Injuns."

One of the passengers spoke up. "You will frighten the child."

"No, sir," I said. "I ain't . . . I mean, I'm not frightened." Although I was, a little bit.

He took me up on the saddle in front of him. "We don't talk," he said, "we listen. Injuns mostly sleep of a night, but sometimes they are late gettin' back to their lodges, just like we are. We want to kind of ease by 'em, like."

"We could fight."

"Yes, son, we could, but fightin's something you do when you've tried everything else."

2

Our wagon was our world. We were six people isolated from all about us as long as the wagon moved. We slept, we read, we stared at the canvas overhead or at one another, and we listened. Always, we listened.

Our stops during the day were brief, and always in selected positions where concealment was possible. Our rules had been laid down before the wagon started to roll.

One or the other of the outriders did the cooking. No pans were allowed to rattle, no voices were raised. Our campfires were brief and built from wood that promised little or no smoke. The side walls of our wagon were higher than usual, but the canvas top was much lower than on the prairie schooner or Conestoga, and the canvas itself was browned by smoke and usage. We wanted no glaring white top to draw the eyes of our enemies.

As we drew nearer the Colorado River, our travel periods were shorter and we were in hiding well before daylight.

We saw no Indians. Once Jacob Finney found tracks, but they were several days old.

My father talked little and did his best to stifle his coughing, yet it was a problem. Opposite us sat Thomas Fraser, a lean, tall Scotsman in a gray store-bought suit that was too small for him. Throughout the day he took notes in a small notebook he carried in the side pocket of his coat.

Hunched over the notebook, his thin shoulders like a buzzard's wings starting to unfold, he hovered in scowling intensity over his stub of pencil. I wondered how he could write at all while the wagon moved, but somehow he accomplished it. When we stopped for the day, he wandered off by himself to sit on a rock or log and stare at nothingness.

On the last night before reaching the river, Mr. Farley led the horses to a secret tank where water collected from the rains. "We've got to water them good," he explained, "else when they smell the river they'll run for it. There'd be no holdin' 'em. We'd have things scattered to hell an' gone, and no end of racket. Bring ever' Injun in the country down on us."

"Are there Indians close by?" I asked.

"I hope not, son. But they're about. Not many for such a big country, but they show up when least expected. Yumas can be almighty unpleasant, and they are fighters. Your pa can tell you."

Jacob Finney came up, his rifle in the hollow of his arm. "Smoke off to the northwest. Thin trail."

"How far?"

"Six, eight miles. Maybe less. This side the river, I'd say." He paused. "Want me to scout the trail to the river?"

Farley hesitated, then said, "No, we've got it to do, and we'll move out quietly as soon as it's dark. No use tipping our hand until we must. With luck we can be across the river before they know we're around."

He glanced over at me where I stood listening. "Y'see, son, Injuns will come out an' study the country after the sun goes down. The glare is gone, everything is still, and things sort of stand out. Sound carries further and any movement is easier seen. You put that away in your skull an' hold it for another time." He spat. "No, Jacob, we'll sit tight and take our chances."

It was very hot and the air was still. The wagon was drawn up among some cedars and the horses were grazing on a small patch of grass. Around us was a forest of sandstone boulders, and beyond them a rocky ridge. There was a good-sized pool of water.

"They've thought it out," Papa said, speaking softly. "The wagon's tight, and if need be we can cut loose from the gear and float all the way to the Gulf."

My father was a puzzle to me. From the start there was a difference in the way Farley, Kelso, and Finney treated him. They seemed to accept him as one of themselves, but the others were not treated so. Why was this so?

Of course, my father had been over the trail before, yet even that did not seem reason enough.

"How much farther?" I asked.

"The hardest part will be after we cross the river. From the river to the mountains is a long way, all of it desert. There are bare ridges, lava beds, some cinder cones, and—"

"What's a cinder cone?"

"Easiest way to explain it is, it's a small volcano. Most of 'em are a couple of hundred feet high, or less, cone-shaped, with a crater inside."

"Is there water in the desert?"

"Here and there, if you know where to look. There's a river, too. Water's not too good, and it isn't much of a river, only a few feet across, and some places no more than an inch deep."

"Where will I live?"

My father was silent for a few minutes and then said, "Your grandfather is a very rich man. He has thousands of cattle, sheep, and horses. He has a big ranch, and then he has a house in town, too.

"Most of the men who work on the ranch are Indians, those in town are Mexicans. Good men, most of them."

I wanted to ask him about Felipe, and what he might have known that he was not wanted to know, but I did not. I could not let my father realize that his private conversations had been overheard, even though I only listened when they spoke about the past or about my grandfather.

We dozed, awakened, then dozed again. Fletcher paced irritably. He was a difficult, impatient man, one accustomed to having his own way, I thought, and he did not like being just one of a group, nor did he like my father. I did not like Fletcher, nor did he like me.

"What's the matter with him?" he demanded once. "He doesn't talk like any boy I know."

My father's expression was bland. "He has spent much more time with adults, so he talks like one, even thinks like one. We've been in few places where there were other children, a fact I regret."

Later, when I had gone to get a drink from the pool, I heard Farley talking to Kelso. "He's trouble, and I don't want trouble. I'm not worried about Verne. He can take care of himself, but I don't want shooting."

"There's been no trouble so far."

"No, and I want to keep it that way. Fletcher looks like a tough man, but he doesn't know anything about Verne, and I don't think he knows much about the West."

There was a pause. "I want to get these people through safely and with as little trouble as possible. I nearly refused Fletcher on sight. I am sorry I didn't."

Fletcher finally seated himself against a tree, removed his hat, and closed his eyes. I watched him curiously, wondering why he was going to California in such a hurry. Yet I had no idea why any of them were going except for my father.

So far, neither of the two women had tried to talk to me, which seemed strange, as women traveling always seemed to fuss over youngsters, and I had been wary of them for that reason.

Miss Nesselrode was a slender, graceful woman who might have been thirty and was probably younger. She wore high lace collars that were always immaculate, no matter how dusty the trail. Her gray traveling dress was much worn and there were signs of raveling at the cuffs. She was rather pretty in a fluttery way, but I did notice that with each day we were on the trail she fluttered less and her eyelashes were steadier. If she had a first name, I had never heard it.

Mrs. Weber was a stout lady in black satin—or what looked like it. I felt sorry for her in that old stiff black dress she wore that seemed to have so many layers. She held a small handkerchief to her nose most of the time, and sniffed a good deal.

Sometimes I tried to imagine why they were all going west, but could not.

It was very still. Not a breath of air stirred. Occasionally one of the horses would stamp a hoof to drive away flies. Jacob Finney, who had been lying under the wagon, got up, and taking his rifle, went out to relieve Kelso.

Farley walked over and dropped to the sand beside my father. "Verne? Did you ever make the crossing this high up?"

"My first time was in Mohave country, but I never crossed in here."

"You know the country west of the river?"

"Some of it. There's some water holes at the west end of the Chocolates." He paused, then abruptly he asked, "Farley? Do you know Peg-Leg Smith?"

"No. I heard of him, but who hasn't? Trapper, isn't he? Mountain man?"

"He's that, but he's more. He's a horse thief, too. He's a mean, dangerous man, and he runs with a bunch of renegades, both Indian and white. He steals horses in Arizona and sells them in California, then he steals horses in California and sells them in Arizona.

"When they take after him, he hides out somewhere in the desert. Vanishes. Just drops off the end of the world and leaves no trail. Nobody's been able to catch him. Obviously he has a hideout somewhere in the desert north of here, a place even the Indians can't find—or don't want to find."

"What has that to do with us?"

"Peg-Leg will steal any horses or mules he can lay hands on. He's attacked at least one of the Spanish gold trains coming down from northern California. He wasn't even thinking of the gold, didn't know there was any, I expect, and just wanted the mules. He got them, too. Wiped out every man, he thought, but two of the mule drivers got away.

"Funny part of it was, they say he didn't take the gold, just dumped out the ore and went away with the sacks and the mules."

"He probably didn't know it was gold. I've seen only two or three pieces of gold ore in my life and wouldn't have bothered to pick up either piece. How many people know gold when they see it in the rock?" Farley was silent; then after a moment he said, "You mean that whole mule train of ore was dumped out somewhere and is just lyin' there?"

"That's the story."

"I'll be damned."

"The point I'm making has nothing to do with gold, but a whole lot to do with Peg-Leg. You've got some fine stock here, and what looks like a wagonload of something valuable, so be careful."

"We're watchin'."

"For Indians. But are you watching for what seems to be a friendly white man?"

3

There was another time when Finney had taken me up on the saddle. "My pa used to ride with me like this. He taught me about cows. More'n I needed to know, I suspect."

He indicated the hills around. "Mighty bare, you'd say. Not much but cedar, but there's always more'n a body would suspect. You've got to look close to see an Injun, if you ever do. Watch out of the corners of your eyes. You pick up movement quicker that way. An Injun never looks over the top of a rock or a bush, always around the base. They don't skyline theirselves. You best learn to do the same.

"Don't wear nothin' bright, nothin' to catch the sun. Shining things can be seen for miles. Buckskin, that's a good color. Stay away from white. Some damn fools want all that fancy, jingly stuff on their horses. Surest way to get killed.

"Your pa, now, he knows an uncommon lot about Injuns. I'd never have figured it of him, either. He looks more like a schoolteacher."

"He was one, for a while."

"You don't say? Well, what d'you know? I wonder if any of them youngsters knowed what a ring-tailed catamount they had for a teacher?"

"A what?"

He drew up to study a wide stretch of country opening before us. "Maybe you don't know about your pa, son. Farley told me, but I'd heard a few stories before that. Seems like somebody didn't want him alive, so they sent some outlaws after him. He killed two of them, wounded another, and got away—wounded himself.

"When he run off with your mother, they took in after him, the old man and about forty tough vaqueros. He played hide-an'-seek with 'em in the desert and got plumb away, and him with a woman with him. There's a lot of folks know about Zachary Verne.

"Farley was thinkin' of that when he taken him on. Just knowin' how to shoot is one thing, knowin' when to shoot is something else again, an' your pa has savvy."

That had been days ago, and now we were waiting, waiting for the last long hours to pass—and then we had the river to cross.

This was the most dangerous moment so far, perhaps the most dangerous we would encounter. Yet the Indians were a danger of which we thought little. They might attack, and the men in the wagon would fight back. Even the women would, for both of them knew how to shoot. Or they might just reload guns for the men to fire. The Indians were a present danger, but it was that fierce old man who was my grandfather that I feared the most.

I fell asleep and was awakened by a stirring about. The sun was already low, and Doug Farley was harnessing his horses. It was something he always did himself, allowing no one to even help. He always wanted to be sure everything was just as he wished it in case Kelso and Finney spotted trouble.

"Check your weapons," he said. "This here's liable to end in a fight. Don't be skeered. Just shoot low and take your time."

"I don't want a fight, but if we get one, we've got to win it or die. I figure we've got a fifty-fifty chance of swimming the river without bein' spotted, but no better than that.

"Just gettin' across ain't the end of it, for they might chase us into the desert, seein' we're only one wagon. We've got to be ready for that."

Farley turned to my father. "Verne? What do you think our chances would be, startin' now? We've got a canyon about three miles long to get through, with some big rocks in the trail. That'll take us the best part of an hour. By that time it will be dark."

"I'd say start now."

"Finney? Kelso?"

Both men nodded. "We can miss some of the rocks if we can see, otherwise we'll bump over them an' make a racket."

Kelso rode out ahead, keeping well to the left, as close to the canyon wall as the fallen rocks would permit. He rode with his rifle in his hands. Fifty yards behind and on the opposite side rode Jacob Finney. Riding warily, eyes searching the canyon ahead and the rock walls and rims, the small group moved slowly down the canyon.

Papa called it a "cavalcade," and it sounded strong and good to me. He had his own rifle out and now he had a shotgun too, which he took from his blanket roll. He put his hand on my shoulder. "Now, Johannes, I have taught you how to load and fire a gun. Today I want you to load for me. As I put down the rifle, take it up and reload. The same with the shotgun. If, when we are fighting, some Indian tries to crawl into the rear of the wagon, take this pistol and shoot him. But you be sure it is an Indian, because Finney or Kelso might have a horse shot from under them."

"Yes, Papa."

My heart was beating with great, heavy thumps. He was trusting me. He was depending on me. I must do it right. Step by step I went through the reloading process in my mind. There might be many Indians, and I would have to work very swiftly and surely.

Surely. Papa had always said not to be too hasty. Not to be nervous, not to waste time.

We were moving at a walk, the wheels grating on the sand. My mouth was dry. I inhaled deeply. My father always said if I was nervous to take a few deep breaths and tell myself to be calm.

Mrs. Weber looked around at me. She was on her side with a rifle in her hands, and surprisingly, she winked at me. "Don't you worry, son. We'll be all right."

"Yes, ma'am. I was worried about Mr. Kelso and Mr. Finney."

"Well you might, son, well you might. If they attack, those boys will take the brunt of it, but they are good men, mighty good men."

She looked around at Miss Nesselrode. "If I was you, miss, I'd set my cap for that Jacob Finney. There's a right upstanding young man. He'd make a good husband for a girl like you. He's knowledgeable, he's steady, he ain't no drinker, and for the right woman he'd make a fine husband."

Miss Nesselrode tried to look shocked. She didn't make it very real. "I am sure he would," she said primly, "but I am not coming to California to look for a husband."

Fraser looked at her; then, as their eyes met, he looked quickly away. Fletcher simply snorted, and Miss Nesselrode blushed.

My father looked at her and smiled. "The young men of California will be the losers, ma'am. It will be a disappointment to them."

"There are other things than marriage," she said with dignity.

"There surely is," Mrs. Weber said, "an' I tried one of 'em. There's bein' a spinster and there's bein' a widow, an' I don't care for neither.

Not that I was ever a spinster. I married when I was sixteen an' seen my man die when a log jam broke on the river whilst he was runnin' logs.

"Two years later I married up with a gamblin' man. Flashy, he was, a handsome man with diamonds and all, an' for a while we had everything. Then he had a run of bad luck and I taken in washin' to he'p us live. Then he hit it big again, a run of luck that lasted three year, an' we bought us a fancy house in Dubuque, had us a carriage drawn by four black hosses, an' then he run off with a red-headed woman from Lexington."

The wagon slowed down and Doug Farley spoke over his shoulder. "A little open through here. Stand ready."

It was dark inside the wagon. Outside it was still light, but it would not be so for long. I saw Doug Farley's hand come back to his six-shooter to see if it was where he wanted it. I could see Jacob, sitting easy in the saddle, but Mr. Kelso was away off ahead of us now, around a bend in the canyon.

Now the horses began to trot, Doug Farley talking easy to them. Rounding the bend in the canyon, we could see a silvery gleam of water far ahead. My mouth was dry, and I tried to swallow.

My father put his hand on my shoulder. "It's all right, son, all right. These are good men."

Farley was talking softly to my father. "You know the place, Verne? Cottonwood Island?"

"I do." My father paused; then he said quietly, "Unless they've spotted us, it's unlikely the Mohaves will be around there at night. That big mountain on the left ahead is Dead Mountain, where the Mohaves' spirits go when they die. They don't like to be around there at night."

Farley slowed the horses through some soft sand. The wheels only hissed slightly as the sand fell from them.

Kelso suddenly came in out of the dark. "Looks good, Doug. Water's no more'n twenty inches deep this side of the island."

"Pray to God we don't have a flash flood upriver," Farley muttered.

It was all downhill now, and Farley held the horses back, saving them, I guess, for a hard run if need be. I had listened to my father talk with other men and with my mother and could understand some of what was happening.

It was dark and still. The stars were bright in the sky, and we could smell dampness from the river. Farley swung the team to avoid a boulder and bumped over another. He swore softly at the sound.

"Deep cuts in the gravel here an' there," Farley commented. "Kelso
will find one we can use, somewhere the bank's broken down. You
know the Colorado—changes all the time. You can't count on the channel one time to the next."

"There are waves of mud underwater, too," my father said, "I've
known them to take down strong swimmers."

After that, nobody spoke. In the darkness of the wagon, I could hear
the people breathing. My father took a drink from a bottle. He was not
a drinking man, but sometimes it stilled his cough, and nobody wanted
that now.

"Is there a road?" Miss Nesselrode inquired.

"Ma'am," Farley spoke over his shoulder, "there ain't even the ghost
of a trail beyond what moccasins leave."

It was quiet again. Even Fletcher was still. I heard him grunt a little
as the rear wheel hit a rock. Then we heard the click of hooves on stone
and Farley drew up, resting the horses. A shape loomed out of the dark.
It was Kelso.

"I don't like it, Doug. I don't hear the frogs."

"Maybe we aren't close enough."

"I was right up there. I haven't heard a coyote in the last half-hour."

"Not much choice now," Farley said. "Better to try it than get
caught out here in the open."

"There'll be aplenty of them."

"Nobody said this was a picnic. There may be deeper water on the
other side. Worse comes to worst, we can cut loose the horses and try
to float downriver."

Kelso agreed. "Water's deeper in Pyramid Canyon, right below here,
but that takes us right into the heart of Mohave country."

"Where's Jacob?"

"Ain't seen him in a while."

My father said, "If it's all right with you, Farley, I'll ride up there on
the seat with you. This looks like close work, and I can handle my pistols better."

"Glad to have you." He clucked to the horses and slapped them
gently with the lines. "All right, Kelso, stay close now. We're going in."

There was no sound but the creak and bump of our wagon and of
the hooves of the horses as they walked. Kelso was ahead and a little to
one side, and I could see he was holding a pistol in his right hand.

"Bank breaks off right ahead." Kelso was back beside us again. He spoke softly. "Keep right ahead, and you can cross the end of the island. No dead trees or fallen stuff in the way."

Suddenly the horses went down before us, the wagon bumped, slid, then went over the edge. The horses were in the water. "Gravel bottom here," Farley commented. "I've crossed here a-horseback."

The current was strong. I could feel the thrust of it against the wagon, high though our wheels were. Once the wagon was pushed and almost swung end-wise in the current, but Farley spoke to the horses and they leaned into their collars and pulled the wagon straight.

We could almost taste the coolness from the water. Farley's voice to the horses was low, confident, strong. How long we were crossing, I do not know, but suddenly the horses started to scramble and pulled us up out of the water.

We could see the dark loom of the trees on our right, a few scattered ones just ahead. It was almost a half-mile across the island at this point, or so I remembered someone saying. We moved on, and there was no sound.

Fletcher swore, slowly, bitterly. Miss Nesselrode spoke primly: "Please, sir, it is no time for that."

Fletcher was silent, and I wondered what Fraser was thinking. Now he would have something to write in his little book. If he got through this alive.

Leaves rustled softly. Kelso was guiding us through brush and fallen logs.

"It's a trap," Fletcher said, "a bloody trap."

They came out of the trees then, a dark wave of them, coming in silence that suddenly broke into a weird cacophony of yells. Farley's whip cracked like a pistol shot and the mustangs leaped into their harness. The wagon lunged forward, and I saw my father's pistol dart flame.

A wild face painted with streaks of white suddenly appeared in the back curtains of the wagon as a warrior attempted to climb in.

Miss Nesselrode thrust her rifle against his face and pulled the trigger. The face, and the head, disappeared.

4

Papa's pistol was empty and he passed it back to me and began shooting with the other. He did not shoot hastily, yet he did fire rapidly, and there was a difference, for he seemed to make every shot count. Swiftly the Indians faded from the scene. Their ambush having failed, they would try other tactics.

The wagon raced on, and suddenly there was a shout. "Finney's down! Finney's shot!"

Deliberately Farley pulled up, and before he could speak, my father was gone from his seat. I saw him running back, I saw an Indian with a club start toward him, and my father fired, the Indian dropped.

In the vague half-light I could see Finney, or someone, pinned down by a horse and struggling to get from under it. My father raced up, fired another shot, and then offered a hand to Finney.

Somehow he got him free, and together, Finney firing now, for I knew my father's pistol was empty, they retreated to the wagon as Kelso raced back, firing.

They scrambled into the wagon and I passed the loaded pistol to my father and took the other. The wagon moved, jolted over a small log, and plunged ahead.

Miss Nesselrode, her heavy rifle in her hands, waited at the rear of the wagon, Mrs. Weber beside her. Miss Nesselrode was lifting her rifle to fire when the wagon pulled up so sharply she almost fell from her seat.

Looking past my father, who had again scrambled to the seat beside Farley, I could see the dark waters of the river rushing by, much swifter here, and obviously much deeper.

The western bank of the river was there, not thirty yards away, but the water looked deep and strong.

"We've no choice." Papa spoke quietly. "There are too many of them back there, and by daybreak we will be surrounded and all escape cut off."

"Steady, boys!" Farley spoke gently to the team. Urging them on, he talked to them quietly. They hesitated, then plunged in. The current caught the wagon and slewed it around downstream from the team, but they fought for footing, dug in, and leaned into their harness. For a moment they simply held their own, and then they began to move slowly. Guiding them diagonally across the current, Farley pointed them toward a gap in the brush.

Slowly, steadily, they gained ground. Suddenly it seemed they were only belly-deep; then they were climbing out on to the shore and up a dry wash that emptied into the river.

"They'll be coming after us," Farley commented. He drew up, glancing back into the darkness of the wagon. "Is anybody hurt?"

"Verne has been shot," Finney said.

"I'll be all right. It is nothing."

The team started again and the wagon rolled ahead; then, when the bank was low, they went over the edge to higher ground.

Farley turned the team southwest and started them out at a steady walk. Kelso came up beside the wagon. "She's all clear so far as I can make out," he told Farley. "And flat—hard desert sand and rock. No problem."

Miss Nesselrode said to my father, "Sir? If you will come back here, I can put a compress on that wound. It will help to control the bleeding until daylight."

"Very well." My father moved back into the darkness of the wagon.

All night long the wagon rolled westward and south. Sometimes I slept, sometimes I was awake. "We can't make more than ten or twelve miles by daylight," Fletcher was saying, "and the horses must rest."

When I awakened, gray light was filtering into the wagon. Fletcher was asleep, as was my father. Farley had crawled back into the wagon, and Finney was driving. Crawling up beside him, I looked out at the bleakness of the desert, all gray sand and black rock in the vague light before the dawn.

"Lost m' horse," Finney said gloomily, "and a durned good saddle. They killed him. That there was a good horse, too."

The horses plodded wearily along, heads low. The fire was gone from them now, and I could see an angry, bloody bullet burn along one's hip. Ahead of us was a rugged, rocky range of mountains, and I could see no way through. I said this, and Finney nodded. "Does look that way, but it ain't so. There's a couple of passes, such as they are.

"Doug Farley, there, he don't make many mistakes, and he's figured this trip mighty close. Right up yonder there's a place where we'll hole up for a while. A few hours, anyway. There's water an' grass. We'll let these mustangs feed a mite and then pull out again."

"Will the Indians come again?"

"Sure." He paused, thinking it over. "Injuns are given to notions, but the Mohaves are fighters, and unless they take a contrary notion, they may follow us for days.

"Y'see, son, they expected an ambush would do it, but Farley bein' what he is, we was ready for them and there were just more guns than the Injuns expected in one wagon."

When I looked from the back of the wagon, I could see the gleam of the river far behind. We had come further than I would have believed, and we were higher, for we had been climbing steadily.

Farley turned the team off into a hollow among the rocks. There was a little grass, and only enough water for the horses in a small tank where the rocks captured runoff water.

Finney, carrying his rifle, went immediately to a place high in the rocks where he could watch our trail.

When I saw my father in the light, I ran to him. He was pale and his shirt was all bloody.

"Here," Mrs. Weber said, "I'll fix that." She helped him off with his shirt, and we could see blood oozing from a hole in his shoulder. The shaft of an arrow with feathers on it was sticking out of his back. "I cut the head off," Papa said. "I thought you could draw it out."

Miss Nesselrode's face was pale. "I'll try," she said. "It got in the way of my compress," she added.

Farley came over. "Better let me do it, ma'am. I've done it before."

Taking a firm grip on my father's shoulder, he drew the arrow out, carefully holding it straight so as not to enlarge the wound. I could see the sweat break out on my father's forehead and face, and his eyes were very wide, but he made no sound. I was sad for him. His shoulders seemed so thin and frail, and I remembered them as strong and muscular when I was in his arms, only . . . I did not know how long ago.

"You saved Mr. Finney's life, you know," Miss Nesselrode said.

"Each of us does what he can," Papa said. "We are traveling together."

"You are a hero!" Miss Nesselrode said positively.

Papa smiled at her. "It is an empty word out here, ma'am. It is a word for writers and sitters by the fire. Out here a man does what the situation demands. Out on the frontier we do not have heroes, only people doing what is necessary at the time."

Kelso squatted on his heels against a rock, his hat off, head tilted back, eyes closed. I thought he did not look like the man he was, but one who my mother would have said should have been a poet.

Fraser was sitting cross-legged on the sand. As Farley walked by him, Fraser looked up at him and said, "I failed. I could not do it. I failed."

Farley stopped, taking out his pipe. "You failed? How?"

"I could not shoot at first, and then I could hit nothing."

"You fired? How many times?"

"Only two shots. I was clumsy. I am a failure."

Farley stoked his pipe and said, "That's two more shots than I got off in my first Injun fight. It all happened so fast I set there with a rifle in my hands and never fired a shot. You done all right, Fraser. Just don't worry about it, an' take your time. If you fire only once, make it count."

Fletcher sat by himself, his face sullen. How many shots did he fire? I did not see. I did not know. Perhaps many.

There was shade where we were, and as the sun rose higher, it was needed. Miss Nesselrode helped my father put on a fresh shirt. It was his last one, and he was a man who liked fresh clothing, and to bathe often. He stifled a cough and Miss Nesselrode said, "You are a sick man, Mr. Verne."

"So it has been said." He smiled at her. "Thank you, ma'am. It was kind of you to help me. I am afraid I shall have a stiff shoulder for a while."

"Your little boy loaded your pistols. How does he know to do such things?"

"I taught him, ma'am. I have also taught him to respect weapons and handle them with care. We wish there were no violence in the world, but unhappily there are those who use it against the weak. I would not be one of those."

He smiled again. "You did very well yourself, ma'am."

She blushed. "I did what seemed necessary."

"Of course. It is that way, is it not?"

"Will you be staying in Los Angeles?"

Papa smiled a faint smile. "Perhaps . . . for a few days. Somehow I do not believe I shall be staying anywhere very long. Men and civilizations are alike, ma'am. They are born, they grow to strength, they mature, grow old, and die. It is the way of all things.

"At least," he added, "I am returning to the sea, where I came from. As a boy I planned to be a ship's officer, as my father was, but then I came to California."

"You changed?"

"I fell in love, ma'am. I fell in love with a gloriously beautiful Spanish girl whom I saw going to church. It changed my life, and hers too, I am afraid."

"She is the boy's mother?"

"She was. We lost her, ma'am. I am taking the boy to his grandparents."

There was a long silence. I sat in the shadow of a great rock with my eyes closed like Mr. Kelso. It was very quiet.

Finney came down from his post and took a pull from a water bag. "Nothin' so far," he said to Farley. "We got us a good view from up yonder."

"Want me to spell you?"

"Sit tight. I'm good for a couple of hours longer." He glanced over at me. "Come up an' join me after you've et. You can help me look for boogers."

"All right."

" . . . you ran away into the desert?" Miss Nesselrode was talking to my father. "They pursued you?"

"Yes, ma'am. There were many of them. They had men watching at the river crossings, in the towns, at the water holes."

"However did you escape?"

My father was growing tired. His voice showed it. "We have never escaped. We only believed we had, ma'am. Now I am taking his grandson back to him because there is no one else."

There was another long silence, and then she said, "I could take him."

My father's eyes opened and he looked at her and said, "Yes, I believe you would, but first . . . first we must try his own blood, his own people."

"Even if they hate you?"

My father shrugged. "What is hate to me? What they feel toward me does not matter. It is my son who matters. He must have a home."

Slowly the day waned on, and after we had eaten a little, I climbed the rocks to where Finney lay, taking his beef and bread to him.

From the crest of the rocks, under some cedar trees, we could look out across a magnificent stretch of canyons and broken, eroded land to where the river was. The mountains were blue with distance, and cloud shadows lay upon the desert.

"It is so dry. How does anything live?"

Finney wiped the crumbs from his lips. "They fit themselves to it, son. They adapt. The animals, the plants, all of them.

"Ever see a kangaroo rat?"

"No."

"Well, he's sort of a ground squirrel, you might say. Has him a tail two, three times as long as his body, seems like. He can jump like you wouldn't believe.

"Now, that there kangaroo rat, he doesn't drink. He gets all the moisture he needs from what he eats. An' off down south of here along the dry streambeds you'll find some trees called smoke trees. That's because from a distance they look like smoke. Well, you take a seed from one of those trees and plant it, and nothing happens. Something in that tree knows that seed will need water to grow, so the trees grow along the dry washes, and when they drop their seeds the seeds are washed away by flash floods, and while being washed away they are banged around by the rocks in the dry wash, smashed against one rock by another, rolled over, and banged again. Then, when that seed finally lodges somewhere, it will be along the bank of one of those arroyos, as we call 'em, and it will grow where from time to time it can get water."

Finney nodded toward the desert. "Look yonder. Some folks start scannin' afar off, and gradually work closer an' closer to theirselves. I do it the other way because if somethin' is close, I want to know it. I look slowly from as far as I can see to one side, to as far as I can see to the other, right close in front of me. I look for movement or something that doesn't fit, some wrong shadow or something.

"Then I look a little further out and sweep the field again with my eyes, and further and further until I'm at the limit of my vision, whatever that is.

"Of course, you pay especial attention to good hiding places or ways that can be traveled without being seen.

"This sort of thing you learn by doin'. Your pa, now, Farley tells me he's a first-rate desert man. None better, Farley says, an' from Farley that's high praise.

"Well, you try to be better. You learn from him. Learn from the

Injuns, they've done lived with it, an' maybe from me, Kelso, an' Farley."

He glanced at me. "Is that Nesselrode woman settin' her cap for your pa?"

"No. I don't think so. She is just being friendly, I think." Then I said, "My father is sick. She knows that."

"I reckon so." He was silent for several minutes and then he said, "I come an' I go, son, but you all just remember. You got you a friend in Jacob Finney. You need anything, you come to Jacob. Or send word, and I'll come to you."

He finished the last crumbs of his beef and bread and added, "Folks out west stand by one another. It's the only way. An' your pa surely didn't waste no time unloadin' from that wagon when I went down.

"Why, I'd hardly hit ground, with Injuns comin' up on me, when he was there, shootin' an' helpin'. That's a man, son, an' don't you forget it."

Suddenly he pointed. "Look yonder! That's desert! Real ol' desert! But let me tell you somethin'. It's been called 'hell with the fires out,' an' that's a fair description, but there's life out there, boy! Life! You can live with the desert if you learn it. You can live with it, live in it, live off of it, but you got to do it the desert's way an' you got to know the rules.

"But never take it lightly, son! If you do, she'll rise right up, an' the next thing you know, the wind is playin' music in your ribs and honin' your skull with sand. You take it from me, son, you just take it from me."

5

My father was asleep when I climbed down from the lookout. The few shadows had thinned and it was very hot. Mrs. Weber sat in the wagon's partial shade, occasionally fanning herself with her hat.

Doug Farley looked up at me from where he sat near the rock wall. "How's things up yonder?"

"We didn't see anything."

"This hour, it isn't likely, but it doesn't mean they aren't out there."

"No, sir."

"You pay attention to Jacob, boy. He's right canny. He's got an instinct for places where there'll be trouble."

Fraser's thin knees were drawn up before him, his back against a rock. His notebook was held against his knees and he was scribbling in it—I wondered about what. From time to time he looked up, as if thinking.

A lizard, its tiny sides pumping for air, seemed to be watching me. In the far-off distance a red-brown ridge edged itself against the sky, but I was tired and looked for a place to lie down. All the good places were taken. I crawled into the wagon, although it was hot under the canvas.

Alone in the wagon, I shivered, for I was very much afraid. I wanted to cry, but Mrs. Weber would hear me and I would be shamed before Mr. Farley and Mr. Finney. Huddled in a tight ball, I tried to forget the weird yells of the Indians and the shooting. I wished my mother were with me, and then I did not, for she would be afraid too. I thought of my poor father, so sick and hurt, lying under the wagon.

Then I heard a faint stirring and my eyes opened and I knew I had slept. It was all dark and still inside the wagon, and when I looked out, it was dark outside, too.

Horses were being moved around, and somebody picked up the wagon tongue. Miss Nesselrode climbed into the wagon, and when I moved almost under her feet, she gasped.

"It is me," I said.

"Oh? Johannes, you startled me. I had no idea anybody was in the wagon. Are you all right?"

"Yes, ma'am. I was asleep."

"I envy you. I tried to go to sleep, but it was too hot. Mr. Farley is hitching the team now. We're going to go on."

Mrs. Weber got into the wagon, and then one by one the others. Fraser helped my father when he climbed in. He sat down near me. "Are you all right, son? I'm afraid I haven't been much comfort."

"It's all right."

Jacob Finney sat beside Farley on the driver's seat. We moved out, Mr. Kelso riding a little way before us.

My father moved to the back of the wagon, where he could watch our trail. Fletcher watched and said, "You ain't in much shape for a fight."

My father's reply was cool. "I hope I shall always do my share."

"You hintin' I didn't?"

"I never hint, my friend. I say what I mean. I was much too busy to observe what you were doing or were not doing. I would assume you did what you could." He paused briefly. "After all, we all wish to live."

After a bit: "You're pretty handy with that gun, I'll have to admit," Fletcher said grudgingly.

"The use of weapons is sometimes a necessity," my father said, and there was silence inside the wagon. We rumbled along, grating over gravel, bumping over rocks.

"Is it far to the other side?" I asked.

"It will take us all night to reach the pass," my father said. "The horses will have a hard time of it, and we may have to get out and walk."

The night was cold. My father told me this was the way of deserts, for there is nothing to hold the warmth, and the heat passes off quickly.

Yet we did better than my father supposed, for by daylight we had come out upon a vast plain, a desert beyond which were distant blue mountains. It was a rocky desert, and there were plants of a strange kind, two or even three times the height of a man, yet with strange limbs, twisted oddly. They were like no trees I had seen before, having, instead of leaves, sharply pointed blades.

"They are called Joshua trees," my father explained. Then he pointed. "There! A day's travel away in those mountains, there is a spring. We shall have no water until we reach there, unless there is some in Piute Wash, which is almost halfway. Usually there is no water there."

Doug Farley squinted his eyes at the distance. "Twelve? Maybe fourteen miles?"

"About that."

"Well, the horses are in good shape." He glanced back. "They don't seem to have followed us."

"I wouldn't trust them," Kelso replied. "Maybe we made it so tough they won't want to try it again, but that's not like the Mohaves."

"We could make another mile, maybe two." Farley looked around at us. "Is everybody game?"

"Let's go," Fletcher said. "It'll be as hot here as there."

Westward and south we walked, beside or behind the wagon, letting the horses have less weight to pull. My father, weak though I knew he was, walked beside me. "We must take care," he said, "when we approach the spring."

"There will be Indians?"

"Perhaps. All who travel in the desert must have water. The Indians know this. They also know where the water is. They might be there before us, waiting."

We had fallen behind a little, and now he stopped. "Johannes, when I leave this life, I shall have almost nothing to leave you, except, in these last months, some little wisdom. Listen well. It is all I have."

We started on again, and he said, "Much of what I say may be nonsense, but a few things I have learned, and the most important is that he who ceases to learn is already a half-dead man. And do not be like an oyster who rests on the sea bottom waiting for the good things to come by. Search for them, find them.

"This desert is a book of many pages, and just when you believe you know all there is to know, it will surprise you with the unexpected. Nor was it always desert. You will see where ancient rivers have run, you will find where villages were, and where they are no longer.

"If you dig down a few inches, you will find a layer of black soil that is decayed vegetation. Once there was grass here, and there were trees. Oaks, I would presume. Along the shores of streams or lakes where men once lived, I have found arrowheads, flint knives, and scrapers for cleaning the fur from hides.

"But remember that men must go where water is, so despite all the vastness of the desert, it is really a very small place."

"Papa? I have heard they could not find you and Mama."

"They could not. Or perhaps their Indians did not try hard enough, for they knew me as a friend. But it was more than that, Johannes.

"There are places in the desert called tanks, where water collects in natural rock basins. Sometimes it is a very large amount of water, sometimes only a little.

"There are seeps where in a week or more a few quarts of water may collect. I would go to one of these places, drink a little, let my horse have what was left, and I would go on, leaving nothing for those who followed. The desert Indians who were guides for those who pursued me knew those places too. They knew I would be gone and there would be no water, and the pursuing parties were six, eight, often twenty men. Some of them would not listen to the Indians, and they died out there for their foolishness."

We moved on into the vast desert, plodding slowly, wearily along behind the wagon and its tired horses. Finally we stopped. We had come to Piute Wash.

Tired as we were, and as were the horses, Farley took them to the far side. "When you come to a stream or dry wash," he commented as he was removing the harness, "always cross to the far side. By morning it may be runnin' bank-full."

My father told me to listen to such things, but I did not need to be told, for it was the way boys learned, and there was much I wished to know.

Miss Nesselrode sat near me when we were eating, and she asked me if I had been to school. "I am six," I said.

"You seem older." She looked at me thoughtfully. "Have you known many children?"

"No, ma'am. We have moved very often."

"Can you read?"

"Yes, ma'am, and write, too. Mama and Papa taught me. And we read a lot together. Mama or Papa would read to each other or to me. I like to be read to, and sometimes we would look for places on the map that we had been reading about."

In the night the coyotes came and howled near the wagon, and I heard Mr. Farley go out to his horses and walk among them so they would not be frightened. My father was lying near me under the wagon, and sometimes when he turned on his wounded shoulder he would cry out in his sleep, but only a little.

The stars were very bright and there were no clouds. Once I got from under my blankets and sat on the wagon tongue, liking the night.

Mr. Finney was on guard then, and he stopped beside me. "Can't sleep?"

"I woke up, and it was so bright. I wanted to listen."

"I know how that is. Get the feeling sometimes myself, but better sleep. We've got a long day ahead."

"Will we stop at Piute Spring?"

"Maybe even overnight. Doug Farley makes up his own mind, and somethin's botherin' him. I can read it in him."

At daybreak we were moving again, heading due west to the low, rocky mountains, and by midmorning we were loading our barrels at the spring. Farley told Kelso to fix a good breakfast, with lots of coffee.

It was a very rocky but pleasant place. From the spring a small stream ran over the rocks and disappeared in the sand some distance away. There was Indian writing on some of the rocks.

With a cup of coffee in his hand, Farley walked over to Papa. "You know this trail?"

"Somewhat. There are springs at intervals. It is used by both Mohaves and Piutes. I believe it is very old. Pueblo Indians used to come out here to work turquoise mines."

"I'm uneasy about it."

"Trust yourself. You know this country. If you're uneasy, there's a reason. Your senses have perceived something your brain hasn't."

Farley glanced at him. "You believe that? I guess most of us do, when it comes to that. Some call it instinct." He sipped his coffee. "Kelso's feelin' it too. Maybe it's that pass when we get to the mountains or that spooky country off to the north, in the Tehachapis."

Farley hesitated, then asked, "How're you doin', Verne? You bein' sick an' all, and then losin' blood."

"I'll be all right. I'll make it." Then he added, "I have to, for the boy's sake."

They did not see me sitting on a rock near the water, but the air was clear and I heard their voices, and I looked into the water and wished my father would live forever.

Sometimes at night I dreamed of that fierce old man who awaited me. What would he do when he saw me? I dreamed of a sunlit ranch house where he would be but my father would not, and I was frightened. I did not know what to expect or what to think, only that I did not want to go to that old man, or even to see him.

Sometimes I wanted to cry when I was alone in my blankets, but my father had troubles enough and might hear me and be unhappy. So I lay wide-eyed in the night, my eyes dry, but the tears were inside me.

We left Piute Spring that day and suddenly, Miss Nesselrode was walking beside me. We were behind the others and alone. "You are unhappy," she said abruptly. "Is it because your father is ill? Or is it something else, too?"

For a moment I said nothing, for this was very private and I did not think I should speak of it to a stranger, but then I said, "Papa is taking me to my grandpa."

"I see." After a minute she said, "Johannes, if it does not go well for you there, come to me. I shall be in Los Angeles. Will you remember that, Johannes?"

I would remember, but then I would have to be afraid for her, too.

As if she knew what I had thought, she said, "I am not afraid, Johannes. You will be safe with me."

I looked up at her, and I believed her.

6

My father was dying and must find a home for me: this I knew very well, and this I understood. This was why we had come on this journey, trusting ourselves to Mr. Farley and his lone wagon. But why had the others come?

When we were walking alone once, I asked my father. "It is a guess, of course, for none of them have said very much, but I would say that Fraser hopes to write a book, and later to lecture.

"He is not well-off, as you can see. He has taught school, I believe, but there is small future in that for a young man with no connections. I think he hopes to write a book that will give him some stature, and use it as a stepping-stone to the future.

"Mrs. Weber? I do not know, of course, but I would suggest that she goes west to marry again. There are fewer women out there, and she feels she would not be lost in the crowd. She is not very bright, but in her own way she is shrewd, and I think she would make the right sort of man a good wife."

"And Mr. Fletcher?" I wondered.

"Ah, yes. Mr. Fletcher. Avoid him, Johannes, and avoid men of his kind. He is a surly brute, quick to temper, violent in expression. If he has not already done so, he will someday kill a man, or be killed. I would surmise that he is running away from something he has done or toward something he expects to do.

"More likely," Papa added, "the former, judging by the way he kept from sight until we were far from Santa Fe."

"Miss Nesselrode?"

He stopped, watching the wagon ahead of us. It was almost a half-mile off now, and Fraser and Fletcher plodded along at least half that distance in front of us.

"A handsome young woman. Not beautiful, but handsome. And she is intelligent. She is unmarried, and the reason is obvious. She is much brighter than most of the men she meets, and unless she becomes very lonely, she will settle for nothing less than the best.

"Unhappily, she is a woman alone. Obviously she has no family, no position. The men she would be apt to meet are marrying to better themselves, marrying money or family or both, which leaves Miss Nesselrode a respected outsider. But I do not believe Miss Nesselrode is thinking of marriage."

I told my father then what she had said to me. He stopped again, quite suddenly.

"She said that, did she?" He swore softly. "I'll be damned! Well, son, I do not think she realizes what she is inviting, but you have my permission to go to her if you wish. And if you can."

He put a hand on my shoulder. "At least you have made a friend, and that is important, Johannes. And she is *your* friend. You made her a friend with no help from me."

Sometime during that day the decision was made to go by a different route than the one planned. Mr. Farley decided, and he told us about it at supper.

We would be longer in the desert. We would come to Los Angeles by a different way. We would avoid some mountains and perhaps some trouble with outlaws. We would be wending a way through the desert where wagons had not gone, and were likely to see some sights others had not seen.

Mr. Fletcher immediately agreed, and Mr. Fraser also. Miss Nesselrode listened carefully and then agreed. "If you think it best," she said, but she turned to my father. "You have experience of the desert. Do you think it wise?"

"I do," Papa said, "although the way is longer."

Later, when we were moving again, she looked over at my father. "Mr. Verne, if you are feeling well enough, perhaps you could tell us something of Los Angeles?"

"Of course," he agreed. "It is a very small town, and you must remember it is nearly eight years since I have been there, and it was changing even then. When I left, there were, I suppose, between two and three thousand people, mostly of Spanish extraction. There were a few blacks, most of them with Spanish blood and Spanish names, and a handful of Europeans and Anglos.

"Water comes to the town from *zanjas*, or ditches. There are wells, also. Several of the Anglos have married Spanish girls from the old families. These Anglos are mostly former mountain men, trappers, and traders who came west when the fur trade ceased to be profitable. They are very shrewd men, alive to opportunity and quick to move.

"The town is twenty miles from the sea, the climate is superb, and the town has room in which to grow."

"There is gold there?" Fletcher asked. "I heard gold had been discovered."

"There is some mining. I knew the man who first discovered it. He was sitting on a hillside and pulled some wild onions and found bits of gold in the earth clinging to the roots."

"There is a harbor?" Miss Nesselrode asked.

"A quite good one, that will be made better. There's some coast-wise trade, and trade with the Sandwich Islands as well as Mexico."

"And China?"

"A little. They buy furs, mostly the sea otter. The business has fallen into the hands of the Russians, I hear."

As we moved, the conversation ceased, then started up again.

Often I slept, awakening to find everybody else asleep, and once when we were walking to ease the load on the horses, my father said, "Your Miss Nesselrode is a very bright young woman. I wonder what her plans are?"

Papa was not the only one who was curious. One morning by the fire, when only Mr. Farley and Mr. Kelso were there, I heard Mr. Farley saying, "There isn't much out there for a single woman except to get married."

"She might teach school."

"She'd have to speak Spanish. Unless maybe she started a private school for the Anglos and foreigners."

Fletcher came over and extended his hands to the fire. He had overheard the comments, just as I had. "She's got money," he said. "I figure she's well-off."

"She has relatives out there, I suspect," Kelso said, a shade of irritation in his tone. I knew he did not like Fletcher.

Fletcher knew he was not liked, but cared not at all. There was amusement in his eyes when he replied. "Maybe, but I am betting she doesn't know anybody out there. She's just got herself a notion. She's one of them romantic females with a notion of finding some Spanish don with a big hacienda. She's got herself a little, and she's figuring to marry rich."

Nobody replied to that, and Farley walked away to harness the team. Kelso glanced at me. "Stay in the wagon today, Johannes. We will be changin' direction pretty soon."

We took a trail that led between a black conelike mountain of cinders and a dry lake. Papa was the guide now, and he often rode Mr. Kelso's horse so he could scout out the trail ahead of us.

On the third day I was walking behind the wagon with Miss Nesselrode, and we had stopped to look at a lizard with some brown bands around him, and we fell behind.

"Miss Nesselrode? What are you going to do in California?"

Her eyes laughed at me. "Have they been wondering about that? I could see they are curious." She smiled again. "Johannes, if they ask you, you can tell them I really do not know. I will make up my mind when I get there."

"Mr. Kelso said you might start a school for the foreigners."

"It is a thought, Johannes, but I am afraid I am simply not the type. It is a bit tame for me, and will not accomplish what I wish."

"Mr. Fletcher says you have money. And you are looking for a Spanish don."

"He would think that." She walked on a few steps. "What does your father say?"

"That you are a very bright young woman."

She smiled again. "I like that. Most men do not give a woman credit for intelligence." And then she added, "And that may be an advantage."

We camped one night where there were many palm trees, and the following day we were among the Joshua trees again, those weird-looking trees with the twisted arms, although I did not think they looked much like trees.

In the far distance there were mountains, and my father pointed to them. "That is where we will go, Hannes, and beyond them."

"Papa? Is the ocean out there?"

"Beyond the mountains? Yes, it is."

"Mama loved the desert, didn't she?"

"She came to love it, Hannes. She was born within sight of the sea, and not many women of her class ever went into the desert, or even the mountains. It was very dangerous, you know. There are outlaws, and also grizzly bears."

"In the town?"

"No, in the mountains a few miles from town. Sometimes we rode there, several of us in a group, but your mother did not see the desert until we eloped. But you are right. She came to love it."

"You ran away into the desert?"

"There was no place else to go, Hannes. We loved each other, and they would have killed me for even daring to speak to her.

"I was a man of the sea, but I went into the desert to look for gold. I thought if I were rich her father would accept me."

"You did not become rich."

"No, I did not find the gold I looked for. I found some, only a very little, but I found the desert. I came to love it. I rode far and wide, sometimes with Indian friends, often alone. I learned how to find water in the desert, and the plants that could be eaten and those that were poisonous.

"Learn from the Indians, Hannes, but with them one must always be strong. They respect truth, and they respect strength."

Yet always he watched the desert, and I saw him walk out to examine the trail, looking for tracks. Mr. Farley noticed it, too. "Keep your eyes open, Jacob," he said to Finney. "Verne's expectin' trouble."

"Injuns?"

"I don't think so. I think this here's somethin' worse."

That night when the stars were large in the sky I went out into the coolness and stood there, feeling it all, loving the night and the stillness. Papa came out too, and stood beside me.

"Papa? Is someone coming?"

"I hope not, but this is Peg-Leg country. He's a bad man, Hannes, and a very dangerous one. Twice I have seen the marks left by his wooden leg, and it is unlikely he would be afoot out here unless he was planning something."

"Would he rob us?"

"Of course. He would if he could, but he is cunning. He will not take a chance on getting killed."

We walked back to the others, and Papa said, "Stay away from the fire." He advised Farley, "Let one man cook. The rest of you stay in the dark. Peg-Leg is out there, and he's watching. He already knows how many men are with you, and he won't attempt anything unless he can make a clean sweep."

We had camped in a thick stand of Joshuas. "The trail is down there," Papa said. "It's the Yuma trail. Agua Caliente is over yonder, at the foot of the mountains."

Later he said to me, "Sleep in the wagon tonight, with the women. If there's any shooting, you'll be safer."

I did not like that very much, but I knew better than to protest. My father was a kind man, but he did not like disobedience or argument.

It was warmer in the wagon. Miss Nesselrode was surprised when I climbed in. "Your father is expecting trouble," she said.

"Peg-Leg Smith is here," I told her. "My father has seen his tracks. He is a robber."

My father came to the back of the wagon. "Miss Nesselrode? Have your weapons ready. This is more serious than the Indians."

"I have heard of him. There was some talk in Santa Fe."

"He's known everywhere, ma'am. He's a very hard man."

"You *know* him?"

"Oh, yes. We traveled across the desert together once. Yes, I know him. He can be very affable, very pleasant. And he is not to be trusted for one minute."

The fire was down to coals before he came. We had the wagon at one side of a rough circle of rocks and ocotillo, a kind of sticklike cactus with very ugly thorns. He came riding up outside the circle and stopped in the glow of the fire.

He was a big, burly man in a greasy homespun shirt, wearing a belt gun and carrying a rifle. He rode a mean-looking roan horse.

"Hello, the camp! All right if I come in?"

My father answered. "As long as you come alone, Peg. If even one other man raises a head, I'll put a bullet into you."

"*Verne!* By the Lord Harry, Zachary Verne! Hell, I thought you went back East!"

"I came back, Peg. My son's with me. I'm taking him home."

"Then you're crazier than I thought. They'll kill you, an' him too."

"Peg, these people are my friends. We want no trouble, but we're ready for it."

He stood in his stirrup. "All right!" he bellowed over his shoulder. "Go have a drink! All off for tonight!"

He swung down. "Hell, Verne, it would have to be you. I was fixin' to kill the lot of you an' steal your goods!" He bellowed a laugh. "An' maybe I'll do it yet!"

7

His eyes twinkled, and he looked down at me. "I'm just a-funnin', youngster. Why, old Peg-Leg wouldn't kill nobody, 'less he was a-shootin' at me!

"Hey? You're a likely-lookin' youngster. You Verne's boy?"

"I am."

He looked at me again, then sat down by the fire, which was smoldering. He added a few sticks, then reached for the coffeepot. "Mind if I do?"

Taking a cup from the kitchen box, I handed it to him. "Thanks, boy." He looked at me again, his hard blue eyes twinkling. "You scared of me, boy?"

"No, I am not."

He chuckled. "Don't s'pose you are, boy, but some are, some are!"

"My father isn't."

He chuckled again. "No, I reckon he ain't. Your papa shoots mighty good, boy. I've seen it. And he takes no nonsense. Hell, if I'd knowed he was along, I'd never wasted time follerin' you all."

Doug Farley came in from the dark, a shotgun in his hands. Coolly he poured a cup for himself.

Peg-Leg looked up suddenly. "Verne, don't be a damn fool! Don't you go traipsin' into Los Angeles! They'll kill you. I'd back you against any three of them, but it won't be three, it'll be six or eight. The old man wants you *dead*."

He held his cup in both hands, his wooden leg stretched out in front of him. He noticed me looking at it. "That there's the third one, boy. Whittled 'em out myself! I busted the first one in some rocks, but the second . . ." He looked up at my father. "Hell, Verne! There was six or seven of them. They come at me in a cantina, aimin' to stretch my hide. They had knives, and so did I, an old bowie, but when there's that many . . .

"Well, I fetched off my wooden leg an' had at 'em! I laid out four before they taken out. Like scared rabbits, they was! But they left four all stretched out, two of 'em with busted skulls.

"Trouble was, I busted my leg an' had to limp out of there usin' a chair. I done holed up in one of them canyons where there's a trail from the San Fernando Valley down toward Rancho La Brea. I set up there until I whittled out a new leg. This'n's better'n the other was."

"How's the trail through Romero's Pass?"

"Romero's? Oh, y'mean the one north of San Jacinto Mountain? It ain't bad. Sandy here an' there, but you can go through, all right."

"Romero . . . I mind him. He was the Spanish captain who went through there first. I mean aside from Injuns."

He filled another cup. "Set down, Verne. I'm peaceful, and them boys out there, they'll be long gone back to camp." He sipped his coffee, then glanced slyly at my father. "You're close to them Injuns at Agua Caliente, so you'll hear it sooner or later. They be sayin' that Tahquitz has come back."

My father did not immediately reply. He took his time filling his cup; then he glanced over at me. "Tahquitz is supposed to be an evil spirit. Some say he's a monster of some kind, even a dragon. Once in a while the mountains rumble and they say Tahquitz is trying to escape.

"Long ago, so the story went, Tahquitz used to come down and steal maidens from the villages. They said he ate them. One day a brave young warrior tracked him into the mountains and found the cave where he lived, and walled it shut with Tahquitz inside."

My father looked across his cup at Smith. "What do you mean, 'come back'?"

Peg-Leg's eyes twinkled slyly and he stole a look at my father. "They be sayin' he's out of his cave, an' that he walks the mountains of a night. They've found tracks up yonder, even down close to the hot springs. No Cahuilla will leave his lodge after dark. Not now."

"There are many such beliefs," Papa said mildly.

"This here's more'n just a belief. Got so no Injun will even hunt in the piney woods. They stay down on the desert. They're scared, Verne, real scared. I know Injuns, an' no matter what folks say, they don't scare easy."

There was a movement behind us, and looking around, I saw it was

Miss Nesselrode. She had gotten out of the wagon and was coming up to the fire.

Peg-Leg Smith saw her at the moment I did and scrambled up with surprising agility. He swept off his hat. "Ma'am! I heard there was womenfolks along, but wasn't expectin' to have the pleasure."

"Please sit down, Mr. Smith. The coffee smelled so good I just had to have a cup. Besides, I want to see the most notorious horse thief in the country."

Smith looked pained. "Now, ma'am, that ain't right. Ain't right nor fair. If you was a man, I'd shoot you for sayin' that, but I can't shoot no woman. Especially no lady. It just ain't fair, you takin' advantage like that. Anyway, I never stole no horses of yours." He looked at her suddenly. "I didn't, did I?"

"No, Mr. Smith, you have not. I hope you never will, Mr. Smith, because you have become something of a legend. I would not like to hang a legend."

"What?" He was startled.

"Yes, Mr. Smith. I may go into the horse business, and if ever I do, and if ever you steal any horses from me, I would follow you to wherever you went with however many men it took, and I would hang you, Mr. Smith."

"Now, ma'am, that's no way to talk! You wouldn't hang a poor one-legged man, would you? After all, nobody's ever catched me with stole horses. It's just one o' them stories that gets around.

"Anyway, that was all years ago. I'm out here huntin' a gold mine I lost." He looked at her, his eyes innocent. "You wouldn't want to invest in a gold mine, would you, ma'am?"

"No, Mr. Smith, I would not." She held out a hand for his cup. "May I get you some more coffee, Mr. Smith?"

He watched her cross to the coffeepot and refill his cup. She returned it to him, smiling. "Tell us, Mr. Smith. How did you make three thousand horses disappear in the desert with men chasing you? That should be a most interesting story."

"Now, now! Ma'am, you shouldn't ought to believe such stories! Them horses were stole by Injuns, driven off by Injuns. I had noth—"

"Please, Mr. Smith! Who led those Indians?"

Smith turned to look at Zachary Verne. "Zack? How come you got this woman along? Whose woman is she, anyway? If she keeps talkin' like this, she could get a body into trouble! Why, I'm an old man now, fixin' to move up to Frisco an' settle down. I can't have stories like that gettin' around. Folks won't trust me!"

Smith was enjoying himself, and my father knew he was. "I d'clare, ma'am, if you was to want to go partners with me, I might just go back into business again!"

She smiled at him. "You're a rascal, Mr. Smith, and a scoundrel, but I like you. You're an interesting man."

She paused. "Tell me the truth, Mr. Smith. Did you really amputate your own leg?"

"Had to. Wasn't nobody to he'p except there toward the end. Milt Sublette, he did some cutting. Injun shot me in the leg, shattered the bone right below the knee. Wasn't no doctor within a thousand miles, prob'ly. It was cut or die, and all the time, them Injuns was around. I'd rather lose a piece of my leg than my hair. So I cut her off."

"You had no surgical training? I'm astonished."

"Ma'am? What you all mean by surgical trainin'? Of course I had! I'd killed an' skinned out maybe a hundred buffler, and as many deer, to say nothing of all the other game.

"Wasn't one of us there hadn't cut arrows out of people or cleaned up bad wounds one kind or another. I'd done more cutting on animals and folks than nine out of ten surgeons. I'd cut meat and I'd cut bone maybe a thousand times since I was a youngster. Cuttin' on a man offers the same sort of problems.

"You civilized city folks live in a world a whole lot different than ours! Why, Ewing Young, him that was our leader a time or two, he was tellin' us one time how a man named Harvey discovered the circulation of the blood. We thought that was almighty funny, amusin' I mean, because every Injun on the Plains and in the woods knew all about it. Hunters for thousands of years understood, and those old priests who performed thousands of human sacrifices, do you think they didn't know? This Harvey feller, he just wrote it up for folks to read.

"I hear folks talkin' about Lewis and Clark and all they 'discovered.' Why, I talked with a Frenchman who was guide to David Thompson, the Hudson Bay man. That Frenchman had been all over that 'discovered' country ten years before!"

"Mr. Smith," Miss Nesselrode asked suddenly, "what is it like in California? Over the mountains, I mean?"

He looked at her, then squatted on his haunches again, nursing the coffee. "It is the best of lands," he said quietly, "and will someday be among the greatest. Don't go there unless you can grow. That's the trouble with the Spanish folks, they've lived too easy all these years, nobody to fight, or reason to. Now some of them smart Yankees are there, things will be different.

"Me, I've been a mountain man and a trapper. Why do you think I left the East to trap for fur? Because that was where the money was! I could make more in a week, if I kept my hair, than I could make in a year back to home! That's why those other fellers come west, too. Now that folks want silk hats instead of beaver, those smart Yankees are lookin' about. They've seen Los Angeles.

"Now, you watch it change! They won't be content to ride horseback or set in the sun! Look at Wolfskill, now. I hunted and trapped with William Wolfskill. Now he's out there with grapes and oranges growin'. You see, he'll make him a fortune. Ben Wilson's there, too, and Workman, Rowland, and others.

"That country is goin' to grow! Folks who are smart are goin' to get rich, and a lot of others are goin' to set by and watch it happen.

"Get hold of some land. It will last and be there when all the rest has changed. Everything else fades with time, but the land stays there. Sure, there's floods, earthquakes, and storms, but by and large, the land stays.

"Get land for the long pull, and look about to see what folks need most and get it for them and make them pay for it.

"I'm an old man now. Never was a hand to hold to money, anyway. I spent it all on drink and whatever, but you watch Ben Wilson, watch Wolfskill, Workman, and some of them others! Shrewd, knowin' men they be! They will make Los Angeles into a city, and all you've got to do is ride the river with them. You take it from me!"

"Thank you, Mr. Smith." She held out her hand to him. I had never noticed how slim and beautiful her hands were.

He took it in one of his, brown and hard and strong, and he looked at it, then at her. "It was a pleasure, ma'am. A pleasure."

Suddenly he got up, walked to his horse, and without touching a stirrup, swung himself into the saddle. Then he looked back at her.

"I have a feelin' about you, ma'am. I shall come to Los Angeles sometime, just to see if I'm right."

And he rode away into the night. For a moment the firelight was on his broad back; for a moment or two after that we heard the grate of his horse's hooves on gravel, and then he was gone, as if he had never been, and we heard no other sound.

Farley looked over at my father and shook his head in what must have been wonder, and Miss Nesselrode simply stood looking into the dying fire for a minute, then looked at Papa.

"He's quite a wonderful man, isn't he?"

"He's an old devil," my father said, "but he is a wonderful man, too, and you, I think, have made a friend."

"I doubt I shall ever see him again."

"That may be, but he will not forget you. And do not underestimate the man." My father coughed slightly; then he said, "Some of the mountain men were finely educated, some were not, but all were extremely practical men whose minds were beautifully tuned. They could not be dull, for to let their wits dull was to invite death.

"One does not need education to be intelligent, and these men might be short on what educated men use in the way of information, but their wits were sharp, their minds were alert, they were prepared to move, to change, to adapt at the slightest need.

"All about them were conditions and circumstances to which they must adjust, attack by Indians or outlaw trappers was an ever-present danger, they lived on the very knife-edge of reality, and when this is so, the mind becomes a beautifully tuned instrument.

"They did not fall into patterns or ruts. There were none. Each day was different, each brought new problems. No two traps could ever be set exactly the same. Whatever else you could say of these men, they were intelligent in the finest sense. Peg-Leg Smith is one of them. The men of whom he spoke were also mountain men, but of different character than Smith. When the money went out of the fur trade, they did not hesitate. They looked about for other opportunities, and in Los Angeles they found them."

Farley stood up and brushed off his pants. "It is late," he said, "and tomorrow we go down into the real desert."

"Good night, gentlemen," Miss Nesselrode said, and she went away to the wagon.

When she was gone, Farley looked at my father. "Do you think he will come back?"

"No." He paused. "Oddly enough, the man's a gentleman, in his own way. If I were you, I'd keep watch, but I'd bet every dollar I have that we will not see him again."

My father turned away toward his blanket roll. "Hannes, I'm tired. You'll have to help me with my boots."

8

In the night I was suddenly awakened—by what sound or sense, I do not know. Listening . . . All was still. From under the wagon I could look out and see the morning star hanging in the sky like a light in a distant window. Then I thought of my grandfather, that fierce old man who hated us so, and whom I had never seen. Under the blankets I shrank, my stomach tied in a knot of fear.

"I am Johannes Verne," I whispered to myself. "I shall not be afraid."

Over and over I said it, and the words seemed to ease the tightness, and after a while I lay quiet, but wide-awake. Carefully, not to disturb my father, who lay close by, I slid from under the blankets and went out to stand alone in the night.

There was a step behind me, and turning, I saw Jacob Finney. "Can't sleep?" Finney asked very softly.

"I was awake." Then I said, "I like it. The desert, I mean. I like the desert nights, and the stars."

"Yeah, me too. No matter how hot it is by day, the nights are cool. It's a resting time."

"Sometimes I think there's something out there, something calling to me, only I can't hear anything."

"I know." Finney got out his pipe and began to stoke it. "Some folks can't abide the desert, but those who love it, like you an' me, for them there's no place like it. Kind of magic."

"My mother loved the desert."

"Spanish girl, wasn't she?"

"Yes, sir. Her name was Consuelo."

"It has a lovely sound." He lit his pipe. "Knowed a Spanish girl once, down Sonora way. I guess I was in love with her, but then there was trouble and I killed a man. Shot him. I had to leave. By now she's married to somebody else an' prob'ly never thinks of me."

He cleared his throat. "I think of her, though. I got something to remember, anyway. There was a fountain in the patio and we used to set there in the moonlight. Sometimes we'd talk, but mostly we just set. Her mama was close by, but that made us no mind. We really didn't need to talk.

"I heard about your pa an' ma, an' how they run off into the desert an' were married there by a priest comin' up from Mexico.

"Can't figure why the old don hated him so. He was an Anglo, of course, and a Protestant. Maybe that's enough for an old Spanish man who is proud of his name and family. An' maybe it was because your pa was just a seaman. I don't know, but it was too bad. But he's become kind of a legend, y'know.

"The way they chased him. Four or five bands of men huntin' just her an' your pa, an' he slipped away from them, time an' again.

"The Injuns he'ped. They set store by your pa because during a starvation time for them he gave them beef cattle. He'd been building a herd, hoped to make hisself wealthy so the old don might accept him. Well, when the Injuns was starving, he gave them beef, so when your grandpa was after him, the Injuns hid him, told him where to hide, like that."

Finney glanced at the stars. "Better roll your bed, youngster. We're startin' early because of the heat."

After Jacob Finney walked away, I turned back to the desert. For a long moment I stood perfectly still, listening. But was I listening? What was I listening for? I did not know. Behind me there was a stirring. Behind me there was movement, activity, but it seemed far away. I walked a few steps further and the sounds seemed to recede. I stopped again, and then I felt an odd coolness, a feeling of something strange, something different.

I shook myself, but it was still there. I looked around and I could see people around the camp. Mr. Kelso was saddling his horse. Mr. Finney was loading his rifle again, and my father was rolling his bed, yet it all seemed far away and in a world different from the one in which I stood. Yet I did not know why.

I waited, expecting something, but I did not know what, and then I saw the shadow out there in the greasewood. A shadow where there was nothing that could offer a shadow. Yet something was there, something a little more tangible than a shadow, something that seemed to be appearing, something that seemed to be happening.

Back at the fire, someone spoke, asking about me. I heard my father say, "He's walked into the desert, but do not worry, he will be back."

Suddenly I was not at all sure if I could go back. That I even wanted to go back. I looked again for the shadow, and it was still there, standing as if waiting—waiting, perhaps, for me?

Turning sharply, half-afraid, I walked back toward the fire, walking slowly, always with the feeling that I wanted to look back, even to go back—perhaps to join that shadow? No . . . not that. Not that exactly.

My father walked out to meet me. "Hannes? Are you all right?"

"Yes, I am."

He stood beside me for a moment and said, "Your mother and I used to walk into the desert at night. We loved it, and loved our time together.

"Long ago, before the Indians who live here now, there were other people. Perhaps they went away, or maybe they died or were driven out by these Indians' ancestors, but they are gone. Yet sometimes I am not sure they are gone. I think sometimes their spirits are still around, in the land they loved.

"Each people has its gods, or the spirits in which they believe. It may be their god is the same as ours, only clothed in different stories, different ideas, but a god can only be strong, Hannes, if he is worshiped, and the gods of those ancient people are lonesome gods now.

"They are out there in the desert and mountains, and perhaps their strength has waned because nobody lights fires on their altars anymore. But they are there, Hannes, and sometimes I think they know me and remember me.

"It is a foolish little idea of my own, but in my own way I pay them respect.

"Sometimes, when crossing a pass in the mountains, one will see a pile of loose stones, even several piles. Foolish people have dug into them, thinking treasure is buried there. It is a stupid idea, to think a treasure would be marked so obviously.

"It is an old custom of these people to pick up a stone and toss it on the pile. Perhaps it is a symbolical lightening of the load they carry, perhaps a small offering to the gods of the trails. I never fail to toss a stone on the pile, Hannes. In my own way it is a small offering to those lonesome gods.

"A man once told me they do the same thing in Tibet, and some of

our ancient people may have come from there, or near there. Regardless
of that, I like to think those ancient gods are out there waiting, and
that they are, because of my offerings, a little less lonely."

When I climbed into the wagon, Miss Nesselrode was sitting up, and
Mrs. Weber was also. Fraser was lying half on his side, still trying to
sleep. Fletcher seemed not to have moved from where he sat. He stared
at me, then looked away irritably. He did not like me, but then, he did
not seem to like anybody.

My father got into the wagon at the last and sat near the back.

Nobody talked. Some of us dozed. We were descending slowly, and
we had been told it would be hot. The sun came up and the coolness
disappeared. Fraser hesitated, then with a mumbled apology took off
his coat. After a bit, Fletcher did likewise, and unbuttoned his vest.

"It's below sea level down there," Fraser said suddenly. "One of the
hottest, driest places in North America."

Nobody answered him. He mopped his face, and then he said, "It
used to be an old sea bottom, or maybe the bottom of a lake."

My father looked around at him. "When we get down a little further," he said, "you can see the old beach line along the edge of the
mountains. There are seashells there, some of them thin as paper, and
they almost crumble in your hands."

"But surely," Miss Nesselrode said, "that was a very long time ago?"

"A very long time," my father said, "yet the Indians have memories
of it. They say the basin has filled up five times within their memory.
There is even a rumor of a Spanish vessel that came in through a channel from the Gulf of California, a channel opened by a sudden break
when the sea poured in. However, when the ship could find no way out,
it returned, to find the channel blocked, and it was trapped."

"What happened?" Mrs. Weber asked.

"The crew were killed by Indians, the ship drifted, hung up somewhere, and was buried in the sand. At least, such is the story. Of course,
according to the story, it was loaded with treasure."

"Nobody found it?" Fletcher asked.

"Not yet. At least there's been no report of it being found."

"There might be something to it," Miss Nesselrode suggested. "Did
not the Spanish believe California was an island? The crew evidently
hoped to sail around the other end."

"It is possible."

"Treasure?" Fletcher muttered. "A shipload of it?"

"That could be," my father said, "but I doubt it. Some pearls, perhaps, as they had just come up the gulf, where there were pearls and pearl-fishing. I cannot think why they would be carrying treasure and going away from Mexico."

"Maybe they were stealin' it. Maybe they just wanted it for themselves," Fletcher suggested.

"In any event," my father said, "the area that was once underwater is very large. It would be there or along the shores somewhere."

"Betcha some of them Injuns know where it is," Fletcher commented. He turned his eyes on my father. "They tell me you know them Injuns. They might tell you where it is."

"They might," my father said. "Indians have their own ways of thinking, and many of the things important to us are not at all important to them. Also, they might not think it safe to tell another white man where Indians had killed white men."

"Scare 'em into tellin'," Fletcher suggested.

Fraser looked at him contemptuously. "From what I have heard," he said, "Indians do not scare easily."

It was growing hotter by the minute. "It's mighty hot," Farley told my father, "but I want to get to the mountains. Once we get to Agua Caliente, we can hole up. Stay a couple of days, if need be." He paused. "Do you know the place?"

"I do. It is likely you'll find some Cahuillas camped there."

"I never knew them to be trouble."

"They are not, if you respect them and their ways."

"They the ones who helped you?"

"One of the tribes. The Luiseños and Chemehuevis did also."

There was no more talk. It was very hot, and I tried to sleep. The wagon rocked, rolled, and rumbled, dragging through sand, bumping over rocks, sliding down banks.

After several hours Doug Farley stopped the wagon and gave a small amount of water to each of the horses.

Fletcher raised up on his elbow at the sound of water being poured. "How about some of that for me?"

"Sorry. We'll have no water until we cross the desert."

Fletcher sat up, grumbling, but Farley paid no attention. Fraser pulled his skinny knees closer and tried to write. Mrs. Weber dabbed at her nose with a flimsy handkerchief, and Miss Nesselrode simply leaned her head back and closed her eyes.

Nobody talked, nobody wanted to talk; they just sat. "Oven!" Fletcher said suddenly. "It's like an oven!"

Mrs. Weber fanned herself with her hat. She had removed it at last, and her hair was drawn tight to her skull except for buns over each ear. Her hair was parted in the middle, and she looked more than ever like a tired bulldog.

Miss Nesselrode opened her eyes to look toward Farley, who sat on the driver's seat. I had not noticed before how large her eyes were. She caught me looking at her, and with a perfectly straight face, she winked.

I jumped. It was so unexpected, and I had never seen a lady wink before, although Papa sometimes did. But her wink from such a straight face was so droll that I had to smile, then I grinned, and she smiled back, then closed her eyes. I decided I really liked Miss Nesselrode.

It was almost dark inside the wagon when my father sat up. I had been asleep, and so had most of the others. Jacob Finney was driving the team, and Farley was sitting in the very front of the wagon behind him, his eyes closed.

"We're comin' up to Indian Wells," Jacob said over his shoulder. "Hear the place started as a spring, but the water level kept falling. Now they have to go down steps to get to it."

It was cool now. It was as if the heat had never been. Mrs. Weber put her hat on, and both Fraser and Fletcher put on their coats, but not before I saw that Mr. Fletcher carried a small derringer in his vest pocket. Later, when we had stopped and were alone, I told my father.

"Good!" He squeezed my arm. "You are observant. I like that, and it is important."

"It is on the left side," I said, "and the butt is turned toward the left."

"Oh?" He paused a moment. "Now, that is interesting. The butt toward the left? That I had not noticed."

9

It was after midnight when we stopped at Indian Wells. My father climbed from the back of the stage, staggering a little.

"Mister?" It was Kelso. "You all right?"

"Yes, yes, thank you. A little unsteady, is all. Will we be here long?"

"We're changin' horses here. Our stock's about played out, an' Farley had planned to get a fresh team for the long pull through the pass." He pointed off into the darkness. "There's the Indian well that gives the place a name, but maybe you know all that.

"You have to go down steps to get to the water, but it's good water. Cold."

"I could use a drink. So could my son."

There was a pause while Kelso removed his hat and wiped the sweatband. "Lunger?" he asked gently.

"I'm afraid so. I've been coughing less since I reached the desert, though."

"Whyn't you stay over at Agua Caliente for a few days? Folks say that hot, dry air is good for lungers."

"I haven't much time, Kelso. I am taking my son to his grandparents in Los Angeles."

Mr. Kelso walked away in the night and my father put his hand on my shoulder. "Hannes? See that big old palm tree over there? The Indians say one of their wise men, when he was growing old, turned himself into that tree so he could continue to serve his people."

"How could he do that?"

"He willed it. He stood very straight and very still and willed himself to become a tree, and slowly he began to change until he became that tree."

"Do you believe it, Papa?"

"I have never seen such a thing happen, Hannes. My reason tells me it could not happen, but my reason can only judge by what I know, and I do not know everything.

"Indians are different from us. They have other beliefs, and other reasons for believing. It is best not to dispute what the Indians say, but to listen and learn, making your judgments later."

He glanced toward the small building where the light shone from a window and an open door. "Stay by the stage, son. I shall be back in a minute."

No one else had left the stage. All were asleep or trying to sleep. Mr. Kelso and my father had both forgotten the cold water, and I was thirsty.

The men who had taken the horses away had not returned with the fresh team. Edging closer to the rift in the earth where the well was, I peered down. Far below I could see the gleam of water.

Carefully I tried the first step, then another. One by one I descended. When I stood on the square of earth near the water's edge, I looked up. All I could see was a rectangle of sky and two stars. When I looked around, straining to see in the darkness, I saw a huge olla or jar, and hanging beside it, a gourd dipper.

Dipping it into the cold water, I drank and drank. Nothing had ever tasted so good. I filled the dipper again, and then realized somebody was watching me.

It was an Indian, a very, very old Indian wearing a loose cotton shirt. His hair was thin and gray, bound with a band around his head and hanging to his shoulders. Suspended from a cord around his neck was a triangle of blue stone with markings on it.

"Oh? I am sorry, sir. I did not see you at first." I dipped the gourd into the water and held it out to the Indian, who merely looked at me. Then my father called, and I put the gourd dipper down and hurried up the steps. "I am sorry, sir. Please forgive me," I said over my shoulder.

My father was beside the wagon and he turned at the footsteps. "You had me worried. I was afraid you'd wandered off."

"I was getting a drink."

When the wagon was moving again, I said to my father, "I saw an Indian."

Fletcher was sitting up. "Ain't likely. They tell me Injuns don't come to the well no more. Not at night, anyway."

"He was very old," I said, "and he had a piece of blue stone hanging from his neck."

"Turquoise," Fletcher said. "They set store by it. More than gold." He glanced at me. "Turquoise is a kind of rock," he said.

The new team moved off at a good gait, Finney driving. Farley had crawled back into the wagon and found a place where he could recline on the blanket rolls. "Next stop is Agua Caliente. You've been there before, Verne?"

"Yes, several times. It's right at the door of the San Jacintos. Some of the Anglos are beginning to call it Palm Springs. There's nobody there except three or four white men and some Cahuilla Indians."

He paused. "I am expecting some mail there."

He leaned back against the baggage, and after a while I did also. I was tired, tired for want of sleep and tired of the wagon. I just wanted to be someplace and not to have to go on, day after day.

Lying awake in the dark, I thought of that lost ship, trapped in an inland sea from which it could not escape, sailing around and around forever until someday it ran aground and could sail no more. I dreamed of finding that ship and going aboard and finding chests of gold and chests of pearls.

Or chests of turquoise like the old Indian wore.

The horses were trotting now, hurrying. We would soon be in Agua Caliente, and then on to Los Angeles. How many more stops? Five, six, a dozen? I did not know. The wagon rumbled along in the night and my father sat up, bringing his holster around to a better position. He took his rifle and placed it beside him also.

Was there to be trouble, then?

A long time later, when I had slept, awakened, and slept again, the wagon rumbled to a stop. Peering out past Mr. Finney's head, I could see a lighted window and a door opening to let light stream out. A man came from the door and hurried toward the wagon.

My father moved to the back of the stage and slid to the ground. He had straightened up when the man came around the wagon.

"Verne? Are you there? Is it you?"

"How are you, Peter? It's been a long time."

"Let's go inside and have some coffee." The man was as tall as my father and had a handlebar mustache of golden brown, and a goatee. He glanced at me. "This is your son?"

"Johannes? This is Peter Burkin. He's an old friend."

"We've got to talk, Zack. Serious talk. Let's all go inside."

"We've only a minute. We're just changing teams again. Farley's in a hurry to get in."

"That's just it, Verne. You mustn't go any further. If you go into Los Angeles, you will be killed. You and the boy as well."

"What?"

"They're waiting for you, Zack."

10

They went inside, and I followed. It was a small store with a bar along one side and three tables. Behind the bar were a few bottles; behind the counter on the other side, were some packages, cans, and boxes of groceries or supplies.

My father dropped into a chair. His face was gray and his eyes hollow. He looked worse than I had ever seen him.

"Peter, I've got to see them! I have to convince them! My son will need a home and he has no other kin.

"I'm not worried about dying. I've accepted that and I expect I'm as ready as a man ever gets. If they kill me, it will only lessen the suffering, but it is Johannes who matters."

"You don't understand, Zack. The way they see it, you disgraced the family by marrying their daughter, and your son is living evidence of their shame. They want him dead, Zack."

Peter went behind the counter and returned with two cups and the coffeepot, filling both cups. I sat on a bench against the wall and almost behind my father, although I could see the side of his face.

His appearance frightened me. He looked so haggard, so exhausted, so drawn. When he glanced around, his eyes unseeing, I was shocked by the desperation in his eyes.

"My God, Peter, what will I do? I've no home for the lad! I've come all this way, hoping desperately they'd take him in. The Californios I've known were kind to their children, and I hoped . . .

"Peter, we've no place to go! No place at all! The last time I saw a doctor, he gave me four or five months, and that's been over three months ago!"

"Zack? Let me get your gear off that wagon. They know you're coming, and they're waiting. There will be four or five of them at the Bella Union and just as many down by the wagon yard. They've men posted on the trails into town.

"You were always handy with a gun, but in your best days you couldn't handle that many at close range. Nobody could."

Peter Burkin got up. "Sit right here, Zack. I'll get your gear." He leaned his big hands on the table. "Look, Zack, I've found a place here. The air is good for lungers, so take a few days, anyway. Get rested, think about it, and we can talk it over. Maybe there's an answer. You won't help the boy by getting yourself killed."

He paused at the door. "You loved the desert, Zack. Give it a chance."

Peter Burkin went outside and my father stared into his coffee, then tasted it. After a moment he drank more. He seemed to have forgotten that I was there.

Behind me the window was open and I could hear a murmur of voices from near the corral.

". . . takin' his duffle off. Yeah, they're waitin' for him. You'll see when you pull up at the Bella Union. Do him a favor and tell them nothing."

Farley said something I did not hear and then Peter replied, "How was he on the trip west?"

"Bad, real bad. He did his share and more, he's that sort of man, but he was coughin' the whole way. Got so's we got used to it an' scarcely noticed. I will say he's coughed a mite less since we crossed the Colorado. I think all that desert before helped him some."

"I'll get his gear."

"Burkin? What's behind it? I know all about Spanish pride and I know Verne wasn't a Catholic and was a common seaman—"

"An uncommon seaman, if you ask me."

"What's behind it?"

"Search me. I've no idea. The old don's filled with hatred, and so's the other one, the man she was supposed to marry. Seems he'd had trouble with Verne before, and when Consuelo ran off with Verne, he was fit to be tied."

Burkin was removing gear from the wagon, and then he said, "Say nothing about it, will you?"

"I can't vouch for the others. There's bound to be talk."

My father finished his coffee and walked outside, and I followed. Peter Burkin waited on the stoop.

"I've a place for you, Zack. It's an old adobe somebody fixed up, and if you can set a horse, you can be there in just a few minutes."

When we mounted, he led us toward the looming mountain, all black and mysterious. Peter saw me looking at it. "That's where Tahquitz lives, boy. Or so the Injuns say.

"He stole Injun girls an' et 'em. Chewed 'em right up. Some young Injuns figured that was an awful waste of girls, so they taken after him, found the cave where he slept, bones all around it. They say a young Injun walled him in. Your pa knows that story."

"He told me. Do you believe it?"

"You get up in those mountains alone, boy, or you get out in some desert canyon, an' you begin to believe most everything.

"There's medicine men who can raise storms, they say, and they can make the dead walk, and some as say they can see the future or what takes place far away. Your pa knows more about such things than me, but I've heard talk around the campfires, spooky talk of ghouls an' ghosts, an' like the Scotch say, 'of things that go bump in the night.'"

The mountain loomed black against the night, with the stars hanging above, and I thought of Tahquitz and shivered. Was he up there now? Prowling in the canyons? Or was he still walled in his cavern, struggling to escape?

11

Peter Burkin led the way through low sandhills to a small adobe surrounded by a living barricade of what seemed to be tall spines of cactus. "Ocotillo," he explained, "makes the best fence ever."

He spoke over his shoulder, as I was close upon him, and my father trailing some distance behind. "Boy? You an' me, we got to keep your pa here. He's a mighty sick man, but if anything can help him, this climate will.

"You tell him you like it here. Get him to stay on. You talk to him, boy."

He pulled up in the yard and stepped down, then lifted me from the saddle, although I could slide down and did not want to be picked up like a baby.

"Do you know anyone who knows the stories about Tahquitz to be true?" I asked.

He brushed his mustache with his fingers. "Well, now. Can't say as I do, but then, the Injuns been here longer than us and they may know a lot we'll never learn. Knowledge isn't a lasting thing. Not unless it's writ down in a good many places. People die, and what they learned often dies with them. Whole races of folks that once lived are now gone, and what they knew we'll not be able to guess at.

"I'm not a book-read man, boy. I never had no proper eddication, but I've listened to those who have had and to those who've traveled.

"Take your pa, now. He's a widely read man. He was a sailor onetime. You know that. He was a sailor on his papa's ship, so he had access to his papa's books, and there were times at sea when he could read.

"He first went to sea when he was twelve, as cabin boy with his pa.

He went to a lot of places with fancy names that just the sound of them makes you want to r'ar up an' go. Places like Shanghai, Rangoon, Gorontalo, Capetown, and the like. Your pa had seven years at sea, mostly in foreign parts.

"You've heard him talk. He's got a way about him, a way with words. He can make the temple bells tinkle for you, and you can just hear them big old elephants shuff-shuffling along, the priests callin' folks to prayer and the like.

"Your pa learned a sight of things most folks never even hear of. I've seen scholars back off an' look at your pa, amazed.

"You take these Injuns, now. You look at the way they live and you'll say they don't amount to much, but what are they thinkin'? What do they know? What memories do they have? They want different things, boy, and they consider different things important. Many a thing we'd give anything to know, they just take for granted.

"Some of these Injuns, maybe all of them, they're in tune with something. I don't know what. But some of them have lost touch with it, and others are losin' touch. Goin' the white folks' way might seem the likely thing to do, but maybe they lose as much as they gain."

Papa rode into the yard, sat his horse for a moment as if he was gathering strength, and then he dismounted, stepping down very carefully.

"I'll put up the horses, Zack. You'll find a candle on the table just inside the door. To the right of the door."

There were three rooms, two very small bedrooms and a large, square living room and kitchen combined. There was a very large fireplace, a table, benches on each side of it, and two chairs. One of the chairs was very large, almost twice the size of any I had seen.

My father stopped, lighted candle in hand, and stared at that chair.

The floor was made of odd sizes of stone beautifully fitted together. No mortar had been used, but the stones were fitted with knifelike precision.

"There's nothing much here at Agua Caliente," Peter Burkin explained when he came in. "There's the hot springs to which the Injuns been comin' for a couple of thousand years, I reckon. There's a stage station, but no stages yet, and it's a kind of two-bit store an' post office. Mail comes in ever' once in a while, sometimes as often as ever' two months.

"There's two or three white men in camp, an' there's the Injuns, mostly Cahuillas." He looked at me. "That's the way they say it, Kawee-ya. Some folks call them Agua Calientes, from the name of the village.

"There's more of them back in the mountains. In the Santa Rosas.

"They know you, Zack, so they'll be friendly, which means you won't see much of them, but they'll not do you any harm, either. As long as you live in this house, none of them are likely to come around."

"What's wrong with the house? It seems uncommonly well-made."

"You won't find a better anywhere about. Not even in Los Angeles. The stable out back is built just as well. There's a spring, cold water, that's runnin' into a fine stone basin, made by the same hands.

"Nobody's lived here for years, though. The house is considered bad medicine. They'll think you a strong man for even livin' here."

Burkin went back outside and brought their blanket rolls into the house.

"Peter? I can't thank you enough."

"Thank me? You done that years ago when you pulled me from under that grizzly." He turned to me. "I was gettin' chawed an' clawed somethin' fierce when your papa came along. He kilt that b'ar an' then he taken me to his camp an' kep' me there until I was able to get around. I was laid up for more than a month, an' your papa put off what he was doin' an' cared for me."

Peter Burkin rode away and I watched him go. Already the sky was faintly gray, and I could see the stark black outline of his figure against the white of the sand dunes.

My father was lying down, and from his breathing, was asleep. Although I had been awake most of the night, I was not tired.

What was it about this house? Why did no one want to live here? Again I looked at that huge chair. Was it that? Did the sight of that chair frighten people away?

Everything about the house was cunningly made. The closets and shelves were cut and fitted with the same precision as the tiles in the flagstone floor. Part of the house was very old. I could see where someone had begun rebuilding it, building up a wall here, opening a window there. An existing ruin had been taken and added to, walls rebuilt, a roof put on, floor added . . . or part of a floor.

Out back there was not only a stable but a corral. There were two horses there, left for our use.

My father had taken off his gun belt and hung it over a chair back close to his hand. His rifle and his shotgun were there, too. There was a blanket hung in the doorway, and I tiptoed back and let the blanket down to cover the door.

This was my home now. For how long, I did not know, for it seemed that now I was not to go to that fierce old man of whom I was so much afraid.

On the table there was a loaf of bread, and beside it a knife. I went to it and cut off a thick slice. With the bread in my hand I went back to the outer door again and looked out upon the yard.

All around it was that living fence of ocotillo with its fierce thorns. There had been rain, so now there was a mist of green leaves along each cane, and a few bright crimson flowers. I stood there, taking bites of the bread and looking out at the yard of white sand.

Where the opening in the ocotillo fence was stood a thick clump of greasewood. I glanced at it, started to look away, then looked quickly back.

Something was there! From behind the bush I could see a bare foot, a foot almost the color of the sand, and the bottom of a pants leg of white.

Lifting my eyes, I found myself staring into other eyes, very black eyes.

It was a boy, no older than myself.

12

Torn between fear and curiosity, I waited, my heart pounding. The strange boy crouched, peering through the leaves at me. I was afraid.

No! I was *not* afraid! "I am Johannes Verne," I told myself, "and I am not afraid."

The boy looked to be no older than I, and no larger. I knew I could lick him. Then I looked again as the boy slowly emerged from behind the bush. The boy looked brown and strong. He looked like a very rough boy. Maybe I could not lick him.

He wore a wide hat of straw, somewhat torn, and a faded blue shirt that hung outside his pants, which were of white cotton. The boy was barefoot.

"Hello," I said.

"*Buenos días.*"

He came a step nearer. I did not know what to do. Trying to appear indifferent, I squatted and took up a twig. With the twig I drew a round head with long hair hanging down. Then I drew a hat on the head. I did not know what to say or do. I had known few children of my own age and did not know what they did. I added eyes and eyebrows, then ears to the picture.

"What do you do?" The boy spoke in English, although with a strange sound to it.

"It is a picture."

He leaned over, studying it. "Is it me?"

"It is."

"The mouth? It has no mouth. I have a mouth."

I extended the twig. "Here. You draw."

He took the twig and drew a mouth like a new moon with the ends turned up. It was a smiling mouth.

"Good! It is finished," I said.

We squatted side by side, looking at our drawing with some satisfaction.

"You live close by?"

"I live where I am."

"You have a house?"

The boy gestured vaguely. "Over there." Then, proudly: "I am Francisco."

"I am Johannes. I am usually called *Hann*-ess."

The boy shrugged. "What else?"

He was a strange boy. I did not know what to think of him. I asked, "Where do you go?"

"I go nowhere. I am here." The boy paused. "And you? You will live *here*?"

"I do not know. We were to go to Los Angeles, but there is trouble for us there."

"Stay here, if you are not afraid."

"I am not afraid. I am Johannes." Then, after a minute: "Afraid of what?"

"The house. Nobody stays in that house. It is the house of Tahquitz."

"What?" I was astonished. I pointed to the mountains. "There is the house of Tahquitz."

Changing the subject, I asked, "Your home is here?"

Francisco shrugged. "My home is where I am. Sometimes it is in the mountains. Often it is the desert."

"You are not afraid of Indians?"

He stared at me. "I am Indian. I am Cahuilla."

I was astonished. "You? An Indian?"

"I am Cahuilla."

"Why do you say this is the house of Tahquitz?"

"Much time ago my people went away into the desert to live. There had been rains and it was good there, but when they returned, this house was here, and it was lived in.

"Nobody saw he who lived here. Only . . . sometimes at night they saw something . . . somebody. Then it went away and came no more. It was whispered that Tahquitz had come to this house. That he built it with his hands."

"It is a good house."

"What will you do if he comes back?"

"He will come back?"

Francisco shrugged. "Who knows? It has been long."

"There was a house before," I suggested. "Part of this house was an older house."

"Who knows? Perhaps."

Francisco squatted by the step. I sat on the step. "I have a horse," I said proudly.

"Of course. Who does not?"

"Someday we will ride."

Francisco took a stick and poked at the ground. From time to time he looked uneasily at the half-open door.

"The mountain is large," I said. "Is it far to the other side?"

"It is far. Two times I have gone with my papa. We go for the chia that grows in a valley there. It grows many places, but not so much as in the valley. Once, the first time, there was fighting. There were others who wished all the chia for themselves. We gathered chia. Some chia."

"Is this your land?"

Francisco shrugged. "It is land. We come here. Sometimes we do not come for a long time. When it is hot, we stay in the mountains, where there is coolness."

"You speak well."

"It is nothing. In the store it is only your talk. My papa speaks much with people. He teaches me to speak."

"Last night at Indian Wells, when it was very dark, I went down to drink. There was an Indian there. He did not speak."

Francisco stood up. "I go now."

"You will come back?"

"I go."

He walked away, slowly at first, then faster. He did not look back.

When I went back inside, the room was light, and for the first time I could really see the floor. It was astonishing in its simple beauty. Around the outer edge was an intricate design and in the middle a black bird with its wings stretched, a bird like a crow.

Sitting down on the bench, I looked at the design. The details of the feathers in the wings were amazing, and the bird had small red stones for eyes.

My father spoke from his bedroom. "Is it you, Hannes? Are you all right?"

"I am looking at the bird."

"I heard you talking, I think."

"It was Francisco. He is an Indian. He is my friend . . . I think."

He came from the bedroom and closed the outer door. "After the sun is up, it is better to keep the door closed so it will be cool inside." He put his hand on my shoulder as he so often did. "It is good to have a friend." He glanced down at the floor for the first time. "Well, I'll be damned," he said.

Squatting on his heels, he studied the floor. He ran his fingertips over the floor. "Beautiful!" he said. "Simply beautiful!"

"It was Tahquitz. This was his house."

My father looked up sharply. "What do you mean? His house?"

"Francisco told me. Nobody will live here because this is the house of Tahquitz. He built it, they say, but when they returned, he went away and did not come back."

"Tahquitz? What was he like, this Tahquitz?"

"They did not see him. Only in the night."

My father was thoughtful, but he studied the floor again as if he would find in its design the face of its maker. He pointed to the design that formed the border. "That purplish stone. That's jasper. It comes in several colors. This is chalcedony. Both stones can be found in some of the canyons near the desert.

"It is fine work. This Tahquitz or whoever it was is a fine craftsman. I should like to know him."

"You do not believe it was Tahquitz?"

He did not reply for a moment, and then he said, "This work is finely done by a man who loves what he is doing. I should like to know him."

Slowly the days went by and became weeks. Sometimes I played in the yard, making friends with a very small blue lizard, and sometimes I wandered in the sand dunes. My father rested in the morning sun, stayed inside when afternoon came, and he read from the books Peter Burkin provided. Sometimes my father walked with me after the sun had gone down. Whenever we met Indians, they spoke to him respectfully, but they did not come to our house.

My father did not leave the house without his pistol. "If you see any strangers, Hannes, come to me at once. I must know."

Another time he took me to the fireplace, where he had loosened a brick. Behind it was an iron box.

"Tell nobody of this. Not your best friend, nor my best friend. In this box there is money. I have saved it since before you were born. If I should die or be killed, get this out, put the box and the brick back carefully, and hide the money. You will need it."

Later, after he had been reading to me from *Quentin Durward*, by Sir Walter Scott, I asked him if we would go to Los Angeles now.

"Not now. Perhaps later. Peter was right. The air and the sun are good for me. I feel better and I have coughed much less."

"Will they come to look for us?"

"Yes, Hannes, they will. Do not forget them, ever. He is an old devil, that one. He will come, but now he is waiting, like the cat with the mouse. He is letting us get over being careful, when we think he will not come at all, then he will come."

My father looked at the bird in the center of the floor. "It is a raven," he said, "and that is a curious thing.

"Far to the south, farther yet than where we came to the Yuma trail, there is a place in the mountains called the House of Ravens. Only the Indians know it, but these later Indians do not often go there."

"What is there?"

"Wait. Someday when I am feeling better, I will take you there. It is well not to go unless you are with an Indian."

He would say no more, and this I had learned of my father: when he ceased to speak, questions would lead him to speak no more. "You will be told in time. First, you have much to learn."

Later, when seated in the sun, he said, "This is an ancient land, older by far than the scholars believe. They trifle with years. They say that before this, nobody was here. They say the Indians have been here but a short time, and for some of them, that is true.

"There have been men here for a million years and more. Before the great ice came, there were men here—and before the ice that was here before that. The wise men among us smile and say no, that men have been on this continent but a short time.

"Who are they to say? Have they dug deeply enough? Have they looked in all the corners? Bah, they have scarcely scratched the surface! They have a Garden of Eden complex, believing that all men came from one source!"

He coughed slightly, waited for a moment, and then said, "There are writings on the rocks, and some of the writings are from Indians whom we know, or their immediate ancestors. Others come from a time far earlier, or have been borrowed from an earlier time. The Indians, just as we, have learned from those who passed this way before.

"And there have been travelers, ships have come here many times, both from Europe and Asia. Chinese junks have come to our shores even in my time."

He sat silent, staring out the window at the mountains. "If they have come in my time, why not before?

"And they have, indeed they have! You must learn to read Spanish, my son. I mean better than you do. Your mother started you, and you speak very well, but to read is better, for there are records.

"Father Salmeron tells of some Spanish soldiers encountering some Asiatics on the shores of the Gulf of California, who were trading with the Indians there, and seemed to think it no great thing, as if they had done so for years. He also speaks of Chinese ships making a landfall on the California coast."

My father sat silent, muttering a little. Then he sat up violently. "Confound it, son! You must have an education! It is time you were in school, but here there is no school! In Los Angeles . . .

"I must forget that. It is impossible. But read. There are books here, read them, all of them. Find others. Many a man has done well with no more of an education than what he can have by reading.

"Your friend Francisco. He is an Indian and will know much you do not."

And when a month had gone by, Peter Burkin returned. He rode swiftly, watching over his shoulder. "Be warned," he said, "they are coming."

13

"Thank you, Peter. Come in, please, and sit down. Will you have a cup of coffee?"

"There's no time, Zack! They can't be more than a mile or two behind me!"

"There's time. Turn your horse into the corral and come in." He lifted his own cup, and his hand was steady. "How many are there?"

"Five, at least. There's maybe more. He's got a way of sending a backup crew to circle around and come in behind."

Peter ducked outside, and I could hear him running as he led the horse to the corral and turned him in out of the way, saddle and all. When he came through the door, he was sweating, and it was still early and the air was cool.

"We've water piped into the house, Peter, and we've food enough. This place is built like a fort, and I expect we'll have a good deal better time in here than they will out in the sandhills. So sit down."

Peter sat down, glancing uneasily out the doorway. "I know about the water. Ain't often you see that. He must have figured on being trapped here sometime."

"That, or he didn't want to be seen."

"Who would see him out here? Who but Injuns?"

My father shrugged. "Perhaps he just did not want to be seen."

"You don't believe that Tahquitz stuff, do you?"

"I don't know. After all, what is Tahquitz, if there is such a being? It is just a name to cover a belief or an idea or a fear."

He turned to me. "Hannes, I'd like it if you'd get back in a corner and sit down on the floor behind the bed there."

"I want to be with you."

"I'm sorry, Hannes. I want you to do as you're told."

"I could load your guns."

"Maybe. Later."

Peter looked at me, smiling a little. "The boy ain't scared, is he?"

"He's my son," Papa said, and I was suddenly very proud. But I was scared . . . a little.

We heard their horses' hooves on the hard-packed yard. I hoped my blue lizard was hiding.

"Halloo, the house!"

My father went to the door, glancing from the window as he went toward it. "They don't know for sure that it's me who is here," he commented to Peter. "No use keeping them in doubt."

He opened the door.

He did not step outside, but simply stood in the door, perhaps a foot inside, waiting.

"You, there!" The speaker was a burly Anglo in a striped shirt. "We're huntin' Zachary Verne. You seen him?"

"I can't say that I have," my father replied mildly, "not since I got up."

"He's here, then? He's been here?"

"Oh, he's here, all right." My father was smiling. "I think he's going to be around for the next few weeks, anyway."

Over his shoulder he spoke in a lower tone. "Peter? Cover the rear of the house, if you will."

"You say you saw him? When was that?"

"This morning, when I looked in the mirror. I was shaving."

It took them a minute. One of the Mexicans behind the Anglo said, "It is heem! He is the one!"

"You? You're Zachary Verne?"

My father simply stood there, smiling a little, and then suddenly he said, "Well? What did you come for?"

"I came to ki—!" Even I, who was not quite seven, even I saw he was clumsy at it. He started to lift the rifle which he held across the saddle in front of him, and my father shot him. Without haste, he shot the third man, for the second, the one who had been quickest to recognize him, had gone around the house.

Peter's gun boomed, and as he started to load it, I took it from his hands and showed him the shotgun, which he took.

Careful to spill no powder, I reloaded Peter's rifle and then crossed to stand behind my father, but those who had been about to attack were

gone. One man, the Anglo, lay sprawled on the hard earth where I had
drawn Francisco's picture. There were spots of blood where another
had bled, and two riderless horses stood in the yard.

Suddenly a horseman spurred by us at a dead run down the lane, and
my father watched him go, gun in hand. "No use to shoot him," my father said. "He's anxious to get away. I do not think he will come back."

"He's lost some fingers," Peter Burkin said. "He dropped on the far
side of his saddle, so I shot off the pommel and took some fingers with
it."

"Thank you, Peter." My father turned to me. "And thank you,
Hannes. You are very cool. I like a man who doesn't lose his head."

My father sat down suddenly, as if exhausted. He looked at Peter and
shook his head. "I don't have the strength anymore, Peter. I lack
stamina."

"You're lookin' better." Peter walked over and closed the outer door.
"No matter what you may think, this air's good for you."

"Possibly."

Peter went out, and when I looked again, the body was gone and the
spots of blood had disappeared.

When we were alone, my father said, "To kill a man is not a nice
thing, no matter what the reason. He would have killed me, and you, so
I had no choice. I hope this will be an end to it."

"Who was he, Papa? He is not the don?"

"No, just a man hired to kill, as they all were."

"Is the don afraid, that he does not come himself?"

"No, he is not afraid. I do not believe he knows fear. Perhaps he has
never had occasion to be afraid. He hires such work to be done, just as
he would hire a man to break horses or trap coyotes."

It was almost a month before Peter Burkin rode again to our house at
the end of the lane. He rode a fine bay gelding and sat well in the saddle, and he brought a sack of good things to eat and three books. "Got
'em from a ship's master," he said. "Your pa dearly loves reading, so I
keep my eyes out for him. I do a mite of tradin' now and again. This
time I had me some sea-otter pelts, prime fur. I made him throw in the
books as boot."

He stripped the gear from the bay, talking the while. "He remembered your pa, and his pa before him. You come from a seafarin' family,
boy. Your pa was more'n seven years at sea before he came to California. Get him to tell you about those places he went to.

"My stars! When I hear him talk, his words are like a song my ears have been wanting. He sailed afar, boy, to places with names like music: Gorontalo, Amurang, Soerabaja, Singapore, Rangoon, Calcutta, Mombasa, and places like that. I d'clare, I could sit and hear him talk forever. It's no wonder Consuelo fell in love with him. The way I hear it, half the girls in California were in love with him. He was a talker, your pa was."

Peter turned the bay into the corral and put his saddle and gear in the small barn. "Listen to me, boy, and gather memories while you can. They come easily now and will warm an old man's heart when the time comes.

"Do not forget the lasses who were good to you along the years. Remember their eyes and their laughter and the way they were with you. It is a good thing not to forget. And remember the shadows on the hills at sunset or in the dawning."

He paused. "Your father is better?"

"I think so. He seems to cough less, but he coughs."

"Aye, it is a miserable thing, the lung disease. Stay in the fresh air, boy." He looked around at me, taking off his chaps. "Have you seen the Indian lad?"

"No."

"Do not worry about it. He will come again. They are strange folk, Indians. Perhaps not so strange as just different from us, but he will come back. I know his father, too. He's an important man among them."

"Will you come in?"

"Of course I shall. Am I interrupting, then?"

"My father reads to me at this hour. Less than he used to because of the coughing, but he reads."

"Good! He can read to me, too. If it's Scott or Byron, I'll prove a good listener. Or Shakespeare. There was a cowhand once who said that Shakespeare was the only poet who wrote like he'd been raised on red meat."

"Shakespeare?" my father said when asked. "Not today, I think. This is a day for Homer. You will like him, Peter. His people were very like those around us now. Achilles or Hector would have done well as mountain men, and I think Jed Smith, Kit Carson, or Hugh Glass would have been perfectly at home at the siege of Troy."

"Troy?" Peter Burkin said. "I mind something of Troy. That's where they fought that war over a woman. Helen, wasn't it?"

"She was the excuse, Peter. Troy controlled travel from the Black Sea into Mediterranean waters, and the Greeks wanted to be rid of Troy. If it had not been Helen, they would have found another excuse."

Those were the wonderful, beautiful days! My father grew better. The clear dry air seemed good for him, and he began to take walks with me, and sometimes to ride. Yet never without a rifle and a pistol.

We saw the Indians from time to time. Once I saw Francisco, and waved. He stood watching us ride away, yet I continued to look, and finally he waved.

My father talked of the desert, of books and men and ships. Peter Burkin returned and rode with us. He was worried about the old don, and warned my father.

"He'll try again. I don't figure he's worried as long as you're here, just among Indians. If you started for Los Angeles . . .

"He don't want you there, no way." He rode in silence, then added, "After what happened here, nobody is very anxious to try you. At first it seemed like money found, just to ride out here and kill a man already sick.

"When that first outfit came back with one man dead and two wounded, those who might have tackled you were short on enthusiasm."

My father tired quickly, so sometimes we sat down right where we were and talked. When he grew tired, his cough was worse.

Often he spoke of the Indians, of how they lived and of their beliefs. "We do wrong," he said, "to try to convert them to our beliefs. First we should study what they believe and how it applies to the way they live. First they must be sure of our respect."

"Francisco does not come."

"Give him time. They believe ours was the house of Tahquitz."

"It was another thing, I think."

My father waited, watching the cloud shadows on the desert. "I spoke of the Indian I saw at the Indian well. The old man who wore turquoise."

"You really saw such an Indian?"

"I do not know if he was an Indian. I *thought* he was." There was a time when I said nothing, and then I said, reluctantly, for I did not wish to be thought a fool, "I do not know where he was standing. I have thought of it since."

"I do not understand."

"At the foot of the steps, beside the water, there is a flat place of hard earth. I stood there. When I took a drink, I looked around and he was standing there."

"Beside you?"

"Facing me. He was standing where there is no place to stand." I hesitated; then I said, "I offered him a drink, in the dipper. He just looked at me."

"And then?"

"You called."

My father was silent for some time and then he said, "Hannes, we know so little. Our world is far stranger than anyone has guessed. We know a little and scoff at much we do not understand, but the Indians are either a simpler people or one far more complex who merely seem simple.

"There are trails in the desert, and mountains, Hannes, trails the Indians no longer follow. Here and there, for a little way, they use them. The trails were made by the Old Ones, the people who were here before the Indians. We do not know who they were or what became of them, and some of the white people do not believe in them at all. The fathers at the missions have told the Indians it is nonsense and they must not speak of them."

"These Indians, too?"

"No, these are not mission Indians. Some of them go to Pala occasionally, but usually they return here. No priests have come here yet."

"Where do the trails go?"

"Nobody knows. To water, probably. Sometimes I believe they go to hidden places where there is writing on the rock walls."

"What does the writing say?"

"Often it is only a few pictures of animals, sometimes there is more. We do not know what it means."

"I shall find out. I want to know what it means."

"There are trails no Indian will follow. Someday you may go, but first there is much to learn." My father got up. "It grows late. Now we will go home."

There were sandhills and cactus where we were, and there was scattered brush. The sun was going down. Something moved in the sand and started a small trickle down the dune toward us. Looking up, I saw nothing.

"If it is the house of Tahquitz," I said, "I like it. Will we stay there?"

"If he comes to claim it," my father said, "we will give it up, although I like it, too." He paused to rest. "It shows much love, that house. It shows the love of a man for his materials and his creation. It is a thing to be respected. There is beauty in the house," he added, "and I envy the skill of the builder."

I thought of the trickling sand. It was probably a lizard. "Will he come back, do you think?"

"Who knows?"

My father took my hand. "Come, we must get home. I am suddenly very tired. I wish . . ."

They were there, waiting for us in the yard. There were four of them. The first was an old man with white hair and a stern face. His eyes were mean and cruel. He said, "It is he. Kill him."

"Sir?" My father's tone was calm, although he must have heard the men behind us. "Let the boy go. He is a child."

"Kill the cur," the old man said, "and kill the whelp. Do it now!"

He turned sharply away as he spoke, and my father shoved me hard away and to the ground, and he drew. His right hand was shoving me from danger, so he drew more slowly. He was hit twice—I saw it— before he could fire. He fired then, once, and a man fell. His second shot cut a nick in the corner of our door, and then he fell.

"Be sure he is dead." The old man spoke quite calmly. "Such carrion is harder to kill than a snake."

Men came around my father and shot into his body. One of them turned his pistol to me.

"Not here," the old man said. "We will take him with us and leave him in the desert. It is better so."

A man grabbed me, and I kicked him. He slapped me hard across the face, smiling past his mustache. "Try that again and I'll cut off your ears before we leave you."

He had a scar across the bridge of his nose, a livid scar that must have almost cut it in two. He was one of those who shot my father as he lay on the ground.

"Take him," the old man said impatiently. "We must be gone. The Indians will come."

"We will kill them, too," said the man with the scar.

"You are a fool! They are many, we are few. Always," he added, "they have liked him as if he were one of their own."

Holding me tight, the man with the scarred nose twisted my arm and smiled when I winced. "Maybe he will give you to me," he said. "Then we shall see you cry. When I move, you will tremble. When I lift a hand, you will scream."

It was almost dark now, and they rode swiftly, avoiding trails. There were nine of them besides the old man.

One was a young man, very handsome, very cold. He had looked at me with contempt. Now he said to the old man, "At last it is done. When this one is dead, it will be finished."

"Leave him to me," the scarred one said.

The old man turned sharply. "Silence! He will die. We will leave him in the desert."

"We are riding east!" the young man said suddenly. "It is the wrong way!"

"It is the right way," the old man said impatiently. "The Indios will believe we are returning through the pass. They will ride after us. They cannot see our tracks, for it is dark. East is the right way."

There was a faint light in the sky when they stopped. It was an empty place of flat sand and broken rock and cactus. All around, as far as I could see, there was nothing but a few great boulders and the empty desert. "Here," the old man said. "Leave him. He is of my own blood, after all. If he dies—"

"Kill him now," the younger man said. "Leave him dead."

"I will not," the old man said stubbornly. "Leave him. Let the desert do it. I will not destroy my own blood even if it is mingled with that of scum. Leave him."

The man with the scarred nose pulled me free of the saddle and dropped me, then sharply turned his horse so that it would trample me, but I rolled away, then ran and hid among some stones.

"Leave him!" the old man said impatiently.

They started off, and filled with anger, I stood up among the rocks. "Good-bye, Grandpa!" I shouted.

He winced as if struck, and his shoulders hunched as from a blow. He started to turn, but the young one said, "It is an insolent whelp! Like the father!"

They rode away, and I was alone.

14

I was in the desert. I was alone. To myself I whispered, "I am Johannes Verne, and I am not afraid."

My father was dead. They had killed him, and they had left me to die.

I was not going to die. I was going to live. I was going to live and make them wish they were dead. The faint light in the sky had increased. I stood by the rocks where I had gone to hide, and I looked around.

Everywhere was desert, sand and bare rock. Here and there was cactus. Those who brought me here had ridden all night, and they had said they were riding east, but I knew it was not only east. It did not matter. I would follow their tracks.

How far had we come? They had traveled at a good gait, slowing to a walk from time to time, but most of the time at what my father called a shambling trot.

I knew something of distance, for we had counted the miles westward from Santa Fe. Mr. Farley had often spoken of how far he must go each day, or how far he had come. I suspected they had brought me forty miles into the desert. Those who rode horses thought it a lot to walk, but I had walked behind the wagon sometimes and I did not think it was so far.

It would be hot. If I was to walk, it must be now when the air was cool. Mr. Farley had rested his horses during the hottest part of the day. He would only begin to travel when the sun was down. When it was cool, I would walk; when it was hot, I would find a place to hide from the sun.

Where? I did not know.

What would Francisco do? He would do as I was doing. He would walk. What else?

There were the tracks of their horses in the sand. I could follow them back to the house of Tahquitz.

Turning slowly around, I looked at where I was. It was a place to start from, a place to begin. In a few days I would be seven years old. In a few years I would be old enough, and then I would go calling. There were three men I would visit. The old don, the young handsome one, and he of the scarred nose. It was a thing to live for.

My mother had taught me never to hate. Hate would destroy him who hated. Nevertheless, I would hate. My mother was gone, my father had been murdered, I had nothing else.

My legs were short. I wished they were longer, and tried stretching my steps. Behind me the sun would be rising. The tracks were there, sometimes plain, sometimes faint. My father had taught me a little of tracking, but here it was not needed. The tracks of ten horses were plain.

I had no water. We had stopped at no spring. I had not been this way before. I did not know where water could be found. I was thirsty, but not enough thirsty to worry. I would wait, and walk.

"I am Johannes Verne," I said aloud. "I am not afraid."

Then the strangeness came. Suddenly I stopped and looked all around. The sand was almost white, the rocks that had seemed black now were brown, the sky was very blue and there were no clouds. I should have been afraid, but I was not. All about me seemed familiar, although I had seen none of it before, and had ridden through it only in darkness.

I sat down on a flat rock. This was where I belonged. My mother had come to love the desert, my father had lived with it, in it, had loved it and its people. Maybe that was it, but there was something more, too. I felt that I was born for this, to live here, to be a part of it.

When I began to walk again, I did not hurry. Soon I must seek shade, and before night I should have to find water. Yet the strangeness was upon me, the feeling that I was not alone, a feeling that the desert was a friendly place.

A jackrabbit started up and bounded away, then stopped, sat up, and looked at me. Then I saw where a snake had crossed the sandy trail, and some kind of bug had crossed over the snake's trail.

It was growing hot. In the sky, no longer quite so blue, but misty with heat, there was a buzzard. He had seen me and was watching.

"Go away!" I said aloud. "I am not your dinner!"

The buzzard could not hear me, but he would not have believed me. I remembered what my father had said, that the buzzard has only to wait. In the end, we all come to him or his like.

I began to look for shade. There was none. I thought of pulling brush and piling it over a place where I could crawl for shade, but everything was stiff and dry and covered with thorns or stickers.

The shadows of the Joshua trees were short. It would be nearing midday and there was no shade. My mouth was very dry. I picked up a little pebble and held it in my hand until it was not so hot, and then put it in my mouth. It would help for a little while. I stumbled.

Some kind of small bird had run ahead of me in the sand. Far off, to the south and a little west, there seemed to be mountains. Were they our mountains? They must be. How far I had walked, I did not know. I sat down again.

By the shadows it was midday, and I had been walking since just before daylight. Jacob Finney had talked to me about the desert, as had Mr. Farley and Mr. Kelso, and of course, my father. I knew I must find shade and rest. A man or a boy could not live long without water.

The trail of tracks I was following dipped down into a dry wash, and the opposite side was steep. By the time I climbed out of the wash, I was very tired. And then I saw the rocks. It was only a small clump of rocks, but they were heaped together and one of them made a shelf that held a little shadow. When I was closer, I could see a hole behind it. Carefully, because of snakes, I inspected it. Taking a stick, and careful before I picked it up to be sure it was a stick and not a snake, I prodded into the shallow hole.

Nothing. . . .

Crawling in, there was room enough for me to lie down. A crack toward the back let a small breeze come through. It felt good.

Finally I must have slept, because when I opened my eyes it was cooler and I could see the sun was down. Crawling out, I looked all around. There was nothing but the desert. Keeping the stick with which I had prodded for snakes, I started to walk.

A little sand had sifted into the tracks. They were no longer so plain. Suddenly I was afraid. What if the tracks disappeared?

Stopping, I remembered what Jacob Finney had said. "Always take your bearings. Locate yourself."

I knew where the sun had gone down, which would be west. So I was facing south. Far away I could see a jagged point of rock, and it was due south. Walking on, night came, and I chose a star that hung in the south right over my point of rocks; then I walked on.

The desert is cold at night, and soon I was cold, but I walked on, stumbling once in a while. A coyote howled and I took a firmer grip on my stick. It was a good strong stick.

My mouth was very dry. Sometimes it was hard to swallow. I took deep breaths of the cool, clear air, which seemed almost like water, it was so fresh. Once I almost fell asleep walking. When I found a flat rock, I sat down. The coyotes seemed close, and I wondered if they were following me.

Somebody had said they did not eat people. My father laughed at that. They were carnivores, he said, and would eat anything available. They were afraid of the man-smell because it meant danger, but they would attack anything they might eat if it could not fight back. If a man or a child is helpless, my father said, he might be eaten. Jacob Finney had agreed.

"No animal has any special respect for man," he said. "It is just that they have learned to fear. Once they lose their fear, a man has to be careful."

Clutching my stick, I waited. If one came close, I would hit him.

Bending over, I gathered some rocks. They were black against the white sand. I piled them beside me on the flat rock.

Sometimes I dozed, yet I tried to stay awake, and several times I heard something moving, but I couldn't see anything. A small wind stirred, rustling the dry leaves on the brush. Something stirred again, closer. I picked up a rock and threw it hard. After that I heard no sound.

A long time later I awakened from dozing and heard a soft sound, so I took my stick and hit the brush near me; then I threw another stone into the darkness. In stories, they always spoke of gleaming eyes peering from the darkness. I saw no eyes. I heard only the soft rustling of something moving in the darkness.

When the first gray light came, I stood up. I was very stiff, and very tired. Also I was hungry, but mostly I wanted a drink. The coolness of the night had made it better, but I wanted a drink, I needed a drink.

Papa had said one could get a drink from a barrel cactus, but I did not see any. Just stiff, dry wood and sometimes whitish-looking grass.

My point of rock was gone. My star was gone. I could not find the tracks, yet I could see where the sun was rising and I started off to the

south. I had not gone far when I saw a coyote track in the sand. It was
a fresh track.

When I topped a small rise, I sat down. My legs ached and I was
very tired. I put a pebble in my mouth again, but it did not work very
well. The sun had come up, and it was very hot.

Heat waves shimmered on the desert, and far ahead I could see a
blue lake that was only mirage. There were rocks ahead, and more
brush. Beyond them I could see the mountains, the San Jacintos they
were called, but they seemed far, far away.

Then, walking on, I found the tracks again. Following them, I fell
down, and when I got up from the sand, my hands were bloody from
the gravel.

There were other, older tracks. I was on some kind of a trail, and it
seemed to dip down into the hotter desert, but beyond were the mountains. My tongue was dry and I could not swallow. My eyes hurt and I
was very hot. I wanted to lie down, but the sand was like a hot stove.

For a time there was a sound, a drumming sound, and then it became the sound of horses, and I turned around.

A half-dozen riders were coming at me. Was it a dream? My eyes
blinked slowly, and I frowned, trying to make them out. They were
only a blur against the shimmering heat waves, and the horses seemed
to have legs enormously long, but that was the heat waves again.

They came up, coming out of the heat waves and the dust, and the
foremost rider had a wooden leg.

They pulled up, and the man with the peg leg said, "Holy Jesus! It's
Verne's boy!"

He dropped from the saddle, amazingly agile, and held his water bag
to my lips. A sip and a swallow, then he took it away.

"Just rinse your mouth this time," he said. "Let it soak in a mite."
After a moment he said, "Where you comin' from, boy? Where's your
pa?"

"They killed him," I said. "They were waiting for him. He tried to
push me away so I would not be hurt, and they shot him."

"He git any of them?" another man asked.

"One, I think." Peg-Leg gave me another swallow and then stepped
back into the saddle, reaching a hand down for me.

"Come on, son," he said. "We'll take you in." Then he hesitated.
"Your pa's dead, boy? What'll you do now?"

"I want to go to our house. Peter Burkin will come."

"Reckon he will, at that. Pete's a loyal man." Peg-Leg started off, leading the way. "You got grub in that house, boy? You got some'at to eat?"

"Yes."

We rode on for a little way, and then he stopped and let me have a drink, stopping me before I drank too much.

"We come on your trail, boy," Peg-Leg told me. "We follered you. You come quite a stretch, you surely did."

He looked down at me. "You got anybody in Los Angeles, boy?"

"No, sir." Then I said, "Maybe Miss Nesselrode."

He laughed. "Say! I mind her! That there's quite a woman!" He turned in his saddle to speak to the others. "Said if I stole any of her horses she'd hang me!" He chuckled. "By damn, I think she'd do it, too! That there was some kinda woman, boy. When the time comes, you find yourself a woman like that. Ain't none any better."

A long time later, after the drum of hooves and my own tiredness had made me fall asleep, we rode up the lane toward our house. All was dark and still.

"Tom?" Peg-Leg said. "Take a look inside. See if there's anybody there. We'll cover you."

Tom swung down, and, gun in hand, walked over to the door and lifted the latch. He stepped inside. A moment, and we could hear him fumbling about for the candles; then light streamed out the door.

His boots went from room to room; then he came to the door. "She's clean as a whistle, Peg!"

Peg-Leg lowered me to the ground. "You'll be all right here, boy? You an' them Injuns get along?"

"Yes, sir."

"I know they set store by your pa. You get some sleep now, boy. Drink a mite now an' again, but don't tank up until tomorrow. Then you'll drink more'n you ever thought a man could hold.

"An', boy? You be careful of that ol' Spanish man. He hears you're alive, he'll come back for you. He'll skin you alive."

For a moment longer he stayed, and then he said, "You see, boy, I dasn't stick around. I'm a man with enemies. There's some as would hang me in a minute if they come upon me. I d'clare, boy, I'm goin' to pack it in an' head north. This here's too rough a life for an old man. I can make a good livin' up there in Frisco sellin' maps to that gold mine folks think I lost."

He turned. "See you, boy! I'm right sorry about your pa. He was a good man!"

For a long time I stood alone in the yard near where my father had fallen, listening to the receding sound of their horses. Then I went inside and looked around.

I was alone in the house of Tahquitz. Would he be angry that I was here? Would he come to drive me away or kill me?

What *was* Tahquitz? Who was he . . . or *it*?

I was very hungry, yet I did not want to eat. I straightened my bed, undressed slowly, then crawled into bed. For what seemed a long time, I lay still, staring into the darkness above me.

Somewhere far off there was a low rumble, and the earth seemed to shake a little. Was it Tahquitz?

Was he angry?

But this was my home. It was the only home I had. What would I do now? What *could* I do? Would Peter ever come again? And why should I matter to him? I was not his boy. He had business of his own to see to.

A low wind moaned around the eaves, and sand rattled against the windows and ran nervous fingers along the roof.

Miss Nesselrode had said I could come to her, but if I did, I should be close to my enemies and they would know I was alive; and that they must not know. To Los Angeles was a ride of five or six, maybe seven days. I did not know just how far.

What could I do? I could stay. I could live here, in the house of Tahquitz.

At least, until he returned. . . .

15

When morning came I went to the cupboard. There was bread in the breadbox, there were two jars of jam, and there was cornmeal, two bottles of wine which I did not drink, and there was coffee which I did not drink either. At least, not often.

I found in the cool place under the floor a big hunk of cheese, so I cut off a piece and returned the rest to the cloth wrapping and the open jar. With the cheese and a piece of bread thickly covered with jam, I sat down by the table and ate. Until then I had not realized how hungry I was. Before, I had only wanted water.

When I had eaten, I went to the door, and Francisco was there.

"You do not see Tahquitz?"

"No," I said.

"He was here. He covered the blood." Francisco pointed to the place where my father had fallen. "Then he went away."

"What was he like?"

"I did not see him. Nobody sees him. He comes in the night, and he goes. He was heard." Francisco looked at me. "He was in the cabin."

Awed, I looked at the cabin. He was *there?* He had been *inside?*

"What do you do?"

"What?"

"You can come with us. You can become an Indian."

"But I am not an Indian."

"You can live like Indian." He glanced at me from the corners of his very black eyes. "You can eat like Indian. At least," he added, "you can eat."

I could eat. When the bread was gone, and the jam and cheese, what would I do?

Father had told me that the Cahuilla collected acorns, that they were an important part of their diet. They also collected chia and other seeds.

"I must stay here. Peter Burkin will come. Then I will go with you and you will teach me what to do."

Francisco stood up, and then for the first time I saw the buckskin bag he had. He held it out. "Is for you." He looked at me. "Jerky?" he said, as if the word were not familiar.

Peering into the bag, I could see the pieces of dried meat.

"*Gracias*," I said, and he smiled, showing his white teeth.

"I go now," he said.

He walked away, and after a moment I went back inside. Tahquitz had been here!

Standing just inside the door, I looked all about me. If Tahquitz was here, what did he do? Why would he come? To see his home, if this was his house? To see what we did here?

Nothing was changed, nothing was different. Carefully, going from room to room, I looked for what he might have done here, and I found nothing.

Anyway, I did not believe in Tahquitz. He was a story, like "Cinderella" or "Jack the Giant-Killer." Even the Cahuillas had not seen him; they had heard him, which was not the same. It could have been the wind, or a coyote. It could have been anything.

Papa's rifle stood in a corner, and I went to see if it was loaded. It was. His pistol belt had been hung on a peg in the bedroom, and I took it down. It was loaded, too. Somebody had loaded it, because my father had fired it. Somebody had loaded it while I was gone.

Taking the pistol belt from the peg, I hung it on the bed. It would be close to me at night, if I needed it. I had shot a pistol, but only with my father helping me. I had shot a rifle, too.

Remembering what my father had done, I got the broom and swept the cabin floor. Then I wiped the windows clean and dusted the furniture. In the desert there is much dust.

When the house was clean, I filled the bucket with fresh water and filled a water bag and let it hang in the wind to keep cool.

Chewing on a piece of the dried meat, I went to the shelf to look at the books. *Quentin Durward* was the book my father was reading. I would try to . . .

It was gone!

There were twelve books on the shelves, and I had looked often at each, but *Quentin Durward* was not among them. Yet there were still twelve. I looked again, and the book that replaced *Quentin Durward* was another novel by Scott, *Guy Mannering!*

Hesitantly I took the book down, and as I opened the pages, I caught a faint odor of pine needles. Holding it to my nose, I sniffed curiously.

Definitely pine, but our books had been nowhere near any pine trees. Very carefully, half-frightened, I put the book down. Who had been here since we had been gone? Tahquitz, Francisco had said, but that was nonsense.

There had been someone else; someone had been in our house, had taken one of our books and left another, hoping no doubt that we would not notice. Especially that I would not notice, for my father was dead.

It was unusual that a boy of my age should read such books, but my father and mother had both taught me, and I had begun reading at an early age, after my parents had read to me.

Why bother to substitute a book at all? Why not just push them together, hoping no one would notice there was one fewer on the shelf?

Again I picked up the book, slowly turning the pages. I turned almost a third of the book, page by page, but there was no clue. The odor of pine needles remained, and there were no pines here. The only trees here were palms, smoke trees, and a few palo verde. In some of the canyons there were sycamores.

Uneasily I put the book down again. Yet, why not read it? *Quentin Durward* was gone, but the new story might be quite as good.

Yet I put the book down for the time and went outside. The horses came to me eagerly, and I realized I had not fed them, and did so. They had water running into a trough, so that was something I did not have to do, yet they were my responsibility now, and I must not forget. But who had fed them when I was gone? Francisco, no doubt, or one of the other Indians.

Turning, I stared up at the looming San Jacinto Mountains, rising so steeply from the desert. If Tahquitz lived up there, why would he come down here? It was high, and must be cooler. Cool enough that there might be pines. The thought frightened me, and I went quickly inside.

My feet were very sore and there were places where my heels had chafed during the walk. I bathed them again and lay down, trying to think what Papa would have wanted me to do.

I was half-asleep when I heard a horse. I heard the clop, clop-clop of hooves and got quickly up, wide-awake. I looked to the pistol and went to stand beside the door. My heart was pounding. Then the rider came into sight, and it was Peter. I put down the pistol and ran outside.

"Howdy, boy. Is it true, then?"

"Yes, sir. There were many of them. He pushed me out of the way before he got his pistol out."

"He git any of them?"

"Yes, sir. One, I know."

He dismounted and I went with him as he walked his horse back to the corral. He watered his horse, then tied it and took his rifle from the scabbard. We walked back to the house with the sunshine on the peaks.

Inside, he got out the pot and made coffee as I told him what had happened and how Peg-Leg Smith had found me and brought me in.

"He's a cantankerous old devil, but he's a good man to have around if you're in a corner." He looked at me. "How you doin', all by yourself?"

"All right. I think I shall go with the Cahuilla. They spoke of it."

"You ain't got no other folks, I know. Your pa said something about this Nesselrode woman?"

"She was in our wagon coming west. She said she would take me, but she may have been just talking. Anyway, I want to stay here."

"Here? Alone? Well, I was on my own when I was nine, and I hadn't as much savvy as you. I brought you some grub. It's in those sacks back of my saddle, but that ain't much, an' I'm not sure I can keep makin' this trip."

"It is a long ride."

"I got to make a livin', boy." He looked around. "No place for you there. It's a mighty rough neighborhood where I live, and all I've got is a bunk in a cheap roomin' house with a bunch of drinkers an' fighters."

"I am all right here. I want to stay."

"Mind if I sleep here tonight, boy? I'm surely tuckered." He looked at me again. "You ain't scared they'll come back?"

"They think I am dead."

"Well, you ain't. No tellin' how long before they find out." He paused again. "You seen anything of that there Tahquitz?"

"No."

Peter stoked his pipe with tobacco, waiting for the water to boil. "Any of that bunch get inside? I mean those folks who killed your pa?"

"No. They killed him, took me, and rode away. They didn't even look inside."

Peter's chuckle was not amused. It was a dry chuckle concerned with something in his mind. "Give 'em a shock if they had," he said.

He did not say anything more, and I did not know what he meant. Sometimes I had a feeling Peter knew more than anyone guessed.

Gesturing at the books, he asked, "Can you read them? I reckon you're a mite young."

"I can read them. Some words I do not know, but if I think, I can find their meanings. Papa and Mama started teaching me when I was three. We traveled a lot and I was with them all the time."

"Well, I brought you some more. I don't know what they are, but a man in town who reads a lot, he said they were good."

He pulled off his boots and sat on Papa's bed looking at me. "Got to get you an eddication. Your pa had it. He knew everything, I reckon. Me, I never had no schoolin' to speak of. I can read a mite, an' I can cipher, sign my name, and the like.

"Read them books, boy. Learn something. I got no eddication, and all I can do is work for the other fellow. I prospect a mite, trap a little fur. It ain't much more than a livin', son, so you get you an eddication."

He dumped some coffee into the pot. "I better find that Nesselrode woman. She will know what to do."

"I want to stay here. I like it."

He smoked and we drank coffee and after a while he pulled on his boots again and went out to the horse and took off its saddle and turned it into the corral. He brought the saddle inside, then the sacks of supplies.

"There's enough here to last you awhile if you use care. You know how to make flapjacks, boy? No? Well, that's one thing I can teach you! Nobody makes no better flapjacks than I do, and I'm a fair hand with bakin'-powder biscuits, too."

He sat staring at the floor. Finally he said, "That there's *work!* I mean, he who done it was a lovin' man. He *cared* about what he did."

He glanced around uneasily. "Kinda spooky place, ain't it, boy? I mean, with that Tahquitz an' all. I never set much store by such things, Injun things, but some of them knew a whole lot we'll never know. Good people, too, although I never knowed 'em like your pa did.

"That black bird, now? Here in the floor? See those red eyes? Those are garnets, boy. Some folks think they're rubies, but no such thing. Garnets. Out in the desert off to the north, there's a crater. Injuns call it Pisgah or some such thing. There's garnets there, boy. I found some."

He chuckled. "I showed 'em one time to a man in a saloon, he grabbed at 'em, studied them a mite, and then, makin' like he didn't care, he offered me a price for them.

"Now, I could see right through him. He figured they were rubies and I was too dumb to know the difference. He offered me a small price for them and I took them up and held 'em in my hand and told him no way.

"They were pretty red stones, and I was going to give them to a woman I knew. Make nice beads, I told him. By that time he was sweatin'. He wanted them stones so bad he could taste it.

"I told him my woman would surely like them. I said, 'Why, I wouldn't part with ary one o' them for less than a hundred dollars!' You know somethin', boy? He jumped at it. That's what he did. He fairly jumped at it. He gave me a hundred dollars apiece for three of them!

"Now, I won't rightly say I did the honest thing, but I never *told* him they was rubies. I never told him different. Was I, a plumb ignorant ol' desert rat, s'posed to know a ruby when I seen it?

"He figured he was cheatin' me, and I taken his money. Fact is, I get myself a fresh grubstake ever' now and again, just that way. I go into a saloon or somewhere, maybe an eatin' joint where there's newcomers, and I take out those garnets and study them. Soon or late, somebody wants to buy 'em.

" 'Just pretty red stones,' " I says to 'em. " 'Ain't worth nothin' except to my woman. She'll set store by them.'

"You know somethin', boy? They try to talk me into sellin' those red stones! And you know somethin'? I must be gettin' weak, because almost ever' time they convince me to sell. With three hundred dollars I can prospect for a year, livin' high on the hog.

"Now, when I leave here, I'm goin' north to that crater and find some more. It ain't easy, for they ain't so easy to find, but they are there."

Peter stayed for a week, teaching me how to make flapjacks, biscuits, and a few simple things, and I learned from him how to find gold, how to pan, what to look for. When he rode away, I did not know that it would be a long, long time before I saw him again.

16

In the passing of days, I rode often to the mountains or desert with Francisco, and often we accompanied his father and other Cahuillas who went to look at the acorn crop, for the oaks provided much of the living for the Cahuillas. It was important they be gathered at once or they would be eaten by squirrels or other animals and birds. Also, if the season was wet, they might rot on the ground before they could be gathered.

We rode along the watercourses to judge the mesquite and screwbean crops, or to see when the tuna would be ripe on the cacti. The Indians knew each plant and what it offered in seeds, fruit, or pulp.

On one day we came upon a dim, dim trail leading off into the remote distance, but when I pointed it out, they rode on their way. "It is a trail of the Old Ones," Francisco explained.

"You do not follow it?"

"It is *their* trail. We have our own."

"It might lead to water."

"It is their trail."

Yet only some of the trails were avoided, and I did not know why. Perhaps the water that had once been there was gone now, or the groves from which the Old Ones gathered had disappeared. And who were the "Old Ones"?

Each day I learned something new, and when we went to the desert and mountains, I watched which seeds were gathered and which plants were avoided. Having crossed the desert with my father, Mr. Farley, and the others, I had learned much, but I began to see that the area in which the Cahuilla lived, partly due to the range of altitude from below sea level to the top of the mountains at more than ten thousand feet, was richer in plants than those held by other Indians whose countries I had passed through.

Occasionally we met other Cahuillas, and once a party of Cheme-huevi, and all knew me because of my father. He had discovered their starving time and had come to them with beef cattle. Flash floods had swept away some of the mesquite groves upon which they depended, and dampness left by the rains had ruined the acorn crop, but the beef my father brought saved their lives.

The days passed into months, and the months into years. In the house, I puzzled over the books, reading slowly, gradually becoming accustomed to the strange words, learning their meanings by their associations. Once a strange Indian came suddenly to the door, warning me of riders, and I slipped away into the dunes to watch.

No doubt it was believed that I was dead, but my grandfather was an uneasy man, and perhaps rumors had come to him that somebody lived in this house. Once, when they would have entered the house, they were stopped by Cahuillas who rose like ghosts from the dunes, bows bent and rifles ready. The riders turned their horses and very wisely rode quietly away, expecting at any moment an arrow in the back and perhaps a pitched battle. The Cahuillas had followed them for several miles, making them aware their presence was not wanted.

Yet I had not begun to understand the remoteness of the area in which I lived. The pass between the San Jacinto Mountains and Mount San Gorgonio was the best of all passes to the coast but was the last one found by white men. From a distance, approaching from the east, the high peaks loomed against the sky, seemingly an unlikely place for a pass.

Once they had arrived, the Californios rarely visited the desert. Some of them had come by sea, others came over the inland route from Mexico that crossed the river near the home of the Yuma Indians, then the desert and the Anza route over the mountains, which lay south of the pass where I lived. There simply was no reason for them to make the long, difficult journey from Los Angeles to the southern desert.

Nor was there anything here they wanted, nothing to incline them to make the attempt. The hot springs from which Agua Caliente took its name had long been used by Indians, but the Californios had access to hot springs that were closer, and the existence of these was scarcely known.

From time to time a book vanished from my shelf, but always another book took its place, and once during my first months alone a sack of piñon nuts was left on my table. Another time a loaf baked from some strange, nutty flour.

Reading became easier, so I welcomed the strange books, but I was careful not to mention the exchanges of books to the Cahuillas, who might not have understood.

Obviously, somebody was hiding out on the mountain who did not wish to be seen but who did not wish me any harm. If he did not wish to be seen, it was his affair.

When my father died, he left some six hundred dollars in gold coins. When the supplies dwindled away and Peter came no more, I took one of the coins from the iron box my father had hidden away to the small store to replenish the supplies.

The storekeeper took my coin; then, glancing around to be sure he was unheard, he said, "I ain't askin' you, boy, but if you got more of these, you'd best not let folks know. Even the best people will talk, an' there's drifters come through who'd kill a man for less than this."

He hefted the coin. "This here will buy you all you want and then some. You leave it with me, and when you are needful of something, just come an' get it. I'll tell you when I need more."

He seemed a kindly man, yet I trusted no one. His suggestion was logical, however, and I did as he proposed.

Often alone, sometimes with Francisco, I wandered the fringes of the desert and deep into the San Jacinto and Santa Rosa mountains. Often I climbed in the canyons, occasionally staying out for days at a time.

One day when alone I heard a horseman coming. The door was open to catch the coolness of the evening, so I took down my father's pistol and stood in the doorway, holding it down by my side, only my shoulder, arm, and one eye showing.

All my life I had been familiar with guns. Long ago I'd been taught that all guns were to be considered as loaded and were to be handled with care, yet any rider might be an enemy. Yet when the rider came within sight, I almost dropped the gun.

It was Jacob Finney!

Tucking the pistol behind my belt, I stepped outside. As soon as he saw me he began to smile. "Well, now! You've growed some! Mind if I get down?"

"Please do, and come inside."

Leaving his horse ground-hitched, he came in, putting his hat on the floor beside him as he sat down. He noticed the pistol.

"You expectin' trouble?"

"Yes, sir. They killed my father."

"Heard of it. From what was said, he taken one or two with him. Well, that's too bad. He was a mighty fine man."

"He would have taken more of them, but he tried to push me out of the way before he drew."

"Like him."

"How is Mr. Kelso?"

"Last I heard, he was workin' a claim in the Mother Lode country. Farley's got him a ranch down San Diego way."

He looked at me again. "You're a couple of shades darker from the sun. How old would you be now?"

"I am ten."

"I'll be damned! You look four or five years older. You been takin' care of yourself here?"

"Yes. The Cahuillas are friendly, and I spend a lot of time with them. Sometimes I eat with them, sometimes I cook, but usually I eat what they do. There's piñon nuts, tuna, and sometimes berries."

"Surely ain't doin' you no harm. Seen the horses out yonder, too. You been ridin'?"

So I told him about the wild country, the desert, the ancient sea bottom, and the old shoreline that could be seen along the sides of the mountains. "I've found lots of shells out there, old seashells from ages ago. The Cahuillas say the sea has been in there several times. Or maybe it was water from the Colorado."

"All right if I stay the night? I'm packin' my own blanket roll."

"Sure. I'll put up your horse."

"Leave it to me. Always take care of my own horse, no offense meant." He got to his feet, turning his hat in his hands. "I come out here a-purpose to see you. Didn't know if you was alive or not, but Miss Nesselrode—you remember her? She's been mindful of you. Sent me to see if you were alive. Said she told your pa she'd care for you." He grinned. "Not that you seem to need much care."

He went outside and I started some coffee. It was good to see him. When he came in and dropped his gear in a corner, I asked, "How is Miss Nesselrode?"

He chuckled, giving me a sly, amused look. "Now, that there's quite a woman, Hannes, she really is. Purty, too. She found herself a little adobe, bought a few odds and ends, and went to church, and the first thing you know, she's been proposed to a couple of times and is cuttin' quite a figger there around town. She walks around with that lacy parasol of hers, and the first thing you know, she's bought herself a horse an' sidesaddle.

"Seems she heard of some hard-up trapper who has ketched some sea otter. Saying nothin' to anybody else, she had me buy those skins from him, at rock-bottom prices. Then she shipped them off to China. Meanwhile she heard of another man up the coast who had skins for sale, and she bought them, got them off on the same ship.

"She's right canny, that woman is. She hired Kelso an' me to do the shippin' for her, an' she's just a mighty pretty young woman, visitin' around.

"You know how womenfolks are, always talking of clothes, babies, marriage, an' what's happenin' around. Well, she listens, she gets acquainted with the families of Abel Stearns, Isaac Williams, Wolfskill, an' them.

"She has me buy about sixty acres of land, and on Wolfskill's advice she plants it to lemons an' oranges. Then she has Kelso buy another piece, which she plants to grapes.

"Los Angeles is a sleepy little town. A lot of ructions down in Sonora Town, time to time, but the Californios don't much care what happens as long as they have a fandango now and again, good horses to ride, and money to spend on fancy clothes.

"They're good folks, but there's never been any pressure on them until now. Times have changed, and most of them can't see what's happenin'. You've heard talk of beaver. When folks over in France and such places switched from beaver hats to silk hats, the bottom fell out of the market. There just wasn't any money in trappin' or tradin' for beaver anymore.

"Now, some folks think the mountain men were just a bunch of big ignorant trappers. You an' I know otherwise. They were mighty shrewd men who went to tradin' an' trappin' because if a man kept his hair, that was the fastest way to get rich.

"Now that beaver don't bring no good prices, what do they do? Keep ridin' a dyin' horse? Not them. Some of them had already been out here with Jed Smith, Ewing Young, and the like, so they come out. They've got a little money, a lot of savvy, and they commence buyin'. Some of them married Spanish girls, but whatever they do, they are in business.

"They open stores, banks, start plantin' grapes to make wine, oranges, lemons, and such. Land is dirt cheap, so they buy land, most of them become Mexican citizens.

"Now Miss Nesselrode arrives in town. She's a mighty pretty woman and she meets folks, and men like to talk to pretty women and they like to show off how smart they are. She sits in their patios, has that beautiful smile working, and she's a good listener.

"Kelso, he takes off for the Mother Lode country, but I stay around. You know something? One reason I stayed is because I just want to see what happens.

"Now, I'm around her a good bit. I notice things. She's losin' weight, gettin' right thin. When I stop by, she always has coffee for me, but she doesn't invite me for dinner anymore. It takes a while to sink in, and then I get it. She's broke. She's livin' on guts and the few dollars she has left. She's invested what all she had in a gamble, a damn big gamble!

"What I'm talkin' about is the first six months she was here. One time I am tyin' my horse to her gate and she doesn't know I'm there. I see her countin' her money. It's mighty little. She counts it an' recounts it, an' there can't be more than ten, twelve dollars there. She stands there, figurin' like, chewing on her lip.

"I knock on the door, she lets me in, we have coffee, and she is all smiles and she tells me she's made up her mind. She's goin' to open a bookstore."

"But you said she had no money."

He chuckled. "Like I said, that woman's got nerve. Real, down-to-bedrock nerve! She's holdin' a busted flush and she bets everything on her last card.

"The next morning she goes to see Abel Stearns. Now, Abel, he's a shrewd man an' he's got more money than he knows what to do with, an' he's made it all himself.

"She goes to him and tells him she intends to open a bookstore and until her 'funds' arrive from Boston, she is short of cash, but she wants to open the store *now*. When she walks out of there, she has the credit, and she already has a few books of her own. She gets more.

"That store becomes a gatherin' place for all of that old mountain-man crowd and some others. She meets the stage, buys books and magazines, even newspapers from people. Her place is the best source of what goes on back in the States.

"Within a few weeks it is the place where Wolfskill, Workman, Rowland, Wilson, Stearns, and all that crowd come for news and to see each other. And she's busy, workin' around, but listening. I tell you,

Hannes, within the next three months that woman knows more about what's happenin' in California than anybody!

"Stearns isn't hurting for money, she's an attractive woman, so he doesn't dun her. When she's in business for about six months, she's been in Los Angeles about a year, you understand, then her ship comes in.

"I mean that ship comes back from China and she has sold those otter skins to the Chinese for ten times what she paid for them. She pays off Stearns and she's free an' clear with money to work with.

"So she stocks her bookstore, orders more books, papers, and such, and then goes up and down the coast, me helping, buying otter skins, cowhides, anything she can sell.

"She goes out to remote ranches which have a time gettin' hides down to the shore where they can be sold to the ships. She buys cheap.

"She lives like she always did, goes about her business with a friendly smile and a kind of wide-eyed innocence. She owns her bookstore building, she owns another building close by, she owns a small ranch, some horses and cattle, and she operates her bookstore like it was a bank. That woman's a caution!"

"I'm glad," I said. "I liked her."

"That's what brings me here," Jacob said. "She wants you to come to Los Angeles. She sent me to get you."

17

Los Angeles?

"I don't know. What of my grandfather?"

Finney tugged at a boot, then stopped. "I asked her that, but she says he believes you're dead.

"He has a place in town, but he spends most of his time out on his hacienda. When he does come in, he rides in like a king, with six or eight vaqueros riding along."

Jacob pulled off the boot and placed it on the floor. "She'd give it out that you were kinfolk from back East. She has dealings with ship owners, ship captains, and the like. She could say you'd just come around the Horn with one of them."

Suddenly I wanted very much to see her. She had been kind, and she had known my father, even if only for a short time. I knew he had respected her.

Also, she was a no-nonsense sort of woman. I remembered the Indian she had shot. Then, for the first time, I was admitting I was lonely.

"She's worried about your education. She says she promised your pa she'd look after you if anything happened to him."

"I like it here."

"You could always come back. Look here, Hannes, you ain't an Injun. This here is all right for now, but what will you do when you're a man? Your pa had education. He could go anywhere. He could have been anything.

"You ain't an Injun, and no amount of livin' out here will make you one. You come along to Los Angeles and have a talk with Miss Nesselrode. If you want to come back, nobody will stop you."

"I like this house, and some of the things belonged to my father."

"Leave 'em. I'll speak to the old gent down at the store, and you can tell your Injun friends."

"They do not come here. They are afraid."

"Afraid? Of what?"

"They say this is the house of Tahquitz. They think because I live here that I have a special power, that my medicine is very strong."

He knew nothing of the story of Tahquitz, so I told him the little I knew. He listened attentively, then said, "I ain't one to scoff at superstitions. To my thinkin' there's always some truth to the stories you hear." He pulled off the other boot. "Then this place will be safe. We'll just leave any truck you don't need."

Lying awake, listening to Jacob Finney snoring lightly in the other room, I wondered about Los Angeles. It had been long since I had visited a town, so long I scarcely remembered anything before Santa Fe except glimpses here and there, little things that clung to the memory. And Santa Fe was nearly four years ago.

When morning came, I would take a hundred dollars in gold and leave the rest hidden. I would have my own horse, my own pistol and rifle. When I wanted to return, I could saddle up and ride. Traveling in the wild country was an old story now.

Francisco appeared as I was putting the rifle in its scabbard. "You go?" he asked.

"To Los Angeles," I said, a little proudly.

"It is far," he said.

"Five days," I said, "perhaps six. I am not sure."

"My papa was there. There are many big houses."

"No doubt."

"You will not come back."

"My home is here, in this house. My father is buried here. I will come back."

"You will not come back." His face was solemn.

"You are my friend, Francisco. You will always be my friend. I shall come back to this house, and I leave my father's things here. I leave even the books."

"Ah, the books." He knew how I valued them. "Perhaps you will come back."

So we rode away when the sun was touching the peaks of Mount San Jacinto and Mount San Gorgonio, and the pass we followed led into the darkness that lay between them.

As we topped the first rise, I looked back at the scattered palms, the mesquite, and the few huts, even the flat roof of the store. My house was hidden among the dunes, and I wondered about my unknown visitor who borrowed books and left others. Well, he would be pleased, I thought, to find two new books on the shelf. I had found them among my father's things and I placed them in the place from which he had last borrowed a book.

Looking back, I could see the Leaning Rock at the mouth of Chino Canyon. Some named it the Calling Rock, and it is said that when one is away the Calling Rock calls you to return. It is also said that if you turn and see it as you leave, you will always come back. I looked long, for I wanted to come back. Francisco was there, and he was my friend.

Jacob spoke of Los Angeles. "Is it by the sea?" I asked, remembering my father had come to it on a ship.

"No, it is twenty miles from the sea. At least twenty miles."

"Will we see the sea?"

"There are low hills and mountains from which it can be seen. There are islands far out across the water. You will see them. It is said that long ago the Chumash Indians made plank boats and went to the islands. They painted them red. I do not know why."

"My father told me of them."

"It was a custom, I suppose. Remember, now! Tell no one you have come from the desert. Do not even speak of the desert. You have come by sea, newly arrived from the States. Before we arrive in town, you will change into your city clothes."

"But they are small for me now," I protested.

"No matter. We will get others in Los Angeles. You have been months at sea. You would naturally have grown. You must be careful! There is always talk, and even the *gentes de razón* have large ears. If it is discovered you are from the desert, if they know you are your father's son, you will be in danger."

"I will remember." After a few steps by the horses I said, "I have no friends in Los Angeles. To whom could I speak?"

"You will make friends. Also, there is Miss Nesselrode, and I, too, am your friend. Most people talk too much, anyway."

We rode on, and my thoughts returned to words my father had spoken, for I was much with him, and being silent, I heard a great many things which I wondered about later. There was much I did not understand and much I came to understand as I grew older. But there was much to think about when I was alone, and often I lay awake wondering about things that were said.

There was a time when a man spoke very impatiently to my father. He had seen a copy of the *Iliad* lying on the table. "You are reading this?" he asked.

"I have read it many times. Now I read it to my son."

"But he is too young!" The man protested, almost angry.

"Is he? Who is to say? How young is too young to begin to discover the power and the beauty of words? Perhaps he will not understand, but there is a clash of shields and a call of trumpets in those lines. One cannot begin too young nor linger too long with learning.

"Who knows how much he will remember? Who knows how deep the intellect? In some year yet unborn he may hear those words again, or read them, and find in them something hauntingly familiar, as of something long ago heard and only half-remembered.

"Yet perhaps it is only that I like to hear those rolling cadences. People, I think, read too much to themselves; they should read aloud from time to time to hear the language, to feel the sounds.

"Homer told his stories accompanied by the lyre, and it was the best way, I think, to tell such stories. Men needed stories to lead them to create, to build, to conquer, even to survive, and without them the human race would have vanished long ago. Men strive for peace, but it is their enemies that give them strength, and I think if man no longer had enemies, he would have to invent them, for his strength only grows from struggle."

My father had waved his hand about at the stark Arizona mountains and the desert where the wagon rested.

"Homer sang of his 'wine-dark seas,' but we, I think, will sing of these. You will find that our Homers will sing of the plains, the deserts, and the mountains. Our Trojans may appear in feathered war bonnets, but none the less noble for them. Our Achilles may be Jim Bowie or some other like him, our Ajax might be Davy Crockett or Daniel Boone."

My father was a tall man, and now he stood up. "My friend," he said, "I do not know what else I shall leave my son, but if I have left him a love of language, of literature, a taste for Homer, for the poets, the people who have told our story—and by 'our' I mean the story of mankind—then he will have legacy enough."

Was this, then, this ride to Los Angeles, was this like a voyage among the Greek islands? Was this to be part of an epic? If so, it was a dusty one! And I was wishing Jacob would decide to rest the horses, because I was tired. Yet, looking over my left shoulder and turning a little, I could see a fine sweep of mountains, and the pines that grew there.

Again I remembered those long plains over which we had passed, the great tower and broken battlements of El Morro, the magnificent vistas of plain, mountain, and forest. Whatever else my father had given me, he had given me a chance to see these, to know them, to live with them.

I thought of Francisco. Who had been his Homer? What stories had he heard beside the campfire when the winter winds chilled the flesh? For it was in the winter the Indians told their stories.

Over the fire that night, Jacob warned me, "Don't you be expectin' too much. It will remind you some'at of Santa Fe, but Miss Nesselrode, she says we shouldn't be fooled by it. She says Los Angeles will be a great city, an' the best thing ever happened to it was when those beaver pelts fell in price. She told me one time, she said, 'Mr. Finney, it will be silk hats that build Los Angeles, because when over in Europe they stopped wearing beaver hats and switched to silk, it started all of those very wise, very bold mountain men looking for new ways to get rich.'"

He added sticks to the fire. "Now, don't you be judgin' all Californios by your grandpa. By an' large, there aren't any finer folks livin'. Generous to a fault, give you the shirt off their backs, and do it graciously and with an air.

"There's another thing. They're proud of bein' Californios. They don't consider themselves Spanish, nor do they think of themselves as Mexicans, although there's plenty of those, too. They call themselves Californios, and although Los Angeles ain't much, right now it is the biggest town in California, and you'll see why they love it.

"But she's rough! I mean, almighty rough! There's good folks aplenty, but there's some of the meanest people unhung. Kill you soon as look at you.

"Pistol or knife, but mostly it's knives in Sonora Town. Back to the east, when a man wants to do you harm, he takes up a shootin' iron of some kind, but out here it can be a shootin' iron or it can be a knife or anything handy. You got to remember that folks were killin' each other with rocks and clubs for a million years before anybody invented a pistol. So be careful. Learn to handle yourself and to handle weapons, but mostly you just learn to guard your tongue. A man out here who speaks careless of others will soon only have a marker in the graveyard."

We had been lying in our blankets, and the last coals were smoldering when suddenly Jacob raised up on his elbow, knowing I was awake.

"You listen to Miss Nesselrode, boy. She ain't no mountain man, but she's one of those who will make the wheels turn. I seen that right off.

"You just set back an' watch that woman operate. Ever' time she flutters her lashes or turns her parasol, she's figured out some new way to make a dollar!"

But I was not thinking of Miss Nesselrode, nor of my father; I was just thinking of how wonderful it was to be riding west into a new land, and to be sleeping under the stars.

My last thought was not of that warm and sunny place called Los Angeles, it was of my grandfather, the one who had my father killed and who created the fear with which I lived.

18

The night was clear and cold, with many stars. The wind off the sea was fresh when we rode down to the water's edge. Out upon the water we could see lights from a dark hulk beneath bare poles, a ship at anchor.

"Brought you roundabout, Hannes. We're ridin' into town like I met you here as you come off the boat. We'll stay the night down here at the harbor."

He turned his horse and rode toward a shack that stood back from the water's edge near a small dock where two boats were tied up. There was a corral beside the house, with two horses already there.

A single light was burning in the shack, and Jacob rapped on the door without dismounting.

"Who's there?"

"Jacob. It's Jake Finney, Cap."

The door opened and a square-shouldered old man stared from him to me. "Is this the young rascal who sailed around from Bedford with me?"

"Yes, sir," I said, "and a fine voyage it was, too, except for that bit of rough weather off the Horn."

The old man stared at me, and then he smiled. "Well! He's got a quick tongue, Jacob. Let's hope he has the brain to go with it."

"I liked stopping at the Galápagos," I said, enjoying it, "and the turtles we took aboard there."

The captain glared at me. "Who did you say this lad was, Jacob?"

"Zachary Verne's boy. Grandson of old Adam Verne, if you remember."

"Remember? How could I forget him? My first two voyages to the

Pacific were made with him. Adam Verne's grandson, eh? Well, I'll be damned!"

He took his pipe from his mouth. "Where's your pa, boy? I knew him well."

"He's gone, sir. Passed away. Murdered, actually."

"That's why the trickery, Cap. The lad's in danger. They believed they'd done for him, too."

"Then why risk it, lad? Come aboard my ship and you can sail to China. I'll sign you on as cabin boy, and before long you'll learn to navigate and be a ship's master like your grandpa."

"Thank you, sir, but I am expected in Los Angeles."

"Miss Nesselrode will see to his education, Cap. She promised Zack Verne she'd do that."

"Nesselrode, eh? Well, I'd not say it of another woman I know, but if she intends to see after the lad, it will be done. If there's ever a woman should wear pants, it's she."

"It would be a pity, sir, lovely as she is."

"Eh? Oh, yes, of course. She's a handsome woman. That's the trouble, Jacob, dealing with a handsome woman is unsettling to a man. When he should have his mind on business, he's thinkin' of other things."

He stepped back. "Come in, lad. You an' me can talk some while Jacob puts up the horses."

It was a long, low room with tiers of bunks along one side, all neatly made up. Directly ahead was a table and two benches, and on the left side a fireplace with a small fire going.

"The bunks are clean. No bugs, I mean. You pick whichever suits you and dump your gear." He seated himself at the table and reached down to the hearth for the coffeepot. "You drink coffee, lad? I don't think much of it for young folks, but there's nothing else hot."

"I'll have a bit, sir. Just a bit."

The captain knocked the ash from his pipe on the edge of the hearth and began to stoke it anew. "Knew your pa, but your grandpa better. They were good men, good men." He struck a match and sucked on the pipe. "Your pa was killed? Must have taken some doin', as I remember him. He was a fightin' man when need be."

"There were several of them, sir, and he took time to push me out of the way. He got at least one of them, wounded another, I think."

"That's like him. There was no quit to him, but always a thoughtful man." The captain puffed at his pipe and glanced at me from quizzical blue eyes. "If you an' Miss Nesselrode don't hit it off, lad, you just be on the beach next time I come to port. You'll be welcome aboard. You've the sea in your blood, and I'll see you've a chance."

"Thank you, sir."

"That Miss Nesselrode, now. Jacob tells me you came west on the wagon with her. She get a case on your pa?"

"I don't think so, sir. I think she liked him, maybe felt sorry for him. He was very sick, you know."

"A takin' woman. Make some man a fine wife if he was up to it. It would take a strong man, a man sure of himself to cope with her.

"She's a pretty woman, lad, and pretty women sometimes can do things no man would attempt. Mighty few men will say no to a pretty woman, no matter what she's after.

"Talked with her some. She come aboard, maybe two years or more ago, said she wanted to talk. Well, now, that old ship of mine is no lady's boudoir. She's a workin' vessel, shipshape an' neat, but no comforts, mind you.

"No matter. She come aboard, drank coffee with me, and asked if I was sailin' to China.

"To *China*? No such idea entered my head. I was buying cargo, selling what I brought, and contemplating another voyage to Hawaii, maybe.

"China, she says, so I ask her why I should go to China. She smiles very nice—she's got a lovely smile, that lady—and says to sell furs. That it is the best market for otter.

"I tell her I don't have any such skins and she gives me that smile and says, 'But I do, Captain. I have three hundred and forty-two otter skins, some beaver, marten, and two hundred cowhides.'

"Lad, I was flabbergasted. Here was this handsome young woman who should be settin' at tea with some other young ladies, tellin' me she had all those skins for sale.

"Next thing I know is, I'm makin' a deal to sail to China. I warned her there was risk. She said she understood that. 'Nothing is gained without some risk, Captain.'

"We talked a bit and she asked questions, very sharp questions about markets, products, and shipping matters. I tell you, lad, there's a shrewd woman!"

Jacob came in, chose a bunk, and then came over to the table. "Weather changing," he commented. "We're in for some rain, and we can use it."

He paused. "Cap, have you heard any talk about war with Mexico? Nobody out here knows anything, but some men came through from Texas who say there's a lot of hard feeling."

"I've heard rumors. What's the feeling here?"

Jacob chuckled. "These are good people, Cap. Good-natured. They want no trouble with anybody, but right now they have closer ties with us than with Mexico. They want to be known as Californios and only that. Push 'em, and they'll fight . . . there's always cuttings and shootings among the rougher crowd in Sonora Town . . . but mostly the people here just want to go their own way. If it comes to trouble with Mexico, I believe California would stay out of it unless some hothead starts trouble. If it becomes a matter of honor, the Californios will fight."

"Their trade is mostly with the States," the captain commented, "and I hear complaints about governors appointed from Mexico who don't understand conditions here."

"They want a California man for governor," Jacob said, "and you can't blame them. It takes too long to get word back and forth from Mexico City, and some of their rulings don't make sense here. These are good people. Let them alone and they'll be all right."

"They won't be let alone, Jacob. You know that. It is too rich a country. Jedediah Smith showed the way across the desert and mountains. Ewing Young and his party got through also, and there have been others. They were just a beginning."

Far into the night they talked, often of things my father and mother had discussed. Everything about California, that mysterious place of menace, had fascinated me, yet finally I fell asleep, curled in my bunk.

When I awakened, Jacob had already saddled the horses.

"Sleep well? There's a place up on the trail where we'll breakfast." He stopped, one hand on the saddle. "They have hot chocolate. Figured you'd like that for breakfast.

"The captain, he went back to his ship last night." Jacob pointed toward it. "He's anchored about three-quarters of a mile out. When the weather's right, he can come right in over the bar, as he doesn't draw more'n about nine feet. Someday folks will get busy and deepen that channel, and you'll see ships in here, dozens of 'em.

"Miss Nesselrode, she thinks this is going to be a big city."

"San Pedro?"

"Well, that or Los Angeles. Get aboard and we'll get going. It'll be nearly a day's ride as it is, us stoppin' to eat."

We rode our horses up the slanting trail from the shore. When we reached the top of the rise, we could see another ship beating in toward the bay.

"Now, don't you be talkin' about Miss Nesselrode an' all she does. First place, folks would think you were storyin', because she kind of keeps it quiet. Womenfolks aren't supposed to be into what she is."

"Don't people know?"

"Here an' there. Don Abel Stearns knows. He's maybe the richest man around. Owns a lot of land. There's a few others . . . men.

"She's canny. Nobody ever really sees her talkin' business. Womenfolks wouldn't approve; neither would most of the men. I do some of it, but mostly it is just a word or two on social occasions.

"The captain, he's been out to China and Japan twice now. He carries other goods, of course, but he does better with the furs he carries for Miss Nesselrode. Otter hides are much in demand there, for they are beautiful furs.

"It was a canny thing, to begin with them, but a frightful risk, too. She could have lost it all, had the ship gone down."

There was a small patch of trees ahead, and off to the left a much larger bunch, a sort of a wild forest of scrub oak and sycamore mingled with what they called chaparral, which was a kind of mixed growth of brush and small trees, all entangled. The trail skirted wide around it.

"Bears," Jacob said. "California's grizzly country, an' a grizzly ain't afraid of nothing. Tackle a man soon's he would a rabbit, but they eat mostly roots, berries, leaves, and suchlike. They'll feed off dead animals, sometimes make their own kills—it depends on the bear. Grizzlies is notional."

We rode over a slightly rolling plain covered with sparse brown grass and patches of brush or trees. Ahead of us there was a low adobe building, some corrals, and a lean-to shed. The roof of the adobe was of red tile.

"See that tile? Injuns made it. Taught by the folks at the missions. The missions are closed now, and the Injuns who made the tile have gone back to the hills, most of them. There's no tile to be had nowadays."

"How big is Los Angeles?"

"Oh, maybe fifteen hundred to two thousand. Varies some. A few years back, 1836, I believe it was, they taken a census. Came to two thousand two hundred and twenty-eight in the whole county, and more'n five hundred of them were tame Injuns. They figured there were forty-six foreigners, twenty-one of them considered to be Americans."

He turned his horse in through the gate and drew up at the hitching rail. "I don't pay much mind to such things, but Miss Nesselrode, she wants to know everything."

Jacob dismounted. "Come along, Hannes. Out here folks eat breakfast at ten o'clock, usually, and what they call dinner at about three. Sometimes they eat supper, mostly they don't.

"I know these folks. Pablo won't be here, most likely. He works on the *zanja*. You know, the irrigation ditch that runs through town. Isabel . . . that's his wife . . . she's a Mexican girl. Pablo's Californio.

"Let's go in. Isabel feeds folks who come along and prob'ly makes as much as Pablo does. Maybe more."

It was cool and still in the stone-flagged room. There were three tables with benches beside them, and as we entered, a young woman came in. She was plump and quite pretty, with very large dark eyes.

"Señor! It is not often you come this way! Would you be seated? I have not much, but . . ."

She left the room, returning in a moment with hot chocolate and some tortillas. "Wait! You like the quesadilla, señor, and you shall have it." She paused, looking at me. "And you? What would you like?"

"The same," I said, embarrassed. It was not often that I talked to a woman.

The hot chocolate was really hot and it tasted good. I had drunk chocolate but once before this and liked it very much.

When she returned with the quesadillas, she said, "You come from the sea?"

"He does"—Jacob gestured to me. "I have just met him at the ship. He will live in Los Angeles and go to school there."

"Ah? You have family?"

I shook my head.

"Miss Nesselrode was a friend of his family. She asked me to meet him and bring him to her."

"She is very pretty, Miss Nesselrode," Isabel said. "I wonder that she is unmarried."

Among the Californios, who often married at fourteen, an unmarried woman of thirty was a puzzle. Yet I had not read romances for nothing. Between bites of quesadilla I said, "He died . . . or was killed. I do not know."

Immediately she was all sympathy. Who understands a broken heart better than those of Spanish blood? "Ah! I see! When she was very young?"

"She was in love," I said solemnly. "He was very handsome. She thinks only of him."

When Isabel had gone to the kitchen, Jacob glanced at me from the corners of his eyes and said very softly, "Now, I never knew that before."

"Neither did I, but she will tell the story and they will have an answer that pleases them. Now they will understand and ask no more questions."

He grunted. "For a youngster no older than you are—"

"It is in many of the stories, and the Spanish are a romantic people. My father knew many of their songs, and so did my mother. They all seem to be of broken hearts and lost loves. I just said what is in the songs."

He chuckled. "Boy, you're a caution! You surely are!"

It was sundown when we came within sight of the town. It lay on a wide, undulating plain, and to the north there was a line of low hills; on the east there were mountains. There was a river flowing near the town, and there were vineyards and many trees. Within the town itself the streets seemed to have no plan or system. The houses were mostly of adobe, flat-roofed and low, yet here and there was a larger frame house or an adobe of two stories. There was a government house and a church.

Jacob Finney led the way through back streets to a pleasant house surrounded by a hedge of willows. The *zanja* ran close by.

The house was of adobe with red tile on the roof. It seemed better built than many of the others. There was a corral behind the house, with several horses.

"You go knock on the door, Hannes. Miss Nesselrode will be anxious to see you. I'll put up the horses."

Hesitant, I stood in the yard, trying to straighten my clothes and brushing them with my hands. There was a low roof over the porch, and a bench with a rocking chair beside it. Slowly I walked up, and just as I lifted my hand to knock, the door opened and a young Mexican girl was standing there.

She stepped back, showing me in, and Miss Nesselrode came to greet me, both hands outstretched. "Johannes! After all this time! Please come in!"

She stepped back and looked at me. "My! You've grown! And what a handsome boy!"

I blushed, shifting from one foot to the other. "How do you do, ma'am?" I asked.

"Sit down, Johannes. I can see we're going to have to get acquainted all over again." She smiled suddenly, beautifully, and I found myself grinning at her. "Tell me, now, what have you been doing? What is it like, this place where you've been living?"

So I told her, slowly at first, then with increased confidence, about Agua Caliente, the Indians, the store, the forests of palms in the canyons, and the house itself.

"A hot spring? Tell me about it."

She had the girl bring us chocolate, and she asked many questions about the climate, the soil, what grew there, and who lived there.

Later, I told her about my father's murder and how I had been left in the desert. "I heard of that," she said. "Johannes, we must be very, very careful! Your grandfather is a very influential man. He is also very wealthy. He does not mix with people here, and particularly not with the Anglos, but there is little he would not know if he wished. The advantage we have is that usually he does not wish.

"He must not see you. You look very much like your father, only you are darker. The Spanish blood, I expect."

She stood up suddenly. "It is late, and you must rest. Tomorrow we must find a tutor for you. Until then I shall see what I can do. In the meanwhile, Hannes, is there anything you want?"

"Something to read?" I asked, and then added, "And when someone goes back to my house, I'd like to send some books back there."

"But why, when you are living here?"

So I told her about the house of Tahquitz and the unseen visitor who exchanged books with me.

She sat down, hands clasped before her, elbows on her knees. "What a strange story! Just think of it! A monster who reads Scott and Bulwer-Lytton!"

"I do not know that he is a monster. I do not know who built the house, or who comes to get the books, or even if it is the same . . . person."

"How long ago was the house built?"

"Only five or six years ago, I think, but there was another house there, or some sort of building. Part of the walls are very old. My father said very, very old."

"The Indians know nothing?"

"Who knows how much an Indian knows? No Indian feels it necessary to tell what he knows about anything. They are good people, most of them, but they think differently than we do."

"You've learned a lot, Johannes."

"No, ma'am. I've learned a little, but I know there is so much more. My father always said that was the wonderful thing about learning, that there was no end to it."

The Mexican girl came in from the kitchen. "Señorita?"

"Yes?"

"There's a man over there, hiding in the willows across the street. He watches the house."

"Thank you." She glanced at me. "You are not afraid, are you?"

"No, ma'am."

She smiled at me. "You want to know something, Johannes? I am not afraid, either."

19

Miss Nesselrode was slender and elegant. I never knew her to raise her voice or make a violent movement. Her dresses were simple, of gray or brown, in the lighter tones. Invariably, when she left the house, she carried a parasol. She smiled often, but her smiles were of several kinds, and I learned to know them.

Of who she was or what she had been, she never said, nor did she ever speak of her plans or what she expected of life. When she came to California she had a little money. Far less money than most believed, although how much that was, I never knew, and I believe I knew more than anyone. It was very little.

She met people easily, and they liked her. In the times of trouble, she was always ready to help, and seemingly always knew what to do. Invariably she took charge, quietly, efficiently, and without seeming to be in charge.

She had what my father would have called a well-ordered mind. I mean, it was uncluttered. She seemed to have an ability to isolate a problem and examine it without anything else intruding, and above all, she could make decisions. She would have been a highly successful gambler. Indeed, that is probably what she was: at first she must always have gambled; later, only on occasion.

She seemed tall. Even when I grew to my full height, she seemed tall. Men always looked at her, at first with hardly concealed excitement, then with respect. I believe that in the first year she was proposed to two dozen times, and often by men of wealth and power, but of that I only heard through gossip or the talk of the girl who worked for her.

She had at once hired a girl. Wages in California were very low, but she looked carefully at a number of girls before she asked one to work for her. In the meantime, she hired Jacob Finney.

I believe she had spoken to him before the wagon arrived in Los Angeles, or at the Bella Union Hotel, where she stayed for the first few days.

Jacob liked California and had commented once that he thought of settling there. Somebody asked him how he would make a living, and he said he was not sure, but he would find something.

She hired him for twenty-five dollars a month. It was as much as he would have earned as a cowhand in Texas, probably more than he expected.

"What am I to do?" he had asked.

"Do as you please, but be there when I need you, and I will need you often. Above all," she had added, "I want a man who does not talk. I want you to say nothing of what we are doing, but not to seem mysterious in any way."

First, she had him buy horses for herself and for him. Then she had him buy two cows for milking and some chickens for eggs. He planted some trees, tended some flowers, and he listened. At breakfast in the morning and occasionally in the evening, he told her what was happening in the City of the Angels and what people were talking about.

She wanted the talk from the cantinas, from the saloon in the Bella Union, and from the corrals. She wanted most of all to know who was doing what when it came to buying, selling, or investing. She listened, and she visited. She attended fandangos, but rarely danced.

She drank coffee with the women, listened to them talk. She watched the handsome young Californios ride into town in their magnificent suits, some of which cost several thousand dollars, and often astride saddles worth as much or more.

After her early moves buying up sea otter skins from trappers she continued to buy more. She bought bearskins and other furs. She bought hides. In none of this did she appear or seem to have a hand. It was always Jacob, although often she sat a horse nearby and listened. They had signals by which they communicated, and when she felt the price was right, she bought.

By the time I came from the desert, she had bought an old adobe to use as a warehouse. She had also managed to buy several acres of land on the edge of the town. These she had planted to orange trees and grapes.

On the second day I was there she had me read to her. When I had read for a time, we talked about the story. She had many questions, but it was mostly fun talk, about the people, their clothes, their horses. And for the next few days we talked a lot, about Ivanhoe, Robinson Crusoe, Robin Hood, things of which I had read or which I had learned from my father.

She was, I know now, trying to judge my education, if it could be so called.

"Do you remember Thomas Fraser?" she said one day.

"Yes, ma'am. He was the man who took notes when we came west."

"That's the one. He is here in town, still working on his book, and he has started a small school. I thought we might send you there. Although he knows your true identity I believe it would be worth taking that risk since I think he would be a good teacher for you."

"Yes, ma'am." A thought came to me. "What happened to Mr. Fletcher?"

Her expression changed ever so slightly. "He is here. I see him occasionally on the street, but he goes to San Francisco quite often."

"I didn't like him."

"Nor did I. And I like him no better now. He is a gambler at least part of the time. Avoid him, Hannes."

Later, when we were alone, I asked Jacob about him. "Yeah, he's around. He's a bad one, boy, a real bad one. He's become a sort of leader for a small group of thugs, but so far he's done nothing anybody could catch him at."

Jacob was currying a horse. He paused for a moment, both hands resting on the horse. "Your grandpa doesn't come to town too often. Only time he's seen much is ridin' to his house in town. Always has six to eight vaqueros with him . . . tough men.

"Rides a black stallion, big, fine-lookin' horse, and the old man can *ride*. Has to, if he handles that animal, and he does. Believe you me, he does.

"Keep out of his sight. You look like your pa, but something like your mother, too, or so the Indians say. Ain't likely he'll see you. He pays no attention to anyone, seems like, but you never know."

Miss Nesselrode was interested in the desert, and she asked many questions about my life there and how I had lived.

"You must remember not to speak of it," she warned again. "Although the chances are the subject will never come up. To Angelenos the desert is far away, and most of them know nothing of it at all. Nor are they interested.

"That is part of the trouble," she added. "This is their world and sometimes they seem to think there is no other. Unhappily for them, there is another world and it is filled with acquisitive people.

"When a Californio wants money, he wants it *now*, and he will pay for it. They do not seem to grasp the workings of compound interest, and they have always bartered for things and there has always been plenty of land, plenty of cattle. They are nice people, but they cannot seem to understand there may come a time when it is all gone."

"Do you lend them money?"

"Yes, and I have warned them. They smile and thank me very pleasantly, but I am a woman and they are merely tolerating me.

"They borrow money and the interest is compounded monthly. When the notes fall due, no effort is made to collect because they who lend money want the interest to continue. Finally the borrowers have to give up thousands of acres of land to pay for comparatively small loans."

She paused. "Thomas Fraser will be your teacher. You read very well, better than most adults whom I know, and you write well. Now you must learn to cipher, and you must learn something of geography. Our world today is growing small. At any time some faraway country may become important to you, to your country, and to your business. Above all, you must learn to be a good citizen, and that means you must learn how your government works and how to go about getting things done, either in government or business.

"The one thing we know, Hannes, is that nothing remains the same. Things are forever changing, and one must understand the changes and change with them, or be lost by the way.

"You have come into this world with good health and a good mind. The rest is up to you."

When I awakened the next morning, I did not get up at once, but lay abed thinking. My enemy was here, close by. A man had been watching our house. . . . Why? Had it something to do with me? Or with Miss Nesselrode? When it came to that, who *was* she? Why was she willing to take me in, send me to school, have me in her home?

Was it kindness? Respect for my father, and pity for him and for me? Or was it loneliness? Or was there some other reason of which I did not know?

The reading of stories causes one to wonder about motives, but I could think of no reason why a small boy would be useful, but many ways in which he might be a trouble or at least an inconvenience.

While dressing, I thought of school. I wanted to go to school, yet I didn't. I had known very few children of my own age, and none very long. Francisco had been the only one whom I could call a friend. We had moved often, and my few ventures into schoolrooms had not been pleasant.

Other children taunted me. Said I spoke like an old man. Teachers were sometimes flattering, more often irritable, usually wary. My father and mother had taught me many things, had read to me from books usually read only by older people. In some ways I knew much more than my teachers; in others I knew less than any of the children. My teachers often realized how widely I had read and were nervous because of it. I did not want it so. I wished only to learn, and to be friendly.

"Today," Miss Nesselrode said at breakfast, "we will buy some clothing for you."

"I have money," I said.

"How much?"

"One hundred and seven dollars. My father left it for me."

"Keep it, Johannes, and say nothing about it to anyone. There are men in this town who would rob you for even one of those dollars."

She seemed to be considering, and then she said, "Perhaps we will invest a little of it for you, along with something of mine. It is never too soon to learn how to handle money.

"Many people know how to get money, but few know how to keep it. Wise investments are always based on information, Johannes, so the more you know, the better. The women know much more of what is going on than their men realize, although most women are simply not interested. Sometimes when we are among ourselves, they talk of such things, and I can learn who is buying, who is selling, and what the city officials are about to do.

"Often men talk to me, wishing to impress me with how much they are doing and how important their activities are. I listen, Johannes, and I remember.

"When you are a man, remember to tell no one of what you are doing unless you wish it to be known. The woman you are telling it to may be relating it all to another man."

She looked at me suddenly. "Johannes? What do you wish to be? What would you like to become?"

I did not know, and I told her so, but the question worried me. Should I know?

"There is time," she said, "but the sooner you know, the sooner you can plan. To have a goal is the important thing, and to work toward it.

Then, if you decide you wish to do something different, you will at least have been moving, you have been going somewhere, you will have been learning.

"What did your father do? I mean, how did he make a living?"

I did not know. He had taught school for a while. I know for a time he had worked for a newspaper. We had moved often, for even in the East there had been attempts to kill him. Or he thought there were.

Yet, I was puzzled. I told her what he had done, but there were other times when he had traded in horses, when he bought and sold things.

"With what, I wonder? Johannes, your father worked at things that paid but little money, yet you seem to have lived well, and you traveled. He paid for your trip west. Three hundred dollars for him, one hundred for you. It is quite a lot. Can you remember nothing else?"

She seemed to have an idea. "Was there no one he went to? Or some place to which he returned from time to time?"

I could remember none. Of course, I had been very young, and of those years there were only memories of places and people here and there. From the years, I could recall only brief moments, none of which seemed important.

Although Miss Nesselrode had said we were to buy clothing for me, yet we went to no stores. She always took a walk each day, and on this day when she returned she told me a tailor would be coming to take my measurements. "You are tall," she said, "and we must leave no clues, so we will lie a bit about your age. You will tell people you are twelve. It is a small lie and will turn away speculation if your grandfather should hear of you.

"In any case," she added, "there is no connection between your father and me."

"Except the wagon," I said.

"Yes . . ." She paused, considering. "There is that."

20

The room was long and low, with two windows that looked across the *zanja* into an orchard. On the other side there was one window which looked toward an empty corral. Inside the room there were two tables and four benches.

There was a smaller table at the far end, and a chair where Thomas Fraser sat. He arose when we entered the room.

"Miss Nesselrode? How good to see you again! And Johannes—?"

"Vickery," she said. "Johannes Vickery. I hope you will find him a good student."

"The classes are for four hours only. You understand, ma'am? I have my own work, and can afford no more time."

"That is understood. I believe you will find him eager to learn. You have how many students now?"

"Only five at the moment. Three young ladies and two young men. Johannes will be the sixth."

"Very well. Tomorrow, then?"

"Eight o'clock . . . here."

He followed us into the yard. He had always been thin. He was thinner now.

"It has been good to see you, ma'am. It was an adventure we shared, one that cannot be forgotten. I would never have believed—"

She smiled beautifully. "It is all very well, Mr. Fraser, but a time that is past. Teach Johannes what you can. None of us might be here were it not for his father. Each time I see Mr. Farley, he assures me that is true. He says he never saw a man shoot so unerringly, so coolly."

"He is a good man," she told me later, "and no doubt he will write well, but if he is to make a living, he must do more than write. His book must sell, also."

"But surely the stores will do that!"

"No doubt they will carry a few copies of his book, as my store will do, but why should they be bought? What is to make somebody come to that store and buy his book, of all that are available? He must give them a reason. He must somehow excite their interest, and then the book must hold that interest."

We walked along the street, sometimes on walks made of boards but more often of hard-packed earth or even of sand. Here and there flat rocks had been placed to make the walking easier when there was mud.

The bookstore was a small place wedged between a general store and a saddle shop, and the books on the shelves were few. There were newspapers and magazines, and she always had coffee on the stove.

"We will be having more books at any moment now. They were ordered long since." She removed her hat and placed it beside her parasol. "You can help me here, Johannes. Look about and see what we have."

"You sell books?"

"Of course, but this is also a reading room. Men come to read the newspapers, to talk business and politics. One can learn a great deal that is useful just by listening.

"It is also a place where people can meet me, although, as you will see, Mr. Finney does most of my business for me." She smiled suddenly, her eyes filled with mischief. "After all, what would a mere woman know about business and politics? A wise woman in these days will listen in wide-eyed innocence, Johannes, ask a discreet question or two, but refrain from comment."

"You shouldn't tell me this," I protested, grinning at her. "I shall someday be a man, and I will know what you do."

"And by then it will have been done, Johannes. In the meantime, listen, learn, and say nothing. Remember, no matter what you do or what you become, you will also have to do business. It is the way of the world, Johannes, so learn what you can now."

Later she commented, "In the course of a week, every man of importance will come in. At first it was the Anglos and Europeans, now the Californios come as well."

"And my grandfather?"

"He does not read. He can, but he does not. There are many who assume that once they have become men there is nothing to be learned from books."

Standing by the door, I could watch people passing in the street: a pescadero, selling fish from the sea; a vaquero in a buckskin suit and broad sombrero, riding a dun-colored horse; a Mexican woman selling panocha, the dark Mexican sugar candy of which I had heard from Francisco. A passing carreta was pulled by a burro who seemed too small for the task.

At sundown we closed the shop and walked home through streets rapidly growing empty as people went to their homes.

One man paused, removed his sombrero with a broad silver band, and told Miss Nesselrode of a fandango that was being arranged, and would she come? When we had gone on, she said, "That was Señor Lugo. He is of an old family here, with much land. He knows your grandfather."

"They are friends?"

"No, I do not believe so. Your grandfather does not seem to make friends, nor care to. He is known, respected, and sometimes feared, but he does not make friends."

"He came from Spain."

"So it is said. You would know more of that than I."

"My mother said he came from Spain long ago, when she was a very small girl. He was given land by the king. He was a very important man in Spain, and very rich."

"I wonder why he chose to come to California? He does not seem the type for adventure, and if he had a strong position in Spain, why would he give it all up to come here, to this outpost?"

My father and mother had talked of this, and they had also been puzzled.

"Was your mother the only child?"

"I do not know. Sometimes I think . . . No, I do not remember."

Yet I did remember something . . . something . . . What?

Now that the question had arisen, I tried to discover a reason why a man of wealth and position would abandon it all and come here. California was delightful, but far from the centers of power. Where had I heard that? My father, I guessed.

My mother had talked much of her family, and I could see in her much of the fierce pride the old hidalgos had, pride of family, pride of name, and of person. Yet too often, it seemed to me, such pride was founded upon events of long ago, or just upon the family's continued existence.

Once, seated in the wagon, I asked my father how such families came to be. What had they *done*?

"Very often," he said, "he who founded the family would not be re-

ceived in any of their homes now. The founder was often a peasant, a
poor soldier or sailor, an adventurer with a strong arm and a sword who
carved his way to wealth and position.

"Usually he was a man of strength, courage, and acquisitive instincts
who rode in the entourage of a king or great lord and was given estates
as a reward for services in the field or court.

"There were few cities then, and everything centered around the castle. Each lord in time of war was expected to furnish so many fighting
men. Shoes, clothing, everything necessary was made by craftsmen at
the castle. The only way for a young man to escape from being a serf
was with a sword. By courage in battle you might win a name for yourself. There were no shops then, or craftsmen outside the castle, and if
you did not own land, your only chance of success was that sword I
spoke of.

"If you did not belong to a castle, you were a landless man, which
meant you belonged nowhere, were fair game for anyone, and almost an
outlaw.

"Some such men became wandering traders. Later some settled down
to practice their trade or craft, and towns came into being. That's
roughly the way it began, in Europe, at least."

Another day, when the newspaper readers had gone, we closed the
shop and I walked home beside Miss Nesselrode. "It is a very small
town," she said to me when we paused to let a girl driving goats pass before us, "but it will not remain small."

"How can you be sure?"

"It has the sea close by, it has many thousands of cattle, almost anything will grow, and the climate is perfect. It will surely become a great
city.

"Above all," she said as we crossed the street, "it has men like Don
Benito Wilson, William Wolfskill, the Workmans, and others. They
are forward-looking men.

"Do not forget, Johannes. It is men who make a town, and bigger
men who make a city."

"I have known one," I said, "and you met him, too. Peg-Leg Smith."

She smiled. "You know, Johannes, he was an old scoundrel, I think,
but I did like him."

"He liked you, too," I said, and told her about his finding me in the
desert.

"During the next few years, Johannes, you should be thinking about
your future. What do you want to be? What do you want to become?"

"To succeed as a human being is not always the same as succeeding in your life's work, although they can go hand in hand.

"You are alone, or almost alone, but that can make you stronger, for you will not be inclined to lean on anyone. You have enemies, but that can be an advantage. Enemies can be an incentive to survive and become someone in spite of them. Enemies can keep you alert and aware."

We ate a small supper, quite late. "You read a great deal, Johannes, so you can be a help to me in the store."

"I'd like to help."

"Good! We will think about that. In the meanwhile, tomorrow you begin school."

The room in which I slept was small, with a narrow bed and two windows. There was a chest in which to keep clothing, a table, a washbasin, and a pitcher with water. On the floor were two rag rugs. The walls were bare, of plastered and whitewashed adobe.

Lying in bed that night, I worried. At no time had school been pleasant for me, although I had an abiding interest in learning. Wherever I'd gone to school, I'd come in after all the others were settled in and knew each other. I'd come along late and would know nobody and frequently I was one of the youngest in the school.

They knew about the same things and the same people. They could talk about them. I didn't know any of those things, and none of the people, and I'd lived in different places and mostly I'd talked with older folks or been talked to by them.

Usually a strange boy in school was teased. Often he had to fight, and twice I got licked. Once we fought until we were both tired out and it was kind of even up, although I had a bloody nose when it was over. I got blood on my clothes and I hadn't any others.

Each time a day was over, I was glad to go home. I said nothing to my parents, and except the time when I was bloody, they did not know about the fights. That time Papa took me out back and tried to show me something about fighting. He didn't show me much, but it helped.

"Most boys in schools," Papa said, "hit for the face. Keep your hands up, and when you can, hit 'em in the belly."

Later he said, "These are rough boys. If they push or shove you, don't talk, don't call names, don't argue. Hit them first, and hard."

I did, and it worked. It worked on that same boy who gave me the bloody nose. He shoved me and I swung a backhanded blow and hit him in the belly, knocking his wind out. Before he could fall, I hit him in the face. That day he had the bloody nose.

Now I had it to do again. There were two boys, and I could be sure one of them would think he was something big.

Miss Nesselrode, I was afraid, would not look kindly upon fistfighting.

Nowhere in Los Angeles was far from anywhere else in those days. The school was only about three or four minutes' walk from Miss Nesselrode's, and it was a little before eight o'clock when I showed up.

Two boys and two girls were sitting on benches outside, but not together. They all looked up when I came into the yard, but nobody said anything. One of the boys was bigger than me, both taller and heavier, and he was older, too, I thought.

"What do you want here?" he demanded aggressively.

"I am going to school."

"Supposin' I said I wouldn't let you?"

This was the beginning of trouble which I did not want, but one does not avoid trouble by backing away from it, not in all cases. I walked toward him.

He had not expected that, and it bothered him a little.

"Mr. Fraser knows me. He expects me this morning."

"Ol' Fraser doesn't run things out here. He runs things in the schoolroom. I run 'em in the yard."

I said nothing, I simply waited. My heart was pounding heavily. Big as he was, I did not think he was any stronger than some of the Indian boys with whom I had wrestled.

"Who are you, anyway? I never saw you before."

"I have just come from the sea. I came around the Horn in a Boston ship."

The other boy was fascinated. "Around the Horn? Gee!"

"My name," I said, "is Johannes Vickery."

"That ain't so much," the big boy said. "Anybody can come around the Horn."

"Of course. But I did it."

I was lying. I had not come around the Horn, but there was need to establish my story. Miss Nesselrode had told me that, and so had Jacob Finney.

At that moment Thomas Fraser turned into the yard from the street. "Good morning, Johannes. I see you have met Rad Huber. And this"—he indicated the smaller boy—"is Philo Burns.

"The young ladies," he said, "are Della Court and Kelda O'Brien." He glanced around. "Where is Meghan?"

"She's coming." It was the girl called Della who answered. "She was expecting her father to come in."

Fraser glanced at me. "Her father is Captain Laurel, of the *Queen Bess*," he explained.

We went inside and took seats at the table. The others had seats occupied before I arrived, and I waited until they were seated, then sat down.

"That's where Meghan sits," Rad said belligerently.

"I'm sorry," I said, and moved over one space.

"You go sit at the other table," Rad ordered.

"Where he's sitting will be quite all right," Fraser said, and Rad shifted irritably, started as if to speak, then subsided, muttering.

"This morning," Fraser said, "we will continue with the study of inflection and emphasis in the spoken language."

That was how my school days began.

21

For three days I attended school, and each day the seat beside me was empty.

On the fourth day, Rad Huber stopped me in the yard as I approached the school. He stood squarely in front of me, feet spread apart. Philo Burns stood at one side, but the girls had not yet come to school. Or I did not see them.

"Meghan's coming back to school today," Rad said. "You move to that other table."

"Mr. Fraser told me where to sit. I shall stay there."

"Meghan's my girl! You move or I'll move you!"

"I do not know Meghan," I said, "but I shall stay where I am."

He struck me. I was not expecting it, and he knocked me down. Dazed, I sat on the ground, and when I put my hand to my mouth, there was blood on it. Angry, I started up, and he hit me again before I got to my feet, knocking me down again.

Rolling over, I tried to get up, and he kicked me in the ribs. Time and time again I tried to rise; each time, he kicked me or knocked me down. Stunned, bleeding, and hurt, I kept trying. I did not know why I kept trying, but something inside me drove me to it.

One of the girls was crying. "Rad! You leave him alone!"

"Come on, Rad! Leave him be!" Philo demanded.

"Shut up!" Rad said rudely. "He thinks he's smart! I'll show him!"

Again I started up, and when I was on my hands and knees, he kicked me in the ribs. I gasped painfully, but struggled to get up.

"See?" Rad sneered. "He ain't so much! Just a big baby!"

He backed off and turned away, and I struggled up, then rushed at him, swinging both fists. Somebody yelled, and Rad turned. One of my flailing fists caught him in the mouth, cutting his lip, but then he pushed me away and rushed at me, swinging both fists. He was larger, and had longer arms. He hit me again and again. Suddenly Mr. Fraser was there.

"Here, here! What's going on? Rad, stop that! Leave him alone!"

"Hah! He had it coming!"

He walked away. Slowly, painfully, I got up and tried to brush off my clothes.

Thomas Fraser came over to me. "Are you hurt?" he asked.

"No," I lied.

"Wash your face, then, and come to school."

There was a washbasin on a shelf around the corner from the schoolroom door. I washed the blood and dust from my face and dried it on the towel. I felt sore and stiff. Limping, I went into the school.

Rad turned, sneering at me. Walking over, I sat down in my usual place. Rad started up, but Mr. Fraser said, "Rad! Sit *down!*"

"You tell him to move, or I'll move him!"

"I shall do no such thing. If there is any more of this, I'll dismiss you from school."

"Hah!" Rad said. "You'll do no such thing. Pa paid for the term, and you try dismissing me. Pa would be down here to see you. He'd be down mighty quick!"

Meanwhile, I opened my books, getting out my slate. Mr. Fraser looked at me but said nothing. His face was pale and he was angry. Perhaps he was frightened, too. His existence depended on the school, and I suspected he hadn't the money to return to Rad's father if he dismissed him.

Rad glared at me, but subsided. He opened his books; then he whispered, "You wait until school's out! You just wait!"

Something fell from my lips to the slate. It was a drop of blood. I wiped it off, staring bitterly at the place where it had fallen.

What was I to do? He would beat me and kick me again when school was out. Nobody would stop him. Still dazed, I hung my head over my slate and felt like crying, but I did not cry. I would not give him the satisfaction. Somehow, I would . . .

He could hit very hard. He would hit me again and again. He would kick me. "Hit them in the stomach," my father had advised, but Rad's arms were too long. I knew so little about fistfighting, but I had wrestled with the Indian boys. I could throw them all, except Francisco, and once in a while I could throw him.

When Mr. Fraser called on me to read from the story of William Tell, I almost did not hear him. Then I stood up and read. Slowly, because of my swollen lips, but I read well.

"Very good, Johannes," Mr. Fraser said.

"Hah!" Rad sneered.

Seated again, I scarcely listened to what was happening. I was thinking, thinking hard, and I was scared. I didn't want to be hit again. I did not want to take a beating and have them all seeing me lying in the dust. I had to do something.

One thing I knew. I was not going to move. I did not know Meghan. I did not care to know Meghan, but I was not going to move. He could kill me, but I would stay right where I was.

Yet, what could I do? Something . . . My father used to say there was always a way. There was an answer to everything. If I could only . . .

Maybe . . .

Soon the class would break up and I must go outside again. Thomas Fraser might protect me here, but away from the school he could do nothing.

There was movement at the door, and I looked up.

She stood just inside, the sunlight touching her hair. It was red-gold. She was slender, graceful as a willow, and beautiful.

This was Meghan . . . and I was in love.

22

She paused for a moment in the doorway, the sunlight on her red-gold hair. Then she crossed the room and sat down beside me. Automatically I arose, stepping back for her. She gave me a quick smile and I trembled. She seated herself and I sat down beside her. The edge of her dress brushed my trouser leg.

"Miss Laurel," Fraser said, "our new student, Mr. Vickery, has just read a part of *William Tell*. You might read the conclusion, up as far as the shooting of the apple."

She read easily, beautifully, in a low, well-modulated tone, but I did not look up. My eyes remained riveted to the lines, although scarcely seeing them. I was conscious of a faint perfume, fresh, flowerlike.

When I did look up, Rad was glaring at me, and I felt myself go sick and empty. He would attack me again, as he had threatened. He would beat me, and I would go down in the dust again, as before. Only now it would be different.

She would be there. She would see it. She would think me contemptible.

In fear and agony I waited for the class to be over. Jacob Finney was coming by for me with my horse. We were riding out to the tar pits along the old Indian trail.

As I started to rise, I turned toward Meghan and she gasped. "Oh, your poor face! What happened?"

"It was a fight. I think there will be another now."

"Rad! It was Rad, wasn't it?"

"Yes."

"He should be ashamed of himself! Picking on someone smaller than himself!"

"He's not so big."

We had started toward the door, but as I stepped back to allow her to go through the door ahead of me, a hand grasped my shoulder and I was shoved aside. Rad stepped into my place and moved up beside her.

Now I was angry. Out in the yard he started walking away beside her. He had brushed me aside as if I were nothing. Inside me there was cold fury. I fought it down.

"What's the matter?" I called after him. "Are you scared?"

He stopped abruptly and turned around. They all did, even Mr. Fraser, who stopped in the doorway as he started back inside.

"*Scared?* Scared of *you?*" He put down his books and started toward me.

Now you're in for it, I told myself. Don't let him hit you. *Wrestle!*

He was larger in every way, and much heavier, but how much did he know? He had his fists up ready to strike, and mine were up too; then suddenly I dove, grasping his ankle with both hands and throwing my weight against his knee as I jerked up on the ankle. He toppled over on his back.

Instantly, holding his ankle in my right armpit, I stepped across his body, half-turning him toward the ground. Then I dropped to a sitting position on his buttocks, facing the opposite way. The Indians had taught me this, and I knew I had only to put more pressure on his ankle and his hip would be dislocated.

I leaned back a little, and he cried out. Fraser had turned and was coming toward us. Out on the street Jacob Finney had come up with my horse and his. He sat his saddle, watching.

Meghan stood with the other girls, their faces showing excitement and shock.

"Let him up!" Mr. Fraser ordered.

"Ask him first if he will let me alone. I want no more trouble."

"Will you let him alone, Rad?" Fraser asked.

"I'll kill him!"

I leaned back again, and this time he screamed. Then he said, "No! No! Get off me! I won't do nothin'!"

Letting go, I got up. Rad lay still for a moment, then got up painfully. Wary, I backed off.

"Now, that's quite enough!" Fraser spoke sharply. "We'll have no more of this! Any more trouble between you, and I shall dismiss you both, do you understand?"

"I never wanted trouble," I said.

Rad glowered but said nothing. Meghan glanced at me, then turned her back and walked away with the other girls, Della and Kelda.

Turning to Mr. Fraser, I said, "I am sorry, sir. I wanted no trouble."

When I reached my horse, Jacob looked at my face. "Looks like you taken a few," he said.

"That was earlier. His arms are too long."

"You done all right, seemed to me. Where'd you learn that fancy stuff?"

"From the Indian boys. They wrestle all the time."

"Feller downtown. Man I know. He's pretty good with his mitts. He's boxed in New Orleans, New York, an' London. We got to get you with him. You fight that boy again an' he mayn't let you get hold of him. Not if he's smart. He'll just stand off an' punch your lights out."

We rode in silence for a few minutes and then he said, "This place we're goin'. They call it the tar pits. Comes right up out of the ground. The water has oil in it, too, seems like. An' gas. It bubbles right up through the water, the bubble floats a minute or two, then busts. Animals get stuck in it. Other animals an' buzzards come there to feed on the ones that get trapped.

"Folks hereabout, Injuns, Californios an' such, they use the tar on their roofs. Use it to watertight their boats, too. The Chumash Injuns who live along the coast, they used it first.

"The Chumash make mighty fine boats. Some carry eight to ten people, maybe more. They use tar along the seams to make the boats watertight.

"They used to go out to the islands off the coast, to Catalina, Santa Barbara, an' the like. The Chumash were right handy with boats, but they're gettin' fewer and fewer all the time."

He pointed off to his left. "Off down there's a big *ciénaga*. Sort of swamplike. The river used to run down there and just spread out. Then about fifteen years ago she broke through to the sea an' drained most of that. Still mighty good grazing land. Green grass and some water down there most of the time. The Californios have some of their roundups down thataway.

"This trail runs all the way to the sea. There's a bay along there, Santa Monica Bay. Not much protection, though, in bad weather. She's too open.

"Miss Nesselrode, she wants you to know the country around, and the folks."

"What's off there?" I pointed toward the mountains.

"There's the mountains, and over beyond, a wide valley. The pass they call the Little Door. The Injun name is Cahuenga.

"There's trails through most of the canyons. Just horse trails, mostly, but there are bears back in there, lots of them, and more than likely they won't get out of the way, in which case you'd better turn around and get out of there, 'less you want to fight."

"I heard there were bandits."

"Oh, sure! Plenty of those. Some just steal horses, some raid lonely stations, murder travelers and the like. You got to be careful."

The day was warm and pleasant. All around us was a wide sweep of grassland dotted with clumps of oak and other brush, with here and there a small grove or a patch where someone was planting. Scattered everywhere, although not in great numbers, there were cattle.

"Once in a while a man has to fight," Jacob said, "but you avoid it if you can. Fightin' attracts attention, and that's the last thing you need.

"This is a small town with not much to talk about. Fortunately the Californios don't pay a lot of attention to us Anglos. There's a few of us here, and although Stearns and a few others are doing well, they go about their business without blowing up a storm.

"The old don keeps to himself, mostly. They say he thinks himself better than the others because he is of pure Castilian blood. Your grandmother has been dead for a good many years, so the old don's house is run by his younger sister, the Doña Elena.

"She runs a mighty fine house, or so they say. Stone-flagged floors 'n everything. I suspect there aren't more'n a half-dozen houses in town with anything but dirt floors. Out here folks make do with mighty little. Nothin' fancy to be had.

"Back t' home my ma never had much to do with, but we lived better than these folks who have thousands of acres. The government doesn't permit trade with anybody but themselves, although there's a good deal of business done with the Boston ships."

"You mean, they're not supposed to?"

"They got laws against it, but what're these folks to do? They are needful of things, and the ships come in. Usually those who are supposed to enforce the laws look the other way."

Jacob Finney drew up. "Back yonder, that's Rancho Las Ciénagas. I told you about the swampland. Francisco Avila owns that, and off to the northwest where those low hills are, that ranch is called Rodeo de las Aguas. Means 'the gathering of the waters,' likely because of the springs. A widow woman owns that. Her husband was a soldier named Valdez.

"La Brea, where we're headed, that's owned by a Portugee named Rocha. Good man. I helped his folks catch up some horses here a while back. Injuns had started to run them off an' we had a bit of a set-to.

"One of these times, you an' me, we'll take ourselves an outfit and ride off up the San Joaquin Valley. That's over yonder. A long, long valley with herds of wild horses everywhere, two, three hundred in a bunch. Some fine stock, too."

"They belong to no one?"

"That's right. Wild as antelope or elk. Comes to that, I've seen herds of over a thousand elk. Boy, that's one you've got to see! Somethin' to remember.

"Tame, too. The Californios don't hunt much. They have all the beef they want and they make do with that. Me, I like elk meat. It's right tasty."

We rode on, lazy in the sunshine. Cattle moved out of our way or turned their heads to look at us with a total lack of interest. We were not chasing them, and they knew it.

"There!" Finney pointed. "See? The trees yonder? That dark pool? That's it. You got to ride careful, there's several smaller patches of tar here an' there."

He waved a hand. "Most anyplace here you can push a stick into the ground and it will come up black with tar.

"The Chumash been coming here for centuries to get tar to calk their boats.

"See? The bones yonder? Something trapped there, buzzards fed off it, and maybe one of them trapped, too. If you set still and watch, you can see the gas bubble up. There! See, yonder? It bubbles up, the bubbles break, and after a bit, another one comes.

"Water isn't fit to drink. Too much oil an' stuff, but this here's somethin' to see. A few years ago a ship's captain from down to San Pedro, he come out here to get tar and he found a tusk. Elephant's tusk.

"Anybody'd told me, I'd not have believed it, but there it was."

"The Indians have stories about hunting them," I said. "Not the Cahuillas, the Plains Indians."

"You don't say? That's one I never heard."

"It was the Osage, I think," I said. "It was a hairy elephant they had killed."

We left our horses cropping the grass and walked over to the pools, but not going too close. The trees Jacob had mentioned were actually some distance away, but grass grew right to the edge of the water in some places. The larger pool was at least an acre in extent. "It was larger when we were here the first time," Jacob said, "but this has been a dry year."

He pointed out two more pools, each no larger than a washtub, and several places where grayish bulges of tar or asphalt had pushed up through the grass.

"There are several oil springs around," Jacob said. "Miss Nesselrode wanted to see them, so we rode over to take a look. Injuns and some of the Californios come there to get oil for some treatments they give themselves."

"It is a strange place," I said. "I'd like to come back again."

"Reckon you can do about as you wish when there's no school. You talk about that with Miss Nesselrode. I don't know what she has in mind, but you can bet she's figurin' on something. That woman's mind never sets still, believe me."

"I like her."

"So do I," Jacob agreed, "but let me warn you, although you aren't likely to need it. Don't cross her. She's almighty pleasant. She's a fine-looking young woman with a lovely smile and all that, but there's cuttin' steel under it, and don't you be forgettin' it."

We mounted up and started back, and Jacob said, "She wants you to ride around over this valley and get acquainted with the locality. Don't ask me why. Maybe she just wants to be sure you don't get lost sometime. Knowin' her, I'd lay a good bit she's got something else in mind."

We were unsaddling our horses when he spoke again. "Did you learn to speak any of that Cahuilla lingo? I mean, could you make them understand?"

"Most of them spoke some Spanish. Francisco and his father know both Spanish and English. They know enough to get along, anyway."

"How about the Chumash?"

"It is a different language, I think."

"She wants you to learn it, Johannes. She's got something in mind."

We started for the house, and Miss Nesselrode was standing in the door, waiting for me. I knew right away that something had happened. Something was wrong.

23

Miss Nesselrode rested a hand upon my shoulder, but she spoke to Jacob. "Will you come in, Mr. Finney? This is something you should know."

Her hand caressed the back of my head. "Johannes? You have a visitor. A guest."

It was dusk and the candles had been lighted. Something in her tone seemed to warn me. In my right hand I held my rifle and pistol belt, for I had been told never to ride without them.

"You will not need those, Johannes. Come in, now."

She stepped aside to permit me to pass, then closed the door behind us.

It was a moment not to be forgotten. The quiet room, the soft glow from the two candelabra, the old carved chest against the wall, the table, the chairs, the rag rugs upon the floor, and that tall, straight woman standing there, looking at me.

Her hair was black, but white at the temples. She had allowed her rebozo to fall back to her shoulders. Her features were thin and what people called aristocratic.

She was a beautiful and stately woman, no longer young, but a woman with presence, to whom years had brought added beauty. She had distinction, more than anyone I had known, perhaps more than anyone I would ever know.

"Yes"—her voice was low, very pleasant—"of course! How like them you are!"

She stepped forward, holding out a hand. "Johannes, I am your great-aunt, Elena. I have looked forward to this moment."

Great-aunt? My mother spoke fondly of her Aunt Elena, but if she was my grandfather's sister, she must be an enemy. Yet she did not seem like an enemy. Her smile made me want to draw closer.

"I am Johannes . . ." I hesitated, then added, "Johannes Verne."

"I know." She seated herself, yet even in that simple movement there was something regal. "May we talk a little, Johannes?" She glanced at Miss Nesselrode. "You have been most kind. I have but little time. If he should call for me . . . at night I am almost never away."

"Of course."

Jacob came in quietly and took a seat on the far side of the room.

"Please, Johannes, tell me of your mother."

My mother? What could I say? What could I tell her? Why should I tell her?

"I loved her very much, Johannes. She was like my own daughter. And I liked your father. Had it been up to me . . ."

"She was beautiful," I said, "like you. We were only three, and we were always together. She was very happy, I believe, except when she thought about home. She told me many stories of Spain, and stories of the sea voyage to California, and of the landing.

"My father offered to take her back to California, but she was afraid for him."

"He was always a bold one. I think he feared nothing. Tell me . . . where did you live? How did you live? I want to know everything."

"We moved often. My father had gone to sea with his father, who was a ship's captain, as you would know, and he had planned to become one himself. Yet he could not return to the sea without leaving us, and he would not do that.

"For a time he managed a livery stable in Philadelphia, and later he trained horses and managed a big farm in Kentucky. He was a marshal in a Missouri river town before that. I do not know its name. I was only a baby then, I guess.

"Often he said he would like to find a permanent job so he could write. Mr. Longfellow, the poet, was also a professor, and Oliver Wendell Holmes was a physician. Mr. Emerson, I think, was a minister. Each had some way of living so he could write with freedom.

"Many of the people who came to our house in Philadelphia were writers, like Mr. Lippard, who had long straggly hair and wore strange clothes. He lived in a big old ramshackle house of many rooms where all sorts of people lived. The house had been abandoned, I think, and they just moved in.

"There was a Mr. Hirst, whom I saw only once or twice, and there was the editor, Edgar Poe. I think he was a writer, too.

"Yes, I know he was because I remember Papa wondering what he might have written had everyone not wanted stories of ghosts, haunted houses, and tombs. Mr. Poe wrote what was wanted, like all of them.

"Papa read me the stories of 'Rip Van Winkle,' and about the 'Headless Horseman,' and sometimes when Papa's friends came around, Mama made coffee or tea for them. Mr. Poe liked to hear Papa talk about his years at sea when he was a boy, and he asked many questions. On one voyage Papa's ship was blown far to the south when rounding Cape Horn, and they found themselves among icebergs and had a terrible time before they escaped.

"Mama told stories, too, and one of them was about Boabdil, the Moor, who was sleeping in an enchanted cave with all his knights, awaiting the moment when he would awaken them to reconquer Spain."

"She sat with the men? She talked with them?"

"It is not the custom. But they all insisted she be with them, for she knew so many stories. Some of them, I think, were stories you told her, for I remember she spoke of you sometimes.

"Sometimes it became very late and they forgot I was not in bed, or maybe Mama just made believe she forgot, for she would say suddenly, 'Oh, how awful! You should be in bed, young man!' But if the stories were very good, she would make believe to forget again.

"There was one story that made her sad. It was a story about a monster—"

"A monster?"

"A woman named Mary Shelley wrote the story. Her husband was a poet, I think. It was a story about a student named Frankenstein who made a man out of pieces of dead people. People thought the creature a monster, but he wasn't really. Mama always felt sorry for the monster. I thought he'd be kind of scary."

For a moment there was silence in the room, and then Aunt Elena changed the subject. "You lived in Kentucky, you said?"

"A man who met Papa at the livery stable gave him the job of training horses for racing. He liked the way Papa cared for the horses, and he said all the trainers he wanted were already employed and if Papa could produce a winning horse he would give him a share of the winnings."

"Did he never talk of going to sea again?"

"Oh, no! By that time Mama was sick and Papa wanted to get out of the city where the air was better. Once when we were alone he said we must be very good to Mama because she was more ill than she believed. Papa would not take any kind of work where he could not look in upon Mama often.

"Once I heard him talk to Mr. Poe about it, for his wife was ill also. Both of them had consumption, and it was considered a kind of aristocratic illness, whatever that is. People became pale and frail and all the doctors did was prescribe fine wines and special foods.

"Papa said to Mama that he had no right to keep her where she was. He said, 'In California you would soon be well. We must go back.' But Mama would not go. She said Papa would be killed.

"He said, 'Do you think I would die so easily?'

"'No,' she said, 'but you might kill him, and that would be just as bad.'

"Sometimes at night when they thought I was asleep they talked of me, worrying about what would become of me when they were gone, because by that time Papa was sick, too, and Mama knew it. After Mama died—"

"How long ago?"

"I was five, I think. I do not remember too well, but we lived in Kentucky then."

For several minutes I could not say anything, only remembering those last, long, lovely days when we could look out over the green pastures with their white fences and the beautiful horses running and playing there. Mama talked to me an awful lot then. I think she wanted to tell me everything, before . . .

Aunt Elena had sat very still, reaching for every word I spoke. Sometimes her eyes filled with tears, sometimes her lips trembled, but she said nothing, and did not interrupt.

"Mr. Poe's wife died, too, someone said. I do not know, only that after Mama died two of the horses Papa had trained won their races and the owner gave Papa a share, as he had promised.

"It was a very damp, rainy year and Papa was worse, so he quit his job and we came west."

"I see." Aunt Elena sat very still; then she looked over at me. "Thank you, Johannes, for telling me. At least she was happy during those years. She had your father, and they had you."

She got to her feet. "I must go. Johannes, if you ever need me, please have Miss Nesselrode or Señor Finney come to me. In the meantime, you must be careful! About him there is nothing I can do. We have had words about this.

"As yet, he knows nothing. I would know if he did. He believes you dead. He even talks of returning to Spain.

"You *must* keep out of trouble! It was because of talk among the women about a fight at school that I heard of a boy named Johannes who was living at the home of Miss Nesselrode. I knew she had come west in the wagon with your father, and that Señor Finney had worked for Señor Farley on the same trip."

She started for the door, but Jacob got up suddenly. "Wait, ma'am. I'll just take a look around outside first."

He was gone only a minute. "It's all right, ma'am. A body can't be too careful."

At the door Aunt Elena stooped suddenly and kissed me on the forehead; then, embarrassed, she slipped out and disappeared in the darkness.

Miss Nesselrode came up behind me and rested a hand on my shoulder. "I believe she loves you very much, Johannes, just as she loved your mother."

"She does not know me."

"She sees your mother in you. Tía Elena has no children, and your mother was like a daughter to her. Now it is you of whom she thinks."

"She is a nice lady."

"Yes, she is. I am afraid she took a great risk in coming here tonight. If your grandfather should discover you are alive and that she came to see you, he would be furious. He might lock her up."

"He could do that?"

"He could and he would."

That night I did not sleep, but thought of Tía Elena. In some ways she was like Miss Nesselrode, yet different, and she spoke English amazingly well, although with an accent. I found I liked thinking of her, for she was a relative, of my own blood, and I knew of no others to whom I could speak.

Yet there was a restlessness in me, a longing for the desert and the mountains. Where was Francisco? Had he forgotten me?

A longing for the wild places was in me, and there was something else, too, some strange yearning, something that whispered to me on the wind, whispered words I could not hear, calling me back to where

the lonely coyotes spoke to the moon and the great cacti would stretch
agonized arms toward the sky.

I could not go back. Not yet. My father would have wished me to go
to school, and Miss Nesselrode had asked me what I wished to become.
I suspected it was not only that she wished to know but that she wished
to start me thinking of it. She wished me to be making up my mind.

When morning came, I walked to the bookstore with Miss Nesselrode, where I was to help her. Two handsome Californios rode past,
splendid on their fine horses with silver-mounted saddles. They doffed
their sombreros, bowing gracefully to Miss Nesselrode, and I watched
them with envy.

Their fine horses almost danced as the riders went down the dusty
street in their fine clothes and large-roweled spurs. Surely no one in the
world could ride like the Californios!

"It is a pity," she said.

"What?" I was startled.

"Their world is going, going very fast, Johannes. They inherited large
ranchos, they live well, they have no worries, they work a little at the
roundups, they go to *fandangos* or *bailes*, they flirt with the girls, and
they give no thought to tomorrow. It is enough that today the sun
shines, that they have a splendid new suit trimmed in gold or silver,
that they have handsome horses. They do not realize their world is
gone."

"Gone?"

"Yes, Johannes, change was sure to occur, and now it has. The Boston men have come."

24

"I do not understand," I said.

"It is very simple. The Californios are wonderful people. They are gracious, hospitable, and to those of their kind they are considerate. Yet in many ways they are like children. Most of them have never dealt with money. They have bartered for what they needed, with each other, with the Indians, and with the few traders.

"The Boston men, as they call them, are shrewd, hardworking Yankees, and they are going to change all this. I will not like it so well, although I am a part of it, but the change is inevitable. There is no malice in it. The Yankees are simply businessmen. When a Californio wants something, a silver-mounted saddle, a fine suit of clothes worked with gold and silver, he does not question the cost. If he does not have money, he borrows it, and all loans are at compound interest, compounded by the month.

"Those young men who passed us? The suits they wear would cost two thousand dollars each. The young man who saluted so gracefully? He used to have a rancho of forty thousand acres."

"Used to?"

"Yes, Johannes. He has not realized it yet, but twenty thousand acres of his rancho are mine. He has borrowed several times, and although he has been reminded that the interest is due, he just smiles. Most of those who loan the Californios money do not remind them when their notes fall due, and their land is lost to them."

We came to the store and I unlocked the door. Inside, Miss Nesselrode removed her hat and the mantilla that had covered her shoulders.

"Their world has changed, Johannes. The time for playing in the sun is over. If they wish to survive in this new world, they must work. They must plant orange or lemon trees as Mr. Wolfskill has been doing, or plant grain."

Two big boxes of books were dropped off at the door by a freighter, hauled from the harbor. My first job that morning was to unpack, list, and place them on the shelves where they could be seen.

As I placed the books on the shelves, I called off the titles to her so she could list them. Suddenly I came upon a copy of *The Narrative of A. Gordon Pym*, published by Wiley & Putnam, in England. It had been previously published in this country but my father had not been able to find a copy.

With some pride I showed the book to Miss Nesselrode. "He was a friend of my father's," I explained. "He often talked with my father about the polar regions because of my father's experiences with icebergs."

"Maybe something of what he told Edgar Poe got into the story."

"I believe their talk was later, after the book was written, but I am not sure. It says here the book was published in 1838. I was just two years old then." I held it in my hands. "May I read it?"

"Of course."

There were still a few books to unpack, but as I worked, I wondered about Miss Nesselrode. Who *was* she? Where did she come from? On the way west when others talked of who they were and what they had done, she listened in silence. There had been rumors she had been a schoolteacher, but that was probably only a guess. The truth was that nobody knew, and the impression persisted that she had come west to find a husband. It was a natural supposition, but I did not believe it. She liked men and enjoyed their conversation but seemed to avoid the younger, more attractive men. Sometimes when I looked up I would see her staring out the window, her lips tight, her face like marble. Of what she was thinking, I had no idea.

Yet I sensed some purpose, some intent, some driving urge, and it matched something I could feel arising within myself. One day when I had come from school to help in the shop, she voiced it herself.

"Thomas Fraser tells me you are doing well in school, Johannes. I like that." She paused a moment, and suddenly her voice was hard, almost angry. "I want you to show them, Johannes! They cast your father out, and your mother because she married him, and you because you are their son.

"Show them, Johannes! Become somebody! Do something! Make something of yourself!

"Listen to the men who come here. Listen well. Education is by no means confined to schools. Listen to such men talk, hear their philosophy, their ideas about the country, about business, trade, shipping, politics. Listen and learn.

"Some people only learn by reading, others by doing or seeing, some by hearing. Learn however you can, but *learn!*

"Mr. Wilson, Mr. Wolfskill, Mr. Workman, all of them. They are the men who will make this town into a city. They have ideas, but they do not merely have ideas, they put the ideas to work.

"You can become bigger, stronger, better than your enemies. You can defeat them by outreaching them, by becoming a more important man, but also by becoming a better one.

"All life is based on decisions. Decide now on what you'd like to become and what you would like to do. The two are not necessarily the same, although sometimes they can be."

As the months passed at school Rad kept his distance but he did not like me and I knew trouble between us was not finished. Meghan Laurel continued to sit beside me, but I was shy. I had little experience talking to girls.

We read better than the others, but Meghan was better at numbers than I.

Rad was smart enough, but disdainful of lessons. Because he was as large and perhaps stronger than Mr. Fraser, he was also disdainful of him, although he did well enough in school to get along. For my part, I avoided him. I wanted no more trouble, and although I had beaten him once, it would not be so easy another time, for he would be ready for me.

Miss Nesselrode, or perhaps Jacob Finney, must have spoken to him in private, for never did Thomas Fraser make any comment on having known me before and having known my father, nor did he speak of the trip across the mountains and desert from Santa Fe.

Often, when we had settled in our seats, he would talk to us very generally on some topic that he considered important or that occupied his mind at the moment.

"Actually," he said one morning, "all education is self-education. A teacher is only a guide, to point out the way, and no school, no matter how excellent, can give you an education.

"What you receive is like the outlines in a child's coloring book. You must fill in the colors yourself.

"I hope, in these classes, to give you an idea of where you came from, how you got here, and what has been said about it."

When we started to leave the room, I found Meghan beside me. She looked around at me and said, "What do you think of him? Of Mr. Fraser?"

"I like him. I think he wants to be a writer."

"I wonder where he went to school?"

"In Scotland, I believe. He is Scottish," I said. Then, fearful of seeming to know too much about him, I added, "Fraser is a Scottish name."

This was one of the first times Meghan had struck up a conversation with me yet I was worried. I did not want to be talking about him because if I seemed to know too much it might start somebody thinking and wondering how I knew.

"Your father is a captain of a ship?" I said.

"Yes. Only he says he is the master. He does not use the word 'captain.' He sails to China," she added. "And he has been around the Horn several times."

I said nothing to that. She glanced at me. "You are from the East?"

"Most of us are. I mean, unless we are Spanish."

"My father thinks you are an interesting boy."

Startled, I said, "Your father? He does not know me!"

"He has seen you. And I have told him about how well you read. He says you remind him of someone."

Suddenly I was scared. I wanted to talk to her but I was afraid of what she might ask, and I did not want to lie.

"I have to read well," I explained. "I work at the book shop for Miss Nesselrode."

"Papa said he would like to meet you someday. He said I must bring you home sometime."

"I'd like that," I said.

We had come to a corner. "I've got to go to the shop now," I said. "I promised to help."

We parted there, but as I turned away I saw Rad standing across the street, glaring at me. Once, when I looked back, he was still standing there, but Meghan had gone on home.

Miss Nesselrode was donning her hat when I came in. "I have to go out for a few minutes, Johannes. Will you mind the shop?"

She left and I gathered up some scattered newspapers and rearranged them, straightened books on the shelves, and had just taken down *Pym* when the door opened.

It was Fletcher.

He was better dressed than he had been in the wagon, and his beard was trimmed carefully now and he had a sense of confidence about him, and seemed less surly.

"How are you, boy? Long time since we come west together."

"Is there something you want?"

He smiled, but it was not a pleasant smile. "Your pa got killed," he said. "I guess he wasn't so handy after all."

"There were a lot of them! I said. "There were too many of them."

"Maybe . . . maybe there was." He grinned at me. "You got a nerve, boy, stayin' here in town with those about who'd like you dead."

My heart began to beat heavily. I was frightened. Yet I tried not to let him know.

"I been watchin', boy. Don't you think I've forgotten." Suddenly he leaned his hands on the desk. "I never liked you, boy, nor your pa either. He thought himself too good.

"Well, he's gone, but I got you. I got you right where I want you, and when it's worth my while, I'll do something about it.

"That Nesselrode woman, now. What's she up to? I figured she was comin' west to catch herself a husband, but now I ain't so sure. Not if what I hear is true."

I said nothing, but I was hoping she would not come back, not now. There was a pistol in the desk drawer. I wondered if I could get to it quick enough.

"I hear she's been dealin'. Makin' herself some money. Makes me wonder what she'd pay to keep me quiet about you."

"Me?" I tried to speak very casually, carelessly. "Why would she pay for me? I was an orphan and she took me in. Gave me a home." I looked up at him. "I work for her."

Taking up some books, I returned them to the shelves. "You must be crazy," I said. "She took me in because I didn't have a home. If you asked her for money, she would just laugh and then she'd probably turn me out. She'd think I was too much trouble."

When I returned from the shelves, I walked right to the desk. He was close to me but I was also close to the gun. He was scowling now and I think what I said had made him doubt. "Nobody cares about me." I tried to sound bitter. "She's the only one who's treated me decent."

"Maybe." He took out a cigar and lighted it. "That house, now, the one down in the desert? That belong to your pa?"

"We stayed in it. That's all."

"I been wonderin' about that. Comin' by there a while back, I saw a light in the window. Thought at first it was you, but it wasn't. I couldn't get close enough to see, but there was somebody in there, somebody big." He scowled as if puzzled. "Real big."

My heart was pounding now but I tried not to seem interested. "Some of the Indians stay there sometimes when they are in from the desert," I said.

Suddenly his manner changed. He smiled in what he probably believed was a friendly manner. "Aw, forget it, kid! I was just funnin' with you! Matter of fact, I thought your pa was quite a man. Quite a man."

He glanced around. "Now, a boy like you, in a place like this, he could make himself a bit of money now and again."

He took his cigar from his mouth and leaned closer. "You an' me, we come over the trail t'gether. We're friends. If you was to hear some talk, somethin' about business deals, somethin' like that, and if you was to tell me . . . ?"

He knocked the ash from his cigar and put it back in his teeth.

"More'n that, there's talk of rebellion. Talk of the Yanks comin' out here. That there Wilson, he'd know about that. Or Stearns. He's supposed to be a Mexican citizen, but . . . You hear anything, boy, you come to me. You tell me what you've heard, an' I'll pay."

He grinned at me from around his cigar; then he winked.

"Pards, that's what we are! Pards! You an' me!"

"Miss Nesselrode will be coming back in a minute," I said.

He went to the door. "All right, I'm goin', but you remember!"

He went out and the door closed behind him.

25

Often at night we heard gunshots. Usually they were from Sonora Town, but that did not mean the antagonists were always Mexican or Californio. Just as often, in proportion to their numbers, they were Anglos. Killings were frequent; knifings and cuttings of varying degrees took place almost every day.

Occasionally groups of vaqueros from one of the nearby ranchos would come galloping down the street to swing down at the nearest cantina and troop inside, spurs jingling and jangling.

Women did not walk on the streets after sundown unless going to or from a *fandango* or *baile*, and then they were usually accompanied by someone of the family. Yet one night, awakening suddenly when it was almost midnight, I heard voices from the outer room.

Surprised, and a little anxious, I listened. But the voices were those of women. "I have come to you for help. There is no one else."

"Of course, Doña Elena. How may I help you?"

"I do not know of business. Of things with money. My people do not think of money. We . . . we exchange. One thing for another, you see? You have the shop. The place of the *libros*, the books.

"I know nothing, but it has been said that sometimes you do business. I do not know of this. There is a woman with a cantina toward San Pedro. She speaks of you with admiration."

"What is it you wish?"

"I wish to use money. I wish to do business. I wish to be rich from my money."

Miss Nesselrode was hesitating, but finally she said, "Always there is risk. If one would make money, one must be prepared to lose, also."

"This I understand. It is like gambling, I think. It is like the cards.

Sometimes they fall one way, sometimes another. I know nothing of business, but I think you do."

"What of your brother?"

"He knows nothing. He thinks of nothing. He would despise me if he knew. He would not allow it. He borrows money, but has contempt for those who lend. He is *hidalgo*. He will pay when he wish. Nobody will ask that he pay."

"The Yankees will ask. They will insist."

"This I hear."

Miss Nesselrode was quiet for a few minutes, as if thinking. "Do you have money? Will not your brother know?"

"I have money, but he does not know. It is from our mother." Doña Elena looked down at her hands. "My mother knows I have no husband. My father and my brother think no one is good enough, so I have no one, but my mother understands and in secret she has given me money, gold money, and jewels.

"The woman from the cantina. She says money can work for money. I have thought you could tell me what to do. You see, I could not appear. I am Doña Elena."

"Of course. You wish me to help. How?"

"Make my money work. I will pay."

Miss Nesselrode changed the subject. "Your rancho? It is large?"

"Very large."

"Your brother borrows money? Has he borrowed much?"

"Very much, I think. He needs much money, and the cow skins, they do not bring much. He waves a hand, says all will be different soon, and he borrows."

"Do you know who he has borrowed from?"

"This one and that. A little here, a little there."

"This work you want your money to do? Is it that you need money now?"

"Oh, no! It is for tomorrow, for a long time off." I saw her lift her eyes to Miss Nesselrode's. "It is for when I am dead."

"If you will risk losing it, I will help." She paused. "Is there any particular thing you wish?"

"One thing, first. I wish some to work, to bring more money. I wish some to buy the old debts of my brother."

"I see."

"He *must* not know. He must never know. He would be furious. He would destroy me. He would destroy the lender. He would destroy you."

Miss Nesselrode smiled. "I do not destroy easily, Doña Elena."

"If he knew I had money, he would demand it from me, and I must give it."

"He will not know. Can you bring the money here?"

Doña Elena took up a cloth bag from the floor. "I have it here. I have some." She placed the bag on the table and reached a hand into it, trickling gold coins to the table. Then from the bag she took a smaller bag, and opening the drawstrings, tilted something to the table that gleamed in the dim light. "I have these, also."

"It is quite a lot. You trust me with these?"

"You are a good woman. I feel this. And you have been good to the niño."

If there was more, I did not hear, for I fell asleep and when I awakened again the room was dark and there was no sound but the soft drip of rain from the eaves, the rain for which we all had waited.

I lay awake thinking of Tía Elena. Women of her class were kept in the background, often knowing nothing of the financial circumstances of their husbands or fathers, having nothing to do with business.

What led Aunt Elena to make such a move? I did not know unless she wished some independence, some security. And how had she known of Miss Nesselrode's knowledge? Or did she know? Did she only come to the one friend she had outside her own circle? The one who would not talk?

Lying there awake with the rain falling softly, my thoughts returned to the house of Tahquitz, far off in the desert.

Fletcher had seen the shadow of someone in the house, a very large someone. Of course, it could have been a passerby stopping for the night, as the Indians would not go near the place at night. It might have been the mysterious exchanger of books.

Suddenly I felt guilty. There had been no new books. I had failed him . . . or it. Somehow I must arrange for new books to be taken to the house.

So much time had gone by! Going to school, working at the shop, riding around the country, exploring . . . The months simply vanished.

When I opened my eyes again it was morning and I could hear Jacob talking. Dressing quickly, I went out to see him. He was drinking coffee and talking to Miss Nesselrode.

"It would take some doin'," he was saying, "but there's thousands of wild horses in the San Joaquin, and some mighty good stock, too. Nobody's bothered them for years. With a trap at a water hole, a body could round up a few."

"How many men would it take?"

"Four or five, maybe."

She turned to me. "Johannes, would your Indian friends help? I would pay them."

"They might. I could talk to them."

"Kelso's in town. I think he'd like a job, and he's a good hand with stock and he's steady."

"All right. You and Johannes plan it, then. I believe that soon Johannes will have learned about all Fraser can teach him, and an adventure like this would do him good."

"How many horses you figurin' on? A couple of dozen?"

She smiled. "I was thinking of four or five hundred. Or as many as you can handle with ease."

"Four or five *hundred?* Ma'am, you must be—"

"I am perfectly serious, Mr. Finney. I want several hundred horses and I want them broken to ride. If you find any mules among them, and I've heard escaped mules do run with the wild herds, I'd want them, too."

"Breakin' that many horses might take a year. Months, anyway. I mean including catchin' time."

"Were you going someplace, Mr. Finney? We have the time. There is plenty of grass, and I believe there will be a market soon. The best stock, I'd like selected for breeding purposes, and we will keep that lot in close to town."

"If you say so, ma'am."

She gathered the papers she had been discussing with Jacob. "I would like Mr. Kelso to work for me here, to fill in for you, Mr. Finney. People are beginning to realize that we work together, and I'd like to use somebody else for a time. You and Johannes can handle the horses."

She stood up, holding her papers; then she looked at me. "Neither age nor size makes a man, Johannes. It is willingness to accept responsibility. Besides, I want you out of town for a while."

She turned to glance at Finney. "Mr. Finney? Have you heard any talk of war with Mexico?"

"War? No, ma'am. I heard talk of some Anglos up north. Seems there's some trappers, maybe soldiers, too, up at Sutter's Fort. There's always rumors, though."

"It is more than a rumor, Mr. Finney. There is a war, and I am afraid there will be trouble here. If we Americans are wise, there need be no fighting."

"How do you mean?"

"Mr. Finney, most of the leaders among the Californios are intelligent men. California is far from Mexico City, and trade is forbidden except with Mexico. The people are denied many of the things they could enjoy, and they lose the profits from foreign trade.

"If the American government is intelligent, all can be accomplished through diplomatic channels. Yet if the Californios are challenged, they will fight. It would be a matter of honor."

"Have you talked to Abel Stearns about this?"

"Not really. Mr. Stearns is a Mexican citizen and will take no part in whatever is done. I believe he feels it is inevitable, but he is loyal and will take no part in activities against the government. Nor will I, although I am not a citizen here. Actually, I have no legal right to conduct a business. I am overlooked partly because I am a woman and partly because the local officials like what I am doing."

"You think there will be fighting?"

"I am afraid so. The leader of one of the groups is Frémont. He is said to be ambitious."

Finney smiled slyly. "Aren't we all?"

Her eyes showed her amusement. "Of course, Mr. Finney, but there are ways of using ambition. One must not be rash.

"Jedediah Smith showed the way here, others followed, and they have prospered, but change can take place quietly and should be handled with discretion. Have you ever talked to General Vallejo, Mr. Finney?"

"Seen him a time or two. Talked to him? No."

"I have. Several times, in fact. General Vallejo is very intelligent, above all he is a realist. He is a Californian first, everything else after. I think our Mr. Frémont or whoever is to handle the situation should sit down and talk to the general. Above all, Mr. Frémont should *listen*.

"Or he should come south, alone, and talk to Pio Pico. After talking to Pio he should get a few of the *gente de razón* together over a good meal, a bottle of wine, and their cigars. Above all, he should not attempt to dictate, but be guided by what the *gente de razón* advise. I believe everything could be arranged as something between gentlemen, do you understand?"

"I do, ma'am, and you may be right. I'm afraid the Anglos are expecting a fight."

When he had gone, I asked, "Miss Nesselrode, what is happening?"

She worked at her papers for a moment, then said, "A few years ago Texas fought a war for her independence. The United States recognized her independence and Mexico was unhappy about it.

"Now, almost ten years later, Texas has applied for admission to the Union and we have admitted Texas as a state. Mexico said that if we did so they would consider it an act of war. Not long ago a Mexican force crossed the Rio Grande and wiped out an American patrol.

"Before coming west, I had talked with some gentlemen from Mexico, who assured me Mexico would go to war if Texas was admitted to the Union. They were quite confident, and with reason, as their standing army is several times the size of ours.

"As a matter of fact, the United States is in no condition for war. We have less than twenty-five thousand men under arms and they are scattered across the frontier protecting settlers."

"Will we be beaten?"

"I doubt it, Johannes. Our Constitution provides that no law shall forbid us from keeping and bearing arms because of the necessity for a militia. We have a militia of a sort, but our greatest strength lies in the fact that so many of our people not only possess weapons but also understand their use, and above all they are prepared to defend themselves against any sudden attack by an enemy.

"You will remember that we won our freedom because we were armed. We were not a simple peasantry unused to weapons. The men who wrote our Constitution knew our people would be safe as long as they were armed."

She gathered her papers and placed them in a leather case. "I was a woman alone, Johannes. I weighed the circumstances and decided to come west, believing California would become a part of our country.

"I told myself I would do nothing against a people who have been friendly to me, nor have I betrayed that promise.

"On the other hand, if such a change took place, I wished to be on hand to accept the opportunity. No matter who wins, California will no longer be isolated. There will be trade, and there will be a need for horses and cattle. Prices here are three or four times what they would be if goods could be imported by sea, and trade will become important."

She paused. "We are two people alone, Johannes. Whatever happens, we must be prepared to move with the tide. We shall be ready. We *must* be ready.

"You were left alone, as I was. I have learned to be strong, and you have also. Whatever is to come, Johannes, each can help the other. We will stand together, you and I."

26

"You are history," Thomas Fraser told us. "Do not think of history as something remote that concerns only kings, queens, and generals. It concerns you.

"Each of you has a history that is part of the history of Los Angeles, a part of the history of California, part of the history of the United States and the world.

"You and your families march across the pages of history, and often he who plows a furrow is of more importance than he who leads an army. The army can destroy, the furrow can feed.

"Los Angeles became a town on September 4 of 1781. The founders were eleven adult males and their families. Their names were Camero, Lara, Navarro, Rosas, Moreno, Mesa, Banegras, Villavicencia, Rodríguez, Quintero, and Rodríguez again. These men were or had been soldiers at the Mission of San Gabriel.

"In all there were forty-six people; twenty were children under twelve years of age. Of the men, two were from Spain, one from China, and the rest from Baja California, Sonora, or Sinaloa.

"Twelve house lots faced the plaza on three sides, the remaining space was given over to public buildings. This was your town.

"On the lowlands near the river, thirty fields were laid out, separated from each other by narrow access roads, these fields to be cultivated by the townspeople. Each was provided with two each of oxen, mules, sheep, goats, and cows. The government at first was largely a military government, and the new citizens, having been soldiers, were accustomed to discipline."

He paused. "Each of you is a part of what is happening here. Do not think you can sit idly by while it grows to a great city, as it assuredly will. A city is made up of citizens, and citizens are so called because they inhabit a city, and if they will, can direct its destiny.

"Is it to be a place where only business is done? Simply a market-place, or is it to be a place of beauty? The great cities, the remembered cities, are the cities known for their beauty."

Our studies slowly became harder and we were given much outside reading and occasional bits of writing to do. In going to and from school we walked only certain streets, staying away from Sonora Town, even though many of the people who lived there were fine people. It was also a hangout for toughs of all kinds. In spite of that, we could see the restlessness in the town, as though trouble was expected. Frémont, I discovered, had been earlier in San Diego and then had gone north.

Often I thought of what Miss Nesselrode had said, that each of us had been left alone. Was that why she had offered me a home? Because she saw in me what she had been? Or was there some other reason?

At another time she had said, "Do not be afraid. A little fear can make one cautious. Too much fear can rob you of initiative. Respect fear, but use it for an incentive, do not let it bind you or tie you down."

Coming and going from school, I had begun to vary my route, taking one for a day or two, then another. The choices were few, but often I cut through orchards or walked paths where no horseman would go, and the Californios were all riders. They disdained walking.

Much time passed before I saw the don. Miss Nesselrode had told me he rarely came to town, staying on his ranch for weeks at a time, sometimes for months. Then there was a day when, about to emerge from an orchard, I heard the clatter of hooves and looked out to see him ride by.

There was no mistaking him. He was a handsome man with a white goatee and mustache, riding a magnificent horse and a saddle loaded with silver. There were six men with him on that day, and one of them I remembered. He of the flat nose and the scarred face, the one who had wanted to kill me.

They rode swiftly past, but it was not until the dust settled that I emerged on the street and crossed it, leaping over the *zanja* and climbing the pole fence that divided Miss Nesselrode's yard from the one behind hers.

Sitting on the top rail I fed a stolen carrot to my horse and thought about my grandfather. Such hatred was unreasonable. As Miss Nesselrode said, such pride was foolish, yet it was present and must be dealt with.

On that day I did not go to the shop, but remained at home, reading.

The hatred was unreasonable, and yet . . . I had an uneasy sympathy for my grandfather. Was it because of that relationship? Or was it something more?

His pride was in his family and his name. From what I had heard both from my parents and from others, it was all he had. His family, the name, and his wealth. To him his daughter's marriage to a common seaman was a disgrace, a blot on the family name not to be tolerated. Having read some of the stories of Sir Walter Scott and similar romances, I could understand what this might mean to a proud man.

Our world was different in some respects. It was based on accomplishment, on doing. His seemed to be based on simply being.

Supposing that was all one had, and suddenly it was threatened? Grudgingly I began to see his side of it, although I had little sympathy for that view.

Later, I explained to Miss Nesselrode what I had thought, and she listened without speaking until I had finished, and then she said, "Johannes, you are growing up. You are becoming a man, and a good man, too."

So much was happening. Thomas Fraser explained some of it in school, very carefully, so as not to seem to take sides.

The Californios had never liked the idea of their governors being political appointees from Mexico. Some of the governors had been liked or at least tolerated; many had come only to get rich and get out. One of those they had not liked was Micheltorena, who, after a bloodless battle fought in the San Fernando Valley, had been driven from California, and Don Pio Pico of Los Angeles had become governor.

Often I saw him near the plaza, a portly, kindly man with rather heavy features, whose genial manner only partly concealed a native shrewdness and skill in handling people and situations.

Suddenly, things were happening. On the seventh of August 1846, Commodore R. F. Stockton, with a small flotilla of ships, anchored at San Pedro, and landing four hundred men and some small artillery, marched swiftly and entered Los Angeles. Governor Pico and General Castro evaded capture and escaped to Sonora.

Later, after Frémont and Stockton had left for San Francisco, the Californios retook the city from Lieutenant Gillespie.

People hurried along the streets or gathered in knots, talking. Miss Nesselrode was irritated. "It need not have happened! Had they been tactful . . . !"

They had not been. Least of all, Lieutenant Gillespie, and he had suffered for it.

Much was happening of which I knew nothing at all. Jacob Finney had ridden in and was staying around our house, in the event of trouble. "Your grandpa's gone back to the rancho," he told me. "Rode out last night. You won't need to worry about him for a few days."

"Have you seen Mr. Fletcher?"

Finney glanced at me. "He's around. You seen him?"

"He came by the bookstore. I don't like him."

"Neither do I." He glanced at me again. "Fletcher? Well, now." Jacob was plaiting a rawhide riata as he talked. "There's a bad one. We'll have trouble with him one day. I feel it in my bones."

"He threatened me." Then I explained what had happened in the store, and Finney listened without comment until the end. "Say, boy? You're growin'! Hadn't realized. If he comes back in, you don't know anything, haven't heard anything, and if he wants more, you tell him to see me."

He put down the rawhide and went to the window, peering out. "Kelso should be in tonight."

Something was worrying him. He returned to his plaiting, then got up and walked to the back of the house to check the corrals. When he came back, he asked, "Have you still got your rifle and pistol?"

"I have."

"Keep 'em handy. I ain't worried about the Californios or the Americans. I mean, I'm not worried about the soldiers. It's that riffraff down in Sonora Town. If they think nobody is around to keep 'em in line, they might start looting. Mostly I worry about the Chinese. They're good folks, but some of them have money. Quite a lot of money."

Jacob Finney spread a bed near the front door and put his pistol alongside his bed.

It was almost midnight when I awakened to hear a scratching at the door. Then a low mumble of voices and a new, familiar one. It was Kelso.

"Jacob! It is good to see you, man! How has it been with you?"

"I'm working. You can see that. You would do well to join us."

"Well . . . join you for what? I am too old to wander around, Jacob. These last months . . . I've been like a leaf in the wind. I believe I was happiest when we were coming west. We were alive, Jacob. There was need for us then, and Farley . . . he was a fine man, Jacob, and Zachary

Verne. I can't get him out of my mind. There was something about him—"

"Of course. We all felt it, I think. He was special."

"But why? I've met a lot of men, but none like him. I've thought about him a lot, coming west when he knew he was going to die, thinking only of his son, even willing to be killed if he could find a home for him."

"He was special. So is the boy."

"Is he here? I ran into Peg-Leg Smith up north, and he was asking about the boy. Said he'd found him in the desert. He'd come upon his tracks and followed them."

"The old devil brought him in. Picked the kid up."

"He told me. He told me something else, too. Somebody was following him."

"Peg-Leg?"

"No, the boy. Somebody was following the boy."

Following *me?* No . . . I had looked back, again and again. I had looked back to be sure I was holding my direction. There had been nobody out there. Yet, there were heat waves and it was hard to see very far.

"What are you talkin' about, Kelso?"

"There's something about that boy. Remember the Indian he saw at Indian Wells? The old man with the turquoise? He told his pa about it?"

"So?"

"I was back there, happened to mention it. Folks there said the boy was dreaming, there were no Indians at the Wells that night, and there hadn't been any for days. There was something going on up in the Santa Rosas, up above Deep Canyon somewhere."

"What are you saying?"

"Just telling you, Jacob. You an' me, we both know there's things out in that desert . . . things happen out there.

"Look, you've been around Injuns enough. There's things they know that we don't. About the desert, I mean, and the mountains."

"Maybe. I've heard stories . . . Hell, Kelso, a man can't believe half what he hears! Who knows what an Indian is thinking but another Indian? Who knows what they believe? I've known men who claimed they knew Indians . . . they were talking through their hats. Nobody does."

Jacob paused. "Kelso? You said Peg-Leg said somebody was following Johannes? Who was it?"

"Peg saw the tracks. Moccasin tracks of somebody with a long stride . . . mighty long, according to Peg."

"Who was it?"

"Maybe you should ask *what* it was. I don't know anything but what Peg told me." Kelso paused. "Thing was, he didn't see anybody, only the tracks."

There was silence in the room, and I lay wide-awake, straining my ears for every word. What were they talking about? What did they mean?

"Look at it this way, Jacob. You've heard the stories about how Verne and his woman lived in the desert, how the old man tried to find them, had dozens of men out hunting, rewards offered . . . everything."

"Did they find them? No. And why not?"

"Hell, Verne knew the desert! He'd roamed out there a lot, and the Indians were friendly."

"I know. Maybe that's all it was, and maybe I'm having pipe dreams." Kelso paused. "Jacob? Is there any grub around? Maybe I'm just hungry. Maybe I just can't think straight anymore."

"Sit tight. I'll roust something up from the kitchen. There'd be some cold frijoles and some tortillas."

"I'd eat a cold horse collar right now. Or even an old saddle blanket."

There was a faint rattle of dishes, then a sound of something being put on the table.

"What are you suggesting, Kelso? What's biting you?"

"Verne took food to those Injuns when they were starving, so they'd want to help him. I run into a Mex up to Santa Barbara and he told me they saw no Injuns. Saw no tracks except the two of them they chased. Only sometimes dust storms wiped 'em out.

"The more I think about it, I've been wondering. Maybe Verne was in touch with something out there? Maybe the boy was?

"Who knows about the desert? Remember the boy being interested in old trails? And why didn't the Mohaves follow us?"

"They'd had enough, that's all. We shot too straight."

"Maybe . . . or maybe they were gettin' into country where their medicine was weak. Maybe they were scared to follow." Kelso paused again. "You been in the desert, Jacob. Did you ever hear of the Old Ones?"

27

There was a long silence in the room, and my ears strained to hear what would be said. The *Old Ones?* Who were they? And where had I heard the expression before?

"Oh, sure! Stories told over a campfire. Spooky stuff, like ghosts an' ha'nts an' such. We've all heard them."

"There's trails out yonder that seem just to wander off an' go nowhere. Sometimes they just fade out into nothing, lose themselves in the heat waves. Sometimes they go into the mountains." He paused. "Ever hear of the House of the Ravens?"

"One time . . . down Yuma way, isn't it?"

"West of Yuma, up in some rocky hills down there. These Injuns around now, they don't know from nothing about it, but they know it's there, like that Tehachapi country.

"Verne was around out there a lot, and those Injuns accepted him as one of their own, as much as they will accept any white man. If anybody knew anything, he would.

"I've wondered some about those trails out yonder. The ones that seem to just disappear? I've been wondering what would happen if a body just kept riding. I mean, why do those trails go somewhere and then suddenly stop?"

"You want my advice, Kelso? Stay away from them. There are some things no man should pry into. Leave 'em to the Injuns, or the Old Ones, whoever."

"One thing I'm sure of. There were people here before the Injuns the Spanish found, and there were quite a lot of them. If they built from adobe, nothing would be left. You know how quick it melts away if it isn't plastered or roofed over.

"As far as that goes, look at our own towns. What would be left after even two hundred years if nobody cared for them? A foundation or two covered with sand, that would be all.

"Iron rusts away. Hell, you let two, three hundred years pass and nobody would ever know we'd even been here. That goes for our cities back east, too. You just notice any old abandoned building and see how fast it falls apart!

"I've heard stories about a city that used to be out in the desert, in the Mohave. It was destroyed by an earthquake and some great rains that followed it. Some of the Injuns or whoever they were took refuge in the Tehachapi Mountains, lived around there for years until the last of them died off.

"You ever been in the Tehachapis or up Caliente Creek? Ever wonder why there's no Injuns there? Well, I've thought about it, but I've got no answers."

Kelso ate in silence, then asked for more coffee. Tired as I was, I was wide-awake.

"Maybe I've spent too much time in the desert and mountains. You get out there alone, and pretty soon you get to wondering. You hear things, little things, you think you see things sometimes, and maybe you do.

"Some of the Injuns have stories about what they call the Thunder-Bird, some great bird or flying thing that makes a noise like thunder. There was a Mexican who said something like that used to land in a lake, Lake Elizabeth, they called it. Used to kill his sheep sometimes. Then later there was a story about two cowboys who killed a flying reptile or something down in the desert in Arizona."

"You been listening to too many stories, Kel. I think it's time you came in out of the hills and settled down with folks."

"Maybe. . . . Again, it may be that I've been closer to some of those Injuns. After all, they've been here a long time, Jacob."

When morning came I went outside and looked for Mr. Kelso, but he was gone into the town.

I kept thinking about what he had said last night. Something or somebody had followed me in the desert. There were trails that seemed to lead nowhere. A city in the desert that had vanished, and the Thunder-Bird . . . the House of Ravens . . . and my own house of Tahquitz.

I wished Francisco was here.

*   *   *

I had been in Los Angeles a long time when one day, our girl Rosa told me she had seen someone lurking under the willows near the house. When I entered the kitchen that morning, Rosa was making tortillas.

She went to the door and pointed. "It was over there!" she said. "He was standing back under the leaves. I could not see him very well."

Walking over to the willows, I prowled around among them, looking for tracks. Suddenly I found them, and not only tracks but cigarette butts, many of them. Some were old, some were new. Some were there from before the last shower; some were fresh.

Somebody was watching our house.

Searching, I found where the tracks entered the willows to come to the place of watching. I followed them back to a narrow lane that led along behind some farm yards to a street.

Whoever was watching us had come up that lane from the street several times, perhaps many times, and he had watched our house while hidden in the willows.

Had he seen Aunt Elena?

Who was it, and why was he watching our house? Was he watching me? Or Miss Nesselrode?

When school was over that day I went to the book shop, and when there were no customers, I told Jacob, who was there, and Miss Nesselrode about my discovery.

"Look into this, will you, Jacob?" she asked.

"The boy's good, ma'am. I'll take a look, but I doubt I'll find anything he didn't."

"I believe," she added, "it is time you took that trip we spoke of once to see the Indians." She stood up suddenly. "Tomorrow morning, Jacob. You and Johannes start tomorrow morning."

"We'll be gone quite a while, ma'am. Don't you think—"

"Mr. Kelso will be here. I want Johannes out of here, and be sure nobody sees you leave. Change horses as often as you wish, but get away from this area very quickly."

She turned to me. "You wished to take some books? Pick five or six and list the titles, if you will. Leave the list on my desk."

Jacob took up his hat. "All right, ma'am, just so you will be in good hands."

"I can handle it." Miss Nesselrode smiled a little. "I believe you will remember that when need be I do not hesitate to shoot."

Jacob smiled. "No, ma'am, you surely don't." He turned his hat in his hands. "Do you want us to check out that wild-horse hunt while we're gone? Might be a good idea to come back by Cajon Pass. Give us a chance to ride up through the edge of the mountains and desert, maybe get a line on where we'd best look."

"All right."

She looked over at me. "Pack what you need, Johannes, and only what you need. I shall miss you very much, but you will have a great adventure, I am sure."

"Yes, ma'am. Will you see Aunt Elena, ma'am?"

Miss Nesselrode considered that, her fingertips resting on the table. "I shall try. She is a very interesting woman, your Aunt Elena."

We rode away before the sun was up, when the last stars lingered in the sky, reluctant to yield their light to the sun. We rode rapidly, and as before, we held to the back roads and trails.

As we rode, Jacob pointed out places he knew or had heard of. We covered a lot of ground, moving at a shambling trot except where we walked up the steeper hills. Wherever possible, we kept to routes that were parallel to the trail, wishing to be seen by no one.

"How you gettin' along in that school?" Jacob asked suddenly. "Had any more trouble with that Huber boy?"

"No, sir. It is a good school. Mr. Fraser is a good teacher, the best I ever had."

"Don't see how he makes it pay with no more students than he has, but if he can hold on, there will be more."

"There are six now," I said.

"I saw Cap'n Laurel's daughter there, didn't I? The pretty one with the gold hair?"

"Red-gold," I corrected. "Yes, she sits beside me."

"Oh? No wonder you had trouble with that Huber boy." He glanced at me with sly amusement. "Wait until you meet her pa. Ol' Cap'n Laurel—now, there's a character!"

There was nothing I could say, although I had heard stories, and Meghan had said he had asked about me.

"Laurel's a canny man. In some ways an uncanny one. Some of his crew were ashore here a time or two, and it seems the old man is either mighty knowing or he's tuned into something. They say he goes places where no cargo could be expected and there is always cargo for him.

"He knows the coast of China and Japan like he owned it. Siberia, too. Sometimes he sails up the rivers, they say. Always something doing with him. 'Uncanny' is the word.

"You know these fellows who go around tuning pianos? They have an ear for the sound, the exact sound? Well, Laurel seems to be that way. He's been known to change course of a sudden, no warning, just a sudden change of course that will take him out of trouble or where there's cargo."

"You mentioned Japan. I didn't think they allowed foreign ships to come to their ports."

"They don't. Only Laurel, he knows somebody or something and he goes. If you get to know him, I'd surely like to hear what you think. So would Miss Nesselrode."

Riding in silence as we usually did gave me time to think, and there was so much to think about. So many puzzling things had come up. My mother had said my father had premonitions. Was that what Captain Laurel had? Or were they what is called hunches? Or was it merely knowledge?

My father had talked to me of his voyages and of my grandfather's, and I knew that sometimes a sea captain kept certain ports of call or anchorages to himself, knowing that at intervals valuable cargo might be picked up there.

"I always listened carefully when your father talked about the sea," Jacob said. "Your father would tell me we will never know how much of the world was explored. The sea was often difficult to cross, but it was never impossible, and it has been crossed again and again by craft of every size and material. The Phoenicians, who were among the greatest of the early navigators, never allowed anyone to know where they went, and only a few stories have come down to us.

"They knew, as did the Carthaginians who developed from a Phoenician colony, sources of raw materials they divulged to no one. For many years they permitted no other ships in the western Mediterranean, or to sail through the straits into the Atlantic. Then a Greek captain named Coleus sometime around 600 B.C. managed to slip by them and went to Tartessus, a port near Gades, which we call Cádiz. He returned with a ship loaded with silver, which left him a rich, rich man.

"Nobody will ever know what voyages were made in the long ago. Hanno, a Phoenician, is reported to have sailed around Africa on orders from Necho, a pharaoh of Egypt.

"Eudoxus was on a ship off the mouth of the Red Sea in the Indian Ocean when some wreckage was seen that included the figurehead of a ship he had last seen in Gades, and that was over one hundred years before Christ.

"You'll like Cap'n Laurel, I think, and he will like you. Get him to talkin' about the sea, if you can. He's made friends with some priests in Japan an' China and they've told him things."

Before sundown we would ride off the trail and camp in a secluded spot, preparing our meal while it was light and with wood that gave off no smoke. By darkness the fire was put out and we slept until morning, trusting our horses to warn us of danger.

We stopped to buy a few supplies at El Campo, a place of one store and a few adobes.

"Stay with the horses," Jacob told me, "and keep out of sight. Folks remember travelers when there's so few."

It was hot and still. The horses stood in the shade of some trees and I sat down against the trunk of a thick old tree. Flies buzzed lazily. The horses dipped their noses in the water and drank; bees also came for water. I looked off toward the store, several hundred yards away, and wished Jacob would hurry.

The warm sun made me sleepy. I tugged my hat lower over my eyes. The horses flicked their tails to drive away the flies. I dozed.

There were footsteps in the dust. A boot crunched in the sand. I put my hand under my coat where the gun was, for the step was not Jacob's.

Boots and legs. From under my hat's brim without lifting my head I saw them. Narrow Spanish boots, large-roweled California spurs, pants split from the knee down.

"Most folks," a voice said, "would think you was asleep, but not Monte McCalla. I've played 'possum a time or two m'self."

Tilting my head back, I looked up at him. He was slim and wiry, not a tall man, but with broad shoulders and the slim hips of a man of the saddle.

"How are you?" I said.

"You can take your hand off that gun, boy. I'm friendly."

"As long as I have my hand on this gun, you better be," I said.

He chuckled. "Now, I like that! That's a proper answer." He squatted on his heels and tilted his broad-brimmed Mexican sombrero back from his face. He was a handsome man, with sideburns and a black mustache and eyes that laughed a lot.

"Sort of curious," he said. "Isn't often a man leaves his horses and walks away to a store when there's a hitchin' rail right out front."

"There's shade here."

"Now, that *could* be it. A boy like you, now. He'd like to look around in that store, maybe see something he wants, but you ain't doin' it. When I was a boy—"

"I was sleepy," I said.

"Maybe," he agreed, "an' maybe you just don't want to be seen. An' why would that be? Isn't likely you'd be a cow thief or a horse thief, not at your age. So who are you, anyway?"

"I'm sleepy," I said.

28

The two-story adobe was shaded by massive oaks whose branches hung above the porch on the second story. In the patio a fountain bubbled. The night was cool and pleasant, and in the main room on the first floor Don Isidro sat with his cigar, a glass of wine on the table close by.

He was a thin man with high cheekbones and hollow cheeks. His hair was gray and his mustache and beard were streaked with it. He was dressed with quiet elegance, and when he heard the sound of booted feet on the patio pavement, he frowned slightly.

What? At *this* hour?

A man appeared in the open door, a man with a flat nose and a scarred face, holding his hat in his hand. The man wore a white shirt, a red sash, and fringed leggings, a big pistol in a holster, and a knife.

He was a man, Don Isidro recalled, who preferred the knife.

"You wished to see me?"

The man turned his hat in his hand; then he said, very softly, "He lives."

An icy chill seemed to touch the back of Don Isidro's neck. He leaned forward and dusted the ash from his cigar.

"Bah!" There was contempt and impatience in his tone.

"I have seen him. I have seen him alive."

"You are mistaken. You have seen another. He could not survive."

"The father survived."

Blue veins showed on Don Isidro's brow. "Nonsense!" Then he asked, "Where did you see this . . . this child?"

"In the pueblo. On the street. It was he. I know it was he."

Doña Elena had appeared, almost ghostlike, at his elbow. There was irritation in his tone. "It cannot be. It is not possible."

"There is a woman, an Anglo. It is Señorita Nesselrode. He lives at her house."

Without turning his head, he said to Elena, "What do you know of this?"

"I know the woman. She has many friends." Then gently she added, "She is a friend to Don Abel Stearns and Don Benito Wilson."

"Bah! Who are they? *Anglos!*"

"You have forgotten, my brother. It is not we who are in power, but the Anglos." Then she added, "Pio Pico is also her friend, and General Vallejo."

"Do you know her?"

"She knows everyone, my brother. She has many friends."

"So you have said. And we have not, is that what you imply?"

"It is well to have friends."

"So you say. So you often say. This woman? This Señorita Nesselrode? I wish to visit her home. I wish to visit it now . . . tonight!"

"Tonight? But it is far. It would be after midnight—"

"So much the better. I wish to arrive without warning." He got to his feet. "You! Get five men and come with me. Five armed men, do you understand?"

"You cannot do this! Go to a woman's house in the middle of the night?"

"I shall do as I please. If the boy is there, he is mine, and I shall take him away. What right has this woman to have my grandson?"

"So you can kill him? Kill him as you have tried before?" She paused. "You do not know the Anglos, my brother. They do not care for you or your name. You would hang."

"Hang? Do not talk like a fool!"

He turned sharply around, glaring at a serving woman. "You! My boots! Quickly now!"

He tugged on the boots, then stamped into them. He turned to his sister. "You are a woman, so I can expect no more, but you are a fool, also! This child's existence is an insult! My daughter and that . . . that *peón!*"

"He was a fine man, and he would soon have been a ship's captain."

"Bah! A ship's captain! Of some miserable little coastal vessel? Married to *my* daughter?"

He strode to the door, turning there. "Do not worry yourself. The child is dead. I go but to make sure."

Doña Elena listened to his footsteps as they retreated across the patio. For an instant she thought of getting her own horse and trying by back trails to reach the town before him. Yet it was no use. She did not know the trails well enough and could easily become lost.

She remembered the cool beauty of Miss Nesselrode. She was a woman, that one. She would not be easily defeated.

Yet, Doña Elena was frightened. What of the boy? Isidro would see him, recognize him, know he was alive, and he would kill him.

Even the courts, even the law, would return a grandson to a grandfather.

Miss Nesselrode awakened suddenly as a rider rode past her window. She sat up. Had Johannes and Jacob come back? What was wrong?

No, of course not! Nobody in her employ would ride past on that side of the house.

Outlaws? Thieves? Quickly she got to her feet and slipped into her robe.

Where was Kelso?

Taking up her pistol and holding it at her side, concealed in the folds of her gown, she went into the living room just as the door burst open and several men charged in. The first one through the door was Don Isidro.

"You have a boy here. I want to see him."

"I do not know what you are talking about, señor, but you have broken into my home. You have broken into a lady's home in the middle of the night, a despicable act, something no gentleman would do. Now I must ask you to leave."

"Search the house!" Don Isidro ordered.

Miss Nesselrode lifted her pistol. "Señor! I am a dead shot! If you or one of your men takes a single step, I shall shoot you through the ear, señor, and tomorrow morning it shall be told all over the pueblo that the noble Don Isidro was shot through the ear by a woman!"

A voice from her right said quietly, "They ain't goin' nowhere, ma'am. I got me a scatter-gun."

Kelso turned up the wick on the lamp, shedding more light into the room, holding the shotgun ready, elbow braced against his right hip.

"You!" She pointed suddenly at a vaquero standing toward the rear, a younger and seemingly somewhat embarrassed young man. "Will you do me the honor of walking through those rooms? If you see a boy, please call out."

He hesitated a moment, then came forward. It required only a minute, for the doors of the rooms stood open. He emerged from the kitchen at the last. "Señor? There is no boy. There are only these, and the cook. No more."

Furious, Don Isidro glared at the man with the flat nose. "You!" He turned back to Miss Nesselrode. "Señorita, I am—"

"Sir, you are a fool. You are also a coward and a disgrace to the name of grandfather. You are proud of a name which you disgrace with every day you live.

"Your story is well known. You drove your daughter from the country, you had her husband murdered, and you have attempted to murder your grandson.

"Do you think it is not known, señor? Do not be such a fool. Behind your back they shrug, they sneer, and sometimes they shudder.

"The son-in-law whom you had killed was a dozen times the man you think you are. You are nothing, sir! *Nothing!*"

Don Isidro's face was a haggard mask, gray and ugly. "If you were a man, I would kill you!" His voice was hoarse with emotion. "I would—"

"No you would not, Don Isidro. You would not face a gun in the hands of any man, or a blade. You would have me killed by one of those!" She pointed at the men at his back. "When did you ever kill a man? Or defend yourself? When did you ever do anything but live on what your ancestors created for you, shielding yourself behind an honorable name?

"Your ancestors, señor, and your countrymen were proud men, they were explorers, fighting men, but what are *you?* What have you ever been but an empty shell?"

The young man who had searched the house had turned and slipped quietly away. The others, shamed, were backing toward the door.

Don Isidro struggled to speak, but before he could find words, she said, "Get out! Get out and stay out and don't ever come to my door again or I shall shoot you myself. Better still, I shall simply set the dog on you. It is what you deserve!"

He turned; his men were gone. Blindly he went to the door and stepped out into the night.

Kelso lowered the shotgun. "Lord a'mighty! Ma'am, I never saw the like! You whipped him like a mangy dog!"

"I am sorry, Mr. Kelso. I did not mean to lose my temper, but that fine boy, and his mother and father . . . It was evil, Mr. Kelso! Evil!"

"Yes, ma'am." He hesitated. "Ma'am? D' you have any idea what

you've done? You've whipped him, ma'am, you've done what no dozen
guns could have done. You've destroyed him.

"Those men with him? They're gone, ma'am. They won't serve a
man like you showed him to be. When you foller a man, you take on
his color. Well, you showed him up, made him to be a coward and a
weakling. When he gets back to that ranch, he will be alone. And you
know something? I'd lay a bet he's never been alone in his life! He had
only to lift a hand to get whatever he wanted. Now he will lift a hand
and nobody will come."

"Will it be that bad?"

"Yes, ma'am. Those men who work for him. They may not have
much, but they have their pride, too. Much of their pride is often in
the man they follow, the brand they ride for. Take that away from
them and they have mighty little, so they will just fade away, they will
go elsewhere."

For a moment, when he reached his horse, Don Isidro leaned against
the stallion. His mind was numbed with shock. Nobody had ever spoken to him like that. No one had dared.

How dare she say such things? Hiding behind the fact that she was a
woman and could not be challenged.

He reached for the pommel and pulled himself into the saddle, then
looked around for his men.

They were gone. He was alone.

Why, the fools! Did they think he would allow such conduct?

He called out. "Andrés! Pedro! Come, we are going!"

There was no reply.

He looked around again, puzzled. They were gone. Gone into town
for a drink, perhaps. Yet there was a sinking within him, a heavy lump
in his stomach as of something dead. He started the horse toward
home.

"That woman!" he said aloud. How dare she! Remembering her, he
shuddered. A witch, that was what she was, a witch! How terrible she
had been!

He looked around. He was alone on a dark road. Nobody followed,
no sound of hoofbeats from his riders.

The patio was dark and still when he reached it. He dismounted,
looking around for a man to take his horse.

There was no one.

He turned, staring all around. The only light showed from the house
itself; all else was dark and still.

"Joaquin!" he shouted.

He tied the stallion to an iron ring. Somebody would come soon. He crossed the patio, his steps echoing in the stillness.

It was very late. No wonder there was no one around. He had not realized. It had been late when he left for that woman's house.

He felt an emptiness within him. What had he been thinking of? She was a respected and respectable woman, well known and liked not only by the Anglos but also by his own people.

His people? Since when had he thought of them in that way? They were Californios or Mexicans. He was from Castile! He was . . .

He now felt sick inside. What was all that nonsense, anyway? He had left Castile to escape the sneers, the things they would say about what had happened. He had run away from a disgrace he could not bear. He had come here, and then Consuelo . . .

That American fellow. That *common* sailor! He had dared to approach her! Dared to speak to her! *His* daughter!

Leaving the stallion, he went into the house. A light burned from the table. He crossed to the sideboard and poured a drink of *aguardiente*, then another. Taking a third glass, he went to the big horsehide chair and dropped into it.

He was tired. Exhausted. It was very late and he was not as young as he had been. He tried to turn his mind away from that woman, but her flashing eyes, her voice, so scathing . . .

There was a soft movement behind him, a hand on his shoulder. "Isidro? It is very late. You had better go to bed."

"My horse—"

"I will care for him. Go to bed now."

"You know? You heard?"

"I heard. When they came back for their things—"

"Their what?"

"They are gone, Isidro. They have left us." She paused. "Their pride was in us. We have failed them."

His mouth tasted bitter. He glared to right and left; he started to rise, then sat back.

The fools! The contemptible fools! Let them go! He would find better! He had the money. He could pay.

Bed . . . yes, he should get some sleep. Tomorrow would be soon enough. He never had been able to think well when he was tired.

He should leave here, anyway. He should go back to Spain.

His men were gone. All of them.

29

When we rode out of El Campo and headed for Agua Caliente, Monte McCalla rode with us. Jacob seemed to accept him easily enough, but I was suspicious. I didn't know who he was or what he wanted.

When we started drawing close to the Springs, I kept standing in the stirrups, looking. "There it is," I said suddenly, pointing. "The Calling Rock."

McCalla made it out. He studied it. "What about it?"

"They say if you turn to look back when you're leaving, you will always return. Some just call it the Leaning Rock."

"I like the first name better. Say, that's a good story. How about it? Did you look back?"

"I looked back a-purpose. I wanted to come back."

When we came closer, I pointed up Chino Canyon. "There's a cave up there with a pool in it. The Cahuillas used to go there to drink the water before they went hunting. Said it gave them greater endurance."

McCalla looked up the canyon. "Have to try it sometime."

He noticed me looking down my back trail, and that Jacob turned in the saddle from time to time. "You boys are riding kind of edgy," McCalla said at last. "You expectin' trouble?"

"You can cut out and ride alone if you're worried," Jacob said. "As a matter of fact, we think we left trouble behind, but we don't depend on it."

"We're ridin' together," McCalla said, "so your trouble is my trouble. You see them coming, and I'll ride back and see if they can chew it."

"This isn't your fight," Jacob said.

"I'm ridin' with you. You don't size up like thieves, and in a fight three is better than two. When I rode up to your camp I taken a hand in your game."

He was a strange man. Half the time, he was singing. His was not much of a voice, but not bad, either. Yet he liked to sing, and he seemed to know more songs than anybody I'd ever met.

When he discovered our plan to catch wild horses, he wanted to come along. "I'm handy with a rope," he said, "and I can ride 'em as good as any man."

Later, when we were alone, Jacob looked over the fire at me. "What d' you think, Johannes? Shall we take him on?"

"I think he's a good man," I said, "and we'll need help."

"My idea exactly."

The next morning we rode through the sandhills to the store at the Springs.

When we walked into the store the storekeeper knew me at once, yet now I could look him right in the eye. "Howdy, son! You've grown some inches."

"Yes, sir. Is my house still empty?"

He hesitated, busy with arranging some items on the counter. "Well, I reckon. Sometimes it is an' sometimes it isn't, although I got an idea it will be empty when you show up."

"And Francisco? Is he about?"

"Comes an' goes. If he wants to see you, he will. Indians are notional."

Jacob bought various items from the shelves—flour, salt, coffee, a ham, and a couple of slabs of bacon.

Walking to the door, I glanced toward the sandhills where the house lay. Did I detect a faint suspicion of smoke? My heart began to pound.

I hesitated a moment; then, turning to Jacob, I spoke as casually as I could. "I think I'll ride over while you're picking up supplies. Don't be in a hurry."

He glanced at me, and Monte McCalla looked over his shoulder at me. "Want me to come along?"

"Not this time. I'll go alone." To offset any comments, I added, "It was where my father was killed. I'd like to ride over there alone."

"Oh? Sure," Monte said. "We'll come along later."

Jacob was not fooled. He knew about the exchanging of books, and he was no doubt as curious as I.

First I unlashed the sack of books and put them on the saddle before me; then I turned my horse and walked it slowly along the trail. When I turned into the winding lane through the dunes, I began to sing some lines learned from my father from an old sea song, "The Golden Vanity."

In the middle of the yard, I stepped down from the saddle and shouldered the sack of books. When I came to the step, I put the sack down and drew the drawstring, opening it. Taking out one book, I looked at it, turning a few pages, then put it down atop the sack, and lifting the latch, I opened the door.

The room was as I remembered it. The floor was freshly swept, there were no cobwebs in the corners. The books were still neatly arranged on their shelves, yet the air was not stuffy as in a long-closed house. It was fresh, clean, with a faint smell of pines.

The beds were neatly made, only now there were sheets instead of simply the blankets I remembered. I opened the cupboards. They were well-stocked. Jacob need not have worried.

The coffeepot was on the coals in the fireplace and the coffee was hot. Taking down a cup, I filled it and sat down, my back to the door.

I was home again. This was the desert, this was *my* desert. My parents, captured by their love for each other, had fled across it, had hidden within it, had survived upon it. And I, too, had survived. And now I was back to the desert, back to the soaring mountains behind my house, back to the loneliness that was never lonely, back to the stillness that held silent voices that spoke only to me.

Slowly, taking my time, I drank my coffee, looking out the window at the dark waves of the rock, pushed high by monstrous tides within the earth itself, waves long stilled that had given birth to pines, and exposed raw edges to the wind, the rain, and the ice.

Enormous tides had built these mountains, but now they were being plucked at, teased, annoyed by wind and rain, by snow that fell and changed to ice, expanding to crack the rock and drop the fragments at the mountain's base. This was as it had been and as it would ever be. Men would come and go, leaving their tiny scars for the wind to hide with sand, men who in their ego thought the world belonged to them, forgetting the dinosaurs who had ruled the earth for many more millions of years than man, and were gone now, leaving only bones.

Some thought them dragons, some thought the bones had belonged to giants, some only shrugged and walked their way, seeking traces of gold and ignoring the mystery of the bones.

Finishing my coffee, I stood up, hearing the coming of horses and the voices of Jacob and Monte, talking.

I stepped outside to pick up my sack of books and saw that the one I had left atop the sack was gone.

Deliberately I kept my mind from wonder. If something or someone was here who so desired privacy, I would not invade it by so much as a thought.

We shared something, whoever it was and I. We shared a community of books, the companionship of gathered thoughts, and for the time it was enough. It did not want more, so I would not ask for more.

Knowledge is awareness, and to it there are many paths, not all of them paved with logic. But sometimes one is guided through the maze by intuition. One is led by something felt on the wind, something seen in the stars, something that calls from the wastelands to the spirit.

To receive the message, the mental pores must be open, and we white men in striving for our success, in seeking to build a new world from what lies about us, sometimes forget there are other ways, sometimes forget the Lonesome Gods of the far places, the gods who live on the empty sea, who dance with the dust devils and who wait quietly in the shadows under the cliffs where ancient men have marked their passing with hands.

Once my father had told me of finding a cliff dwelling built high in the rocks, the bricks plastered with mortar from clay, and in the clay were the marks of fingers.

Who left those prints in the clay? Who pressed his hand here and then stepped back to view it? Why did he leave his signature here? To show that he, too, had a hand? To tell others that a man had gone before, had passed some brief time in this place, and then gone on? My father had found human bones there. Did they belong to the possessor of the hand? Or were they the bones of another, following long after?

Why did he impress his hand upon the clay? Did he hope to send across the centuries a thought? A dream, perhaps? Or just to say that "I, too, was here. This was my place. This I built with my hands."?

I knew the image of that hand would be with me forever, for we who pass do not own this land, we but use it, we hold it briefly in trust for those yet to come. We must not reap without seeding, we must not take from the earth without replacing.

My father told me of a Navajo once who found an arrowhead on the sand and took it up, but then he took from his pocket a small buckskin sack and from it a pinch of dust to replace what he had taken.

Jacob Finney rode into the yard with Monte McCalla, and they swung down, leading their horses around to the corral. I followed, and suddenly Monte stopped, holding up a hand.

There, in the dust, was a footprint, the print of a gigantic moccasin!

"Lord a'mighty!" Jacob said in an awed whisper. "Look at the *size!*"

"Make two of mine," Monte said, placing his boot beside it. "Hell, it would make *three* of mine!"

I looked, then looked away. That footprint, I told myself, was no accident. Like the hand in the clay, it was a signature. It was a hint, a warning, the opening of a story.

Never before had there been a footprint, never before an indication, only the missing books.

This was a statement. This was saying to me, "This manner of man am I. If you would go no further, you may leave the trail here."

Within me there was a pang, a sharp pain of sympathy. Where would such a one find a companion? Who could bridge the awe of size to share a meeting with this man, this being, this creature? Could I?

How lonely he must be! How cut off by strangeness, by difference!

Yes, I thought, the footprint had been deliberately left.

Yet I, in my own way, had been a stranger, had been cut off from others of my age by the circumstances of my parents. Wherever I had gone, people had thought me strange, except in the desert, except, so far as I knew, the Indians.

Yet no doubt the Indians thought all white men strange, for our ways were different from theirs and each people is apt to consider their own ways as "human nature," not realizing they were merely a pattern imposed upon them by rearing, by education, by the behavior of those with whom they associated.

"Got a nice place here," Monte commented thoughtfully. "Somebody taken a deal of trouble. Clean, too."

Monte glanced over at Jacob. "You know these Indians?"

Jacob indicated me. "He knows 'em. He takes over where Indians are concerned. They know him, and his pa was a big man among them. You'll see."

As dusk came, we lighted the lamps, and I took the other books from the sack and arranged them on the shelf. I removed some of those that had long been there, planning to take them to the book shop for those who might not have read them. Reading material was too highly valued and scarce not to be shared.

"Your pa was killed?" Monte asked.

"Right out in front," I said. "He got one of them, might have taken more, but he took time to shove me out of the way. He was a good man with a gun."

"Zachary Verne? I've heard of him." Monte glanced at me. "How about you? With enemies like you've got, you should learn to use guns."

"I do all right."

"Maybe I can help. You should be one of the best. Then you don't have to worry."

"All right."

They spread their beds on the floor near the fireplace and I went into my old bedroom and closed the door. When I was in bed I looked up at the ceiling, which was lost in darkness, and remembered Meghan.

When we had rounded up the horses, we would go back, and maybe then I would see her, and would meet her father.

In the night, the wind came up, blowing softly in from the desert to the east, that strange, empty desert where the old trails were and where the sea had once been. Soon I would be out there, far out on the sands, wandering.

And in the night, when the winds whispered around the eaves, I lay awake in the house of Tahquitz and wondered where he was, and how he fared.

Where was Francisco, who had drawn the smiling face? And when we met again, would that face still smile?

Would he still be my friend? We were older now, and it had been long since we talked.

By Indian standards he would now be a man, but was I not a man also?

The swift-paced years had gone by and left no footprints on the sand that had not blown away. I could only hope there would be some traces, some memory in his mind.

Tomorrow, I hoped, I would see Francisco.

My eyes opened suddenly from near-sleep. What of the old man with the turquoise? Would I see him also? Or was he only a ghost figure in my imagination?

Why had he come to me that one time? If I had stayed, would he have spoken?

Would he come again?

30

My father had prepared me for marvels. He was a cool, logical man, but life upon the sea and the desert had left him with the realization that man thus far has but scratched the surface of knowledge and of his possibilities.

"Keep an open mind," he told me, "for no man can say what can or cannot be, nor can he say what does or does not exist.

"Landlubbers make much of what Columbus did, but many longer voyages had been made under more difficult circumstances. Landlubbers might believe the world was flat; any seaman knew otherwise, for he had seen ships disappear over the curvature of the earth.

"Landlubbers would have you believe that ancient seafarers hugged the coast, when any fool knows that is by far the most dangerous place. For thousands of years men have known the stars and how to travel using them as guides. The open sea had no dangers that compared with the reefs, offshore or onshore winds, baffling currents or floating objects, which were much more common close to shore.

"The farmer, the hunter, or the deep-sea fisherman always had his eyes upon the heavens. He lived with their vagaries as much as with the trails he followed or the furrows he plowed. He could read the weather in the clouds, locate distant islands or lagoons by their appearance. He knew the flight of birds and which lived upon land and which upon the sea. Long before there was a compass, he understood how to locate the sun on an overcast day. He who sits at a desk and tries to understand by logic often loses touch with the realities.

"Remember this, my son: our world is one where the impossible occurs every day, and what we often call supernatural is simply the misunderstood.

"When you go into the wilderness or out upon the sea, keep your mind open. Much can be learned from books, but much remains about which no book has been written. Remember this: the poor peasant, the hunter, or the fisherman may have knowledge that scholars are struggling to learn."

All this was in my mind when I pulled on my boots that morning. Jacob was already stirring about, and Monte had been outside.

He came back in while Jacob was frying some ham. "That track," he said. "I found where he put his other foot down."

"Another track?" Jacob inquired.

"Not exactly. He stepped on a rock in a place where the ground was soft. Pressed it deep. I took it up and could see it was freshly done. Judging by the stride, that thing must be seven or eight feet tall!"

"Jumped, maybe?"

"Ain't likely," Monte replied. "That rock would have been tipped a mite when he landed. No, that man or whatever it is is *big*. I checked that track again. It must weigh twice what I do. Maybe more."

"Don't worry about it," I said. "Whoever or whatever it is hasn't bothered us. Let's return the compliment."

Monte started to speak, but Jacob interrupted. "I'd say that's good advice. Let's just forget it, shall we?" He glanced around at Monte. "And don't ask any questions or even mention it."

Monte shrugged. "Hell, what difference does it make? I've already forgotten it."

We switched over to talking about wild horses and how they could be trapped, how canny they were, and the necessity for picking out the good ones.

"If they're too old," Monte said, "even if they're in fine shape, we'd be fools to bother. The old ones are tough to break. Some of them will die before they'll give in."

"There may be some horses that have escaped from ranches," Jacob suggested, "and that will almost surely be true of any mules we find."

"There are wild, unbranded cattle out there, too," I said. "My father told me that some of the cattle he rounded up for the Indians had been running wild."

"How are we going to find those Injuns?" Monte asked.

"We won't," I said. "They will find us."

"You mean we just sit and wait?" Monte asked.

"Let them choose the time," I said. "They have their own ideas about things. And don't judge these Indians by others you've known. They're different.

"They're changing, and some of the old ways are being forgotten, and some of the wise old men have not passed on their knowledge, partly because they found no one worthy of it."

"What's it mean? Their name?"

"Cahuilla? It's an open question. Some say it means 'power' or the 'people of power' or 'the power way,' and by that they do not mean physical strength, but wisdom and something more, the power from the mind."

Monte shrugged. "Maybe. I never knew any Injuns who were much on the mind. Smart . . . yes. Mighty smart when it comes to that. Of course, it depends on what you mean by mind."

"You just may not have known them well enough," I commented. "My father used to say that just about the time you decided you knew all about Indians, you would discover you'd only begun to learn, and then after you'd learned an awful lot more, you would realize you really did not know anything yet."

"Maybe . . . maybe."

Jacob was like the Californios in that he preferred to work with a rawhide riata, so he was busy plaiting the rawhide. He was a skillful man who worked fast. All of us had much to do to be ready for the wild-horse hunt. We must wait for the Indians to appear, but I had no doubt they knew of our presence and Francisco or one of the others would meet us "accidentally" at the store.

Yet there was something in me that I did not quite understand. Mentally I was more content than I had been at any time since leaving the desert, yet at the same time restless to be out there in the really wild country. Was there an affinity between myself and the desert? Was it true, as some believed, that men had lived other lives? And that one of mine had been lived in the desert? Or—and the thought left me uneasy —had I left something there that now I must find?

Of these thoughts I said nothing to my companions. Yet Jacob was puzzling to me. He seemed a simple man, yet on occasion he brought forth ideas that were far from simple. I knew that many men of the wilderness have much time to think, and their thoughts may wander down strange byways. My own father was an example.

More and more I was wondering about him, and why he had done certain things, why he had often spoken to me as he had, suggesting ideas rarely shared with someone so young as I.

Still, he had known, at the end at least, that his time was short. He had no doubt been trying to pass on as much of what he had learned as possible.

No individual completely acquires the experience of another, but if even a small part may be carried over to the next generation, much time can be saved. In technical ways, methods of working and such, knowledge has been passed on, but too few have learned from experience. I remembered my father once saying that perhaps in the future some device might be constructed into which all historical knowledge could be fed, particularly all knowledge of government, of diplomacy, of statecraft, and then this device might tell us what mistakes have been continually made and what situations to avoid.

Men have passed on the knowledge of how to mix cement, lay brick, splice a line, navigate a ship, make steel, and dozens of other crafts, yet in politics, statecraft, and social relationships we continue to repeat old mistakes.

Wandering outside, I gazed up at the looming mountains, at the distant haunts of Tahquitz. Up there, somewhere, was Tahquitz. Both the fabled creature of whom the Cahuilla spoke and the creature who sometimes inhabits this house where now we lived. When the person or creature or whatever it was wished to be known, he or it would make itself known. Until then its privacy would be respected.

Seven feet tall? It seemed impossible. Yet I myself was almost six feet now, and still growing. Who could say? I had never seen a man so large, although occasionally stories were heard of huge men.

Walking around to where the track was, I studied it with care. I must remember, for sometime it might be important. Then with my boot I brushed out the track. I could not escape the feeling that it had been deliberately left, for there had been no others. Only that one, as if it were a hint, a warning, or even a signature.

Our waiting was not in idleness. Jacob taught me how to plait a rope, and Monte already knew, although he favored a hair rope, as many from Texas did. We would need a number of them, for some would surely be broken, no matter how well done. Listening to Jacob and Monte talk, I learned much about wild horses and their capture.

That night when Monte returned from the store he said, "We got company. Neighbors, I mean."

We looked at him, waiting. "Paulino Weaver, he's moved in over yonder. Been here for some time."

"Mountain man," Jacob said. "I mind meeting him some while back. He's a good man."

"A man named Sexton with him. They've made friends with old Juan Antonio. They're trading, cutting timber and what-all." Monte looked around at me. "Paulino knew your pa back when your pa was on the dodge from the old don."

They were good men, yet in a mild way I resented them. I was jealous of my Indians, jealous of my canyons and desert, yet even as I thought that, I was amused by it. People would come, and my deserts would not remain empty, yet that thought made me irritable, and I got up and went outside. The stars were out, and the wind off the mountain was cool.

If more men came, crowding the desert, what would happen to the Lonesome Gods? Where would the spirits of the ancient ones go? Would they fade into the old trees? Into the rocks? Or, being worshiped no longer, would they fade gradually away?

When I went back inside, I said, "It's bound to be, I suppose, but I don't like the country getting crowded up. It seems to me we're losing something."

Jacob nodded. "I know how you feel. I'm gettin' so if I see another rider on the trail, I'm jealous, but we can't be that way. It's here for all of us."

"There's something out there, Jacob. Something I've got to find before it is too late. There's something out there for me."

He said nothing for a while, and then he said, "Your pa and ma found something for them. They were on the run, but no matter. Your pa told me. They found happiness out there, happiness with each other. Maybe they didn't have it long, but they had it good. Don't you ever forget that."

Thinking of them led me to think of Meghan. Where was she now? Did she ever think of me? I smiled into the darkness beyond the door, thinking how foolish that was. Why should she think of me? I was just a boy who had sat close to her in school, a boy too shy to talk, too awed by her presence to do anything but grow red and embarrassed if she so much as looked at me, which she rarely did.

How did my father meet my mother? Had he been shy, too? I doubted it. He seemed the essence of confidence, of assurance. Months had gone by with Meghan, and I had said nothing, yet . . . there had been communication of a sort. We read better than others in the class, and Thomas Fraser had often had us read aloud, first one, and then the other. It was not much, I realized.

Restless because Francisco had not appeared, I saddled my horse the next morning and rode down to the store. As I walked up the steps, a man came from the store. It was Fletcher.

His smile was not pleasant, and there was a kind of a taunting in his expression that irritated me. "Been keepin' an eye out for you," he said, "wonderin' when you'd head for the desert."

"Does it concern you?"

His smile was there, but the amusement was gone from it. "Maybe," he said. "Maybe it does. Your pa, now, he spent a lot of time in the desert. Him and those Injun friends of his. I been wonderin' why, and there's some who figured that was where he got his money."

"Money?" I was puzzled. "What money?"

"Him an' your ma. They lived it up back east there, an' your pa had money to pay your way west. Now, you take what your pa paid for you an' him on the wagon. That's a good year's income for many a well-off man these days.

"Where'd your pa come by that kind of money? I figure he had it when he went east. I figure he got it out of that desert."

I simply stared at him. My father had had a difficult time during those years back east, barely having enough to keep us alive at times. There were periods when he had, briefly, done quite well, and then at the end the windfall from the races the horses had won, and the generosity of his employer.

"You are mistaken, sir," I said. "My father had nothing when he went east beyond a little he had saved from cattle sales and furs."

Fletcher took a cigar from his pocket and bit off the end. "Maybe, an' maybe not. Why'd he stop here instead of ridin' right into Los Angeles with the rest of us?" He waved a hand. "Why stop in this godforsaken spot? I say he had reason. I say he'd found gold, or those Injuns showed him where it was.

"I say your Miss Nesselrode knows about that gold. Why else has she been keepin' you? Why are you goin' into the desert with that there Finney?"

He put the cigar in his mouth and struck a match on his pants, bringing up his knee to draw the material tight over his thigh. "You go ahead. I'll foller. Maybe there's enough for all of us."

"Fletcher," I said, "you're a fool."

For a moment I thought he would strike me, and I said, "Don't try it, Fletcher."

Something in the way I said it seemed to warn him, for he suddenly looked at me again. "Hell, you're a man now. 'Least you've growed up. Now I can kill you."

What happened within me, I do not know, but I was suddenly light-hearted. I smiled at him. "Whenever you're ready, Fletcher. Whenever you're ready!"

31

What I thought of as the store was really nothing of the kind. It was merely a sort of dwelling where the owner kept a few supplies which he sold to the Cahuillas or to passersby. Under the counter he kept a jug from which he dispensed occasional drinks.

When Fletcher walked away, I turned to see him go. Already I had learned that one does not become careless around such men. There was murder in the man; I accepted the realization and was careful.

Yet when I turned, I was surprised. Francisco was there.

For a moment we looked at each other, and then I drew a quick round face in the dirt. He took the twig from my hand and added the smile. Then we looked at each other, and slowly he held out his hand.

His was not a muscular handshake. For that matter, few Indians whom I had known more than touched palms. The strong handshake that many think is an indication of character is not so at all. Many very strong men merely clasp one's hand. Theirs are not limp handshakes, nor the firm grip one hears of in fiction.

We walked over and stood in the shade of some mesquite. "We're going up-country," I said, "to catch wild horses."

He squatted on his heels, and I did likewise. "We hope to catch many horses," I said, "and we will need help." With a twig I dug in the soil for a pebble, turning it over. "We would like to find five or six Cahuillas to help us."

Francisco pushed his hat back and squinted at the pebble I had dug from the hard-packed earth. He picked it up and turned it in his fingers.

"We are thinking of three or four hundred horses. We would build a long fence of brush to guide them into a corral. There would be much work, but we would pay or share the horses."

"We do not need horses," he said. After a silence he said, "You catch cows, too?"

"Maybe."

"Catch cows, we take some cows."

"All right."

We sat silent, watching a raven plucking at something in a palm tree.

There had been times when I was a boy that I had gone with them to the oak groves to gather acorns, or to the mesquite for their beans. I had worked beside them and learned to know them, a little.

There were old men I remembered who sometimes talked to us as they worked. I remembered the stories of the coyote who had planted mesquite beans after the sea disappeared from the basin and left it dry. The fish and the seabirds on which the Cahuilla had lived were gone, but there were forests of mesquite soon. Yet, until the mesquite grew, times must have been hard. They did not speak of that, only the story of the coyote planting the mesquite.

Later, talking to Monte, I mentioned the story. "A legend," he said. "The Plains Injuns, too. They have many stories of the coyote."

"But in all the legends there is some truth. As for the coyote planting the mesquite, it could be true."

He took the cigarette from his mouth. "You mean you believe that?"

"Why not? The coyote eats the mesquite beans. He goes into the desert to hunt rabbits. Where he stops to do his business, he leaves some undigested beans, perhaps? They grow. Why not? That's the way plants are often scattered, through bird and animal droppings."

"Didn't think of that," Monte admitted. "Runoff water would bring down some seeds, too, I suspect."

He glanced at me. "You think those Injuns will come?"

"You can depend on it," I said. "They will come and they will be ready."

"You've been in their villages?"

"Time and again. Lived with them when I was a boy. I stayed in this house but often went hunting with them, gathering nuts and seeds, listening to the old men tell of when the water disappeared, little by little.

"It came and went several times. Sometimes it came slowly, and at least once it came with a great rush, carrying great logs on a vast wave that swept up the valley. Many Indians were lost. The only ones saved were those hunting in the mountains or close enough to the mountains to escape."

Gesturing toward the mountains, I said, "They have villages up there. In the Santa Rosas, too.

"There are old trails in the mountains and on the desert. A few of them I have followed, and there are more I shall follow."

"Why?"

Why, indeed? Turning that over in my mind, I shrugged. "How do I know? It is my destiny, I think. All I know is that I shall never rest easy until I have gone into the desert alone. Until I have followed some of those trails to wherever they go."

"I know," Monte said wistfully. "It's something around the bend in the trail or over the next ridge. I feel it, too."

We would need extra ropes, so we bought hides from the Indians or the Mexicans and we made ropes. We worked, waiting for the day. Our horses were in good shape, as we knew they must be for the work ahead.

The next morning, when we went outside, Francisco was there, and five Cahuillas were with him; with them were their horses.

"Come on in," Jacob invited. "We're fixin' some grub."

Nobody moved. One Indian lit a cigarette; the others simply looked across the desert toward the mountains. Francisco looked at me and shrugged. "It is the house of Tahquitz," he said.

Jacob walked over and looked at their horses. They were good stock, mustangs all, and built for the work they must do.

"Tomorrow we go," he said. He glanced at Francisco. "All right with you?"

"Bueno."

There were still a few supplies to get, a little work to do. When my part was done, I sat down with *The Last Days of Pompeii*, by Bulwer-Lytton. It was one of the books I was leaving for my unseen visitor, but I wished to read it first. However, I was scarcely reading, for my thoughts were of him.

Who was he? What was he? A giant? A monster? An evil spirit, as some presumed? Had my father known him? Had the Indians *seen* him?

If he was so large a being, how could they not have seen him? Where did he live? How did he move back and forth without being seen?

At night . . . of course, he did travel at night, at least until he returned to the mountains. That he came from the mountains, I was sure, for there was the smell of pines about him.

Where had he come from? Where had he learned to read? Or to lay mosaics as he had here? Or to build so beautifully? How did he pass his days?

The only thing I actually knew about him was that he was or had been a builder, a worker in tile and timber. Also, that he liked to read, and read good books. Presumably he was a thoughtful man, but I did not know. Nobody knew.

Suppose he was mad? Suppose on some occasion he should suddenly go berserk? Or decide that I was spying upon him? What then? He could—he had—come into this house in the night. Suppose he did it when I was here alone?

Inadvertently I glanced over my shoulder. What did I know of him? Nothing. . . .

By the time I closed the book, all were asleep. I extinguished the candle and went outside. The Cahuillas had chosen to sleep in the shed, so I walked along the path that led into the sandhills. It was very still, the stars bright as only desert stars can be.

Alone, I stood, feeling the stillness, the softness of the night. Far off I heard a faint music. Straining my ears, only half-believing. . . . It sounded like a flute, like one of those I had often made as a child. I listened, but the sound faded, vanished.

The night was empty again.

An Indian? Some of them played flutes, but the music had a sound . . . It must have been European or American music.

At last I walked back to the house and went to bed. Tomorrow the desert, and after that the northern valley—the San Joaquin, some called it.

Captain Pedro Fages had been there, probably the first one. Others had followed, but very few. The northern desert was the haunt of the Mohaves, at least at times. In the mountains a few Piutes remained, although from what Francisco had told me, they were leaving, going away. There was something about that Tehachapi country they no longer liked.

"I do not know it," Francisco said. "Ramón does."

"Ramón?"

"He will meet us. I do not know where, but he will." He glanced at me. "He comes when he will. Of you I have spoken, and he will come. He will know where the horses are. Ramón is of the desert," he added, "and the mountains. He comes alone to join us."

"He is Cahuilla?"

"No Cahuilla, no Chemehuevi, no Piute. I do not know."

"There are wild horses there?"

"Muchos. There is grass, amigo, and from there to the north and in the mountains there are horses. There are also cattle."

"We will touch no branded cattle."

"Of course. It is understood."

I thought over the situation, and what lay ahead. It was good to be with Francisco again, and I must come to know the others. And in the morning before we left, I must sweep the floors, leave all as we had found it.

At daybreak I was up and dressed, going outside to saddle my horse before Jacob had started breakfast. Monte joined me, and the Indians were already trooping into the yard, bringing their packhorses to tie to the corral bars.

As they rode, I followed, trailing behind. Glancing toward the store, I saw four saddled horses at the water trough.

Whose horses? Why? It was unusual at this hour, and the sight of them disturbed me. The Indians, too, were noticing them and talking among themselves. As the last of them disappeared down the trail into another clump of mesquite, I glanced back again.

A man had walked out from the store and was shading his eyes after us. It looked like Fletcher.

My thoughts returned to Los Angeles, and I wondered where Miss Nesselrode was, and Aunt Elena.

Aunt Elena, who had never been married, a strange, lonely, yet lovely woman, so tall, so remote, so very quiet.

What did she think to herself when she was alone? What did she think of that brother who had kept her so? And Miss Nesselrode. Who *was* she? Had she ever been married? Was the story of a lost love and a broken heart true? What was it that drove her? And was it her loneliness that caused her to reach out to me?

Whatever the reason, I was grateful. She had given me a home when I had none, had given me something of stability, of understanding, of sympathy, and of assurance, too. Just to see her standing alone, so quiet in her simple yet so elegant gowns, smiling gently. One would never suspect the iron that was in her soul, the cool efficiency of her mind.

She had guided me a little, suggested a little, and had helped me to bridge that gap from being a boy to becoming a young man.

What of her? What did she really want? Security, yes. No doubt of that. She had spoken to me of our being alike, of each being left alone, and there had been a hint of sadness, a hint of rejection, a hint that somewhere behind her there had been those who rejected her because of lack of money, of position, of whatever. This was supposition, but it was a possibility and might account for much.

Whatever the reason, she had gambled her little money on a fast trip west, had come to California believing in it, determined to make a place for herself there.

Was it because she had been known in the East? Had she come west to escape all that? To start anew where nobody could point a finger or demean her because of what she was or had been?

Whatever else she was, she was certainly a woman of fine courage and of no uncommon ability.

Riding along a desert trail gave one time to think, to consider. Talking became difficult because most of the trails were for riding single file, and talk also created thirst. So one rode and dreamed or thought or simply dozed.

Overhead flew an optimistic buzzard. In the distance was a curious coyote, and far behind, barely visible against the sun-glaring sky, lay a dust trail.

A very thin trail, hanging like a mute question mark against the sky.

Francisco was leading now, and Jacob fell back, waiting for me to come up to him. I turned in my saddle and nodded toward the rear. "Lots of travel these days," I commented.

"Hunters," he agreed. "I wonder what they expect to find?"

The sun grew hotter, dust devils pirouetted across the desert, and the distance created enchanting blue lakes that lost themselves as we drew nearer.

Sweat trickled down my face. I mopped my cheeks with a bandanna and wiped the sweatband of my hat.

Far ahead, unbelievably tall in the blue water of a mirage, was a man on horseback.

Francisco turned in his saddle and pointed toward the still black figure, so far off, yet so visible.

"Ramón," he said. "You will see."

32

"What do you know of this Ramón?" I asked.

"He is Ramón." Francisco added no comment for several steps and then he said, "He is a shaman, a man of magic." He paused again. "He is also a fine horseman."

We drew closer. Ramón did not move, simply sat his horse, waiting. Was he young or old? I could not guess at a distance, but he sat very erect, and his sombrero was hanging from his saddle horn.

"He will know where are the horses," Francisco said.

As we approached, the mirage of blue lake retreated but Ramón remained where he was.

"He knows you," Francisco said at last.

Ramón? I knew no Ramón.

He was slim and he looked tall. It was not until he dismounted that I saw he was not tall, but of less than medium height. He wore a shirt open at the neck and something suspended from a rawhide cord that was behind his shirt. He wore buckskin breeches and a wide leather belt. He had a knife in a scabbard at his hip, but no pistol. A rifle was in the scabbard made of fringed buckskin and beaded.

"I am Ramón," he said.

"And I am Johannes Verne," I replied. "This"—I turned in my saddle to indicate them—"is Jacob Finney and Monte McCalla. The others you know."

"I do not."

Surprised, I added, "This is Francisco. The others are Alejandro, Martìn, Diego, Jaime, and Selmo."

He looked from one to the other as I mentioned their names. His hair was nearly white, his eyes intensely black, his skin a smoky brown, more like East Indians my father had pointed out than our own Indians.

It had become a custom for Indians to take Spanish names, although they had their own, often known only to their families. The custom had no doubt begun at the missions, when the fathers, for their own convenience, had given the Indians Spanish names.

Ramón turned his horse about and rode away, leading us.

Francisco came up beside me. "He does not look like a Cahuilla," I said.

"He no Cahuilla. I said it. He is Ramón, and that is all."

"I do not know him."

Francisco eased himself in the saddle. "I did not say you know him. I said he knows *you.*"

It was a difference, of course, but how did he know me, and from where? From when?

He stayed well ahead of us, riding a line-back dun with black mane and tail as well as black hairs around the hooves. The horse had a thicker neck than most horses I'd seen, and looked strong.

Throughout the long afternoon we rode, and Ramón did not stop until suddenly he turned from the trail and led the way into some tumbled boulders. There, in a small cove almost surrounded by giant rocks, was a small pool of water, and water trickling into it from among the rocks.

He stepped down, drank from the spring, and watched us do likewise. When I got up and wiped the drops from my mouth, he was looking at me.

"Johannes of the desert," he said.

"Perhaps," I acknowledged, and then added dryly, "Let the desert say."

We made camp, each tending to his own horse, Selmo preparing a meal.

"The horses," Ramón said, "will be here." He drew a quick map in the earth, indicating where we were, where the horses would be, and the trail between. "Here"—he put a finger on a spot—"are mountains, and there is a pass, very narrow. A trail leads to the sea." He glanced at me. "To Los Angeles.

"All this"—he gestured to the north—"is the valley of San Joaquin." He gestured to his right and east. "There is desert"—he glanced at me again—"the desert you crossed."

He looked at me again. "How many horses?"

"Four hundred, if possible. Four hundred of the best."

"It is many."

"We will need many. People will be coming, and they will need horses."

"No doubt." He looked over at me. "You can read? You can read books?"

"I can."

"I have never seen a book," he said, a note of wistfulness in his tone.

"The wilderness is a book," I said. "It has many pages."

"Yes," he agreed, "but the pages are never quite the same."

"You live near here?"

"Wherever," he said. "My home is where I lay my head."

"But your family? Your people?"

"All gone. I am alone." After a moment, when the fire was crackling and a bit of smoke rising, he said, waving a hand toward the desert, "Out there was a city. When I was small, it was my home. There was a shaking of the earth. A small shake, then a very strong shake, and much came crashing down. There were other shocks. For days the earth shook. Some of us ran away to the mountains, my father among them, taking us.

"The rains came, and the winds. The winter came, and the bitter cold. With my father I went to the ruins to find food, clothing, weapons. Others would not go, for they were afraid.

"We had grain stored for the future. We took it. We returned to the mountains, and my father was killed for the food we had. My brother, my sister, and two others ran away and hid.

"It was very cold. We found a small hollow among the hills where there were two springs. Below the hollow was a stream. We hid there and were not found. The winter was very cold, but we dug into the hill and built a shelter before it.

"Sometimes when hunting for food we would see others, but we did not trust them, so we hid and watched them. They did not fare as well as we, for some of them had never hunted."

"Indians?" I said. "Who did not hunt?"

"They lived in the town," he said. "Do your people hunt who live in towns?

"We built another place. It was up a narrow canyon among the trees, and there was the second spring. We did not go there, keeping it in reserve. There were nine of us.

"In the spring, one was killed by a spotted cat, what you call a jaguar. There were many around here in those years. Now it has been years since I have seen even one.

"Three of us went back to the town. The walls were of mud brick and they had fallen. Now they had returned to earth. Only a few were left. We picked around, but there was little to find.

"The fields were gone, some washed away, others buried in dust.

"When we came back, two more were dead and somebody had been there to kill them. The others had retreated to our other place and had hidden there."

Food was passed around, and we ate. He ate sparingly, and spoke no more of those bygone years. How long ago? I did not know, but the more I saw of him, the older I believed him to be.

On the second day after that first camp with Ramón we came to where the horses were. We saw them out on the grassy plain, thousands of them, and for a time we sat our horses in the shade of trees along the mountainside and watched them. Our eyes picked out this one and that, judging, by the way they moved, their grace and speed.

In droves of one hundred or even as many as two hundred they fled across the plain, wheeled, and turned back, manes and tails flowing. They would come charging across the plain and come within a hundred yards or less of us before pausing, heads up, studying us to see what we were, then wheeling and rushing away like the wind.

It was a magnificent sight, and nothing I had seen equaled it. They seemed to flow across the plain like a varicolored wave, with often as many as a thousand horses within sight at one time, but each divided into smaller herds. A few of them stood out. One, a splendid black stallion with one white stocking, must have weighed a thousand pounds or more, whereas most of the horses were somewhat smaller.

One particular herd, numbering well over a hundred, wheeled and darted about us several times, as though challenging us to a race, but we made no effort to accept the challenge or to draw near, wanting them to become accustomed to our presence. They showed no evidence of ever having been chased, although Selmo suddenly pointed at a fine-looking bay who wore a brand on his hip.

The area through which we now rode, walking our horses and studying the land, was covered with grasses. Once, nearing the mountains, we saw a herd of elk that must have numbered nearly a thousand, and as they moved, it was a veritable sea of horns. Some of these seemed as large as the horses themselves. Toward nightfall, coming up to the place where we would camp, Monte killed one that would dress out to several hundred pounds of meat.

We saw several wolves, not at all afraid, for they had not seen our like before. They seemed to be following the elk to pull down any calves they could find straying from the herd or lagging behind. They were big gray wolves, moving like ghosts along the flanks of the elk herd.

Ramón led us again to our camp, this time beside a small but swift-running stream, several acres of grass and near the stream a spot of less than an acre surrounded by tall pines and a few scattered oak, although we were almost too high for the latter.

We staked our horses on the grass after watering them, and went about preparing our own camp. With Ramón and Francisco I walked out to look over the area.

After a minute, Jacob walked out to join us. "This is their watering place." Ramón pointed to a bunch of tules further along the stream. "The water spreads out and sinks into the ground over there."

Jacob studied the long sweep of the valley, the trees, and the brush. "We could build our corral to straddle the stream so they'd have water, filling in with brush between the trees, and some poles to fence them in."

We walked along, studying the lay of the ground. Our plan was to build a wide-mouthed funnel down which they would go to water, a funnel that would narrow at the corral itself and which we could close off once enough horses were gathered.

"Take us a while," Jacob said finally, "but we can pull back to camp each night and let them come down to water if they like. And if they get thirsty enough, they will come.

"They'll leave when they wish, and they will get over being scared. Finally, we'll just close them in. We should be able to get two, three hundred horses in there all to onct."

It was not all that easy, but we didn't expect it to be.

Going out there with axes, we cut brush and filled the spaces between the trees. Here and there it needed poles. We took our time, working steadily, pausing for coffee now and again or simply to tell stories. We could see the horses from time to time, and when evening began to come, we'd stop work so our movements and the ring of the axes wouldn't frighten the game.

We were not thinking only of the horses, for in dry country water belongs to all living things, and we moved off from the creek to our own place, farther up. Then the horses would come in, moving along slowly but warily, alert for any movement. Along with them were a few elk and a deer or two.

Sometimes, while it was still light, we'd lie up on a rock and watch them come. Wolves would come, too, and in the morning sometimes there would be bear tracks.

Occasionally we killed an elk or a deer, but never close by. One of the boys, often it was me, would ride off a few miles and do our shooting there so as not to scare the game.

It was hard work, but the air was clear, the sky blue, and the days went by like the drifting clouds, so we scarcely noticed they were gone. Finally our corral was ready, and the drift fence, too.

We'd made a swinging gate of poles and brush that we swung wide to one side, and then we rode away up the valley. We wanted not only the horses that had been coming there, but a good many more.

We started from ten miles up, the lot of us, spread out across the valley, and after we'd fixed ourselves a spot of grub and drunk some coffee we rode out across the country, turned and began to drift, walking our horses down toward our corral.

This was wild stock, but we'd been moving around and not bothering them, so they hadn't, after the first day or so, paid us much mind.

Now, spread out maybe a half-mile apart, we started drifting, and they moved ahead of us. After all, this was their country, and most of them had lived their lives here. Wild horses are, more than you'd believe, inclined to be homebodies. They didn't like to get too far from where they were born. They knew that country, and if driven away, would come back.

Gradually the valley narrowed, and gradually we cowboys moved in closer together. Not so much as they'd notice at first, but by the end of the first hour we were only a hundred yards or so apart. Ahead of us the horses were bunching a little, and here and there some wild old stallion was beginning to be bothered by it.

Once in a while one would stop, stand head-up looking around, but the way ahead was clear and we were coming along behind. We didn't seem to be anything to worry about, but they just didn't want us getting too close.

At the last, just as he went through toward the water, that black stallion decided he didn't like that crowd of horses up ahead and wheeled. He made a dash for the opening, but Alejandro and Martìn were already swinging the gate closed.

It had been easy, just too easy. Later, when they had become wary of men, it would prove much harder, but we had them. We didn't know how many, but we guessed around three hundred horses.

There was grass enough for a few days, and there was water.

33

"It will never be that easy again," Monte commented.

"They just aren't used to people. Nobody's tried to catch them before."

"And they always drink from that stream," Jacob agreed.

We sat our horses, studying them. We would have to cull them, turn the rejects back to their freedom, and then start breaking the others.

Watching them from where we were, we could see a few that could be turned out, but by and large they were in good shape, a well-built bunch of horses. "Give 'em a few years," Monte said, "and you'll look a long time to find any horses you want to keep. We'll cut this bunch for culls, and the next bunch, too. Then along will come some other wild-horse hunters, and they'll cut for the best stock, too. It won't be no time at all until all you find out there will be culls."

"Do you suppose Miss Nesselrode was thinking of that?" I wondered.

Jacob shrugged. "Maybe, maybe not. I've given up trying to second-guess that woman. I just know that seven times out of ten she's right, and when she makes a mistake, she swallows it and never tries to blame anybody else."

The quicker we could get rid of the culls, the better off we'd be, as there would be that much more grass for what remained. We stayed away, watching from a distance, letting them get settled down.

"Funny thing about wild horses. Folks think it's the stallion who keeps them together. It's true that he herds them around, fights off varmints and any other stallions who want to take over, but there's something more going for them. Take away the stallion, and the others will fight to get back together.

"They've become a family. Good neighbors, at least, and they want to stay with their friends. Watch 'em, you'll see."

Jacob indicated the black stallion. "That one's a troublemaker. He's too smart. I think we should get rid of him."

"I want him," I said.

"Look," Jacob warned, "that stallion is anyway six years old. He's been runnin' wild all that time. He's tough and he's smart, and he looks to me like a fighter. He'll make you no end of trouble."

"He's right, Johannes," Monte said.

"I want him," I insisted. "Leave him to me."

"Your funeral," Jacob said, "and it could be just that."

The weather held. It was bright and clear, day and night, and we took our time. Nobody was in a hurry, nobody was waiting for us. Nobody had a watch and nobody had a calendar. We just forgot all about time except for dawn and sunset.

When we quit work, we'd eat, and then I'd stroll down to the corral. I'd already learned that singing will quiet a herd, mostly because it knows where that sound is coming from and that you're not some varmint sneaking up on them.

I'd lean on the gate and keep my voice low. I wanted them to get to know me, and especially that black, who seemed to know that gate was the way out. He watched it like a hawk, never far away, always watching his chance.

We started weeding them out on the first day, two of us riding into the corral and just easing the culls out, with a man on the gate ready to open and close it. Some of the culls ran away; others hung around looking for their friends, like Jacob had said.

We tried not to make any fuss. We wanted them to get used to our moving around and to the feeling that we didn't represent trouble. We spotted a couple wearing brands, and there were three mules in the lot which showed signs of having been worked.

Even in the pasture we'd created, they separated into bunches. The black stallion kept his lot to one side, but never far from the gate.

"Horses may seem stupid," Jacob said, "but they know what they have to know to get along, and you can teach them a lot if you take time. Wild horses have learned a lot by just surviving out there, so be careful."

By the fourth day, taking our time and raising no dust, we had weeded out most of the culls. We were sitting by the fire considering our next step when Ramón came in and squatted near us. He accepted a cup of coffee, sipped a little, and then said, "Somebody is out there."

Jacob looked over at him. "Injuns?"

"White men. Six, maybe seven. They watch us."

"Could be Fletcher," I said.

"I never liked that man," Jacob agreed.

Monte reached for the coffeepot. "Why don't we take turns standing by with rifles? Maybe two at a time?"

Fletcher it could be, but there was also my grandfather. His holdings were vast and he had many riders, few of whom I knew by sight. There were other dangers, too, the Mohaves, who raided deep into the settlements at times, and the few lingering Piutes who came down from the Tehachapis.

There was also, somewhere around, old Peg-Leg Smith. Supposedly he had left the country, but one could never be sure. He was a wily old pirate, and if I judged him right, he would wait until we had our horses broken to ride, and then steal them. They would bring more money.

I said as much, but Jacob doubted his presence. "Heard he was up Frisco way. You know, that little town on the bay?"

"Monterey?" Monte suggested.

"North of there. Yerba Buena, they called it. I heard the name was changed."

There was good talk around the campfire, and occasionally the Indians joined in, but usually it was Alejandro who did the talking. He had left the Cahuilla country as a young boy and worked on the west side of the mountains; then for a time he had gone north and worked for a doctor up there, often riding with him when he made calls on the sick.

We moved our camp closer to our horses, both to protect them and to let them become familiar with us. Jacob decided after studying the horses that aside from the mules there were at least four horses that showed signs of having been ridden.

Separating them from the others, we brought them outside, and Monte offered to ride them.

Ramón was quiet, speaking rarely. He had an easy way with horses and occasionally led one out of the corral, walked it around, let it graze where the grass was green and fresh while he held the picket rope himself. His way of gentling horses took time, but when he called them, they came to him.

For three weeks we worked hard, breaking horses to lead and to ride. The Cahuillas we had were all riders, but Francisco was the best of the lot.

Even Ramón avoided the black stallion. "He is a devil," he warned.

"I'd say turn him loose or shoot him," Monte advised. "He's been wild too long and has been leading that herd too long. Look at the teeth scars and hoof scars. He's a fighter."

Nobody needed to tell me that. It showed in every line of him, and he was wary, watching his chance to escape and take his bunch with him. Sometimes I'd gather some green grass from near the water and drop it over the fence, and his mares would eat it, but not him.

At night when I was on watch I'd move over close to the corral where I could keep an eye on the horses. They would know if trouble was coming before I would, and it was a lot easier to watch them than to stare into the shadows under the trees. Sometimes I'd talk to them, low-voiced. Mostly I was talking to him, and I had an idea he knew it.

I've known men who thought horses stupid, but it's been my impression that horses are only as stupid as their masters. A riding man in wild country becomes very close to his horse, and most talk to them as to another person. The horse listens, and although he may not understand, there is communication and he senses the kinship of interests if no more.

The black stallion was wild and might have been wild all his years, yet sometimes I wondered about that. Sometimes I had a feeling he had belonged to somebody sometime, maybe when he was very young.

Each morning we roped a few head and took them out of the corral, where any fighting they did wouldn't get the others wrought up. Monte McCalla was a first-class hand, more experienced with breaking horses than any of us. Alejandro was good, too, as he'd broken horses for the doctor up north.

We were settling down to eat when we heard a horse walking. Jacob stayed where he was by the fire, but Monte an' me, we faded back into the dark. The Cahuillas were already there.

We waited, and then somebody called out, "Hello, the camp! How's for some coffee?"

"Ride in," Jacob Finney said, "but ride easy, with your hands in sight."

He was a tall, very lean man, a little stooped. He had quick, ferretlike eyes and he rode a dapple-gray gelding, a fine animal. There was no blanket roll behind his saddle.

"Get down and come up to the fire," Jacob said. "Coffee's on, and we've got some grub, such as it is."

"Thankee, thankee much! I've been ridin' all day and I'm mighty tired an' almighty hungry!"

Monte, his rifle in his left hand and his pistol in its holster near his right, came in from the dark, flanking the stranger. Then Francisco and Alejandro came in. The rest stayed out, away from the fire. Diego was with the horses, and I suspected Jaime was, too.

He came on up to the fire, taking a look around as he did so. Seeing those men coming in from the dark seemed to make him a mite nervous, and you could almost see him counting.

"Come from Los Angeles," he said, although we did not ask. "Headin' for the Colorado."

"Well, that's different, anyhow," Monte commented. "Since that gold strike up north, everybody is headin' that way."

"Gold is where you find it," the stranger said easily. "I figure they've got to eat, so I'm thinkin' of drivin' cattle north. No matter whether they find gold, they've all got to eat."

Nobody had much to say to that. He drank coffee, seemed about to speak, then changed his mind. Finally he said, "Seen a corral yonder. You catchin' wild stuff?"

"Here an' there," Jacob said, "catchin' an' breakin'."

"Must be gold down here, too, feller knew where to find it."

"Like you said," Jacob said mildly, "gold is where you find it. We figure folks will have to ride to get anywhere, so we're breakin' horses to sell."

"Seen any Indians?" I asked innocently. "I mean Mohaves? Or Piutes? This is nervous country, so many of them around. Although," I added, "they don't often come this side of Tehachapi Pass."

He looked around as if seeing me for the first time. "No? Why not?"

"Superstitious," I said, "or what we'd call it. They don't like the spirits up yonder." I indicated the Tehachapis. "There's a spell on this country."

"You don't seem much skeered," he said contemptuously.

"We aren't," I said. "We've got our own medicine man. He's out there now," I added, "casting spells on our enemies, whoever they may be."

"I don't put no stock in such things," he said.

"I didn't either," I replied. That this man was a spy, I had no doubt. He carried no blankets, yet he was supposed to be traveling for days. His horse hadn't even worked up a sweat, yet he implied he had come far, and he did not eat like a man who had missed even one meal.

"I didn't either," I repeated. "Until that man"—I was lying cheerfully now—"stole our medicine man's horse.

"This fellow just rode up and threw down on him with a pistol and took his horse. Our medicine man just stood there and said, 'Did you ever have a broken back? Somehow I see you with a broken back.'

"The horse thief, he laughed sarcastic-like and said he'd had no broken back. At that moment the medicine man lifted a hand, and that horse started to buck. Next thing you know, that horse thief was on the ground.

"He started to get up and he cried out and sweat broke out all over him. Our medicine man, he went and mounted his horse. He said to that horse thief, lyin' there, he said, 'You said you didn't have a broken back. Well, you've got one now.' And then he just rode off an' left him lyin' there."

"What happened?"

I shrugged. "What could happen? It was August. It was the Mohave Desert. If he was unlucky, he'd have lasted two, three days. If he was lucky, he'd have died the first night."

He glanced from one to the other of us, but nobody was smiling. Monte said, "Aw, he's a good feller, long as you don't cross him."

My eyes dropped to the stranger's gun. The thong was slipped off the hammer. Now, a riding man would want that thong in place unless he expected trouble.

Alejandro had moved slightly. He was now seated right behind the stranger. He spoke softly. "You didn't tell us your name."

"Just any name will do," I said. "We need something for the marker."

"What?" He started to get up, then sank back. "What marker?"

"Suppose horse thieves rode in and attacked us now?" I said. "We might be suspicious of you, or the thieves might think you were one of us. At least you'd be one less to share things with. We'd have to have a name for the marker on your grave. Shame to bury a man without leaving something to show where he passed."

He put down his cup. "Maybe I should be ridin' on," he said, "ride while it's cool, y' know?"

He got to his feet very carefully. He started to brush off his pants, which would put his hand near his gun, and then thought the better of it.

"Mount up," I said, "and ride. When you see Fletcher, tell him to come anytime he's ready."

34

When it was daybreak, I walked down from our breakfast fire carrying a piece of bread, and when I reached the corral gate, I held it out to the black stallion. He shied away, tossing his head and rolling his eyes, but I talked quietly and held the bread out to him.

One of the mares came up and reached for it, and I broke off a bit and let her have it. This mare was one that had been handled quite a bit, I thought. Anyway, she took the bread from my hand.

The stallion seemed interested, but he was wary. I talked to him a little, but he held off, and finally I left the bread on the top rail of the gate and went away. I suspect the mare got it, but did not know.

Jacob was getting up from the fire, holding his cup in his hand. "I figure we should move 'em," he said. "I don't like that crowd."

"Me neither," Monte said. "I think they had something in mind last night. I think they were out there, ready to come in. I think he was going to start it."

"Martín saw something moving out there, and the horses were restless." Jacob sipped his coffee, his eyes on the scattered oaks along the mountainside. "Maybe it's the Injun stories, but I don't like this place. Or maybe it is just that I want to go back. I'd never have believed it, but that woman's got me thinkin' of business, wheelin' an' dealin' like she does. It's like poker, only it takes longer to rake in the pot."

He looked at me, a faint twinkle of humor in his eyes. "Anybody told me I was becoming a city man, I'd of been ready to shoot him, but there it is."

My thoughts were on Meghan, and I agreed. "Why not?" But when I said it, I was looking at the hills. There was a place back there where a creek came down a canyon, with oaks on the mountainsides. I wanted to ride up that canyon alone sometime and drink out of that stream.

Ramón came up to the fire, leading a line-back dun from the herd. It was a horse to which he had given special attention. He dropped the reins, and getting his cup, poured coffee from the blackened pot. The others had gone, wandering off to catch up their horses. Most of them had already rolled their beds.

"We go now?"

"Jacob does not like it here."

"And you?"

"I like it." Nodding toward the hills, I said, "There is something up there for me. And in the desert there is something."

"You come back?"

"When I can." I threw the rest of my coffee on the ground. "It is an old place. I can feel that. It has changed, but it has been here. When I look at those mountains, I see the centuries pass like seasons.

"My father often said that men talk of what they call the 'Old World.' It is no older than this, if as old. Men had the Bible and they had the Greeks. They knew of the Egyptians and Babylon, so when the scholars began to dig, it was to find familiar things, things of which they had read. Whatever they found tied into something, and when they found something strange, they shied from it because it would have no place, no connection.

"Who knows when men first came here? Who knows how many people were here before you whom we call Indians? So much decays. So much disappears in the passage of years."

"You must come back."

The coals had burned down to nothing, only a few faint fingers of smoke rising. I looked at the dying red of the coals and thought of Meghan.

Did she ever think of me? Why should she? I was only a boy who had sat beside her.

I looked around. What would she think of my desert? Of these, my mountains? Was it vain to think of them as mine? Yet they were mine in a secret place in my mind. They were mine because I belonged to them and them to me. Or was this simply a romantic idea I had because my father and mother had sought a refuge in the desert?

Taking up my saddle, I kicked sand over the coals.

"You are one of us."

"I am Johannes Verne. Beyond that I know nothing. What I am to be is something I must become. I must create myself from this that I have." I glanced around at him. "We are nothing until we make ourselves something."

"No doubt."

"I do not know what I shall be except that I wish to be something, to be someone."

"Before the world? Before other men?"

"Perhaps. Sometimes that also comes, but what I wish is to be complete in myself."

Ramón took up his saddle. "Not too complete—to be too complete is often to be lonely. A man needs a woman, and a woman a man. It is the way of things."

We walked down to the corral and caught up our horses. Francisco was there, and he walked over to me. "You will take the stallion? He is trouble, I think."

"Let him be my trouble. If he escapes, let him go."

Monte walked over to me. Jacob was already in the saddle. "We're going to let out a few of the tame ones first, and I think the others will go to them with a mite of urging. We'll head them toward Tejon Pass."

"They'll be watching," I said. "They may try to stampede the horses."

"Maybe, but I think they will try to steal them at night, after they're trail-broke. They won't have men enough to handle a herd of this size. Or the horses."

We let a few of the horses out, and Francisco and Martín headed them off and held them; then we let a few more out and they fled at once to join them. After a few minutes we let out some more, and then some more, and Jacob led off, leading the herd down the old Indian trail.

Francisco and Martín flanked them, and we let out more and then more. By the time we let the stallion out, the herd was trailing along in good shape, with Jaime and Diego falling in beside them.

His mares were already with the herd, so the black stallion went after them and we closed in. Selmo started from habit to close the gate.

"Leave it," I said. "Other animals will want to get to the water."

"Of course," he agreed.

Monte McCalla was waiting. He had his rifle in his hands, and I the same. "We'll sort of bring up the rear," Monte said, "just in case we have visitors."

Ramón had mounted up and disappeared, and when I looked around for Alejandro, I did not see him.

"Scoutin'," Monte said. "He thought he'd have a look around, but he'll be along."

A dapple-gray mare had taken the lead. She was older, and had been saddled and ridden in some bygone time. There was a strange brand on her shoulder that we could not make out. When she shed some more of her winter hair, we would see it better.

"You going to ride that stallion?" Monte asked.

"Sooner or later," I admitted. "When the time seems right."

"Give it plenty of time," Monte advised. "He's a fighter."

We kept them moving at a good gait. "Get them tired," Jacob had said, "so when we bed down they'll be ready to rest."

The trail we followed was old, leading through low hills crested with boulders. Larger rocks were scattered across the low ground among the hills. There were only scattered oaks, but the grass was good.

Selmo was bringing up the rear, close behind the last of the horses. Monte and I fell back.

"You ever been in a fight, kid?" he asked me.

"I lived through a couple, loading guns for my pa. Miss Nesselrode was there, too."

"Her? In a fight?"

I told him about the Indian she had killed trying to crawl into the wagon. "And that wasn't the only one," I told him. "She can shoot."

"I'll be damned. You'd think she'd faint at the sight of blood."

"Not her," I said.

Late in the afternoon we slowed the pace and let the horses scatter out a bit. There was good grass in that little basin, and some water. They ate and they drank a little, and we moved them on.

Alejandro came up to us just as we were going into camp. There was an old horse corral, half of natural boulders and pieced out with poles. We let them graze a little more and then bunched them into the corral. There was room enough for all of them, but not much more. Each of us roped another horse and picketed them outside for easy access in case of trouble. I chose a dark dapple-gray that I had been watching.

Martín put together a small fire and Francisco squatted on his heels nearby.

"They come," Francisco said.

"You've seen them?"

"They come. Maybe tonight, maybe tomorrow."

Well, we had understood that. We had known they would come, and we were ready, as ready as anyone can be. When it was not quite

dark, I took my rifle and went down to the corral with a couple of tortillas. I fed half of one to the mare, with the black stallion looking on. I
held out a piece to him and he took a step forward, then shied away.
The mare wanted it, but I would not give it to her.

Francisco came over to me. "There are Mohaves out there."

Surprised, I said, "Mohaves? Indians?"

"Sí. Maybe ten, maybe twelve."

Mohaves, too? I thought about that. Were they working with
Fletcher? Or were they on their own? More likely the latter, but if so,
did Fletcher know they were there?

When I had taken a circle around the area, I went back to the fire,
took my coffee, some tortillas, and jerky, and backed off from the
firelight.

When Jacob came over, I told him what Francisco had said. He
squatted on his heels beside me, and Monte came over, too.

"What d'you think?" Monte asked.

"I say we catch an hour's sleep, then get the herd down the trail.
Alejandro just came in and he says there is a good place with grass and
a seep of water down the trail about an hour's drive. We can leave the
fire burning low." Jacob straightened up. "I'll go tell the boys."

He glanced at me. "That set all right with you?"

"It does." I drew the back of my hand across my mouth and looked
up at the stars. There would be light enough.

Ramón came in from the darkness. The blackened coffeepot still sat
by the coals. He took his cup and filled it and came and sat near me.

He sipped his coffee as the others scattered to what they must do.
"What is it you wish?" he asked.

"To be a complete man."

"And what is that?"

"I do not know yet. One lives so long to learn so little."

"So you will come again to the desert and the mountains?"

"I will." I looked off toward the east, where the morning would
begin, and then to the west, where along the distant mountains we
would see the first light.

I was thinking then of Meghan, but I was remembering the vanish-
ing books. I spoke abruptly. "Do you know the house of Tahquitz?
Where I live?"

"I know it." He sipped his coffee and was silent, watching the rim of
the mountains for the first light. "Of course it is not Tahquitz," he said
then, almost impatiently.

"Of course," I agreed; then added, "They say he is a monster."

Ramón shrugged. "Which of us is not a monster to something else? To the ant in my path, I am a monster. Do you think this Tahquitz a monster?"

"No," I said. "He reads. No one who reads can quite be a monster. Or," I added, "perhaps he is only partially a monster."

"I cannot read."

"But you think," I said, "and you listen."

The Cahuillas were in the saddle. I got up and walked over to the dark dapple-gray and saddled up. The stallion was watching. "One of these days," I said to him, "this saddle will be for you."

He snorted and tossed his head, almost as if he understood, which might have been nonsense.

We trailed the horses off down the dim track, with Monte and me bringing up the rear again. Francisco fell back beside us, holding his rifle.

Then suddenly from far behind us there was a quick rattle of distant firing. Sharp, quick explosions, very close together. Francisco turned in his saddle and looked back, but all was still darkness and we could see nothing.

We heard other firing, but much less, and then silence, and after a bit, a single shot.

Death had come in the morning, death blowing gently across the hills like a breeze at dawn.

Had those who died been ready? Was one ever ready?

Monte glanced at me. "Maybe we won't have trouble after all."

"Not now," I agreed, "not this time."

The Mohaves and Fletcher's men. But somehow, I knew, not Fletcher.

Somehow I knew he was for me or I was for him, yet I said nothing of that.

"Come on," I said. "Let's go to Los Angeles!"

"Somebody would think you had a girl there," Monte said, smiling.

"I have," I said, and then I smiled, too. "Only she doesn't know it."

"You never know about a woman," Monte said. "You never know."

35

How long the green, green valley! How veiled with distant haze the hills beyond!

From the back of the dark dapple my eyes searched out the place where the pass was, so narrow a pass, so small an opening, and so much a place where trouble might be.

The horses were tired now, and they had found their places in the pecking order of the herd. The old mare still led and the rest trailed out behind, only my black stallion aloof, alone, watchful but accepting, too. He was growing accustomed to the long drives, to the night camps, to the presence of men whom he had come to recognize and not to fear.

"Will the Mohaves follow us? Or will they go back?"

Francisco shrugged. "Who knows? They lost men, I think."

Of course. There had been much shooting, and all the shots could not have missed, so they might have turned back, no longer sure of their medicine, even though they had probably won.

At noon I changed horses and took from the herd a sturdy bay with a black mane and tail. He had been ridden but little, and when I hit the saddle he ran forward, stopped suddenly, then, switching ends, spun in a tight circle. I stayed with him, rather enjoying it, and when he quit, I patted him on the neck and said, "Take it easy, boy, it's going to be a long day."

He was a good horse, a tough horse, and he moved well. He was very quick to pick up any horse that started to cut out from the herd.

We saw an old cow and two lean steers coming down a trail from the green hills. I watched them along a narrow trail, wondering how they could make it at all, yet they did, with no more trouble than so many mountain goats.

At night we made camp in the open, not liking it very much, but the valley was wide and flat and we were hours from the pass that opened into the hills. From here on we would be climbing slowly. Atop a small rise I studied our back trail and all the country we had left behind. I saw no dust, no sign of movement.

We had only a rope corral, but when we had eaten I took a tortilla and walked down to the corral and stood near the black stallion. He tossed his head and watched me from the corners of his eyes, but after a bit I moved closer and held out the tortilla to him.

He showed no interest, so I let my hand fall, waiting. After a bit I edged closer and held it out again. Tentatively he stretched his neck toward me, sniffed, and drew sharply back, shook his head, then reached his neck toward me again, and this time he nibbled cautiously at the tortilla. He got a bit of it, seemed to like it, and reached for more. I let him have it all, then walked away from him and back to the fire.

It had been three days since we had seen Ramón when he rode in from the darkness.

"They are behind us, and they need horses."

"Mohaves?" Monte asked.

"The others. The white men. Three were killed, and one Mohave, I think."

"They need horses?"

"Four men, two horses. Two ride, two walk, then they change."

It was still dark when we moved out, keeping the horses moving at a good gait until the pass opened before us and the trail grew steeper. It was a narrow place between high, grassy hills dotted with clumps of oak.

"Further along," Ramón said, "there is a spring and the burial place of a French trapper, Peter Lebec. There is a carving on a tree which says he was killed by—" he drew an "X" on the ground with his foot to show us the way it had been carved—"a cross bear."

Monte chuckled. "You'd be cross too, if a bunch of fur trappers started setting traps around your home!"

"It is the rancho of José Antonio Aguirre and Ignacio del Valle," Ramón explained, "but they are not often here. Too many raids by Indians."

It was a stiff climb up through the pass, and we let the horses take their time, grazing a little as they moved.

Taking my hat from my head, I mopped the sweat from my brow and looked back to where the tall V of the canyon opening looked out upon the vast sweep of the San Joaquin Valley. Far away there seemed to be a tiny plume of dust.

Riders? Or a dancing dust devil?

Topping out on a small hill, I saw the long line of horses going down the slope before me and around the side of the low hill. Despite the dust on their coats, they were a fine lot of horses. Suddenly, far ahead of us where the pass widened into a valley, I could see a small cloud of dust.

Riders! Several of them. Turning in the saddle, I said to Ramón, "Stay with us. I think we're going to have trouble."

Pulling out from the drag end of the herd, I rode swiftly along the flank until I came up with Jacob, who was in the lead.

"Riders coming," I explained. "Quite a few of them."

Jacob turned and motioned to Monte McCalla, who rode up beside us.

"Trouble," Jacob said, "or it could be. There are more bandits in this country than bears, and there's a lot of grizzly."

From where we were we could see no dust cloud as I had spotted it from the top of a rise. Jacob dropped back, speaking to Francisco, and they began bunching the horses.

We walked the horses forward, and my eyes swept the terrain ahead. There was a low hill crowned with a few cedars backed by the steep grass-covered mountainside. To the east of it there was a deep gully cut by runoff water.

"Jacob?" I pointed.

"Good idea." He turned in the saddle and pointed, and Francisco moved up and began to turn the herd. They went into the few acres of grass against the hill, and almost at once Jaime and Martín faded into the cedars. Francisco stepped down from his horse behind a boulder where there was also a fallen, decaying tree trunk with its web of branches. The others found their places, and we waited.

The riders came on. That they had seen us from afar was obvious, for two of them were standing in their stirrups, searching for us. There were seventeen or eighteen men in the lot, a mixed bunch of Anglos and Mexicans, heavily armed.

"Bandidos," Francisco said.

We waited. Suddenly one of them pointed, and they turned and rode toward us in a wide skirmish line.

"If there's trouble," Jacob said, "the tall one with the red scarf is mine."

"I want the two on the paint horses," Monte said.

They rode nearer, slowing their pace as they took in the situation.

"Looking for something?" I asked.

The man who answered was a thin, wiry man with a pockmarked face. He smiled quickly, his even, very white teeth showing under his black, trimmed mustache. "We are looking for lost horses," he said, "and we have found them."

"Good for you," I said. "We've been lucky, too. We captured some wild horses and broke them. We're taking them into Los Angeles."

"It seems there is a difference of opinion," he said.

One of the Indians up in the cedars cocked his rifle. The sound was sharp and clear, and I saw several of the men turn their heads in surprise. From where they sat their horses they could have seen no more than four of us. Now they knew there were more, but how many more?

My heart was beating slowly, heavily. Sweat trickled down the side of my cheek, yet I did not feel nervous. I was curiously relaxed, ready.

"It is a lovely day," I said mildly. "The way is clear for you to ride on."

"Give us the horses," the pockmarked one said, "and you will not die."

"We watched you coming," I said, smiling at him, "and we have a bet among us. Selmo," I said, "is almost behind you now. He was betting we could kill twelve with the first firing. I am more modest. I believe nine or ten only. The rest we will have to get later."

"Ten," Monte said. "I figure we can get ten, settin' out in the open like that, and our boys under cover."

"We got you outnumbered," the pockmarked man protested.

"Have you, now?" I said. "You're a guessing man. If you were a gambling man, I'd lay you three to one you're wrong, but I'd never collect, because three of the rifles are on you. Right on you, and that's too bad, because I wanted you for myself."

He shifted his eyes to right and left. I saw him look at Monte, then look quickly again. Obviously he recognized him.

My rifle was in my hands, directed toward them but at no one in particular.

"You know," I said, "it's strange what a moment can do. Right now you've got it all on the table. You can turn your horses and ride quietly down the trail and live for years. There are a lot of women, a lot of wine and whiskey down that road, and if you stay here, there's only a mouthful of blood, teeth, and the dirt you'll bite into while dying."

"You talk too damn much!" he said, but I could just feel him trying for a way out.

"I want to live," I said simply, "and if you don't turn down that road, a lot of you will die. Most of my men will live, because you can't even see them."

Suddenly I smiled. "Now, why don't you save my life?"

"Save *your* life?"

"Sure. I'm right out in front, like you. We're going to catch it, sure as hell, so why don't you save my life by riding right off down that trail?"

He stared at me for a moment; then he lifted a hand. "Adiós!" he said, and rode away, his men following.

We sat there, our guns ready, and watched them go. As they reached the trail, some of them looked back, and I lifted a hand. Their leader lifted a hand in return.

"Now, what the hell?" Monte spat into the dust. "I thought we'd bought ourselves a scrap."

"A man can always fight," I said, "but sometimes there are other ways."

"We *were* outnumbered," Jacob commented.

"He didn't know that, and all he had to show was right on the table. We could see what he was holding, but he didn't know what we had. Also, our men were on the ground, which gives us the advantage over men on moving horses."

We moved them out and headed off down the trail. As we moved on, that day and the next, the country became increasingly broken. Ridges, hills, jagged rocks, which I indicated to Jacob. "Earthquake country?" I asked.

"It happens here," he admitted.

Ramón heard our conversation and said, "It is often the ground shakes, but soon a big one. Maybe this year, maybe next. The Old Men are agreed, the next one will be bad."

"That one," Monte said suddenly, "the one with the pockmarks? I remember him now. He rides with Boston Daimwood, a very bad one, and he himself is bad. His name is Steffens, Turkey Bob Steffens."

The name meant nothing to me, although I had heard of Boston Daimwood.

Yet now I wished to be finished with the drive. I wished to be in Los Angeles again, and to see Meghan.

Other trails fed into the one we now traveled, and from time to time we saw other travelers, some headed toward Los Angeles, some riding away.

All day I rode abreast or right behind the black stallion, and from time to time I talked to him, letting him grow accustomed to my presence and my voice.

"Wait until you try to ride him," Monte said. "He'll kill you if he can. He's just bidin' his time."

Of that I was not so sure, but Monte had more experience with wild horses than I, and caution was advisable. Thus far I had made no effort to approach him beyond offering him bits of food from time to time. These he only occasionally accepted, and once when I seemed to get too close, he started to rear, as though to strike with his forefeet. Casually I walked on past, ignoring him.

We drove our horses to some brush-and-pole corrals west of Cahuenga Pass. Monte and the Indians agreed to stay with them while Jacob and I rode into town.

Months had passed, and I noticed Jacob looking at me. "You've taken on some beef," he commented. "Miss Nesselrode will hardly know you."

Francisco strolled over and squatted on his heels. "We go home soon," he said.

"You've got money coming," Jacob said. "Better stick around until we talk to the boss."

"We want cattle," Francisco said.

Along with the horses, we'd rounded up a few head, but they deserved more.

"You'll get them," I said.

Jacob came up, leading my horse. Mounting, I lifted a hand to them and we rode away. Smoke lifted from the town. I stood in my stirrups, looking to see farther.

"You can't see her from here," Jacob said.

Embarrassed, I glanced at him. "Just wanted to see the town," I said. "We've been gone a long time."

"It's still there. Don Isidro is still there, too, so ride easy." He glanced at me. "Monte says you're pretty good with that gun."

"We didn't work much," I said.

"The way he talks, you didn't need it. Your pa teach you?"

"Some."

"Watch yourself, anyway. Last year Los Angeles averaged a killing a day. I don't want one of them to be you."

"Or you," I said, grinning at him.

36

Miss Nesselrode looked up when I came through the door, then sat back in her chair, her eyes on me. "Johannes! It has been almost a year."

She stood up and extended her hand. There was gray in her hair that I had not seen before. I felt a sharp twist of pain, for somehow she had seemed ageless, and she was my family, she was all I had.

"Come and sit down. I want to hear all about it."

"I've just come from the corrals," I protested.

"Don't be foolish. Sit down."

Curiously, I was shy. "We've some fine horses. They are beautiful, wild and wonderful, and I've loved every minute of it."

"Even the hard work?"

"Why not? The work is part of it. I suppose a woman wouldn't think of it that way, but I like the smell of my own sweat, the dust, riding the rough stock. I am afraid I am a man of the hills, after all."

"We must talk of that." She was a beautiful woman, I thought, and wished my father might have lived to know her better. "Have you decided what you wish to do? It is time, I think."

"No, not exactly." Changing the subject I asked, "Have you seen Aunt Elena?"

"Yes, as a matter of fact I have seen her several times. She loves you very much, Johannes."

"How could she? She does not know me."

"You are your mother's son, and despite Don Isidro, she always admired your father. She has told me how romantic he was, how exciting a man. I believe she was half in love with him herself, without knowing it."

She paused. "Anyway, Johannes, she is a lonely woman and you are all she has." Hesitating again, she said, "I gather she had much sadness long ago. Something about a relative. Would you know anything of that?"

"I know very little about her. I remember my mother talking of Tía Elena, but she was only a name to me."

"You must be careful, Johannes. Don Isidro is still here, rarely in the town, but on his ranch. All the men he used to have with him left him. Now he has a new lot—a very bad lot, if all we hear is true."

We talked long and I told her of Ramón, of the Tehachapis, and of the desert. She listened, as always intent upon any information she could obtain. Finally she stood up.

"You must get some sleep, and tomorrow you must see a tailor. You will need clothes, and you have outgrown everything you had."

She measured me with her eyes. "You've grown a lot, and you're a bigger man than your father."

Picking up my hat, I had taken a step toward my room when she said, "Johannes, I have been dealing with a man named Captain Laurel. He has a ship that often comes to Wilmington and San Pedro."

Starting to speak, I stopped abruptly. Then, more carefully, trying to seem casual, I said, "Oh? I have heard of him, I believe."

Her amusement showed. "Yes, I believe you have. I believe you went to school with Meghan. She's a beautiful girl, Johannes, and very interested in you."

"In me?"

"We've been riding together several times, in fact. She is very curious about you, Johannes."

"It's been a long time. We sat beside each other in school for months and months. Sometimes she was away on voyages with her father."

"And you had a fight over her."

I blushed. "Well . . . maybe. I can't say it was over her, although it was because of her. I mean, there would probably have been trouble between us anyway. Rad seemed to be hunting trouble."

"He still is, Johannes, so be careful. He killed a man in Sonora Town a few weeks ago, and he's been in two or three other shootings, and some rather ugly brawls."

I wanted nothing to do with him, and after I had gone to bed I thought of him and of Meghan. She was a young woman now. Many at her age were already married.

Was she married? Miss Nesselrode had said nothing of that. I sat up suddenly. She couldn't be! Miss Nesselrode would have told me! Yet, would she? Why should she?

I started to get out of bed to go ask, and then realized how foolish that would be. Besides, Miss Nesselrode would be asleep.

Kelso was at the table when I came out in the morning. The hot bath I'd had made me feel better. He looked up from his coffee as I came in.

"Well, now! You've grown some!"

We talked about the horses, laying plans to break them more thoroughly, and I told him about the black stallion.

"Heard about him. That's a mean horse, boy."

He paused, and then he said, "Be careful around town. This has been a quiet week, and four men were killed. Since you've been gone, we hung twenty-two murderers or thieves, some were hung legal, some were just hung because they needed it.

"Down there in Sonora Town they'll kill you for no reason at all, and believe me, it ain't just the Mexicans. There's fifty or sixty of the meanest Anglo outlaws you're liable to find who hang out down there, Boston Daimwood for one."

"I've heard of him."

"You'll hear more. Vásquez is runnin' around the country, too. The law can't seem to catch up with him."

As we sat over coffee, Kelso told me what had been happening in town, new businesses starting up, new people coming in from across the isthmus. "Carry your gun," he added. "There's renegades of all kinds driftin' in. Some of them run out of Frisco are comin' down here."

West of the town, where I liked to ride, the hills were almost bare. Main and Spring streets had been laid out past First Street, but there were only a few scattered structures there, and east of Main and along that street there were many vineyards. From Spring Street west to the coast there was a wide area of swampy land, the *ciénaga*, miles of tules inhabited by wild cattle, occasional deer, and great flocks of ducks and geese at certain seasons.

Nearly every house had heavy wooden shutters that could be closed and barred at night. The houses were almost all of adobe, bricks made of clay mixed with straw, and the roofs were covered with tar from the tar pits on the La Brea Rancho, now owned by a man named Hancock, whom I saw about town but did not know.

Water was still obtained from the *zanjas*, but it was also peddled from door to door by a waterman. If he had been there earlier, I did not remember him, but now he went from house to house filling the *ollas* that hung in the shade of a porch. The water was cool and pleasant, even in the hottest weather. Riding about town after my long absence, I noted the changes that had been made, yet some things remained the same. Despite the laws against it, women still washed clothes in the *zanjas*, and more often than not some Indian children were found splashing naked in the water ditches from which the drinking water was obtained. Bill the waterman supposedly drew his water from the Los Angeles River or some of the springs he knew of in the hills around.

Thomas Fraser was no longer conducting his little school. William Wolfskill had hired teachers and opened a school for his children and those of some friends, but there was at least one other small school.

Business was slow, and I saw several storekeepers playing cards on the wide windowsills.

Further along the street were several gambling houses, the El Dorado and the Montgomery being two of the busiest. Turning suddenly to go back, I caught a glimpse of the flat-nosed Mexican with the scar. A glimpse only, and the man was gone. Was I being followed?

Walking on, I turned a corner and stopped. Only a moment later, the Mexican appeared. He started around the corner, but seeing me, stopped abruptly.

"Looking for someone? Maybe I can help you." I took a step toward him.

He stood his ground. His hand was on his red sash and the hilt of his knife.

"I am not a boy any longer," I said. "You wanted to torture me once. You intended to kill me. Now you have the chance."

"Someday," he said.

"Why not now? I am ready."

"Someday." He gestured around. "You have friends. I can wait."

"Whenever," I said.

He turned away, then stopped, and when he looked back, his eyes were ugly. "You think you are man now," he sneered. "You are nothing! *Nothing!* You think you brave? Who did you ever fight? Who did you kill? Bah! To kill you is like a kitten! A sheep! You are nothing!"

He disappeared around the corner, and I stood there hot with anger, yet as the anger cooled, my ego was pierced by a thin shaft of cool logic.

Who *had* I fought? The flat-nosed vaquero might have had a dozen, two dozen, three dozen fights. He would be skilled with a knife, perhaps with a gun as well. Only his own caution had saved me.

Walking along the street to the book shop, I stepped inside and sat down. Long ago Jacob Finney had spoken of a man, a former boxer who lived in Sonora Town.

Boxing alone would not be enough. My skill with a gun was far beyond that of the average man. Part of this was due to a natural aptitude for which I deserved no credit, and a part was due to practice. Coordination was a gift, and my physical strength, which was considerable, had been not only a birthright but also developed during those years of living with and among the Cahuillas, climbing mountains, running in the desert, and wrestling.

Yet Rad Huber had already given me one lesson, and the fact that I had triumphed the second time did not fool me. I had won because he had been too ready for an easy repeat victory and my sudden attack had taken him by surprise. If we met again, as I was sure we would, he would whip me again. He had probably grown even more than I, and he, too, handled himself with natural ease.

There was only one answer. I had to learn something that would give me an edge.

Finney's boxer, if he was still around, would be one way, but my father, who had traveled much in the Far East, had told me of skills each people possessed, known to them alone.

In both China and Japan as well as in Korea the fighting arts had been widely developed by various schools, each claiming its system the best, each possessing some tricks known to them alone. These included not only bare-hand fighting but fighting with all manner of ingenious weapons.

The world in which we lived was a violent one; furthermore, it had always been violent. Much as I wished to avoid trouble, it would surely come, and I must be prepared to meet it.

Sitting alone at the back of the shop, ignoring the conversation that went on, I considered myself with some irritation. People might have said I was brave to face Flat-Nose as I had, but it had been the bravery of ignorance. No doubt he had been fighting since he was a child, and in bitter win-or-die fights. He had sneered at me, treated me as a child, but he had been right and I was wrong.

Had he chosen to attack, I would now be dead, and the only reason he had not attacked was that we had stood among Anglo stores and shops or places where the *gente de razón*, the gentlemen of reason among the Californios, were to be found. In Sonora Town it would have been different.

When we walked home that evening, Miss Nesselrode was silent until we were almost at the door. "You are quiet," she said. "Is something wrong?"

"It is never nice to realize one has been a fool," I said.

"If you have done something foolish and realize it, then you are not quite the fool you were," she said. "May I know what happened?"

Inside, seated in that quiet room I had come to think of as home, I explained.

"Your flat-nosed vaquero is a bad one. Only last week Vicente Lugo pointed him out to me as a troublemaker who had been driven out of his own town in Sonora. He uses the name of Valdez, but it is not his own. Chato Valdez is well known in Sonora Town, and much feared. You did well not to have trouble."

"He was the wise one, not I," I replied bitterly.

"And now?"

"Now I try to learn. With the gun, I shall not worry, but otherwise? And here, in the town, it could be otherwise. There is also Rad Huber."

We talked long, of that and other things, but through it all there was a nagging thought, something said in passing that I had not noted at the time. Some reference to a man who lived near the mountains. He was Chinese, if I remembered correctly.

Miss Nesselrode told me then, for the first time, of her meeting with Don Isidro.

"And now?"

"He has not forgotten," she said, "but I think he is a little afraid. I do not think he has ever been afraid except of being shamed, of being made to seem ridiculous. To be laughed at or pitied—that he could not stand. I think it has been the ruling motive of his whole life. But he is a small man—small in character, I mean. He hates you, and he now hates me as well, and I do not believe he has forgotten us."

"Nor has the flat-nosed one, the one you say is Chato Valdez. Nor, for that matter, Fletcher."

She smiled. "We have enemies, Johannes, but enemies can make one strong. And we will be strong."

For a moment she was silent. "Your Aunt Elena, now? She, in her own way, is very strong. Yet, I think she has a secret. Perhaps it is her brother's secret as well, but there is something . . ."

Her voice trailed off; then she said, "Have you ridden your black stallion yet?"

"Not yet," I said, "but soon. I think he likes me. I think, somehow, that he expects me to ride him. When I saddle the other horses, he comes to the corral bars and watches. He follows along inside the corral as I ride away, and I do not believe it is just because he wishes to be with the other horses."

Wind stirred the leaves in the trees outside. Miss Nesselrode got to her feet, then said suddenly, "I almost forgot. Captain Laurel was by the shop earlier. He wants to talk to you."

Meghan's father wished to talk to me? And about what? It did not matter. I would see him.

Perhaps I would see her.

37

When it was discovered that I had lately been rounding up wild horses in the San Joaquin, many wished to question me about what I had seen and what the country was like. The area from the mountains to the Colorado was virtually unknown, although some of the citizens, particularly those like Ben Wilson and William Wolfskill, who had been trappers, had crossed it at least once.

Yet why did Captain Laurel wish to see me? Was it this? Was he interested in those inner lands? Or was it some other matter?

On an early afternoon I walked my dark dapple-gray along the dusty street to his door.

An attractive Indian woman opened the door for me and I was shown into the shadowed quiet of a rectangular room carpeted with Oriental rugs. Other such rugs were thrown across the hidebound chairs. The inner walls were whitewashed, and over the mantel was an ancient shield and two samurai swords, which I recognized from drawings I had seen.

One wall of the room was covered with books, and I crossed to them at once. It needed but a glance to realize that I had discovered a first-class mind, one who had read far beyond my limited opportunities. Somewhat awed, I studied the titles, choosing a volume published in Spanish in 1621 of the journals of Matthew Ricci, covering his travels in China from 1583 to 1610. I knew nothing of the book, and opening it, was soon lost in its pages and scarcely heard Captain Laurel enter the room, nor was I aware of his presence until he appeared beside me.

"You are interested in China?"

"In everything," I admitted, "but I've read nothing about China but *The Travels of Marco Polo*."

"Then you should read Ricci. His may be the first book to come to Europe since Polo. The first about China, I mean. If you are interested, you may read it."

"Thank you, sir. I'll treat it as though it were my own."

He lifted an eyebrow at me. "I was afraid of that. Please remember it is not your own. Too many people borrow books and come to believe they are their own."

"I wouldn't—"

He waved a hand. "Forget it. Will you sit down?"

When we were seated, the Indian woman brought hot chocolate. He glanced at me several times. "I knew your grandfather," he said abruptly, "and knew your father slightly. They were good men. Two of the very best."

He changed the subject. "Tell me about this foray of yours into the interior."

Briefly but with care for the major points, I told him of the country, our capture of wild horses, and of the Cahuillas who helped us. He listened, asking but few questions; then he said suddenly, "You know my daughter, I believe?"

"Yes, sir. We attended the same school."

"Fraser's a bright young man. A good teacher, I believe." He looked at me again. "You are finished with school?"

"I can go no further here, and in any event, I must make my way in the world. I am a boy no longer, and whatever future I have lies in these"—I spread my hands—"or in what I can learn."

"You have no wish to go to sea?"

"No, sir. I have chosen California, or it chose me, I do not know which."

He emptied his cup and put it down. He stared at me, lighting a cigar. "You have enemies."

"Yes, sir. Enemies I have not made myself. They have chosen to be my enemies."

"No matter. The reality is that you have enemies." He paused, staring at me from under his brows. "Perhaps more than you realize, and that is unfortunate. A man can protect himself against enemies of whom he is aware. It is the others who can be most dangerous. In this case, *most* dangerous."

"I do not follow you, sir. I know my grandfather—"

"Of course. He is an old fool, not only because of his attitude toward you but because of his acceptance of others."

He took the cigar from his teeth. "Have you given thought to what would happen should your grandfather die?"

"Die? No, sir. It had not occurred to me. I should certainly have one enemy the less."

"What of his estate?"

"I have not thought of it, sir."

"You'd better! You'd better give it serious thought. Your grandfather is not a young man. Moreover, I suspect there are those who do not expect him to live much longer. If he should die, you would be his heir, or one of his heirs."

"I had not thought of it, sir. My Aunt Elena—"

He dismissed her with a wave. "She is a woman. She would be left a modest pension, I suspect." He paused, dusted ash from his cigar, and asked, "Do you know of any other heirs?"

"No, I don't," I admitted, "but I've given it no thought. My grandfather hates me, sir. He would leave nothing to me."

"Perhaps. Perhaps he has been no more careful in that than in other business dealings. Perhaps he has no will."

He paced the floor, then turned abruptly and said, "What do you know of your grandfather's Spanish properties?"

"I wasn't aware there were any."

"There are. Your grandfather, in property, is a very wealthy man. His cash position is, I believe, not so good. Not that a skillful manager couldn't straighten it out very quickly."

He sat down again, leaning his elbows on his knees. He was a stocky, powerful man with fierce gray brows and a shock of gray, curly hair. "What do you know of Don Federico Villegra?"

"It is a new name to me."

He drew on his cigar, dusted the ash again, and said, "It is good that you have friends. You'd last no time at all without them."

Irritated, I said, "I can take care of myself!" Yet even as I spoke, I thought of Chato Valdez and honesty made me remind myself that I'd been a fool once. Was I about to be so again?

"I have some good friends," I agreed.

"You have more than you realize of those, too. Why do you think you are here?"

"I've no idea. Frankly, sir, I have been puzzled, although I have wanted very much to know you."

"You have, have you? Well, you know me now, thanks to Meghan. She decided you needed help."

Meghan thought I needed help? Did she think me a child, then? Or did she think me weak? I said nothing, waiting.

"You see, young man, Meghan and I knew things you did not. You must not blame yourself, for there is no way you were likely to know.

"Don Federico is the man your grandfather wanted to marry your mother. When she ran off with your father, he was insulted. He was furious." He drew on his cigar, then put it down beside the empty cup. "And not only because of your mother.

"You see, Don Federico is a relative. A distant one, it is true. Distant enough so he could marry your mother, but close enough to inherit if you were dead."

For a moment, I just stared. Slowly it sank in. "You are sure of this?"

"My first trip to California was around the Horn, from Spain. Before that I spent several months sailing to Spain from Tripoli. I am a man who listens well, and there is much gossip. There was a lot of it when your grandfather suddenly decided to sail to America so suddenly that he arranged to leave Cádiz at night."

"On *your* ship?"

"No, my ship was to come later. I was to bring cargo that belonged to him. I was also to bring his sister."

"Aunt Elena?"

"It was she. We carried five other passengers on that voyage. An old man, a Spanish lad several years less than twenty, three women, and a sick boy."

"Then you know Aunt Elena?"

"Only slightly. She kept to her cabin much of the time, as did the woman who was caring for the sick boy. Occasionally when the weather was fair she would come on deck, and sometimes she helped the woman care for the sick boy. If he was really sick."

"You do not think he was?"

"I've no idea, although he seemed active enough when on deck, and quick enough when he needed to be. You see, one night the other Spanish lad tried to stab him. At least, that was what my mate thought, and the helmsman, too. The sick boy was alone by the rail, and it all happened very fast. According to the mate, the Spanish lad suddenly drew a knife and tried to stab the boy, but the boy turned so suddenly the attempt failed, and the boy twisted the Spanish lad's wrist and forced him to drop the knife. And he did it almost without effort.

"The mate called for me, and when I came up they both refused to

admit there had been trouble. Under the circumstances, there was nothing I could do but warn them."

It seemed a story without point except that Aunt Elena's voyage had
not been without incident.

"Some more chocolate? I shall have some."

"Please." I did not know what to say except to comment, "There
must have been some quarrel between them."

"Perhaps." He accepted the cup from the Indian girl and waited
until I had mine and then said, "The Spanish lad was Don Federico."

Was that it? Was he warning me?

"The other boy, the sick one, simply dropped off the world. Perhaps
he died. There was much sickness here for a while. When I asked about
him, nobody knew anything, and the woman who cared for him had
also disappeared. Later, I heard she married a vaquero."

"There has been much moving about. Every day people have left for
Monterey or San José, and of course for Yerba Buena. Half the people
who have come here have gone on. Why, even among the first settlers,
three families were sent back as useless to themselves or the town. Another, an Indian from Mexico, simply ran off. There are many such
stories."

"Of course." Captain Laurel got to his feet. "You will eat with us?
Meghan will be back soon, and I know she would enjoy seeing you."

"I'd be pleased." I stared into the chocolate. What was he trying to
tell me? That Don Federico was my enemy, and was dangerous? I could
accept that. He had been among those who pursued my father into the
desert.

"It does not matter," I said. "I want nothing from my grandfather."

"Do not be hasty. What you may not want, others may need."

Now, what did that mean?

"You have sailed in Chinese waters?" I asked. "I have heard of a system of self-defense known to the Chinese. I'd like to learn it."

He smiled. "It might take years. And you would have to decide what
it was you wished to learn, for each country has its own system, almost
every province in Japan or China, in fact, almost every city has its own
system. Some vary but little, some very much indeed.

"Chi'in-na is one of the best, for if one attack fails, another is ready
to follow. Tai-chi, kendo . . . you can choose what system you like.

"However, if you are serious, I have just the teacher for you. He is the
boatswain on the *Queen Bess*, my ship."

"I heard of a Chinese who lives here. Lives over against the mountain somewhere."

Laurel smiled. "I know him, but he will teach no one, and he is not a Chinese, although he comes from what is part of China. He comes from Khotan."

"Khotan?"

"It is far west, in Turkestan, against the Kunlun Mountains. It is on the way to India. Long ago it was a center of Buddhist culture."

"I remember, I think. I believe Marco Polo was there. It is on the old Silk Road that led from China to the Mediterranean."

"The Silk Road branched at Khotan, to Syria, and over the mountains to India. It was a pilgrim's road, also, for the Chinese Buddhists who went to India to learn."

"I should like to know that man."

"He will teach no one. He has found a place he loves, and he lives there. He lives alone, I believe."

The evening had come, and shadows were falling. The Indian woman came in and lighted the lamps. Their light was uncommonly bright, and I commented on it.

"It is an oil from petroleum. The Chinese have been using it for centuries."

He changed the subject, and we talked of ships and men, of the far sea and of strange foreign ports whose names were music. Some of them I remembered from my father; many were strange to me. Others I remembered from stories I'd read.

A door opened at the far side of the room and Meghan came into the room. Instantly I was on my feet. She was even more lovely than I had remembered.

She came to me, holding out both hands. "Johannes! It is so good to see you!"

She was no longer a little girl, but a young lady, and if she had confused me before, I was even more confused now.

"You will have supper with us? Do you remember Kelda? She is coming over, I think, and Philo Burns as well."

"And Rad Huber?"

"No, not Rad Huber. I am afraid he has found friends in other quarters. I have seen him on the street a few times." She glanced at me. "He's very big, you know. And very strong."

The comment irritated me. I was pretty strong myself.

Kelda O'Brien came in with Philo Burns. She still had a few freckles over her nose, with deep blue eyes and black hair. Philo had changed but little except to grow older. He was an erect, handsome young man, looking very polished and at ease. "I am the Los Angeles representative for the Adelsdorfer Company, and through them for the Hamburg-Bremen Company."

I knew enough to know that Adelsdorfer was an importer and the Hamburg-Bremen Company insured ships' cargoes.

"You've a good job, then," I said.

"I like it, and there's a future in it, I believe." He glanced at me, smiling suddenly. "Have you seen old Fraser? He's hardly changed, and he's finally finished his book. He's written some things that were published in London, and I believe in Germany, as well."

Fraser had finished his book, Burns had an assured future but what about me? Where did I stand? What was I?

38

Excusing myself, I went out into the night. I led my horse to the *zanja* for water and then tied him at the corral with a bit of hay. For a few minutes then I stood beside the dapple, idly scratching under his mane. The night was cool, the stars very bright.

Don Federico? I could scarcely place the man, although I had seen him about town and no doubt he knew me. It was hard to think of a man whom I did not know as an enemy.

Captain Laurel's story of the sudden treacherous attack on the other boy had been intended as a warning. Obviously he wished to place me on guard against such a surprise attack.

The idea of inheriting from my grandfather had never occurred to me, nor was it likely. A man who hated so much would take no chances on such an inheritance falling to one he hated.

How much of what had happened had been due to Don Isidro, and how much to Don Federico? When I was abandoned in the desert, he had accompanied my grandfather. He had been younger than my father and was still a relatively young man, and strikingly handsome.

A door closed, and turning, I saw Meghan on the step. When I started toward her, she came to meet me.

"You were gone so long, I was beginning to wonder what had happened."

"I watered my horse and then got to wondering. It's not easy to believe a man I do not know might wish to kill me."

"I know. My father has been worried that you might be attacked without warning. He is concerned about you." She paused, then added, "You see, your other grandfather, the one who was a ship's captain, taught my father navigation, helped him to his first command. There was a strong bond between them. He feels almost as if you were one of the family."

Without thinking, I said, "I wish I were!"

Teasingly she said, "I wouldn't know how to act toward a brother."

"I wasn't thinking of being a brother," I said.

"We'd better go in. Respectable young ladies do not talk to gentlemen when unchaperoned."

We walked back to the porch, not talking, and the evening passed quietly with casual conversation with Philo Burns, a few words with Kelda, and at the last, with Captain Laurel again. "If you are serious about learning," he said, "I'll have my boatswain up from the port. There's much to do aboard ship, but the mates can handle it." He paused. "We do not have much time, so you will have to work hard. I will suggest he dispense with the formalities. Formalities and ritual are very important to the Far Eastern peoples, you know."

So it began. For the next six weeks I worked with Liu Ch'ang six to seven hours a day. Liu Ch'ang was a big man, enormously strong, and agile as a monkey. He was from somewhere in northern China and had trained from childhood. He spoke but little English, a few words of Spanish, and he taught me some Chinese as we worked.

Wrestling for sport was not considered. My purpose was to defend myself and to retaliate as swiftly and brutally as possible. There was no time to learn any system of self-defense completely. That would come later. What I wanted now were a few throws and blows to be used in an emergency, and to practice these until their use became as natural as the act of swallowing.

Occasionally when Liu Ch'ang was busy with other things, I rode to the corral and worked with Monte McCalla at breaking horses. Often Jacob was there as well.

The black stallion now came to the bars looking for me. He shied from my hand but accepted a piece of bread. So far, I had found but two horses that I would keep for myself, the dark dapple-gray and the bay with black mane and tail. How fast either horse might be, I did not know, but both had stamina, and both were smart, quick to learn, and very quick in their movements.

"Watch that stallion," Monte warned. "He's ready to go at the slightest chance. One of these days he's going to try it, and I just hope I'm not in the way when he starts!"

*　　*　　*

Change was in the air, and no amount of concentration on one's personal affairs could prevent one from realizing it.

Miss Nesselrode was crocheting when I entered the shop. "Johannes! I see very little of you these days."

"We've some fine horses out there, ma'am. Monte's working them hard, and he's got about three dozen as good roping horses as a man could want.

"We've picked out some others, paired them up for teams. We've been working them together, getting them used to each other."

"We'll need them, Johannes. There's a man on the other side of town who has started building wagons. It will take time to make the change, and the Californios may want to stay with their *carretas*. I am depending on the easterners to want wagons, and later, buggies."

Glancing over the new books that had come in, I looked across the street and saw a tall man in a dark tailored suit. He was just standing there, apparently reading a newspaper, but he was watching the shop, too.

"Ma'am? Do you know that man?"

She glanced up at me, then followed my gaze to the street. After a moment she said, "I am not sure, Johannes. He does look familiar."

Several vaqueros rode by; then a *carreta* passed. When I looked again, he was gone. Miss Nesselrode put down her pen, placed her palms flat on the desk as if she was about to rise, then relaxed. She was disturbed.

"Someday," she said, "we must have a talk."

"Have I done something wrong?"

She flashed a quick smile. "No, Johannes, but I may need some advice."

"Advice? From me? If there is anything I can do . . . ?"

"I value your judgment, Johannes. I have no one else to turn to."

"Whatever I can do. You have only to ask."

Yet I was puzzled. She had always seemed so thoroughly in command of herself, so self-sufficient. I looked again at the street. The well-dressed man was gone.

Who was he? Was it he who had triggered that comment by Miss Nesselrode? Or was it merely a coincidence?

For that matter, the very question of who Miss Nesselrode was still left me with a sense of guilt. What, after all, did I know of her? What did anyone know? As far as I was concerned, her life began when she appeared for our ride west in Farley's wagon.

Who *was* she? What had she left behind? To all appearances she was a lady. Obviously she had education. Of her intelligence there could be no doubt, but where had she come from?

Fletcher had been suspicious, yet he was suspicious of everyone. As with many a dishonest man, he suspected everyone of duplicity.

Our horses were held in a series of corrals near a spring at the edge of the mountains. There was a small grove of sycamores and oak nearby that offered shade, and the water was good. It was far enough up the side of the mountains to offer a good view of the wide-open country, below which was grasslands and *ciénaga,* dotted with clumps of trees, some of them quite extensive. On a clear day we could actually make out riders or *carretas* along the old Indian trail from Santa Monica Bay to Los Angeles, the same trail that led to and past the pits of *brea.*

Francisco and his Cahuillas had taken their cattle and the rest of their payment and returned to their own country, far away on the desert's edge.

Jacob Finney came up to the fire in the coolness of the morning, stepping down from his horse and trailing the reins. He extended his hard brown hands to the fire's warmth. "I don't like it, Johannes. We need more men, good men. Coming in from the La Brea Ranch, I saw tracks, fresh horse tracks coming this way."

Monte looked up at him from where he squatted, cup in hand. "How fresh?"

"Last night. Maybe sundown or after. They were scouting us." He reached for a cigar from his breast pocket. "I think they're holed up down there near the old Anza spring, eight to ten of them."

"Stearns and Wilson have both lost horses," Monte said. "Stearns thinks it's some outfit from over on the Mohave River."

"Kelso should be back in town tomorrow," Jacob said. "He's been up to Santa Barbara for Miss Nesselrode."

"The Yorbas have lost both cattle and horses," I said. "They think it was some of the old Jack Powers outfit."

"He lit out," Jacob said. "Powers, I mean. He went down to Baja just ahead of a posse with a hangin' noose."

"I can stay around," I said. "We've put in too much hard work on these horses to lose them."

"How you comin' with that stallion of yours?" Jacob asked.

I shrugged. "He'll take bread or a carrot from my fingers, but if I go to put a hand on him, he shies away."

"Be careful. You can't trust a stallion."

"Odd about people's notions of riding," I said. "Most Americans will only ride geldings. I'm talking about working riders. The Spanish conquistadors favored stallions, and the Arabs, I hear, favored mares."

Jacob took up the reins and led his horse to the corral, where he tied the reins. "You know the Yorbas," he said to me. "Did Raymundo tell you anything about that bunch of horses they took back from outlaws over at Tujunga Canyon? A couple of hundred of them, somebody said."

"Hundred and fifty, the way Raymundo tells it. Mexican and American outlaws. Maybe some of that same bunch we ran into over near the Grapevine."

Jacob dropped to his heels by the fire. "Monte? You know those folks over at El Monte? Why don't you take some time off and ride over there? If you can find three or four good hands, hire them."

"They're a tough lot of Texas boys, but they're good hands, too."

"That's what we want, isn't it?" Jacob smiled slyly. "Although with Johannes takin' all those fightin' lessons, we may not need anybody else. He should handle four, maybe five all to onct."

"Give me time," I said. "Somebody has to protect you boys from the boogers."

Sunshine lay along the slopes, and from Los Angeles a few thin trails of smoke pointed fingers at the clouds. Where we sat under the sycamores, sunlight and shadow dappled the earth.

"It has to change," I commented, "yet I wish it were not so. This is my kind of country. This"—and I waved a hand toward the distant hills—"and what we saw out there. Maybe I'll go to horse ranching. There's nothing prettier than a bunch of colts playing in a meadow."

"It's a livin'," Monte said. He looked from me to Jacob. "You really want me to ride over to El Monte?"

"We do. But don't waste around. You'll miss all the fightin' if you do, and Johannes will have all the fun."

Monte walked to the corral and took his rope from where his saddle lay. He went into the corral and roped a mouse-colored mustang with three white stockings. He led it out and saddled up. We sat by the fire, watching while slow smoke drifted up from the dying coals.

"You serious abut that?" Jacob asked. "Horse ranching, I mean?"

"I am. At least it is something I can do until I find my way. My trouble is the wild country, and there's no money in trapping anymore. Prospecting . . . well, I don't know. Since they've found gold up north, everybody is hunting it."

"Is it the gold? Or is it the country?"

With a small stick I poked at the coals. "The country, I guess. There's something out there, something I've got to find. I feel sometimes like I'd lost something out there, but I don't know what it is."

He got up, dusted off his pants, and looked around at me. "Will you be all right here? Monte's ridin' in, and I think I'll go along and see Miss Nesselrode. I can make it back before sundown."

"Go ahead, I'll be all right."

When he had gone I walked over to the corral and talked to the stallion. He had to have a name, but what would it be? Standing near the corral, I let my eyes slowly sweep the country to the south, east, and west. North and west, the mountains were close, and the timber was thicker but rarely dense. A few vague trails reached toward the canyons.

I stood my rifle near me and against the corral bars, sweeping the country again with careful attention. Many times before I had watched that country down there. The view was unbroken except for the occasional clumps of trees, and I could see anybody approaching from afar.

The trouble was that I could not keep a good watch down toward the Anza spring. From there attackers could hold to low ground and groves, coming around behind me, and there was no need to wait until dark. Many previous raids had been by daylight.

Vásquez was somewhere around, and Joaquin Jim. Joaquin seemed to be a popular name for outlaws for there were at least three by the name. Probably that was why John Rollin Ridge, the Cherokee writer whose Indian name was Yellow Bird, had chosen that for the name of his outlaw. He had written a story for *The Police Gazette* about an outlaw named Murietta, and many people had come to believe he was a real person.

Pancho Daniel was around, and Juan Flores, both known men, and dangerous. Three-Finger Jack, whom Ridge had attached to the so-called Murietta gang, was actually riding with Vásquez.

Far away I could see the plume of dust that would be Monte and Jacob. Taking up my rifle, I turned toward my fire.

For a moment my heart stilled; then I felt its slow, heavy beat.

A man was standing by the fire, a square-shouldered man with a thick neck, a man no longer young but whose shoulders were shocking in their intimation of quiescent power.

How he had come there, I did not know, but he was standing, as if waiting. Rifle in hand, I walked toward him, walking slowly, very slowly.

39

He wore dungarees such as were worn by sailors on the China ships, a broad leather belt, and a white cotton shirt stretched tight over unbelievable muscles. So far as I could see, he carried no other weapon.

"Good morning." I gestured toward the pot. "Will you have some coffee?"

His features had an Oriental cast but he looked unlike any Japanese or Chinese I had seen, although my knowledge of both peoples was limited. He had high cheekbones and a scar on the side of his jaw. When he got that scar, he had also lost an earlobe.

He squatted on his heels and accepted the cup I brought from an arbor we had built to add to the tree's shade.

"I am Johannes Verne," I said.

He tasted the coffee. "You grandson to Captain Verne?"

"Yes."

"Captain my friend."

"I wish I had known him. All I know is what my father told me. He sailed off the China coast for many years, I believe."

He watched the horses moving inside the corral. We took some of them out to graze each day, returning them to the corral at night. A few of the horses had already been driven to the corral in town, others to land held by Miss Nesselrode on the old Indian trail to Santa Monica.

"You have many horses."

"If we can keep them. There are many thieves, too. I am told there are some bandits down near Anza spring."

"Eleven," he said.

Surprised, I said, "Eleven?"

"Yes. I count. They wait for somebody who comes from the town."

"You know them?"

"I see them. I come by, see, go to look. I listen."

"They did not see you?"

"Did you see me come here? I am Yacub Khan."

Apparently that was explanation enough, and he was right, for I had not seen him until he stood at the fire. It irritated me that I had been so careless. How could I not have seen him? I was alert. I was a damned fool. He had done it, somehow. If he had, others might.

As if he read my mind, he said, "You watch good. I see it."

He emptied his cup, then stood up. He watched the horses for a few minutes, then walked to the corral. He put his hands on the bars and then called; he called to the black stallion and it came right up to him. He put his hand out and the stallion did not shy. "He is a good horse," he said. "Yours?"

"He's unbroken. Some say he is a bad one."

"He is good horse. Very strong. He run very far, very fast."

"You have had experience with horses?"

"In my country everybody rides, from tiny baby, we ride. I am of Turkestan, what the Chinese call Sinkiang. We have the best horses in the world. There are no better horses than those of Karashar or Bar-Kol."

When I was a small boy my father often showed me maps and pointed out places on them, some of them places he had visited, others places he simply knew about. Turkestan I remembered because Marco Polo had crossed it.

The black stallion had remained close to us, and putting out a hand, I scratched its neck.

"He is a good horse," Yacub Khan said. "He is the best of them."

It dawned on me suddenly. "You are from Khotan? You are the fighter?"

"I have fought." Abruptly he turned and started away. Having no idea what to say or why he had come or why he was going, I simply stood and watched him go.

When he was some fifty yards away, he turned and looked back at me. "You are strong. Become stronger."

Then he walked away, his shoulders very straight, walking with a curious flat-footed style, toes turned out.

Why had he come? He, whom I had heard was a recluse, seeing no one, wishing to see no one. Captain Laurel had said he was the best, and Liu Ch'ang agreed. Now he said: *You are strong. Become stronger.*

When I looked again, he was gone. Of course, he could have gone into the trees. No doubt he had.

Eleven outlaws, he said. It was too many. For a few minutes I stood looking about me as if seeing the place for the first time.

Suppose they came now to run off my horses? What would I do? What could I do? The corral, which opened on a small pasture fenced with rails, stood on a level spot among low, rolling hills close to the mountains. One of the several canyons that offered trails to the San Fernando Valley was close by, and Los Angeles was less than ten miles away. In the clear air it was not easy to judge distance.

Between where I now stood and Los Angeles there were numerous clumps of brush and trees and some vast stretches of prickly pear. Against the mountains and around Anza spring, named for the explorer who stopped there on a trip to the north, there were trees.

By this time the outlaws must know I was alone, so if they attacked, how would they do it? Our fire could be seen for miles, and they would judge that I was nearby. A sudden charge might kill me and run off the horses, needing no more than minutes.

My position close to the corral was not a good one, for riders could split, ride around the corral, and take me from both sides. Thinking of that, I recalled a spot I had seen while gathering firewood.

No more than fifty yards from the corral, it was a low knoll covered with rocks and chaparral, backed by a few trees and some fallen logs. From one of these I had taken bark for kindling, and broken some small branches.

Building up the fire and adding fresh fuel, I then retreated to the knoll and found the view I had of the corral and my camp was better than expected. Carefully I looked around, choosing several possible firing positions, for after firing, I must move at once. My movements could be covered by the way the hill fell away as well as by the brush and rocks.

Checking my field of fire, I settled down to wait, and was scarcely in position before I glimpsed three riders come out of the trees and ride slowly along the dim trail that led from the southwest. They were ambling along as if going nowhere, and in no hurry, yet I was suspicious.

Where were they going?

The route they followed would bring them close to our camp, and the trail led on past and into one of the canyons that offered access to the valley beyond. Yet, at this hour, where were they going? There were ranches in the valley, and a stage stop at Calabasas.

Curiously I watched them draw nearer. As I watched, one of them drew his rifle from the scabbard. My own rifle eased forward. At the corral the black stallion was restless, and glancing that way, I saw he was not watching the three riders, but something off to my right, head up, ears standing.

Turning sharply, I saw five riders, rifles in hand, less than a hundred yards away. While my attention had been riveted on the three riders, as was no doubt intended, the others were approaching under cover and from almost behind me.

Eleven, Yacub Khan had said, and there were but eight in sight. Where were the others? By now they all must know I was not at the fire, and were waiting until I gave away my position.

They did not know how I was armed, but would assume I had a rifle, which, once fired, must then be reloaded. They would also assume that I had a pistol capable of five or six shots, depending on whether all cylinders were loaded. Thinking of that, I drew each pistol, for I had two, and in each I loaded the extra chambers while watching the riders.

The five had drawn up. One man was standing in his stirrups, peering around.

That I was not in sight disturbed them. If they could surprise me, they need not fire a shot. Otherwise they could draw my fire and leave me with an empty rifle. That I had two pistols and my father's shotgun loaded with slugs, they could not guess.

Monte and Jacob had expected to be back before sundown, and any firing would bring them on the run. Yet now I was alone, very alone.

Where were the other riders?

The three riders drew abreast of our fire, but a good hundred yards off, then walked their horses past it. Glancing around swiftly, I saw the five riders were moving forward.

Sweat broke out on my brow. My heart was pounding heavily. What should I do? To shout a warning meant to give away my position, yet it went against the grain to shoot an unwarned man. Yet, they had come here to steal, and so were taking their own chances.

The three riders suddenly turned and started for my fire. The first of the five rode around the near corner of the corral and trotted his horse to the gate. He reached to unfasten it, and I yelled, "*Get away from there!*"

Instantly I rolled over and three bullets struck into the brush or the log near which I'd been lying. Quickly I took aim at the rider at the gate. Just as he leaned over to pull the pin, I squeezed off my shot, the bullet directed at the small of his back right above the cantle of the saddle.

The moment I fired, I dropped the rifle and, picking up the shotgun, fired one barrel at the rider nearest the fire.

He raised up in his stirrup, looked right at me although I was deep in the brush, and then, as his horse wheeled, he toppled from the saddle and fell at the fire's edge.

They were gone, vanished! Two men lay on the ground, one near the fire, the other some distance away, where he had fallen from his running horse. Swiftly I reloaded my rifle, then the empty barrel of the shotgun.

All was quiet. A stick fell in the fire, and sparks flew up.

The horse of the man near the fire walked slowly away.

Moving carefully, I shifted my position to have a better view of the corral and the fire. I could see along both sides of the corral for most of the way, but some of the riders were grouped just beyond the end of it farthest from me. As the ground fell away there, I could not see them, although I could detect occasional movement. Nor did I dare fire, for the horses were milling about. Had they been loose in our pasture, the outlaws would have been driving them, a mile away by now.

Slowly the moments passed. I lay quiet, sweating, straining my ears for any sound. Some of them were pinned down at the end of the corral, and to emerge would bring them within sight, but where were the others?

The sun was going down. It would soon be dusk, and then dark. They had only to wait. Uneasily I glanced over my shoulder. It was already growing dark under the trees. I saw nothing, heard nothing.

When I looked back, the man near the fire had moved. So he was not dead then, only wounded.

Again I looked over my shoulder, searching the trees and brush for some movement. There was nothing.

The wounded man at the fire had put out a hand, and digging his fingers into the earth, was trying to pull himself along the ground. His rifle had fallen from his hand when he was shot and lay in plain sight.

Where were Jacob and Monte? How far could our shots be heard? Over a mile, I assumed, but could not be sure. I simply did not know, and so much depended on the terrain, the vegetation, and the general surroundings. I dried my sweaty palms on my shirtfront, and drawing my spare pistol, I placed it on a rock near my hand. The other was in my waistband.

Again I checked all around me. . . . Nothing. The wounded man had crawled several feet. My eyes swept the trees. Our horses had bunched at my end of the corral, away from the outlaws.

How many were down there? Three? Four? Brush crackled behind me, and two men burst out not thirty feet away. Whipping around at the first sound, I fired the shotgun point-blank at the nearest man; then, forgetting the other barrel, I caught up the pistol and shot into the next man.

A bullet burned my ear, another plunked into the earth beside me, and then I felt a sharp impact on my leg. I fired again, and that man went down. He got up, staggered a few steps, and fell again.

At that moment there was a burst of firing from out in front, then a second pounding of gunfire, and silence.

The fire smoldered, almost out. Slow smoke arose from the coals. The wounded man was gone.

A dark spot in the dust near the fire showed where he had bled, and there were drops of blood further along. When I was attacked from behind, he had chosen the moment to stagger away. His tracks were visible from where I lay.

The man hit with the shotgun slugs was dead; the other one was alive and conscious, his eyes wide open. "You goin' to kill me?" he asked, his voice almost casual.

"You were trying to kill me," I said, reloading the shotgun.

"You had us in a bind. We didn't know where you was."

"When a man sets out to be a thief, he sets himself up in a shooting gallery. He's any man's target.

"I never saw so many damn fools," I added, "men risking their lives for so little. If you stole all those horses, with today's market there wouldn't be enough left for one good night in a saloon. Any man who would risk his life or prison for so little has got to be soft in the head. At least two men are dead, two who will never see another sunrise, eat another meal, or know another woman, and for what?"

"I don't have to stand for no preachin'."

"Like hell you don't! You have to stand for whatever you get! You've got no more choice than a rabbit."

A call came from the fire. "Johannes?"

"Up here," I said. "I've got me a pigeon. He's lookin' toward his rifle now, wondering if he should chance it. I may let him try."

They came up the hill then, and through the brush. Only it was not just Monte and Jacob. Kelso was there, and two other men, two strangers.

"Looks like you had you a time," Monte said. "Your pa couldn't have done better."

40

During our early years in Los Angeles, with a population not exceeding three thousand persons, there was an average of fifty to sixty killings per year; yet when we moved our horses to Miss Nesselrode's rancho, there was no trouble. Even the black stallion behaved himself, shying only slightly when, riding beside him, I reached over and put a hand on his back.

The ranch was a quiet place with an old adobe house standing under the shade of huge old sycamores, and with a good view back toward Los Angeles.

On the morning after the delivery of the horses, Miss Nesselrode was busy with other things, so it was I who opened the shop and laid out the newspapers just in from Wilmington on the morning stage.

The streets were virtually empty, as I had come early to the shop. Down along Commercial Street, only one man was visible, a tall man, wearing an apron, who was sweeping the boardwalk. I had just taken a book from the shelf and was settling down to read when the door darkened and I glanced up to see the man whom we had seen watching the shop from across the street.

He was a man of what we then called middle age, a neatly dressed man in a gray suit and a narrow-brimmed hat. Nodding a greeting, he asked if we had a Boston newspaper he might see.

"It is ten days old, which is very up-to-the-minute news for us."

"For me, also." He smiled, but his gray eyes were sharp, penetrating. "You have a nice shop. Are you the owner?"

He was leading up to something, and I was wary, yet something else disturbed me also. There was a faint suggestion of an accent in his voice, something vaguely familiar.

"Mind if I sit down? This is a reading room, is it not?"

"Of course." Opening a box of books, I began taking from it several volumes by Bulwer-Lytton and a collection of tales by Poe. I glanced at it again, as he had been a friend of my father's and a man whom I had known slightly.

He saw the name. "Is that Edgar *Allan* Poe? He has become very popular in Europe, suddenly."

"These are the first of his books we've had. My father knew him, and I have met him."

"He died, I think. A few years ago."

"I had not heard." For a moment I straightened up. Another thread to the past, gone, lost forever. "He was a soldier once, so my father said. For as much as two years, I believe, and a sergeant."

He glanced at me. "Surely you did not know him here?"

"We lived in the East then. My father said that as a boy Poe was a noted swimmer, and thought of swimming the English Channel."

"Well for him he did not try. Nobody could swim the channel! That's preposterous!"

He changed the subject. "You have a nice shop. Is it yours?" It was the question I had avoided.

"It belongs to Miss Nesselrode."

"Nesselrode? An interesting name. Have you known her long?"

"Long enough. She's a fine woman."

"I do not doubt it, but I am curious. The name is not common, you know. I have seen her, I think. A tall, attractive young woman?"

"Yes."

"Most women of her age are married," he commented.

The comment deserved no reply. He was seeming to read his paper, making idle conversation the while. Yet he was prying, he was seeking for something, and it seemed to be about her. It occurred to me suddenly that she was no longer such a young woman, yet she seemed ageless. I had never thought of the passing years affecting her in any way at all.

"I wonder"—he spoke casually—"how she came by the name?"

"As most of us do, I presume." I spoke rather brusquely. "As you, no doubt, got yours." Straightening up from my work, I said, "When it comes to that, I do not believe we have met. I am Johannes Verne."

"I am Alexis Murchison."

An interesting name. The Murchison would be English, no doubt, and the Alexis? It could be Russian.

He shook out his paper, settled himself as if to read.

"You are not a cattle buyer. Is it horses in which you are interested?"

"We have many horses in Russia."

"You are from Russia, then? Not England?" Was that the accent I detected? But where could I have heard it before?

He was irritated. "Does it matter?"

"Not at all. We have had Russians in California from the beginning. I believe they had thoughts of claiming the area at one time.

"As to the name, I was simply curious, as you were. California is welcoming many strangers these days. Some come for gold, the wise ones for land, and others are simply buying or selling. Of course," I added, "others are merely prospecting."

"I am a traveler. The name Nesselrode intrigued me. It is uncommon."

"So you said. I knew some Nesselrodes back east when I was a child. Quite a large family. If the name interests you, I believe I could provide their address, in Philadelphia. He is a painter, I believe, and his wife taught ballet, when there was anyone to teach."

He folded the newspaper and put it down. "Thank you very much."

"Not at all," I replied. "When you want to know anything, please feel free to ask."

He gave me a look that had a whip in it, but I smiled and he went out, his back very stiff, and when he closed the door, it was with an emphatic bang.

Feeling pleased with myself, I returned to putting books on the shelves. The streets were growing busy now, people coming and going about their trading and shopping.

That accent, now. Russian, was it? Where had I known any Russians? I hadn't.

The thought returned. Who *was* Miss Nesselrode? Was his interest romantic? Her age . . . It gave me a sharp feeling of discomfort to realize she was not what people called a young woman any longer. Yet she was as slender and graceful as always, unchanged so far as I could see.

She came in suddenly, yet not so suddenly, for I had been hearing the distinctive click of her heels on the walk.

She closed the door behind her and glanced around, then looked at me with sudden awareness. "Hannes? What is it?"

"There was a man here . . . the one we saw across the street. I think he was trying to find out about you. I do not believe his interest was romantic, although I could be wrong."

She smiled beautifully. "Romantic? I am afraid it is late for that."

"Is it ever?" I paused. "His name was Alexis Murchison."

She was drawing off her gloves. There was a moment of stillness.

"No," she was thinking aloud, "it cannot be. Not after all this time." She came through the gate in the railing that divided her desk and the shelves from the reading room, where there were easy chairs and a table. "What did you tell him?"

"What could I tell him? That you are a beautiful woman. That you own the shop. What else do I know?"

She was amused. "I haven't told you very much, have I?"

"I do know a little more than before he came in," I commented, "because he had a very slight accent. I was puzzled as to where I'd heard it before." I glanced at her. "You are Russian, are you not?"

"I was once, a very long time ago. Now I am an American. A Californian."

"But you were a Russian."

"When I think back now, it seems another world, another life, and almost another person."

"You will go back?"

"I cannot. You see, Hannes, I was sent to Siberia, and I escaped. There were nine of us who started and only three who made it. I was a young girl when we escaped to China. My brother was killed in Siberia before we even got away, another died of hardships, and a third was killed in Mongolia by men who robbed us. I am the last of my family, and there is nothing to which to return. And I would be arrested."

She looked into the sunlit street, watching an old *carreta* rolling past. "When I reached China, I was taken in by an English family and earned my keep teaching French to their children. When I got older, I hired out as a governess. I saved my money, determined to come to America.

"I have been poor, Hannes, and I do not wish to be poor again. I work, I plan, I save."

We sat for a long time watching the people passing, and then she said, "We were so young, Hannes, and so very naive! We wished to change everything! I was too young to take part, but I listened to my brothers and their friends. They were excited. They were filled with enthusiasm. They wanted to reform their government. They wished it to be more liberal, and to follow the path of England and France.

"My mother was English, you see, and we had spent vacations in England. We pitied our serfs and we thought our government too rigid, but we were naive, and we had no idea how deeply embedded in Russian nature were the ideas we wished to change!

"My brothers belonged to a secret society called the Union of Welfare, which had been organized among the Semonovsky Guards officers, but it came to nothing and disbanded in 1821. My oldest brother had belonged. He was transferred to Tulchin in the Ukraine, and Colonel Paul Pestel was also located there. They organized what was called the Southern Society.

"When Alexander I died, they planned a revolt, but they were idealistic dreamers, they had no contact with the troops who they believed would join them.

"It was called the Decembrist Revolt and it was put down quickly and harshly. Five men were hung, including Pestel, and of the 121 men tried for treason, 109 were under thirty-five. Some were sentenced to hard labor, some sent to Siberia."

"But you were a young girl!"

"It made no difference. In Russia if someone in your family was involved, it was taken for granted you all were. We were sent to Siberia and we learned through sources friendly to us that we were to be eliminated. It was then we chose to escape."

"And now?"

"I could not go back. We are still considered enemies, and the fact that some of us escaped has compounded the evil."

"Would they come here? Would they try to get you back?"

She hesitated, biting her lip. "I do not think so. I was not that important. Still, I do not know. It would depend on the situation there. If by bringing one of us back to trial they could embarrass someone politically, it might be.

"You see, there were others of our family, very distant relatives but of the same name, who were very active. Count Nesselrode was at the Congress of Vienna. He was very active in the government."

"You must be careful."

She studied me for a moment. "Do you think of Don Isidro?"

"He is never far from my mind, but . . . there are other things." I stood up suddenly. "I am restless for the desert."

"But what is out there for you, Hannes? Beauty, of course, but what else?"

"I don't know." I frowned. "Maybe that's the trouble, I just don't know." I walked across to the window, then turned to face her.

"There's something out there for me, something unfinished, something I must do.

"All of this"—I waved a hand—"I can feel it happening, it's in the air. A man could become rich and successful here, but is that what I want? Or is there something else? Something my father and mother found?"

"Are you sure? Did they find anything? Or were they simply escaping from here? They had happiness with each other . . . we know that, but was there anything else?"

I remembered that time in the desert when Peg-Leg had found me, so long ago now. I tried to remember if I had been frightened, but could not remember fear. I had been in trouble, but I had known what I had to do, and was trying. I might even have made it.

No . . . no, I could not have made it. Peg-Leg had saved my life. I would have died out there, for there were too many miles and I had too little knowledge of the desert.

What was drawing me back? The house by the springs? The desert itself?

"Someone is coming," Miss Nesselrode said suddenly. "Be careful!"

Stepping away from the window, I turned to face the door. It opened tentatively and a small boy peered in, a small boy with very large dark eyes and a very large straw hat. He glanced quickly from Miss Nesselrode to me, then thrust a folded paper at me and ducked out the door before I could speak.

The handwriting was familiar, the note brief:

Can you come? I need you now, desperately!
Meghan

Passing the note to Miss Nesselrode for explanation, I went out the door.

Her home was but a short distance. I could be there in minutes.

41

An obviously frightened maid opened the door for me. "Oh, señor! Come quickly! But be careful!"

She pointed the way, and I crossed the patio to the *galería*, pausing in the doorway.

Meghan was facing me, and also facing a man whose back was toward me. There was no need for him to turn for me to know him. It was Rad Huber.

"Good morning, Meghan. I am sorry to be late." I moved on into the room, and as he turned toward me, I said, "It has been a long time, Rad."

He would outweigh me by forty pounds and was at least an inch taller. There was brutal power in his physique and in his features as well, but there was something else . . . A faint shadow of weakness, perhaps? A sense of something incomplete, unfinished?

"Get out." He did not speak loudly, and he jerked his head toward the door. "Get out while you're able."

"I'm sorry, Rad, but Meghan and I have business to discuss. Captain Laurel asked me to stop by and arrange matters. Do you mind?"

He faced squarely toward me, his feet a little apart. He had always been rather obvious, and he had not changed. He was expecting a shooting, and welcomed it. The trouble was that Meghan was there, and bullets do not always go to their intended mark.

"Go ahead. State your business, then get out."

I smiled at him. "Our business is confidential, Rad, and has nothing to do with you. I am here by invitation, Rad. Are you?

"If you will recall, there have been several hangings this past year, and at least three of them were of men who tried to force their attention on ladies. You could be next."

"I'm courtin' her!"

"He was asked to leave," Meghan said. "He has only come because he knows my father is away."

"That was one of the matters we had to discuss. Your father," I was inventing as I went along, "wished me to find a couple of the El Monte men to be around in the event of trouble."

Turning to Rad, I added, "A couple of the Texas boys from El Monte are coming by. It would not be wise to be around when they arrive."

He stared at me. "Someday," he said, "we'll meet somewhere. It'll be just you an' me."

"Of course, Rad. We've both known that, haven't we? And when it is over, I shall be able to get on with so many of the important things."

"*You* will get on? You will be dead."

I smiled tolerantly. "You're really not very good with a gun, Rad. There's a little way you have, an odd way you use your hands. You lose time, Rad, and time is the essence of it all."

As a matter of fact, I'd never seen Rad Huber in action, but he didn't know that, and it was in my mind to get him worrying about himself. If he became self-conscious, he would be hesitant, slow. He might try to dismiss the idea from his mind, but it would still be there, haunting him. He might review his method of drawing a gun, trying to discover what I indicated was a bad move. I had no idea whether it would have any effect, but it was worth a chance.

"You ain't nothin'," he said. "You never was."

"Ask the men who tried to steal my horses out by Coldwater," I suggested.

He walked to the door, turned as if to speak, then walked away, spurs jingling. I waited until the outer gate closed behind him.

Meghan came over to me. "Oh, Johannes! I am so sorry! I've gotten you into trouble again, but I just didn't know what to do or whom to call upon!"

"Who else but me?" I took her hands. "I'd have been disappointed had you called anyone else. I hope whenever anything is wrong you will call me."

"But because of me you're in trouble with Rad. I was the cause of that other trouble, too."

"We would have clashed anyway. He had started making trouble even before I sat down in your seat. You just gave him one more reason."

"Will you have some coffee?"

The *galería* skirted the patio on three sides, and we sat at a table under the arches, looking out over the sunlit patio at the fountain. We talked of her father, far out on the seas bound for China, and then we talked of Kelda O'Brien and Della Court, and all that lay outside the walls seemed far away.

Despite the violence of Sonora Town and such places as the Calle de Los Negros, ours was a town of flowers, vines, and trees, an island of people and problems lying between the mountains and the sea. Despite the furor off to the north in the Mother Lode country, Los Angeles remained a pleasant cow town. Phineas Banning had opened a stage line from Wilmington to Los Angeles, and later had begun building a railroad. Many of the Californios such as Andrés Pico had become out-standing citizens, and despite the seeming quiet of the town, it was stirring with ambition, realization of possibilities.

"You should not be here alone with your father gone," I suggested. "The talk about the El Monte boys was just talk, but why not let me get one of them to live on the premises? They are a decent lot, but very tough, and nobody wants trouble with them. There should be a man here."

"One is coming. He will be here tomorrow."

"Someone your father knows?"

She hesitated only a moment. "Yes, Father knows him. A friend is sending him to live in the cabin by the corrals."

"When your father returns, I wish to talk to him again. He seemed to know more about my family than I know myself."

She hesitated, then said, "He is afraid for you."

"He implied something of the kind. He seemed to think trouble might come from directions I did not suspect."

She was silent; then she added, "Father is often suspicious where he should not be."

"Perhaps. He seemed to me to know much that I did not. Until he told me I'd not heard the story of Don Federico trying to kill the other boy aboard ship."

"It was just a story. Father has many such stories, picked up at sea. It was just a disagreement between boys, I think."

"I wonder what ever happened to that other boy? Don Federico is here, of course."

"Father suspects the boy is dead. He has always intended to ask Aunt Elena."

"She knows?"

"If anyone does. The boy was taken away by the older woman who traveled with him. Nobody seems to know where they went, but it is not important. No doubt he is somewhere about, someone we know, perhaps."

"I do not really know Aunt Elena, but I believe I would like her very much."

"I like her. She comes here sometimes." After a moment's pause she said, lifting her chin slightly, "So does Don Federico."

"What?" I was startled.

"We met at a *fandango*. He's quite a marvelous dancer."

Unreasonably, perhaps, I felt betrayed! I gulped coffee and burned my mouth. Mentally, I swore. Who was I to object? She could see whom she wished. But when had this begun? Since her father left, I was sure.

"He can be charming when he wishes," Meghan said. "And he seems to think a great deal of your grandfather."

"I have not seen him since I was a small boy. That is, not to be sure of him."

"Of course. He is older, but there is not as much difference between us as between Don Abel Stearns and his wife."

Astonished and shaken, I protested, "You're not thinking of marrying *him*?"

She smiled teasingly. "I think that is what he has in mind. A girl cannot be sure, but he has been very correct."

After a long moment of silence I said, and my tone had changed, "He is my enemy. When I was a small boy he wanted me killed."

"Are you really sure he was the one? It has been a long time, and you were very young."

"I remember him well, very well."

"You must be mistaken. Once when I mentioned you he did not seem to know who you were. He did not, he said, know many Anglos."

Suddenly I wished to be away from here. From here, where I had most wanted to be. Beside her whom I loved or thought I loved. After all, I thought bitterly, what did I know of such things?

"He is a fine horseman," she was saying, "and one of the most handsome men I have ever seen."

The charm was gone. The water still fell from the fountain into its basin, the leaves still rustled, but my enemy had been here. He had sat, perhaps, where I was sitting, had drunk from the same cup.

I got to my feet. "I must go."

Surprised, she turned from the plants she had begun to water. "Must you? But you have only just come!"

"I must ride to the ranch."

Her eyes searched my face, but I hoped nothing showed. Who was I to object to whom she might entertain?

"I have been told of your black stallion. Have you ridden him yet?"

"Not yet. He has taken bits of food from my fingers and I have watered him from a bucket held in my hands."

Something was gone from the afternoon. She knew it now as well as I. We stood for a moment, facing each other, each wanting to say something but finding no words.

Being alone here with Meghan—this was a dream come true. I had wanted nothing more, and the reality had been, for a short time, even greater than the dream. Turning abruptly away from her, I started for the door.

"Johannes? Hannes?"

I stopped at the gate from the patio to the street. "You cannot know how it is with me," I said. "My grandfather and your Don Federico harried my parents into the desert, hunted them there like animals, trying to kill them. Finally, after a long time, they did find my father and kill him."

"But that was your grandfather!"

"Don Federico was there, too. He was the one who wished me killed, not just left to die. He wished it done then. He wished to do it, or have it done."

"I cannot believe that. I do not believe it. I know him."

"Of course. He is a handsome man, and a very good dancer."

"That has nothing to do with it!"

"I must go."

"You will come back?"

"If you need me, I will come. Otherwise . . ." I hesitated, then said, "I shall not. What if I met him here?"

"I'd trust you to act the gentleman. *He* would."

"How does a gentleman act in the presence of one who wished him killed? And who left him to die in the desert?"

"I told you I did not believe that. You are mistaken in your man."

"What does a murderer look like? He can be a handsome, smiling boy or a gentleman of style. It is not what is outside that makes the murderer, but what is within him."

"Nevertheless, I would *know*."

"No doubt you have some special gift. I hope it always works for you."

When I was in the saddle, I held still just for an instant. She was at the gate, looking after me. But he had been there. No doubt he would come back. Her father would not approve, but he was far away on the high road to China. I rode away, and I did not look back.

My day was ended, my beautiful day. Nothing in my life had prepared me for this. For much else, but not this. I had never been in love before. I did not know how to be in love, but I had thought, I had believed this was it, that Meghan was the one I wanted, what I had dreamed of, and now . . .

I would still dream of her. I had seen no one else to make me look twice. I had wanted no one else, and now . . .

Don Federico . . .

My eyes went to the mountains, as they always seemed to do on the plain of Los Angeles. I would go to them. I would lose myself in them. I would go back to the desert. Let her have him. Let him . . .

I swore bitterly.

Suddenly I realized I was running my horse, and slowed down. There was no use to kill a good horse because all had not gone well for me. What kind of a man was I? I had told myself I was strong, that I could be brave. I had thought of myself as having character, and here I was shattered to nothing by a few words from a girl!

Slowing my horse to a walk, I looked around. I was nearing the tar pits on the old Indian trail.

In the distance there was dust, a dust cloud coming toward me.

My rifle was in its scabbard, but I wore a pistol in my belt, and today, of all days, I was ready.

It was Monte, and one of the El Monte boys. When they saw me coming they pulled up.

"Hannes!" Monte shouted. "We were coming for you! He's gone!"

"Who is gone? What has happened?"

"There was a raid at the ranch. We fought them off, but they drove off some of the horses, and others simply escaped.

"It's your stallion," Monte said. "He killed one of the thieves who tried to take him, and he escaped. Your big black has gone back to the hills!"

42

My beautiful black horse was gone! Well, he had waited long for this moment, ever alert, ever watchful, eager to escape. Perhaps the wilderness out there was the best place for him. Yet I missed him, for I believe we understood one another.

He had, I always believed, belonged to somebody at some time. He seemed to respond to some overtures readily enough, and he might even have been ridden. To say he was beautiful might be stretching a point, yet he was magnificent. His coat was scarred by teeth and by hooves from his many battles with other stallions, too many for him to be called beautiful, but his conformation was perfect, he had a fine arch to his neck, delicate flaring nostrils that spoke of Arab blood, and eyes that spoke of intelligence.

First, we had to ride on to the ranch and discover just what had happened, then take steps. How many horses were gone? How long ago did the raid occur? How many attackers had there been? Then we had to organize pursuit.

At least forty horses had been taken. Tomás Machado, who worked on the ranch for Miss Nesselrode, stopped me. "The stallion? He not go with them. He escape. He round up two, three mares and run off. He has gone back to the wild."

"Finney and Kelso are here, they rode in just before you did," Monte said. "Do we go after them?"

"What else?"

"They'll be looking to ambush us like they did with Sheriff Barton," Finney suggested. "This is a bad lot. I think it was some of Pancho Daniel's outfit."

"We'll have to be careful." I pushed my hat back on my head. "I can go alone. The fewer of us, the better, if we're to slip up on them and avoid an ambush."

"We rode over from El Monte because we figured there'd be some action," Owen Hardin said. "You tryin' to deal us out of it?"

He was a short, barrel-chested man with a thick neck who at twenty-two was already growing bald. "Monte said we'd see some action. Now you're tryin' to hog it all."

"Come along, then. Kelso," I said, turning to him, "I wish you'd stay. Miss Nesselrode will need you, and there's no telling how long we will be gone."

"How long you figure?"

"As long as it takes to find our horses."

"That may take you clean into Sonora."

"Fine! I've never seen Sonora. Nor Chihuahua."

"Ain't nobody waitin' for me," Myron Brodie said, "and I ain't been to Sonora neither. Although," he added, "I did ride down Chihuahua way one time."

"You know that country?" Finney asked.

Brodie grinned. "Not too well. I was ridin' mostly at night."

"Tomorrow morning," I said, "we leave before daybreak."

The ranch house was long, low-roofed, and pleasant, adobe plastered with white, and a tiled roof made with tile the fathers had taught the Indians to make. It was a trade quickly abandoned when the fathers lost their autocratic control over the Indians. Several rooms opened on the *galería*, which was shaded and cool. Inside, there was a central room with a fountain, a table, some chests, and a few hide-covered chairs. The rugs on the floors had been woven by Indians.

Dropping into one of the chairs, I dropped my hat on the floor nearby. Elfego brought me coffee. After a sip or two I leaned my head back.

I did not like it. Raids upon outlying ranchos were not uncommon, but such a raid on our horses so soon after the other was unlikely. Several of the would-be thieves had been killed, and it was strange, I thought, that they would strike again so soon. The object lesson from the previous raid would make them wary. Yet there had been a raid and some horses stolen. What was I to make of that?

Something about it made me uneasy. There were a dozen horse herds more vulnerable than ours and less well-guarded, so why us? And why so soon?

It was cool and pleasant there. I thought back to Meghan, and shied from the thought. She had not betrayed me. She was her own person and could do as she wished. No doubt Don Federico was a handsome and exciting man. Because he was my enemy did not make him her enemy. I was stupid.

Nevertheless, the thought irked me, and I opened my eyes, staring at the ceiling for a moment, trying to bring my thoughts back to the problem at hand. I sipped coffee. Suppose . . . ?

No, that was unlikely. Yet, to consider . . . Suppose the stealing of the horses was a deliberate plan to kill me? To lead me into a trap, as Barton had been led and shot down?

Friends of those who died in the previous attempt? Or Don Isidro? Or perhaps even Don Federico? Suppose when Meghan had mentioned me he decided to eliminate me from that field, too?

Or was I too involved with my own problems and not seeing clearly? Suppose it was simply a case of horse theft?

Play it that way, but remembering the ambush of Sheriff Barton, be very cautious.

Long since, I had learned that one needs moments of quiet, moments of stillness, for both the inner and outer man, a moment of contemplation or even simple emptiness when the stress could ease away and a calmness enter the tissues. Such moments of quiet gave one strength, gave one coolness of mind with which to approach the world and its problems. Sometimes but a few minutes were needed.

Long walks can provide this, or horseback rides, reading a different book, or even just sitting. Here, in the pleasant coolness of this *galería*, listening to the waters of the fountain, I could gather my forces again, and perhaps reach some conclusions about myself.

Hatred is an ugly thing, more destructive of the hater than the hated, and this I had tried to avoid. I did not hate Don Isidro, I did wish there were a justice that would see him pay for what he had done to my parents. Yet in his pursuit of them he may have given them a closeness, a needing of each other they might not otherwise have known.

Although I did not hate, neither did I wish evil to succeed in its evil. Don Isidro had fierce pride in a name whose reputation had been won by others and to which he had contributed nothing. He had fled to this country to keep from his peers a knowledge he deemed disgraceful, and he had driven his daughter from his doors for the same reason. Now, a lonely and embittered old man, he was left with nothing.

The old family servants had left him because of his actions, and those now around him were men he could not control and who showed him outward respect while secretly holding him in contempt.

Thus far I had been occupied in growing up, learning a little, avoiding enemies, but moving no farther, and it depressed me that I was not moving. Nor had I found my direction. From my window I could look off across the grassland, spotted with groves of trees or patches of prickly pear. In the distance lifted the smoke of Los Angeles. Someday, Don Benito Wilson had said, this would be a great city. Perhaps, but it must find other industries than cattle and grapes, which provided its income now.

Nor was I sure I wished it to become a great city, for we who are among the first always yield reluctantly to the latecomers, seeing our meadows fade, our trees cut down, our horizons obscured. We who were the first-comers accepted the dollar prices but bemoaned the loss of beauty, yet what was happening was inevitable, I suppose.

Yet we must never forget that the land and the waters are ours for the moment only, that generations will follow who must themselves live from that land and drink that water. It would not be enough to leave something for them; we must leave it all a little better than we found it.

Never did a tree fall that I did not feel a pang, and rightly so, for when the trees are gone, man will also be gone, for without them we cannot live. The very air we breathe comes from trees, and when they are gone, the air will thicken and men will die and our great towers of stone will fall away to rubble and there will be only weeds, and then grass to cover the unsightly mounds we leave behind.

My coffee was cold, and Elfego was off about his business somewhere. As I turned my head to look out across the meadow, I saw some of our horses run by, biting playfully at one another, bright flashes of color upon the green of the meadow. This was the good life, this I could do, raise horses, watch them grow, and perhaps have a little to do in shaping the destiny of our country.

For it is not buildings that make a city, but citizens, and a citizen is not just he who lives in a city, but one who helps it to function as a city. My father had often talked of the town meetings in New England and of the discussions that helped to shape the destinies of cities and states. For this I must prepare myself, for I knew too little of law, too little of governing, too little of the conducting of public meetings. There is no greater role for a man to play than to assist in the government of a people, nor anyone lower than he who misuses that power.

*   *   *

The shadows were reaching out toward the edges of the fields, the trees were losing their forms in the darkness, and night was coming.

Night, and I was alone. Restlessly I walked to the window, then hurriedly turned from it, for to expose myself there might give some hidden marksman an opportunity. Grimly I reflected. There was the dream, but there was also the reality, and all men were not men of goodwill.

Where was Meghan now? Did she think of me at all? And why should she?

Why Don Federico, of all people? He was twice her age and more, yet that was almost the custom here, and most girls married when fourteen to sixteen. Meghan was younger than I, although we had gone to school together. Rad Huber had been older than all of us, for ours was a small school and there were no subdivisions.

Tomorrow at daybreak, another venture into the unknown, five men after a band of at least ten and our horses. Unless it rained, highly unlikely at this time of year, there would be a trail. And if this was, indeed, a trap, there would certainly be a trail.

Was it over between Meghan and me? Had there ever been anything to be over? Had I been foolish? I could not escape the idea that had Captain Laurel been at home, Don Federico would never have been permitted to visit. And that did me no good whatsoever.

My thoughts strayed again to the desert. Where was Francisco? Was he married yet? Indians took wives early, in most cases, and he was a man of growing importance among his people.

How was the acorn crop this year? I wondered. And the mesquite and chia? Would they fare well this coming year? And had my visitor come again to the cabin with the mosaic floor?

Odd, that he should have that talent. Had he been instructed? Or did he conceive and plan and originate himself? Had *he*, my monster, actually laid that floor? Someone else, perhaps?

He returned to the mountains in the dark. How well he must know them! And how sure of foot he must be, for all his size.

What if some night he fell along the trail? Who would find him? Who would look? Who would even wonder? Was there someone, somewhere, who cared?

I cared.

I would send word to Francisco, I would learn if anyone had been in the house or near it.

And my great black horse? Where was he? Was he glad to be free? Glad to be running once more over his wild, wonderful hills? Grazing beneath the oaks where the acorns fell? Watering at lonely streams?

Standing in the middle of the room, I looked around. I was alone. I felt as if I had always been alone, always.

Don Federico . . .

Why had it been him? Why, of all men?

Meghan, I love you. I spoke the words in my mind, but they fell into silence and left no echo behind.

Had I told her that? I had not, in so many words. Yet, I believed she knew. He would tell her. He would tell her easily and with skill. He was a man who would be good at such things.

It was just as well I was going to the mountains.

Settling myself in a corner away from view of the windows, I tried to read, but on this night I could not. Often I read aloud, loving the sound of the words, amazed at how beautifully some writers sounded when read, how impossible it was to read others aloud. Yet now I could not read.

Meghan, I have lost you.

Long I lay awake, staring up into the darkness where the dark-beamed ceiling was, hearing the faint sounds from outside, a mocking-bird singing the long night through, a movement of horses in the corrals, the sound of water from the fountain.

Tomorrow I ride to the hills again, to the long green hills now fading to a tawny brown, hills that looked like the flanks of some great lion sleeping.

My father had fled to the hills, had lost himself out there where the silent gods awaited, eyes hollow with loneliness for the worshipers they no longer had. Out there under the sky, under the stars by night, they waited for the click of a stone thrown upon a pile, for arms lifted in prayer.

Men need their gods, but did not the gods also need men?

43

We rode into the morning while the stars were there, like anchor lights of ships afloat in the harbor of the sky. We rode with a soft wind blowing, our horses stepping quick and light, eager for the trail.

We smelled the dampness of fallen leaves and of disturbed grass as we wove our way among the clumps of boulders and prickly pear.

Over coffee and the campfire we had talked that morning of what was to come, our faces heavy with sleep, our lips fumbling for words. We had said what needed to be said and were on our way, five young men armed for the work we had to do.

"They will be waiting," I told them. "This wasn't just a horse-stealing. There are a dozen ranches around where they could have rounded up more horses with less trouble. You boys would be better off to let me go it alone."

"Are you crazy?"

"I am the one they want, but I am better out there than they know. I grew up with the Cahuilla. I can find them and I can bring the horses back."

"When we hired on," Owen Hardin said, "we put our money in the pot. We're not likely to throw in our hands until we see what the other feller is holding."

"Glad to have you along." I said it with sincerity, although I'd have preferred going alone. Then I should have to worry about no one but myself.

A man alone can become a ghost in the woods; others, no matter how skillful, will make some sound. Also, he who leads is responsible. How many riding out on a dangerous venture would ride back? I must think of them as well as myself. If alone I made a foolish move, there was none to pay but me, but with others? Good men might die through some error of mine. Yet these were warriors, veteran fighting men who knew the risks as well as I . . . or better.

What would Sir Walter Scott have thought of us? I wondered. Yet those who rode with me were fit men to ride with any of the clansmen of whom he had written. They were men of much the same stripe, driven by many of the same motives.

Those fierce clansmen of Scotland were often driven by pride to actions as foolish as those of my grandfather, and for much the same absurd reasons. I recalled the story of Donald the Hammer who when he saw his son actually working in the fields rushed across the stream intending to kill him to erase the shame.

Reading had done that for me—that even when I disapproved of what my grandfather had done, I could understand him. It made his crimes no less, but left me with a clearer view.

We rode into the morning, but we rode alert for trouble and aware of the tracks we followed, all too plain, all too easy. The problem was, how far would they lead us before laying the trap?

The sun was rising when we came down the narrow trail off the mountain into the San Fernando Valley, a vast waste of sparse grass and prickly pear with a few cattle scattered here and there. In the distance lay the old San Fernando Mission.

They were moving fast, keeping the horses at a trot, following along the base of the mountains.

"They've chosen the place, I'm thinking," Finney suggested. "Some special place to hole up and wait for you."

"They've a full day's start on us," Monte added.

We held to a steady pace, took a short nooning, then pushed on. The trail was rarely used, and from the top of each small rise we could see the tracks several hundred yards in advance.

Short of sundown we saw a trickle of water coming down from some rocks among the oaks and willows. There was grass for the horses and a good place to camp.

Myron Brodie came over after staking his horse. He hunkered down beside the fire. "Notice the tracks back by that big lichen-covered boulder?"

"They've got company."

"Two more," Brodie said. "Probably whoever was in town watching to see if we left, and when. That'll make maybe a dozen men they've got."

"That figures about right."

"And there's five of us?" Monte lifted an eyebrow.

The coffee was coming to a boil. I pushed fuel under it and glanced at him. "The way you talk, I figured you'd be good for two, anyways, and those El Monte boys—"

"No more'n five," Hardin said, straight-faced, "an' do tell 'em not to bunch up. I like to take 'em single and straight up."

There were oaks behind us with a lot of fallen branches. Some of those blue oaks, as they called them, shed branches like leaves, sometimes good-sized limbs. All of which made a place nobody could come through without making noise. Backing up against that with the stream from the spring before me and some rocks lower down, I felt good.

The others scattered out, so if the thieves came at us at night they wouldn't get us all crowded together. Each chose his own bed in his own way and back from the small fire we'd had.

"I'm not sleepy," Brodie suggested, "so you boys roll up and catch some shut-eye. I'm good for two, maybe four hours."

When Monte was bedded down, he spoke out. "They don't care about the horses, like you said. What they want is a battle. They want to kill you."

"They'll let us catch up," I said, "and maybe they will set up a camp that is a trap. They'll corral the horses in plain sight, making them easy to get at, and they will bed down early, then slip off in the dark and wait for us."

"It's better not to have any preconceived ideas," Finney suggested. "There's no telling what they might do."

He was right, of course, but I was trying to foresee. There were many possibilities, and I hoped to consider them all.

From now on our travel must be extremely wary, for an ambush could be mounted at any place. Each night before dropping off to sleep, I tried to work out the possibilities of the following day, but Finney had been right. We must not expect any particular course of action, but be prepared for the unexpected.

Owen Hardin awakened me at what must have been about three o'clock, judging by the position of the Big Dipper, but he was in no mood to sleep. While I tugged on my boots, he sat beside me.

"Finney tells me you spent some time down in the desert with the Cahuillas? He says there's a big pass down there opens right into the desert. How come nobody knows much about it?"

"Folks out here are just not interested. Who cares about the desert? To most people it is just a big desolate place."

"Never figured that way myself. I've prospected some, never had any luck, but there's a-plenty to keep a man interested, old riverbeds and the like. Found some old camps, too, and some Injun writing on the walls."

"Ben Wilson has been through that pass. You know, the man they call Don Benito. He chased a bunch of horse thieves through there at one time, and long ago a Spanish man named Romero went through. I suppose he was the first white man, but you never know."

"Weird country," Hardin said. "I was sixteen when we come through from Texas. Started with a herd of four hundred head of cattle. With the deserts and all, we got through with less'n seventy head.

"My brother Pete, he died out yonder. He was maybe seven year old. Wandered off from camp an' we hunted for him most of two days. We'd about give up. Came back into camp all wore out.

"Ma, she was beside herself. So were the girls. We figured to start huntin' again when morning came, but about midnight the dogs set up an awful barkin' an' me an' Charlie, we rolled out, tired as we was, to see what was happenin'.

"We rushed out, gun in hand, and there was Pete. He was settin' up against a rock wrapped in a great big old coat, and it taken only a look to see he was in bad shape.

"He'd fallen and hurt himself and he'd been snake-bit into the bargain. Odd thing about that, he'd busted his wrist and that was all bound up with a splint and all, and whoever taken care of him had tried to fix that snakebite, but I reckon he was too long gone.

"We taken him into camp and we tried to do for him. He was conscious from time to time when he wasn't delirious, and he told us about fallin', breakin' his wrist, and gettin' snake-bit.

"He said he yelled for us, yelled for help like, and then his mind kind of wandered off. We never could make head or tails of what he was gettin' at. He said he was yellin', scared as could be, when a giant showed up."

I sat up. "A what?"

"A giant. Oh, I know! It sounds crazy. That's what we thought, too. He said that there giant came right down into that hollow in the sand where he was lyin' and fetched him to where there was some shade from rocks, and then the giant set his wrist and worked on that snakebite.

"Well, some little time had gone by. That poison had a chance to get through him. Wonder was he was even alive. The giant picked him up an' carried him to us, then set him down an' left him."

"You never saw him?"

"Never. Nor any sign of him. All we had to go on was what Pete could tell us. He said that was the biggest giant ever, that he carried Pete, a pretty solid chunk of boy, like he was a baby. To get him back to us fast, he climbed over a ridge in the dark that I wouldn't tackle by day, an' him carryin' Pete."

Hardin shrugged. "I never believed in no fairy tales, no giants or the like, but Pete swore it was the truth."

"You say Pete died?"

"Had that poison all through him. The giant or whatever had done all he could and then brought him to us, but there was mighty little left to do."

I slung on my gun belt. "Is that all? Nothing more?"

"One thing. Pete never lied, and he wasn't crazy in the head when he talked of giants. When we found Pete, he was wrapped in a buckskin huntin' coat, fringed and all? Well, that coat was *big*! Pa, who weighed about one-sixty and stood about five-nine, him an' another man close to his size, they put that coat on. Standin' shoulder to shoulder, that coat was a fit for the two of them across the shoulders."

"Have you still got that coat?"

"No, sir. We surely ain't. Ofttimes Pa wished he had it so folks wouldn't think he was lyin', but Ma, she said maybe that poor man needed his coat, so we taken it back and hung it over a rock near where we'd camped."

I walked down to the fire for coffee, and Owen joined me. "Where did that happen?" I asked.

"South of here. Down in the desert about a day's travel this side of Indian Wells."

Finney rode up beside me. We had been in the saddle for several hours, and the tracks had suddenly veered left into the hills. "I rode this way a few years back. There's a valley off yonder, all surrounded by hills, a mighty pretty little hidden valley."

"How little?"

"A few thousand acres, with a spring or two. I've had an idea of moving in there and settling. It's a likely place to hide stolen stock, too."

"Do you suppose that's where they are headed?"

"I'd bet on it."

We rode off the trail and into the oaks. It was very hot. With my bandanna I mopped my face and neck, squinting my eyes against the glare. When I turned in the saddle to speak to Finney, the cantle was too hot to touch.

"Used trail"—I indicated it—"but they didn't go that way."

"There's a ranch down there. They wouldn't go near it." He sidled his horse into deeper shade. "They're surely going on into the valley."

He pointed to some even deeper shade where several oaks had clustered together. "Let's ride over yonder and take a breather. It's too hot."

We walked our horses, occasionally ducking our heads to avoid a low branch. There were several deep pools of shade, and a faint stir of wind was coming off the shoulder of the mountain. Our shirts were soaked, and when the wind touched them, it was mighty cooling.

We stepped down from the saddle and Owen Hardin took his rifle and walked out to the farthest point of shade and hunkered down to keep watch on the trail. We all took our time in sizing up our situation. There was no protection where we were, except for the occasional fallen trees or the tree trunks themselves.

"We'll take it easy," I suggested. "No use killing ourselves or our horses. If you ask me, they're holed up someplace, too."

Monte stretched out on the thin grass and put his hat over his eyes. The water in my water bag was cooled by evaporation, and it tasted good. I took only a swallow.

"After sundown," I said, "we'll move on. Catch some rest." Turning to Brodie, I said, "You want to give Owen a break in about an hour?"

"Sure."

With my back against a big oak, I tilted my head back and closed my eyes, wishing for another breeze through my wet shirt.

Finney was close by. "Couldn't help but hear what Hardin was sayin' last night," he said. "Do you reckon that was your big man from near the palm springs?"

"Isn't likely there'd be two such. Not so close together."

There was silence for a while and then Finney asked, "Are you goin' back that way?"

"Uh-huh. I love that country, Jake, and there's nothing holdin' me in Los Angeles."

"Nothing?" He glanced at me.

I thought of Meghan again. "No, Jake, there's nothing to keep me. I'm going back to the desert. I don't want to have to kill anybody, and there's nothing keeping me, nothing at all."

44

For as long as she could remember, Aunt Elena had been rising at daybreak. She supposed it was her father's influence. Although he had been an *hidalgo* with vast estates in both Spain and Morocco, it had been his custom to ride each morning with the rising sun. Often, as a small girl, she had ridden with him.

Her breakfast was frugal. Habitually she drank one cup of maté, a tea imported from the Argentine, and ate one tortilla and a piece of fruit.

She supervised the house of Don Isidro, although she and her brother had never been close. Each Saturday morning she checked her accounts as she had learned from Miss Nesselrode. She kept a careful record in one small book of what she was doing with her money, and on another page of the book she listed possible investments. She had learned from Miss Nesselrode but now went her own way, made her own plans, and in a time when much was growing and expanding, her small investments accumulated.

Although she went to mass regularly, she did not consider herself a religious woman. She loved the quiet of the church, the voices of the priests who officiated, and the subdued rustling of garments.

Often she took walks along the *zanjas* or under the oaks. She loved the tranquillity of those moments alone. Occasionally she was joined by a young priest, Father Jaime. They were, she suspected, kindred spirits. It was a term she had heard but had never applied to anyone until meeting Father Jaime.

On this morning she had walked alone, and upon returning to the house decided upon another cup of tea. Scarcely had she seated herself when she heard the jingle of spurs. For an instant, caught in the act of pouring, she hesitated, and a flicker of annoyance touched her eyes and mouth. She knew the step, the hard-heeled arrogance.

Don Federico, dressed for riding, came into the room. "Ah, Tía! You rise early?"

"As always."

"I was not aware."

"Of course."

He gave her a sharp glance, but she was replacing the teapot. She did not offer him a cup.

"It will soon be over now." He spoke with satisfaction.

"Is anything ever really over? Do things ever really end? No lingering aftereffects?"

He shrugged. "Johannes Verne has ridden into the desert to recover some stolen horses." His eyes were upon her. "He will not come back. The stain will be erased."

She tasted her tea. "Yes?"

"This time it will be finished."

"Have you talked to Don Isidro? Is he involved?"

He made an impatient gesture. "He grows old! He is too slow to act, and we could not wait! He thinks too much, and sometimes I am afraid he weakens. No matter. I have done it."

"You assume too much. Don Isidro wishes to be consulted."

"He wavers and hesitates. Besides, I know what he wishes done, and am I to sit idly by while this . . . this *peón* lives?"

He turned on her suddenly. "You have never liked me, Tía."

"What is there to like?" she asked mildly.

He flushed and his eyes turned mean. "You shall see! When I inherit—!"

"Ah?"

"Who else? They are gone. Consuelo is gone. Alfredo is gone. Now this other one, he who could never inherit anyway, he will be gone. Who else is there?"

Her shrewd old eyes taunted him. "I shall be here," she said gently.

He made an impatient gesture. "You are a woman. What can you do?"

"I can inherit. What will you do? Kill me, too?"

He stalked across the room, standing with his back to her. "You need not worry. You shall have this place. I shall return to Spain.

"To Spain, do you hear? Who would live in this place when he can live in Madrid? Or Rome. Or Paris. I have thought it all out! I shall live in style! In elegance! Bah! What do I care what you do here? All but this house I shall sell."

"Don Isidro is still alive. Have you plans for him, too?"

He shrugged. "He is old . . . old."

"He is sixty-seven. His father lived to be ninety-five, his grandfather to eighty-nine. Don Isidro may live thirty years more."

Don Federico made an impatient gesture and strolled to the arch, where he could look into the patio, but he made no reply.

"He could live another thirty years, Federico, and you would be an old man then . . . if you live so long."

"You talk too much."

"If I talk, it is to stir some grain of sense in you. Do you not *see?* You dream. You cannot win. You build castles. You cannot defeat Johannes, as you could not defeat his father.

"You wished to marry Consuelo to ensure that you would inherit, but she would not have you. Then she married Zachary Verne."

"A common sailor! A *peón!*"

"A man."

"A *man!* Am I not a man?"

She lifted a shoulder. "Who knows?"

He took a step toward her, his face twisted with fury. "Someday I will—!"

She showed him the small pistol in her sewing bag. "Be careful, Federico. I do not like you very much."

"You talk the fool."

"When your mother died, Don Isidro provided for you, sent you to school, treated you as one of us."

"And I hated you! All of you! Why should you have so much and me nothing?"

"What is so special about you, Federico? Is there any reason why you should have *anything?*"

He brushed it aside. "What is so special about you, then. Or Don Isidro?"

She poured tea into her cup. "Not very much, Federico. Really, not very much. In Spain we are of the nobility, but what is that? It means that we had an ancestor or two who were bold men, energetic men. One fought against the Moors and so became wealthy.

"He was a poor lad who helped a tanner with his hides, and when war came he proved a good man with a sword. He killed a Moor and took his armor, weapons, and horse. He took a gold chain from his neck and a ring from his finger. He captured another Moor, and the man was ransomed, and our ancestor was no longer a poor *peón*, but a young man of wealth.

"He rode his horse to war, and with the money from the ring which he sold, he hired several men-at-arms who followed him. He fought with great strength, and perhaps with great courage, and was made a noble. He married well and his son was a captain in the armada, commanding a warship. He was one of the few to bring his ship back intact. Largely, I think, because he avoided battle and fled to a safe harbor at the first sign of a storm. His grandson was a skillful manager of their estates, and what he inherited, he doubled."

"So?"

"The one who began it all was a peasant. You have nothing, so why not do something yourself? Many of those whom you respect are the sons and daughters of leather-jacketed soldiers."

He did not respond, and she said, "You tried to kill Alfredo on the ship."

"A pity I did not succeed. Nobody wanted him. You cannot tell me that you did. Consuelo made a fuss over him just to show off."

"She loved him. We all did."

He shrugged. "So you say. You all wished to be rid of him, and now he is gone. I see no tears."

She hoped he would go, but he lingered. . . . Why? Her fingers closed on the small pistol butt. He was arrogant, greedy, and completely selfish. For such a one there were no limits, and she was alone but for the girl in the kitchen. Yet she was not afraid. He hated her, and she despised him for all that he had become.

"Take my advice," she suggested, "and leave Johannes alone. You do not know him. He is stronger than his father was, and infinitely more dangerous."

"Bah!"

"You are being foolish, Federico. Don Isidro would give you more land. You have some. Today all is changing, and it is a time to become rich.

"Drop all these foolish thoughts of revenge and hatred. There is money to be made in a growing land. Many of the Californios are already prospering. They have found their place in business, in politics—"

He snorted his disgust. "What do you think I am? A *tradesman*?"

She leaned back in her chair and looked at him. Her fingers held the pistol in the folds of her dress. "I think you are a very conceited, vain man, with empty hands and an empty head. You are not a tradesman. Perhaps you could not be.

"You dress very prettily. You strut. You ride well, so perhaps you could become a vaquero, but if you have other talents, I have not seen them. You are, despite what you seem to believe, no longer a young man by present-day standards. From childhood you seem to have had no other idea than to inherit the wealth of Don Isidro."

"And I shall. I shall have it all. Now that you have shown what you are, and what you think of me, you shall have nothing. Nothing at all!"

For a moment she held the pistol. Suppose she killed him now, here? Would it save Johannes? Or would she simply drag them all through the disgrace of a public trial? For a moment she looked at him, weighing the possibilities. He needed killing, he deserved to be killed. Yet slowly, reluctantly, her fingers relaxed.

"You may go," she said.

He turned sharply around. "What?"

"You may go. I will not kill you now."

"What?" He stared at her. "Kill *me?*"

She lifted the pistol. "I have been considering it, but you are not worth the trouble. But go . . . please go before I change my mind."

He was shocked, yet as his eyes went from her to the pistol and back, he became suddenly aware of how vulnerable he had been.

But *Aunt Elena?* Kill *him?* He looked at her suddenly with a realization that this quiet, strange old woman was not known to him at all. She had seemed a frail shadow hovering somewhere near Don Isidro, someone you passed by, someone you acknowledged, something dim and ghostlike. Now suddenly her voice had changed. There was iron beneath those rustling garments. She could have, might have, killed him.

Abruptly he turned and walked away, and he did not look back. Out on the patio he stopped. Suddenly he shivered. She could have done it. She might have done it.

His mouth was dry with shock. There had been a tone in her voice he had not heard before, and he shivered again. She could have killed him, she might have; the idea appalled him.

He went to his horse, and stopped after gathering up the reins. For a moment he stood there; then he swung into the saddle and turned away. He must be careful. There were enemies everywhere.

But Aunt Elena! It was impossible!

*   *   *

Tía Elena finished her tea and then went to her room. Now, more than ever, she was sure she was doing the right thing, but she should consult the *alcalde*, or perhaps one of those American attorneys. Miss Nesselrode had showed her what a woman could do, and other Californio women were in business and doing well.

Coolly, carefully, she considered what she was doing and its consequences. She had watched Federico for many years and knew the kind of man he was. She also knew their conversation would not deter him in any way and might even act as a spur.

With the desertion of Don Isidro's loyal workers and the subsequent weakening of Don Isidro's position, Federico had become more assertive, more confident, and he had, to all intents and purposes, taken command. Her brother had withdrawn more and more, eaten by his hatred.

She must move a little faster now, even at the risk of being discovered. Of the properties in Spain, she knew little, although when the time came she must learn more of them. They were her brother's concern, and when she had left Spain she had no reason to interest herself in them. Of the house in town and the ranch, whatever other property there was—these were the focus of her attention.

"Somehow," she whispered to herself, "I must save them. I must protect the young ones."

Federico had stated his intentions clearly. Of his intentions there was no doubt. For Consuelo she could do nothing. Consuelo was gone, but for . . . She would see.

At the same time, she must be careful. Now she had presented herself as an antagonist. Federico recognized her as an enemy, and he would not hesitate to do what he felt needed to be done; only now he would be cautious.

One thing more remained to be done. She must find the woman.

But how to find a woman gone these forty years or more? Where to look?

She would be dead by now, or gone to Mexico, or taken by Indians. In all those years, there had been no word.

She had been a strange woman, a woman alone in the world. Where would such a one go? What would she do? Elena remembered that night, a stormy night when the rain came down in torrents and the wind blew. It had been one of the worst storms ever known along the Pacific coast of California.

A man had come with two black horses, a man whose face she never saw, and she herself had opened the door that the woman might leave. She, with little Consuelo at her side.

She had seen the horses plunging in the rain, their coats streaming with it, their eyes rolling, their teeth gnashing at the bits. Lightning had flashed, and in a roll of thunder the woman had climbed into the saddle with her bundle, and the horses had raced away, their iron shoes striking fire from the pavement.

Gone! But where? And nothing . . . nothing left after all those years? No sight, no sound, no word.

Vanished. . . .

45

Miss Nesselrode unlocked the book shop only just after daybreak. The street outside was deserted. She had seen a lone horseman riding along Aliso Street, and a man had been sweeping the boardwalk in front of a store on Main Street.

Half the night she had lain awake worrying about Johannes, yet explaining to herself there was no need to worry. Johannes was born to the wilderness. He knew it and was at home there. He had lived with Indians; he had survived several ordeals in the mountains and had shown himself capable of handling difficult situations.

Scarcely was she seated at her desk when the door opened and Meghan burst in. "Where is he?"

"You quarreled with him?"

"Well . . . I guess. Maybe it could be called that. Don Federico had called on me, and Johannes did not like it."

"Did you expect him to?"

She avoided that. "Where is he?"

"He has gone to the mountains, following some horses that were stolen from us. I have no idea when he will be back."

Meghan sat down, eyes wide. "Stolen horses? But he might be killed!"

"He is aware of that. He is also aware the horses were stolen to lead him into a trap. Those who stole the horses hoped he would follow. They will be waiting."

"But why, then? Why would he go, knowing it was a trap?"

"He caught those horses, helped to break them. They were to be the beginning of a horse ranch for him. I am sure he can handle the situation." Even as she spoke the words, she was praying she was right. "Jacob is with him. There are others."

"But who would do such a thing? Was it Don Isidro?"

"Not this time," Miss Nesselrode replied coolly. "It was Don Federico, or so we believe."

"That's absurd! Why should he do such a thing? Oh, I know Johannes believes Don Federico tried to kill him once, but—"

"And you do not?"

"Of course not! Federico is a gentleman! And why should he do such a thing?"

"You should know. It was your father who warned Johannes of what he might expect."

"My father does not know Federico! He has never even *met* him!"

"Well, we shall see." Miss Nesselrode pushed her mail to one side, folding her hands before her. "Where is Don Federico now? Do you have any idea?"

How should she know? He had not said when he would call.

"How could Johannes leave like that? He did not even say good-bye!"

"He left very quickly. And if you quarreled—"

"It was not really a quarrel! He did seem upset when I told him Federico had been calling, but I did not think it mattered that much."

"He felt betrayed. I know he did. It is very hard, Meghan, but you must decide where your loyalties lie. Hannes *knows* Federico tried to have him killed. Not once, but several times. When Don Isidro was leaving him in the desert, Don Federico wanted to kill Johannes and then leave him."

"I do not believe that. He was only a small boy then. He cannot remember."

"He does remember. Also, where is Don Federico now? I believe he has gone into the desert to make sure of his trap."

Meghan stood up. "That's a hateful thing to say! I don't believe it!"

"Your father did. He warned Johannes."

"I must find him."

"Meghan, no one could find him. Perhaps Mr. Kelso, who works for me. He will be trailing those stolen horses and riding very fast. It will be in wild, wild country."

"I didn't think he'd go off like that. I thought I'd be seeing him again. I—"

"Meghan, you must try to understand. From his earliest memory Johannes has known his life was in danger, that his own grandfather wanted him dead. He saw his father killed, and he himself was carried off and left to die. Whether you believe it or not, he is sure Don Federico was one of those who abandoned him.

"He seems relatively untouched by all this, but that isn't the case. He has no waking moment when he can feel safe, and he has become exceptionally wary as a result. I am sure he is, or was, in love with you, but suddenly he discovered that even that haven was no longer secure, and he discovered that you, whom he loved, were welcoming an enemy.

"Now he has gone into the desert, and if you have learned anything about him at all, you must know he has an affinity for the desert and it for him."

"He has talked of it."

"The first happiness his parents knew together was in the desert. Even in flight they found a peace there, and a quiet. Johannes has experienced the desert himself. He has lived with Indians, and where others might feel lost and terribly alone, he feels at home."

"What are you saying?"

Miss Nesselrode rested her hands on the desk. "What I am saying is that even if he survives, he may never come back."

"What? You mean he might *stay* out there?"

"That is exactly what I mean. Human relationships are often fragile, they need to be nurtured until they can put down roots, and Johannes is one of the most complete human beings I have known. He has understanding, compassion, and strength. He possesses an inner tranquillity and poise such as no one I have ever known, with the exception of a Buddhist monk I met in crossing Mongolia as a girl.

"What you must understand is that Johannes does not *need* anyone."

"Then what chance would there be for me?"

"I said he did not need anyone. I did not say that he did not want someone. He told me once that happiness was born a twin, that it must be shared. He had the example of his mother and father, who found happiness in each other no matter whatever else they discovered.

"You and Johannes were just finding each other. Each of you, I think, was reaching out. Johannes, I think, with less confidence than you. You are a beautiful girl. People come to you. Your finding of people has been natural, easy, without strain. You have never had to work at it.

"Johannes has lived in many towns. He has met people, but before liking or understanding developed, he had to move away. Close relationships are strange to him. He has no foundation of security on which to build. The result is that through sheer loneliness he has had to become more secure within himself. He has learned to live alone, to be alone."

"You have known him a long time?"

"Longer than anyone here. Only Mr. Kelso and Jacob Finney have known him as long, and they did not live in the wagon with him as I did."

Meghan was quiet, and Miss Nesselrode gathered her papers together and began checking her correspondence, some of which had come by sea and some overland from the States. "I guess I do not know him at all," Meghan said at last. "I thought—"

"That he was like the others? He is not. He is vastly more complicated and much more simple. He has read more than anyone I know, but what is more important, he thinks.

"He thinks about what he has read, about what he has seen, and about what he has learned."

For a time they sat silent, Miss Nesselrode working over her correspondence, checking notes on future business dealings and projected plans. She missed Jacob Finney. Kelso was good but not as astute. He carried out her orders to perfection, but he was less aware of the nuances of business and less aware of indications of weakness or strength on the part of those with whom she dealt.

"I do not know him either." She spoke suddenly. "I think Elena is the wisest of us; she does not pretend to understand him, nor wish to. She simply loves him. First, she loved him because he was Consuelo's son; now she loves him for himself. She would die for him. I know that, for she has risked much, risked all, in fact."

"I must find him!"

"It is impossible. I do not know where he has gone, nor does anyone else. He is following a trail left by thieves, wherever it takes him.

"He lost his great black horse, too. The one he has been hoping to ride. When the thieves stole the other horses, the stallion escaped. It has run away into the hills, nobody knows where."

"Why did he have to go? Why did he not at least tell me!"

Now there were people on the streets. Horsemen were riding by, a wagon or two, and a *carreta*.

"He is the son I never had," Miss Nesselrode said suddenly. "I scarcely knew his father, but there was an affinity between us, an understanding, if you will. And with Johannes also."

"His father was very ill?"

"He was dying, and he knew it. He was desperately worried about Johannes, so much so that he risked his life to find a home for him. I believe he would cheerfully have died if he could have been sure Johannes was cared for. He need not have worried, for the Indians accepted him as one of their own."

"I wish he had not gone."

Wind stirred dust in the street, and a man walked down to the door and stood there, not looking in. It was Alexis Murchison.

For a moment he looked around; then, turning quickly, he lifted the latch and stepped in. A quick glance to where Meghan sat brought an irritated frown to his face.

"Ma'am? May we speak alone for a moment?"

"Whatever you have to say, sir, you can say here. I can think of no reason why we should be alone."

"I am from Russia!"

"Of course. And so?"

"We wish you to come home. We want you to come back to Russia. To your mother country."

"Russia is no longer my home. And the czar sent me to Siberia."

"That is all forgotten. You are wanted at home."

"No doubt. What would it be this time? Siberia again?"

"Please! I can arrange transportation. You would see your family again."

"I have no family. They died in Siberia. This is my home, and here I shall stay."

"Please, I have been sent to see that you return. I am not alone in this. Your country wishes you back."

"You are wasting your time."

Murchison was silent, glancing at Meghan; then he said quietly, "My advice would be to come now and come willingly. We will give you a few days to settle your business here, whatever it amounts to, and then you must go. Do not make us go to your government."

She smiled. "Mr. Murchison, you amuse me. By all means, go to my government. Go to any official you wish. I suggest it. In fact, I entreat you, please go to them. Tell them what you wish.

"I can think of no reason why anyone in Russia would want me back unless my presence, and perhaps a trial, would be embarrassing to someone, but I have no intention of returning, nor is there any way you can force me to return. You may know your government, sir. You do not know ours."

"I have been sent to get you. I cannot return without you."

She smiled again. "Then why don't you stay? Why go back at all?"

His lips tightened. "Madam, I am an official. My duty—"

"You are not an official here, Mr. Murchison. Over here I think we would call you a bounty hunter." She got to her feet. "Will you leave now?"

"And if I do not?"

She smiled again, amused. "Mr. Murchison, I need only step to that door and call out. There would be a dozen men here within the minute. They might simply rough you up, but they might shoot you or even hang you."

He was coldly furious. He stared at her; then slowly he moved toward the door. "I shall go, but I shall begin the proper steps. You shall see."

When he had gone, Meghan stood up, her face pale. "How can you be so strong? I would have been frightened."

"Once, I also would have been frightened. It is so no longer. I have friends. My advice to you, Meghan: make friends. Wherever you are, make friends."

"You have seen the last of him, I think."

"No, I have not. He will go to our officials, I believe, and he will get nowhere. Then he will try force. I know them. It is their way. It has always been their way.

"A thing to remember, Meghan: governments may change, but a people do not, nor does their basic thinking change. My people, the Russians, have always had a suspicious government. The Russian government has never trusted its people—and they have always been suspicious of outside influences. This is not a new thing, but it is a way of life for them. The czars have always ruled with cruelty and repression, no matter what kind of government they have, that will remain the same."

"I shall go now. If you hear of Johannes, if you hear anything, will you tell me, please?"

"I shall."

Miss Nesselrode hesitated and then said, "Your father's friend . . . Yacub Khan? I believe I shall ask him to come to your house and stay there while your father is gone. Do you mind?"

46

The oaks were islands of blackness in the pale moonlight. We had made coffee and eaten jerky and then we had left our fire behind and ridden about two miles before camping on a small bench among the scattered oaks.

It was a good place. Below us the long hill sloped away to the trail, all white and empty in the stillness. The slope above us was steep and rocky, impossible for riders and not easy for men on foot, who would be sure to set a stone rolling.

As usual we had scattered, not bunching together but bedding down in our separate areas of darkness under the trees. Several of the oaks had fallen, others had shed massive limbs, and we had chosen a spot where these could make easy breastworks in case of attack. Our field of fire was excellent.

It was a dry camp, but our canteens were full and at the foot of the long slope there was a stream. Further along, the canyon grew narrow and the walls too steep for a horse. The tracks we left to ride up to our camp were fresh. Our stolen horses were not far ahead.

"They won't go much further," Finney suggested. "We're already a whole lot farther out than I expected."

That thought was a worry to us all. We were many days' ride from Los Angeles and there'd been no need to lead us so far that we could think of. An hour out of Los Angeles was wild country in almost any direction but the seacoast.

Was it our alertness? That could be it. Maybe they were just waiting until we grew careless.

We took off our boots and our gun belts but we kept both close at hand. Wherever I rode I carried a pair of moccasins with me. They were light of weight and took up no space to speak of, and they were handy in the woods or at night. When in wild country I often slept with them on in case I had to move out fast. I pulled them on, then lay down with a six-shooter close to my hand.

The moonlight made black-lace patterns of the leaves against the sky. Sleep never came easy for me on moonlight nights in the open. No one is entirely free of atavistic memories left in the subconscious from primitive times, when men had to fear not only others of their kind but wild animals as well. I lay awake, resting, yet alert. Wind rustled the leaves, then died away. One of the horses stamped a hoof. I put my hand out in the darkness and touched the butt of my gun.

Then I heard the sound—a faint beating of horses' hooves against the turf. Rising on an elbow, I looked down toward the trail that followed the creek.

Three riders, black against the pale grass.

They drew up at the stream, watering the horses. A faint rustling from nearby told me at least one of my crowd was also listening. The men by the stream were talking, but they were a good hundred yards away and we could hear nothing but a distant muttering. Then they mounted again and rode away.

"Three of them," Monte McCalla said. "That means three more to deal with."

"Get some sleep," I suggested. "Tomorrow will be soon enough."

Somebody chuckled, blankets rustled, and then there was silence again.

Three men, traveling late and traveling fast. It was unlikely they were not involved. To be traveling this late meant they were expecting to be someplace at an appointed time or were close enough to someplace they knew to keep riding.

Lying on my back, staring up into the lacework of leaves, I considered the situation. A trap was being laid, probably no more than an hour's ride, for I doubted they would ride farther in the night. Their horses would be tired as it was.

So then? Somebody wished to be in at the kill? Don Isidro? It was a possibility, but fine a horseman as he was, I doubted if he would ride half the night to get anywhere. Don Federico was another matter.

Until Captain Laurel warned me, the idea that I might be wanted out of the way because I was a possible heir had not occurred to me. But with the known negligence of some of the older Californios insofar as business was concerned, it was possible Don Isidro had made no will. He was growing old, and Don Federico would wish to inherit, so he had a very good motive aside from hatred for wishing to be rid of me.

Had he only realized how little I cared! The idea of inheriting had never entered my mind, and I could not care less. Great wealth had never been one of my ambitions. It was more important for me to become a good human being, and to learn, for there was so much to learn, from the Cahuillas, from the desert and mountains, from books, and from the people around me.

There was also the mystery of Tahquitz, a mystery that haunted me and was never far from my thoughts. Who or what was this strange creature who lived in the night? Who read the books I read, who created that beautiful floor, who left that gigantic footprint? Did he truly live in a cave somewhere atop the San Jacinto Mountains?

When the horses are recovered, I must ride back to the palm canyon where the hot springs are, back to my lonely house near the mountains. I must take books with me to replace those he must have read.

When I awakened, a small fire was burning from smokeless wood, and the coffee was on. I sat up, pulled off my moccasins, and tugged on my boots. Monte was at the fire and Myron Brodie had taken the horses down to the creek for water.

"Quiet," Finney said, sitting up, running his fingers through his thinning hair.

"It will be today," I said.

Owen Hardin stood up, slinging on his gun belt. "I think so," he said.

Squatting by the fire, I warmed my hands on the cup. Nights in the desert or near it were always cold. Uneasily I studied the rim of the hill above us, studied the scattered oaks, patches of prickly pear, and the rock outcroppings.

"I don't like it," Finney said. "It doesn't feel right. What will we do if that trail goes up the canyon?"

I had been thinking of that. "Tough," I said. "It leaves us wide open to anybody up on those slopes with a rifle. They can get us going and coming."

"We can wait," Monte said. "We can just set an' make them come to us. We can outwait them."

The coffee tasted good. I chewed on a piece of jerky. The morning was bright and clear. The sun was not up yet, but the bits of mist were fading away under the trees. A tuft of redbud pushed its way out of the brush near the creek.

Finishing my coffee, I stood up and threw the dregs on the ground. "Take your time," I said. "I'm going to shave."

"Shave?" Brodie asked, swinging down from his horse.

"I like Monte's idea. Let's let them wonder what we're going to do. You boys do what you want, just stay close. They are expecting us, so let's give them a chance to worry about us."

There was a clump of willows and several large cottonwoods on the creek, and I went down to them with my rifle, scouted the patch thoroughly, then leaned my rifle against a tree and propped a small mirror in the fork of the tree.

The water was not warm, but I'd shaved under worse conditions. As I shaved, I listened, but could detect none but the usual, natural sounds. It was quiet but for an occasional gurgle from the stream or bird sounds in the willows.

Squatting by the stream to rinse off my razor, I considered what lay ahead. I wanted my horses. I had worked hard to get them, as had a lot of others, and we had worked to break them. Given a chance, many of them would go back to the wild, and this was their country, and this was, if he had the chance, where my stallion would come.

Finding a fallen log from which there was a good view of the canyon slopes ahead of us, I sat down with my rifle beside me and watched the hills, studying them with care. There was, or seemed to be, a dim trail along the side of the ridge above the canyon. I looked away, then looked again. Yes . . . it was a trail. A game trail or an Indian trail. Did the horse thieves know of it?

Carefully I studied the ridge for landmarks, knowing that from different angles the view can be very different. When I returned to camp I studied the ridge. The trail was no longer visible.

Finney had made coffee, and I collected a cup of it and sat down on a log. "Maybe," I said to him, "just maybe . . ."

As they gathered around, I explained what I'd found. "In another light or from another angle, I'd never have seen it. My guess is that it's an old Indian trail, and I'm also guessing they don't know about it."

"Where does it go? Maybe it angles away from where they are?"

"Look, Indians liked to travel high country when they could, but they also need water. I figure that outfit have camped on water, and I'd make a small bet that trail branches off to water. It's a chance, a wild chance."

"Suits me," McCalla said. "I sure don't like riding up the bottom of that canyon with them settin' there waitin' for us."

Monte and Owen Hardin went back down to the creek with me and I found the exact spot where I'd been sitting when I spotted that trail. It took some time for them to locate it.

"Then it won't be today, like I promised," I said. "We'll try it at daylight."

Owen Hardin studied the trail. "I've an idea," he said, "and I think I'll scout the country to see where that trail starts. At least, where we can find it."

When he was gone, we napped, drank coffee, and loafed the sultry, lazy afternoon through. Each of us knew what was coming tomorrow, each of us was aware that when the shooting starts all men are vulnerable. Bullets are not selective, but we were hard men, reared to a hard school.

Owen came in just before dark. "Found it!" He stepped down from his horse, smiling. "Those Injuns, they always knew what they were doin'! That trail takes off from a bit of a branch canyon back yonder where there's trees an' brush. Doesn't look like anybody has been there in years! If I hadn't known about where to look, I'd never have found it, takes off from behind a tree, like."

He squatted on his heels by the dying fire and filled a cup from the blackened pot. His shirt was sweat-stained and had a fresh tear from the brush.

"Thanks, Owen. You've saved us a lot of hunting."

"You'd never find it in the dark," he agreed, "but we'll have to ride easy. Somebody has been comin' down the canyon tryin' to throw a loop on what we're about."

He drank his coffee, then stretched out under his tree and was asleep in minutes. Moving over to the fire, I dowsed the coals with dust and the last of the coffee and set the pot in the shade to cool off. Then I backed up to my own tree and checked both pistols and my rifle.

Brodie was on watch, shaded by a low-growing juniper that had an enormous trunk and a wide spread of branches. It was deep shade and he had a view for a half-mile of the canyon.

Owen was dozing, but suddenly his eyes opened. "Forgot to tell you. I seen some tracks down yonder."

Jacob Finney opened his eyes, listening. I spun the cylinder on my gun and then reloaded it.

"Tracks?"

"Well, I can't be sure. I only seen them a couple of times, and these weren't complete tracks. I mean, I saw only a piece of them, here and there."

"Well?"

"Looked to me like that black stallion's tracks. The one that got away."

Here. . . . But why not? This was home to him, this part of his old range.

Finney sat up. "I'd of bet on it. Given a chance, a horse will always go back to where he comes from. They are homebodies, horses are."

He looked over at me. "I never told you what Ramón said. He said that black was a ghost horse, whatever that means. Kind of a ha'nt, like. He warned me nobody could ride him 'less he wants to be ridden."

"Sounded like some of the stories I've heard of that pacing white stallion from the Plains country. He told me never to try to ride him, that the stallion would kill anybody he didn't want on his back."

"Superstition," Hardin said. "Injuns got stories about everything. Up where I come from in the Nova Scotia country, their stories are all about somebody or something called Glooscap."

"Did Ramón say anything about me riding him?" I asked.

Finney took up his hat and wiped the sweatband. He put it on his head and tugged it into place.

"He surely did. He said he thought that horse wanted you to ride him. He said he thought that horse wanted to take you somewhere."

47

Under a starlit sky we rode to find our trail. The air was cool, a hoof clicked on stone, saddles creaked, brush fingered our clothing. It was a steep scramble along a bare slope after we escaped the brush of the river bottom.

Single file we rode along a vague whitish streak through sparse grass still gray with night. No horse had been here, nor did we see track of any other animal. Haunted by a warning from our senses, we paused to listen, heard nothing, and rode on.

Scattered oaks were islands of blackness on the rolling gray sea of the hills. At last we topped out on a narrow ridge, and on my left there was a loose pile of stones. Swinging down, I picked a fist-sized stone from the earth nearby and threw it on the pile.

"What's that for?" Hardin asked.

"The Old Ones did it. Offering to the god of the trail."

"D'you believe in that stuff?"

"I like doing it." For a moment I stood beside my horse, my hands on the saddle. "I have a feeling for them. The old gods, I mean. It must be hard for them, with no worshipers left, their lands invaded by strangers who don't know their ways, or care."

"Throw one on for me," Hardin suggested. "We'll need all the help we can get."

We would be five against at least twelve going against them on ground of their own choosing.

I thought of them then, those four young men who rode with me, four young men carved from the same oak of trouble seasoned by the same winds, yet each as different as could be. They rode forth to battle without a flag except that flown by their own courage, loyal to the last fiber of their being, and strong with the knowledge that if men are to survive upon the earth there must be law, and there must be justice, and all men must stand together against those who would strike at the roots of what men have so carefully built.

It is all very well to say that man is only a casual whim in a mindless universe, that he, too, will pass. We understand that, but disregard it, as we must. Man to himself is the All, the sum and the total. However much he may seem a fragment, a chance object, a bit of flotsam on the waves of time, he is to himself the beginning and the end. And this is just. This is how it must be for him to survive.

Man must deal with himself. It is his reality he must face each morning when he rises. It is his world with which he must deal. Perhaps his end is only years away, or even months, yet he cannot more than acknowledge that, for it is the now with which he must deal, unless like a spoiled child he is to fall on his face and beat his fists against the earth. He must *be*, he must move, he must create.

If man is to vanish from the earth, let him vanish in the moment of creation, when he is creating something new, opening a path to the tomorrow he may never see. It is man's nature to reach out, to grasp for the tangible on the way to the intangible.

We have hedged ourselves round with law, for we know that if man is to survive it must be through cooperative effort.

We walked our horses down a steep, grassy, rock-stewn hill, across a narrow gully, and were angling along the slope opposite. At times the trail faded or vanished utterly, and once when we lost it, Monte spotted, a hundred yards down a gully, one rock placed atop another. We chose that way and found the trail again. The rocks as we passed were, I saw, coated with the desert varnish of many years. Suddenly my horse pricked his ears and looked to the north, nostrils flaring. I spoke warningly, sharply, and my horse tossed his head, irritated with me.

It was growing light now. We waited, listening, catching a faint smell of wood smoke, then a clink of metal against metal.

"Close," Brodie whispered. "Only a couple of hundred yards or less."

The trail we followed branched suddenly, as I had foreseen, and one branch dropped sharply down into a shaded hollow that opened into the wider canyon. Sunlight sparkled on the creek there. Each of us had drawn his rifle; we looked one to the other.

We looked down into the hollow through the trees and brush, down a steep trail made by men on moccasined feet for other moccasined feet. There was no easy way down, and from the moment we started there would be a trickle of rocks and gravel falling, warning them.

Dismounting, I walked to the rim and looked down. A horse could make it, but we could not. We'd be shot out of our saddles before we got halfway down. Slowly my eyes searched for a way.

A man on foot, if he was careful. A faint sound of voices came, a laugh; they were right below us. Yet that one man with a rifle . . . Maybe he could pin them down, scatter them, leave time for the riders to make it.

There were oaks along the steep mountainside. A man would have to be careful to start no pebbles rolling. Even one might cause a man to look up, and the descending man would be pinned against the slope, an easy target.

Studying the ground, I saw my way. Yet if the others did not manage it, I'd be trapped. Yet the horses stolen were my horses, and a trap, if such it was, was set for me. I walked back to my horse, got out my moccasins, and taking off my boots, slung them to the saddle horn. Then I donned the moccasins.

"What are you thinkin' of?" Monte asked.

"One man can make it. I'll pin them down, then you boys come."

Jacob Finney spat. "You let me go, boy. I'm an old hand at this game."

My eyes picked out a flash of sorrel from among the leaves. Moving over a bit, I could see the horses, all neatly gathered behind a makeshift gate in a small box canyon. There seemed to be somewhat of an obstruction further along the canyon, an improvised brush-and-timber fence across the upper end of the corral.

If a man could . . .

"Jacob?" I pointed. "If a man could get down there and open that gate—"

"He could stampede those horses right through their camp and down the canyon," Brodie interrupted.

"And we'd have our horses," Hardin accepted the idea.

Monte McCalla had ridden off along the ridge. Now he returned. "Yonder," he pointed, "there looks to be a way down to the upper canyon. I figure we can make it down a-horseback. It's a steep slope, but away from their camp, and it doesn't look to be as steep as this."

"Take my horse with you," I suggested. "I'll take this route down." Pausing, I added, "We all know what this is going to be like. If anybody gets separated, go back to town. If we shake the horses loose, get away with them."

Monte caught up the reins of my horse. "Let's go," he suggested, and they rode off along the ridge and I was alone.

For a moment I stood there in the lemon light of early morning. The sky was slightly overcast. It was still cool, and I looked around, inhaling very deep. The air was fresh, and I filled my lungs with it, then walked to a big old blue oak and stood beside it, looking down the way I must go. Taking my rifle in my right hand, I started down the hill, taking my time, putting each foot down with care, lifting it with equal care.

If they found a way down, it would take them a while to get to the corral gate, which was out of sight of the camp below but had been a convenient place to hold the stolen horses.

Twelve or more men, eager to kill me, and for a minute or two I'd be facing them alone. Supposing that route Monte had found proved impossible? It could. . . . Many a time I'd seen an apparently easy way down end in a fifty-foot drop with no way around. If that happened, I'd have something to sweat about.

My moccasin came down on gray, dusty earth and pine needles. These were the needles of the Digger pine, eight to ten inches in length. Step by step I worked my way down for fifty feet, then crouched by the trunk of an oak to study the way I should take.

Three men were loafing about a small fire. A short distance away, two more were playing cards on a blanket. All were armed, all had rifles close by. There was a pot of coffee on the fire. There was no way I was going to get down there without getting my head blown off. What the hell was I doing here, anyway?

Where were the other men? I had figured on at least another five. There might be a dozen more, or there might be no more.

The trouble with a situation like this was that a man kept going forward until there was no turning back.

From where I now waited their camp was about a hundred yards away, more than fifty yards of it almost straight down. Lowering one knee to the earth, I studied the route I'd have to take, then moved quickly to another vantage point behind part of a huge old oak that had broken off about five feet above the ground and lay where it had fallen.

The concealment was better, I was closer, and there was some cover from the thick trunk of the remaining stump as well as the fallen part and its branches.

A stone trickled past me. Startled, I looked up, half-turning to see a Mexican in a big sombrero and a serape aiming a rifle at me.

In half-turning I had thrown myself off-balance, and I just let go and fell. The rifle above blasted, and whipping over on my left elbow, I fired my rifle like a pistol. He was looming above me, not more than thirty feet away, and I could scarcely miss.

My bullet caught him in the brisket and he fell toward me. Twisting to one side, I let him fall, then whipped around to face the camp.

From the canyon I heard yells and shots, and then I was shooting into the camp. One man near the fire had leaped up, and my bullet spun him around. Twisting position, I fired at one of the card-players. I missed and so did he; then I triggered another shot and he fell back, blood turning his pants leg crimson.

Leaping up, I plunged down the slope toward the camp. A bullet hit a tree near me and spat bark into my face. I hit level ground and went into the camp firing. These men had, after all, prepared a trap to kill me.

There was a wild yell from the main canyon, and horses went streaming past. A man leaped up to try to head them off, and I burned him with a shot that spun him around and made him dive for cover. Horsemen went streaking by, there were more shots from down canyon, and I glanced quickly around.

Two men were on the ground. Another was gripping his leg and trying to stop the flow of blood. I ran down the canyon, looking for a horse.

Men were coming up the canyon from some post below, and turning, I ran up the canyon, hoping for a horse, any kind of a horse. There were none.

Rounding the bend, I came on a Mexican down and dead, and a little beyond him, Brodie.

A glance was all I needed. Brodie was dead, too. I could hear men coming, and I ran up canyon, holding to the soft sand to make no sound. Seeing a crevice in the wall, I darted into it, pausing to catch my breath, and then went scrambling over the rocks, trying to get higher, to escape the canyon.

Brodie gone! He was a good man, a damned good man.

I paused again to catch my breath. Did they know I was still around, and afoot? If they did, they could soon round me up. I checked my rifle and my cartridge belt. Then I climbed on, up the canyon, keeping to whatever cover was available. My one desire was to get away, to find a horse.

Brodie gone . . . and what of the others? What of my old friend Jacob? He whom I had known since boyhood, who had taught me so much, who had been and still was my friend? The place where I was climbing was, during hard rains, a steep runoff for water. Soon I would top out on the ridge. Would some of them be waiting?

Under some trees near the crest of the ridge I studied the situation. I had been seen, no doubt recognized. The man with the wounded leg, if he did not bleed to death, would have recognized me. They would know I was here and afoot.

They would come seeking me. The horses they could afford to lose, but I was the game they had planned to hunt down and kill.

Turning to the trail, I glanced at it, disappearing among the rocks, appearing on the grass beyond. The canyon would be a trap from which there was small chance of escape. The bald hills where I now was offered no place to hide. There would be several mounted men hunting me, and I was on foot. What I needed was a change of scene. I started to run.

Often, when living with the Cahuillas, I had run with Francisco or others, run mile upon mile in all sorts of weather, over all kinds of terrain. Automatically I used every device for hiding my trail, leaping from rock to rock, running along occasional fallen logs, but moving swiftly. The ancient trail had once gone somewhere, and now I hoped it would take me away, take me to a place where I could hide.

Jacob, Monte, and Hardin had the horses and would drive them back to Los Angeles or at least to a rancho where they could be held for us. They might come hunting me, but it would be better for them if they did not.

Ancient men had run this trail, to trade, to visit, to attend places of worship; in war and in fear they had run where my feet now ran. Once, topping a razor-backed ridge, I paused to throw a rock on the pile. Only minutes remained to me, only minutes until they would be upon my trail, mounted and hunting.

Slowing to a walk, I looked back. Nothing yet. Miss Nesselrode, Aunt Elena, Meghan . . . I thought of them. They were my family. Yes, Meghan, too.

I had loved her. I still did.

Turning, I ran on into the bright crystal morning; I ran on into the face of the rising sun.

Behind me, the pound of hooves. . . .

48

Was this to be the end? Here in this high, rocky country above the desert? Had all my dreams and plans come only to this? To die here, alone, killed by my enemies? Had all the sacrifice of my father and mother brought me only to this?

Yet I fled not in fear but to find a better place from which to fight. The odds were great against me—how great, I did not know. Many times before, I had run with my friends, the desert Indians. My breath came evenly and strong; the rifle was heavy, but I would need it.

A mile, another mile. Thicker, taller, rougher rocks, great crags jutting out, trails that dipped between them. Topping out on a great ridge among some rocks, I glanced back and saw them coming, single file, issuing from a narrow place. I counted six, and more followed behind.

"You want a chase," I said aloud, "I'll lead you one."

Running with an easy stride, I knew I could go on for miles. I also knew that although a horse was faster, a man could run a horse to death over a distance. Deliberately I turned to a route that would keep me parallel to the old track I'd been following, but one that led into much rougher terrain.

Barren crags loomed above the way I chose to go, and there were no more oaks, but here and there ancient cedars and patches of cholla cactus. We were nearing the desert now, the harsh Mohave that lay off to the south, mile upon mile of the Mohave, until it merged with the Colorado desert.

Now the coolness of early morning was gone and the heat was coming. Turning sharply to the right, I went down a steep slope among the cacti, crossed a wash, following it through a natural gate in the rocks, and then found what I sought, a place among the rocks and a gnarled old cedar.

There was more than expected, for in a shallow pool scarcely an inch deep and a foot across was water left from a recent rain. I wet my lips, then sucked some up as I waited.

With my rifle trained on the natural rock gate, I heard them coming, slowing a little, but coming on. A rider loomed in the opening, and I squeezed off my shot.

My intent was not to kill, nor was it mercy that guided my bullet, but to give them a man to care for, a wounded man who would be a trouble to them.

He was a good three hundred yards off when he came through the opening, and I shot for his shoulder. His body jerked with the bullet's impact and he lurched in the saddle. I put a second shot through the opening for good measure, then went down the rocks behind me and ran off down the slope, weaving among the trees.

They were not within view of me now, for the slope fell away and they must come forward a good hundred yards to have a view of the mountainside. Unexpectedly I came upon a trail, a companion or perhaps even an extension to that which I had followed earlier.

I hesitated a moment. It led into the desert, and I had no canteen, nor, I was sure, did they. Yet I was but one, needing little water, and they were many.

Would the wounded man be sent back alone? Or would he try to keep up with them?

The dim track I followed led along the mountainside, dropping slowly down, yet occasionally climbing. My gait slowed to a walk. Several times I paused for brief rests, once sitting down to study the ridge above me for a way down if they chose to hold to high ground.

Also, I tried to study the desert into which I was going. At all costs, I must keep to cover or concealment. There were places where runoff from the mountains had cut deeply into the desert; at other places there were shallow washes that still offered some slight shelter behind their banks.

There would be men among them who knew the desert, some who knew the country better than I, although not many of the Californios ventured into the desert regions.

Why should they? California offered all they needed, and there was no reason to come into these wilderness areas. Far into the desert I could see other mountains, bare ridges pushed up through the sand. There were springs and water holes in the desert if one knew where to find them, and I had learned from my friends the Cahuillas where they were likely to be. In the barest of rocky ridges there were often natural tanks that collected rainwater. Often in sheltered places they kept the water shaded and cool. Those tanks often held thousands of gallons. To find them was not easy, yet they were often there.

Rising, I moved on along the slope. Glancing back again, I saw them cresting the ridge far behind and above me. They were scattering out now, with an idea of cutting me off from the mountains, of herding me into the desert.

It was noon by the time I reached the desert's edge. The sky was clear and blue. It was very hot.

The men would be suffering less than I, their horses more, yet now they were thinking of what lay before them. The dim track I followed disappeared, appeared again, vanished again, but its direction was plain. It led into the desert, and those who made that trail would have needed water as much as I. Of course—and this I knew from the Indians—the climate had changed, grown drier over the centuries.

Pausing beside some rocks fallen from the higher ridges, I glanced back. They were gaining on me, closing in.

I was tired now. I needed rest but could get along without it. They had a man's hatred to drive them; I had my wish to survive.

Again I paused and looked back, measuring the distance and their strength. Suddenly I smiled. They were coming into the desert. They were mine now, they belonged to me.

This was my world, this barren, lonely place, this vast pink-and-copper silence, this land of dancing heat waves and cruel ridges. Here where even the stones turn black from the sun, if they followed me they would leave their bones to mark their trail.

Far to the south of here in another desert they had driven my father and mother, who had survived. And so would I.

Squinting my eyes against the glare, I saw them coming down that last slope. Into a wash I went, and along the bottom, hot as an oven. Deliberately I left my trail. Let them follow.

Once I went to my knees, struggling to get up. It was done with intent. Let them whet their appetite. Let them think they had me. No longer was I alone, for this was the land of the Lonesome Gods, and they were my friends. The desert itself was my friend.

"Come on!" I begged. "Follow me!"

Yet when I left the wash in the shadow of a cloud, I saw them hesitating at the mountain's foot. There was argument among them, I was sure. At least there was reluctance. Would caution or hatred win?

One man turned back; the rest came on. Perhaps the wounded man? Or one wiser than the others?

When I came down off the mountains, I'd been somewhere near Lone Tree Canyon, and heading into the desert, I had a dry lake north of me, and beyond it, a range of ragged mountains. There were occasional clouds now, and when possible I used their temporary shadows, moving into the desert.

The low range ahead of me could have caught some of the brief showers that had fallen within the past few days. Often when I was with the Indians there had been talk of the desert and of places where water might be found at certain times of year. By this time such water would have been scarce or nonexistent had it not been for those brief showers.

The mountains ahead of me had no tanks that I knew of, but there would be hollows here and there, some of them shadowed by higher rocks. Water ran off these mountains like off a tin roof and gathered in whatever hollows there were.

Holding the dry lake on my left and the low range on my right, I moved along the mountains, following a dim trail that was, more often than not, invisible.

It was very hot. I had a lead of several miles and needed every inch of it. My shirt was soaked with sweat, but that was a help, as every slight stir of wind cooled my body. Turning into the mountains, I began searching for hollows. Several were dry; then under a slanting rock I found a half-shaded hollow with at least two gallons of water. I drank, waited, then drank again. Resting, I drank again, bathed my face and neck in the cool water, then started on.

They were closer now, but they would need water more than I, and there was none. Turning away, I walked along the rocks, then down into the sand. Almost ten miles, if I had understood correctly, from where I now stood, was Bed Rock Spring. It was northwest, a bit out of my way, but there would be water.

Keeping Red Mountain on my right, I started. Had it been left to me, I should have holed up somewhere in the shade and waited until sundown before starting, but the choice was not mine.

Steadily I walked. Sweat trickled down my spine and down the sides of my face. As long as I could sweat, I was not worried. Once, crossing a dry wash, I saw some horse tracks. Most of them were unshod horses, wild stock without a doubt. The desert at this season was an unlikely place for them, so they must have been pursued by somebody or something.

Several times I saw the tracks of bighorn sheep, and the tracks of coyotes were common enough. I walked on into the heat waves, only occasionally looking back. My pursuers were gaining ground. Coming to a stretch of hard-packed ground where the wind had swept away the sand, I started to dog-trot. The hot air seared my lungs; soon I was gasping, and slowed again to a walk.

Glancing back, I saw them stopped. They were grouped together, obviously arguing. If they turned back now, they could make it to water by sundown . . . with luck.

Stubbornly I pushed on. In places the sand was deep, but whenever possible I moved where the trail was, and there the ground was hard-packed from long years of use. Changing my route slightly, I kept in the shadow of a cloud until there was no more shadow, then sought another, working my way steadily toward Bed Rock Spring. Emerging from the shadow of Red Mountain, I saw Dome Peak ahead of me. The spring was somewhere just beyond it.

Again I glanced back. Two riders still followed; the others had turned back. Undoubtedly these two would try to keep me in sight and the others would return for fresh horses and for water.

The trail, merging with another of later vintage, ran off to the northeast. Only a little of daylight was left, and weary as I was, I knew what had to be done. I turned abruptly into the lava beds near Dome Mountain. Keeping to the rocks to leave no tracks, I worked a careful way eastward toward the spring.

Coming down off the rocks, I studied the area around the spring. There could be one among them who knew the desert better than I, and who might be waiting for me. I had watched for several minutes when I saw three bighorns walk out from where it lay, one of them pausing to lift a hind foot, and bending his neck, scratch behind his ear. Obviously there was nothing to fear. As I came down off the rocks, they moved away, unhurried but watchful.

At the spring, I drank deep. The water was brackish but cool, and anything wet was welcome. Placing my rifle close at hand, I settled down to wait. If they wanted me now, they had only to come, and they would come.

For the last half-mile I had walked on rock, leaving no tracks. For at least a mile before that I had left few, but there were two of them, and casting about, they might find some indication, and their horses would be sure to sense the water.

Again I drank, and rising from the water, I heard them coming. Shadows were gathering, and the sun was going down. Moving into some rocks near the spring, I waited. I was tired, as tired as I had ever been, moving almost continuously over rough terrain since before daylight, and I had come a long, long way.

Yet I had known desert Indians to run a hundred miles in a long day, and there were Indians south of the border, the Tarahumaras, who were not reckoned as men unless they could run a hundred miles in a day. Well, they were better men than I.

A sombrero showed above some rocks, and I put a bullet into it and the hat disappeared.

Moving slightly to a prechosen position, I waited, but nothing happened. All was still. They would want water, but they were having none of it until after dark, if they had the courage to come after it.

All was still. I could hear the horses moving on the rocks, restless for the water they were denied. Night drew its shadowy shroud about us, and I drank again; then I took up my rifle and moved off into the night.

There were low, ragged mountains before me. Well before dark I had chosen a sharp-edged rock for landmark, and now I walked toward it. The night was cool, but every step was an effort, and sometimes I felt like a sleepwalker, yet I pushed on, trying to leave no trail but unable in the darkness to judge how successful I was. When I crossed the low, rocky ridge, I could see Pilot Knob against the sky.

They would not leave the water in the darkness, not knowing where I had gone, and no doubt they would wait until almost morning before they took the chance to approach Bed Rock Spring. Lying down on the sand, I went to sleep.

Night was a time for prowlers, a time for snakes and such, but I was so tired I simply did not care.

An hour or two of sleep, and then I would move on. To travel at night was best when it was cool and pleasant. The sand was soft, and I was very tired. With my rifle cradled in my arms, I fell asleep.

In the distance, a coyote howled. A stone rattled down the rocks and something scurried in the night.

49

Cold awakened me. My muscles were cramped and stiff. Sodden with sleep and exhaustion, I rolled over and sat up.

The sky was very clear, the stars unbelievably bright. Listening, I heard no sound in the night. Staggering to my feet, I leaned for a moment on my rifle. The sand was very white, and there were dark patches of greasewood. Slowly, for I was still stiff from yesterday's running, I began to walk toward Pilot Knob.

Careful to leave no tracks, stepping on rocks whenever possible, I pushed on. There were springs up ahead if they knew where to find them, but I did not intend to be their guide.

From my conversations with the Cahuillas I knew that Pilot Knob was something over ten miles, yet exact distances were always hard to get from Indians. Yet with luck I could make Pilot Knob by sunup, and those who pursued me would not start before then. As the sun lifted to the horizon, I was drinking from a small spring near the base of the Knob.

Escape from those who would kill me was first, yet I must conserve my strength. There was no guessing what ordeals might await me, yet I was gambling I knew the desert better than they. One thing worried me: what of those who had turned back? Had they quit? Gone for fresh horses and water? Or to plan some other device, some other way in which to entrap me?

Indian Spring would be my next stop, and it would not be easily found, but now I would begin the destruction of those who followed me. I suspected they had found Bed Rock Spring, but I had traveled by night and left few signs; the slight winds that stirred the sand would remove those.

They had followed me into the desert to kill me; they had tried to trap me, and were themselves trapped. Few in California knew the deserts except for the Indians. The Californios kept to their lands along the seaward side of the mountains, and the interior was as strange to them as the surface of the moon.

I had only myself of whom to think; if the others returned they would have six horses and as many men.

Looking back along my trail, I thought I saw them, but it was likely to be my imagination. "Go back while you can." I spoke aloud.

My muscles had loosened with movement and heat. I walked easily now, although my moccasins were wearing through. By nightfall they would be gone.

It was very hot. Off to the south where the dry lakes were I saw dust devils dancing. Heat waves shimmered, obscuring the distance and the mountains.

By midday I was at Indian Spring. There were many boulders in the wash where it lay, and high brush hid the spring itself, offering no indication of the presence of water. Indians had placed stones to wall the spring, and the water was about three feet deep. No stream, not so much as a trickle, escaped it. No doubt it was just a seeping to the surface of water running down the wash from Eagle Crags.

Kneeling by the water, I drank. Scooping up handfuls of water, I bathed my neck, face, and chest. Then I drank again. Resting in the shade of the brush, I continued to soak up water. Several times I crawled from my shelter, and keeping under cover, studied my back trail.

At last I saw them. Even at this distance I could see they were walking and leading their horses. I counted the horses.

Five. . . . *Five?*

One was gone, then. One horse had gone down. "I am sorry for the horses." I spoke aloud, as a lonely man often does, hungry for the sound of some voice, even if it is his own.

Reluctantly I yielded my shade to the lizards and went away from the spring, stepping from rock to rock. I doubted they would find it. Without my friends the Indians I would never have imagined water in this place.

The sky was molten brass, the desert a vague, dusty copper where heat waves shimmered. Looking down at my own ragged moccasins, I could scarcely see my own feet, but I went out into the desert, going east now with the knowledge that before me was a long and bitter trek to the next water of which I knew, at what was called Garlic Springs.

My rifle was heavy in my hands, and it was a temptation to discard it, a temptation I resisted. Pausing briefly in the shade of some rocks, I looked off to the east in the direction I must go, squinting my eyes against the glare.

Nothing but bald, open desert. In the distance, far away, some low, ragged mountains if such they could be called.

I sat down, staring again at that awful waste that lay before me. Could I make it? Could anybody make it? Anybody at all?

There might be water closer than Garlic Springs, but I knew of none, and my enemies were coming behind me. I looked back again but could see nothing; then I did. I saw a man leading a horse, enormously tall, an impression of height created by heat waves.

It would be hours before I would have another drink, if I ever did. Yet, before I was halfway across, night would come with its coolness and its dark, so I must think of that. I must endure. I must wait for it.

Yet, if I waited, I might fight them off. I might get all of them.

"Don't be a fool!" I told myself irritably. "One or two, but not all."

Standing up, I took a step, and taking it, I gave myself to the desert, to the heat, to the thirst. I walked boldly into the desert and took step after step, my eyes upon those distant mountains, shimmering in heat waves like some weird land beyond imagination. Slowly, steadily, I walked. I chose little goals for myself. That greasewood with the weird shape. If I could get that far. . . .

A white rock as large as my two fists. I made it to the rock, and chose another, and then another. I kept my eyes from the awful distance and chose just the near goals. It was midafternoon before I stumbled, minutes later when I fell.

The heat on the face of the desert was unbearable. Struggling up, I started on again. Once I turned to look back. They were there, they had seen me, and they were coming.

Squinting again, I saw but three. Only three? I was winning, then.

I was winning? Grimly I laughed within. The desert was winning. Whatever killing was done, the desert would do.

How long since I had eaten? I could not remember, but the thought of food nauseated me. I fell again, but I got up.

Glancing back, I could see they were closer now. They had gotten into their saddles. They were riding to catch me, but the horses were walking. I did not think they could run.

Walking on into the heat, I staggered, almost fell, but caught myself on the rifle, using it as a staff. Turning then, I lifted the rifle, holding to the wood, for the barrel was too hot to touch, took careful aim, and fired.

A man lurched in the saddle. I had scarcely hoped to hit him, but then he fell.

Stumbling, staggering, I kept moving. Once more I fell, and from somewhere a thought came to me. "I am Johannes Verne. I am not afraid."

I got up to my knees, lurched to my feet, and walked on, nor did I fall again. "I am Johannes Verne, and I am not afraid."

Over and over I said it, and over and over like some weird litany it chanted itself in my brain, and then from somewhere came coolness, and the day was gone. The low, ragged mountains were not that far away.

In the coolness of the early evening when the stars were just appearing, I came to the springs. There were two of them, only a few yards apart, lying at the edge of some low hills near the Tiefort Mountains.

Dropping to my knees, I bathed my face and neck. I swallowed a little water, then a little more. I put my head down into the water, then withdrew it, dripping. I turned around and sat down to face the desert from which my enemies would come. I got out a piece of dried beef and worried a piece from the end with my teeth. Slowly, methodically, I chewed.

My foot moved, and I gasped with sudden agony. I looked again. My moccasins were gone. My feet were raw and bloody, the broken skin cracked and the cracks filled with sand.

Scooping water with my left hand, as my right held the pistol, I bathed my feet. Slowly, for what must have been an hour, I bathed them.

Listening into the night, I heard nothing. Peeling off my buckskin shirt, I got out my knife and cut the shape of my moccasins from it. One, then another. It was something I had done before. Sitting there in the darkness beside the Garlic water, I cut and made myself moccasins, and used the laces of the shirt's neck and lower sleeves to bind them on.

Again I drank, and drank.

Moving away from the water, I found a place in the sand. Dared I sleep? I slept.

And in the night the stars moved, and a night wind stirred the dried leaves on the scarce brush, and sand sifted, and in the night, something stirred, and my eyes opened.

A man . . . moving . . . coming nearer.

I sat up. There was a pale gray light in the eastern sky. I held the gun in my hand, and out of the desert a scarecrow of a man, staggering, with wild, staring eyes. He saw me and stopped.

"Water?" he pleaded. "Water?"

"Drop your gun belt. Your knife."

"Gone . . . back . . . back there."

"Drink, then, and be damned."

He drank, drank too much. Taking him by the hair, I dragged him back from the water. "Wait, you fool. You'll kill yourself."

Yellow crept into the sky. He was an Anglo, a man burned red by the sun, a man whose boots were leather rags about his feet, an evil man with a knife-scarred face.

"Where are the others?"

"Gone . . . dead . . . back there." He lifted a hand toward the desert. "Gone. All of them."

"Was Federico among them?"

"He went back. For horses and to come again for you." The man stared at me. "You are dead, too. He will have men waiting for you when you come from the desert. If you do not die here, they will be waiting at each water hole. He has a man who knows where you must come. They will be waiting."

Careful not to turn my back on him, I recovered the sleeves of my buckskin coat, and using rawhide threads cut from the remnants of the back after the moccasins were made, I doubled one sleeve over to make a bottom for the other sleeve and threaded it through holes in the sleeve.

He watched me, staring. "If that's s'posed to be a water bag, it won't work. It'll leak."

"Maybe. Some of it."

"You're a fool. They're goin' to get you."

My hand waved toward the desert. "That's what they thought."

He started toward the water, and I let him drink. "You're a fool," he said.

"A live fool," I said.

I dipped my water bag into the water and lifted it out, full. Water ran from it, dripped from it.

"See?"

Yet much water remained inside. I lowered it into the water hole again and left it there to soak.

"You . . ." I lifted my gun. "Get up."

He stared at me. Slowly he got up.

"There's another water hole right over there. It's a part of this spring. You go over there and set. And you stay there. If you stand up again after you get there, I'll kill you."

He stumbled over to the other hole and sat down. "You try to walk out of here, and you'll die," he shouted at me.

It was only about thirty or forty feet away, but it gave me breathing room. After a while he stretched out on the sand to sleep. My back against a bank, I did likewise, dozing, sleeping, waking. He never stirred.

All through the day, I rested, letting my feet heal, saturating myself with water. When the sun went down, I filled my water bag again, and holstering my gun, I turned into the desert.

The man got up and stared after me. "You'll die!" he shouted. "You'll die out there!"

There was no need to waste time looking back. I had far to go.

"You'll die!" he screamed.

He ran a few steps after me. "You'll die out there!" he screamed hoarsely. "You'll *die!*"

My crude water bag slung around my neck and hanging against my chest, I walked on.

". . . die!" he screamed.

Far off there were mountains, and where there were mountains there might be hollows where water had been caught. The water in my bag would not last. Now it was saturated; soon the buckskin would dry and shrink. Would it help? At least there would be a few swallows before it was gone.

A few swallows . . . Then?

I thought of Meghan, and I said aloud what I had never dared say before. "Meghan, I love you."

My feet were bleeding again. Each step was agony. I chose a distant star above distant mountains.

I walked on, into the night, into the desert.

50

Miss Nesselrode made coffee in the large pot. Soon the stage would come to the Bella Union and the newspapers would be brought to her. Several of her regulars were sure to drop in. A dozen of the town's most prominent men had made her reading room a place of meeting, away from the noise of the saloons.

The news of the day was discussed here before it appeared in the columns of the *Star*. In the beginning she had been merely a young woman who kept a book shop, but more and more she had been accepted into their conversations, although when more than two men were involved she retreated behind her desk.

English had long been her preferred language, although every young woman of her class in Russia spoke French in common conversation, yet she kept her books and her notes in Russian for the sake of privacy.

In Russia she would have been making tea in a samovar. How long ago it was! What if she had not been sent to Siberia? What if her brother had not been involved in that rather silly plot? By now she would have married, had children, and would be spending much of her life in France or Germany, perhaps Switzerland.

She remembered her mother, that slender, beautiful woman with her kind gray eyes and her stately manner. Her father had been terribly proud of his wife, although he affected to disapprove of some of her too-liberal British ideas. They had met when he was on a diplomatic mission to England, and it had been immediate love. He had not even waited to be presented but had crossed the room and introduced himself. It had been shocking, but exciting, too. Her mother had often told her the story, a story that never grew old and which she had delighted in hearing.

So far, far away, so long, long ago!

She remembered playing croquet on the lawn, and while waiting for Mikhail to make his play, she would look off down the avenue of firs toward the lake. She loved that view, and how often she had walked to the lake with her father on a Sunday afternoon!

By now she might have been a great lady, received by the czar and probably living at court. Although she had always preferred their country estates to living in St. Petersburg.

Nor had Siberia been the cold, dismal place they all expected. In the town to which they had been exiled the winters were less rigorous than in St. Petersburg and she had found the people more open and friendly, and the countryside beautiful in summer. Although exile was considered the worst of things, she had found it not at all bad, but then word had reached them of what was to happen, and they fled.

So lost in her thoughts was she that when she turned and saw a man standing inside the door she was completely surprised. It was a man she had not seen before but immediately recognized for who he was— Yacub Khan.

Her first impression was one of power, not muscular power alone, although that was obvious from his massive shoulders and mighty arms, but from something emanating from the man itself.

He was no taller than she, but wide and thick. He stood facing her, his feet slightly apart, his loose shirt hanging outside his trousers. His face was broad, strongly boned, and his head was either bald or shaved.

"You are friend to Meghan Laurel?"

"I am."

"She goes to look for Johannes Verne."

"What? *Meghan*? But she cannot! She must not!"

"She takes four men. One is Tomás Machado, a good man. Three packhorses."

If Meghan had gone into the wilderness looking for Johannes, she had not one chance in a thousand of finding him. He was pursuing horse thieves and would follow wherever the trail led. Meghan, having never been into the back country, could not appreciate the immensity of it, nor have the vaguest idea of what she was undertaking. She had ridden the trails in the Los Angeles Valley and into the San Gabriel and San Fernando valleys, but beyond the mountains it was something quite different.

"She must be found before she reaches the desert."

"I go."

"You? Only an Indian could find them!"

A glint of amusement showed itself. "I am born on the desert. My people were of the Taklamakan and mountains bordering it."

"I know of the Taklamakan. I crossed the Gobi as a young girl. I know of your people, but this desert is different, although less dangerous than yours."

"I shall find them."

"Johannes has been gone three weeks. No one has returned, so there will have been trouble." She looked down at her desk, then looked up at Yacub Khan. "Johannes knew it was a trap. The stealing of horses was deliberate. They wished for him to follow."

"He will not be trapped."

"Yacub Khan, please bring her back. She is a young girl in love and she is my friend. She is very dear to Johannes, too."

When he had gone, she sat very still, remembering not the desert she had crossed with Johannes and his father, but that long-ago crossing of the Gobi. The Taklamakan she knew only by reputation; some said it was the worst desert on earth. In the far west of China it was reached by the Silk Road, which went around its border. That road had been taken by pilgrims from China proceeding to India to study Buddhism at its source. There had been great schools at Khotan, and the Buddha himself had been a Saka, an Indo-European people from Central Asia whose tribe had settled in Nepal.

Such a man as Yacub Khan might find Meghan.

But where was Johannes? Actually, now that she thought of it, he had been gone more than three weeks.

Meghan herself had been worried about Johannes having enemies of whom he was not aware. At least he had been unaware of the true reason for their enmity, and she had herself been partly responsible for her father's warning to Johannes, but that had been before she met Don Federico.

After meeting him, her fears seemed ridiculous. Intrigued by his courtly manner and his obvious interest in her, she had accepted a contrary view, unwilling to believe that such a polished gentleman could also be plotting murder.

Johannes had gone. He had left abruptly. Miss Nesselrode remembered that she herself had implied he might not return.

Meghan had returned home sick and empty at the thought that she had driven him away, that he might not come back. She was used to the young men of the town, but Johannes was different. He possessed a quality she had not fathomed, a strangeness and a sort of inner quiet. Her father respected him, which was astonishing, as her father was rarely impressed by anyone.

Yet she was not her father's daughter for nothing. If Johannes would not come back, she would go after him. She told no one but the maid at her home, but she suspected Tomás had told Elena.

Miss Nesselrode walked to the window and looked into the street. The idea that Meghan would follow Johannes into the desert had not occurred to her. Nor could Meghan have any idea of what she was getting into. Few Angelenos had knowledge of what lay over the mountains, nor were they interested. Nor was it the kind of conduct one expected from a well-behaved young lady.

She heard the steps on the boardwalk and recognized them at once. Impulsively she started for the door as Jacob Finney pushed it open and stepped in.

"Mr. Finney . . . !"

"He's still out there, ma'am. We recovered the horses, but they took out after Johannes. He told us if we got separated to bring the stock back here, that he'd take care of himself."

"He's out there alone?"

"We weren't ready for the desert, ma'am. Neither were they. Don Federico and a couple of his men came back for fresh horses and outfits. I think they plan to locate on water holes at the desert's edge and wait for him to show."

"How is it out there?"

"Upwards of one hundred degrees, ma'am. If I know Johannes, he'll come out of that desert alive, but nobody else will. I've heard him talk about it a time or two. Those Injuns and his pa, they taught that boy aplenty."

"Meghan has gone looking for him."

"Meghan? What in God's world . . . ?"

"She's a young girl, Mr. Finney, and she's in love. She knows nothing of what is out there. The man she loves is gone and she is afraid he'll never come back."

Jacob Finney swore softly, bitterly. How far had she gone? He asked quick, pointed questions. His thoughts raced. She would be impatient, and she would push it. Tomás was all right, but what if something happened to him? She'd be out there alone, with three men whom she did not know, and in bandit country. And how could she even dream of finding Johannes?

Of course, Finney had been planning to go back. He had not wanted to leave Johannes out there, but they had the horses to consider, and Johannes in many ways was better off alone.

He was dead beat. He'd just come in, and the trip had been a hard one. It was the same with Monte and Owen Hardin, and Hardin was upset because of the loss of his friend Myron Brodie.

He needed rest. "You're not as young as you used to be," he told himself. Still, he was far from an old man, and he knew the desert somewhat.

"Tomás will slow her down if he can. Maybe by the time she sees some of that country she will begin to understand what she's up against." He paused. "I'll get the boys, but they're dead beat, Miss Nesselrode. They came in off the trail all wore-out. We'll do what we can."

"Yacub Khan went after her."

Finney wiped the sweatband of his hat, thinking. Yacub Khan? Some kind of an Oriental foreigner who had a small place over against the mountain. He had only seen him once that he remembered.

"He is a friend of Captain Laurel's."

"Some kind of foreigner, ain't he? What good will he be out there?"

"He grew up in a desert worse than the Mohave, a good deal worse."

"Can he sit a horse? I mean, most of those foreigners don't know one end from the other, 'less they're Englishmen."

"His people live on horseback. They are nomadic herdsmen, following the grass from the desert's edge to the high mountain country. Mountains," she added, "that make these look like prairie-dog mounds."

Finney was doubtful. "I been in the Sierras," he said, "and the Rockies. There's peaks in the Rockies that top out at fourteen thousand, a lot of them."

"Where he comes from they are twice that high," she said quietly. "In the Kunlun and the Pamirs there are many peaks over twenty thousand feet. He's used to rough country, Mr. Finney."

"Maybe. But can he fight?"

"He can. His people all carry broadswords and rifles. They protect their herds from bandits and other nomads. He grew up fighting. They tell me, too, that he's a master at several kinds of hand-to-hand fighting."

Finney was silent. Finally he dropped into a chair. He did not want to go back out there, but how to explain that? He had been constantly in the saddle for three weeks. There had been a short, hard fight, and above all he knew finding Johannes would be impossible. He would lose himself in that desert. He would go places no man on horseback could go unless he had three packhorses loaded with water.

He did not know Meghan Laurel, but in his own mind he was sure she would give up and return. No young girl was going to buck the heat, the sweat, the sleeping out . . .

She had to be crazy. Almost automatically he accepted the coffee Miss Nesselrode offered.

Other men were coming in. Matt Keller, De La Guerra, and then Ben Wilson.

"Captain Laurel's daughter?" Wilson asked. "What in the world . . . ?"

"She's in love," Miss Nesselrode said.

Wilson shrugged, with a wry smile. "I suppose that explains everything. I've been across that desert, and I would say somebody had better bring her back before she dies out there."

A young girl out there alone? Finney swore under his breath. Tomás was all right, but who were the others? And there were bandits out there, several roving bands along the fringe of the settlements, to say nothing of Indians.

He put down his cup and got to his feet. "I'll get some boys together," he said. "We'll go after her."

"Johannes will thank you for it. So will I."

"Yes, ma'am."

There were so many routes, so many trails. Could he find hers now?

He got to his feet. Wilson glanced at him over the rim of his cup. "It's a big country," he said.

"Yeah," Finney said dryly.

Wilson glanced at him again. "If she's in a hurry, as she probably is, they will need fresh horses."

Their eyes met. Ben Wilson knew this country as well as anybody could, and he knew the only ranch where they could get fresh horses. It was a hangout for outlaws, for Vásquez and his lot, and Ben Wilson knew it. He also knew that Finney knew it.

Jacob Finney walked to the door. He glanced back at Miss Nesselrode and lifted a hand.

When the door closed, she said, "He did not want to go."

"And I don't blame him," Wilson replied.

51

On a cool brown ledge in the shade of a jagged upthrust of rock, I looked out upon a desert turning gray with the coming of night. It had been four days since I left my last enemy shouting threats and obscenities as I walked away.

Those who pursued me were dead, and some future traveler could mark their trail by their whitening bones and the sound of a desert wind moaning in their empty rib cages.

My moccasins had worn out again. As I watched the desert that tomorrow I must travel, I made a fresh pair from the buckskin of my sleeve-canteen. That water bag had leaked, yet retained enough water to get me across three long stretches where there were no springs.

Torn on the rocks when I fell, the water bag lost the last few drops and I was near my end when I glimpsed some salt grass at the lowest part of a blistering desert basin. As I drew closer, I saw arrowweed and crawling mesquite, two more evidences of water. And then I found a spring that offered no other sign of its presence.

That had been two days ago. Now I sat within a dozen feet of a rock tank containing water, a place visited by bighorn sheep, coyotes, and other wildlife. Their converging tracks, scarcely to be seen in the sand, had brought me here. I had drunk deep, splashed my face and chest with water, and then I'd moved off to sleep the night through and leave my animal guides access to the water. In the morning I returned to drink and then settled down to rest, study the desert, and wait for night.

The changing light on the desert had let me pick my route. Tonight there would be a moon, and I would start for the mountains on the skyline. Now I was close to the southern edge of the desert and must move with extreme care.

Every instinct and a bit of common sense warned me somebody would be waiting. At least three men had turned back, and one of them would have been Don Federico. He had tried too often and had a fierce hunger to see me die. The logical thing would be to watch every water hole at the desert's edge until I appeared, as eventually I must.

Odd, but I had never thought of myself as an heir. Nor had I wanted anything from Don Isidro, although the irony of it appealed to me, to inherit after all his efforts to see me die. It would serve him right.

On the horizon were the San Gabriel and San Bernardino mountains. If I could reach those mountains I could travel south to join my friends the Cahuillas with less trouble. Not only would I be traveling among the pines, but water would be easily available. The thought of traveling with water and shade was tantalizingly beautiful.

Now, studying the desert from my high point, I tried to decide where my enemies might await me.

Not more than five miles from the low range of rocks where I now rested was Old Woman Springs; near it, Cottonwood Spring. Beyond them were the mountains where I wished to be.

Twenty-five or thirty miles away was Rabbit Springs, but in the wrong direction for me. Don Federico would rightly guess that I would attempt to reach my friends the Indians at the hot-water springs at the mountain's edge. Not these mountains, but the San Jacintos further south. He might or might not know about the Indians in Morongo Valley, closer, and also my friends. It was near there, I believed, that Paulino Weaver had settled. Don Federico would have men watching these springs.

That I would be in desperate need of water they would realize, and they had only to wait. Yet there was now an advantage for me. This was country I had ridden and walked with the Cahuilla.

By the time I reached the vicinity of Old Woman, I would be thirsty and needing a drink, yet I would pass it by in favor of a more hidden spring with even better water, Saddlerock Spring, where the water flowed right from the granite in a hidden place in the mountains. Only a few miles further south and I would be safe among my friends the Indians.

Now I rested. My belt was drawn four notches tighter than when I left the others. The last piece of jerky left to me was now in my mouth. I chewed slowly, to make it last as long as possible. During the days in the desert, I had found seeds that could be eaten, and with my small supply of jerked beef they had kept me alive.

One more stretch of desert to cross, one more group of watchers to evade, and then I was safe.

Now . . . I sat still, dreading the moment when I must leave this water behind and once more endure the desert.

I arose. On a rock face near where I had been sitting there was Indian writing, faded by blown sand, almost obliterated by time. Here, long ago, Indians had come to drink. There was no pile of stones, what some unknowing people had called "shrines," but I placed two stones, one atop the other. Then I turned away into the desert.

San Gorgonio Mountain, something over eleven thousand feet above sea level, was almost due south of me. For a moment I looked at it, then chose a star just east of the peak and started walking. Once I paused to stretch, trying to stretch some of the stiffness from my muscles. I was tired, very, very tired.

Until now all my effort had been directed simply to the next spring, water hole, or tank. At each I had fallen, exhausted. One spring upon which my hopes depended had proved to be dry. A tank I had hoped to find containing some water had been a bed of sand.

Before me, beyond this stretch of desert, were the mountains. A forest, even if a sparse forest at first, but the cool, cool shade and cool, cool water! I longed to lie on pine needles beneath a tree and rest, just rest.

A little further, just a little further! Into the night and the coolness I walked . . . and walked. Sometimes I found my eyes closing even as I walked; I stumbled and awakened, but on course. There was my star, there were the mountains.

I smelled smoke.

Wood smoke, the smoke of a campfire. There, not a half-mile away, perhaps even less, Old Woman Springs, and a faint gleam through the brush.

A fire. My enemies awaited me. They were resting, drinking water and coffee at their leisure.

Yet suppose these were not enemies? Perhaps some other travelers, merely camping at the water hole. They would welcome me, give me something to drink and to eat.

Should I chance it? It had been days since I'd had enough to drink, and I was always hungry. I hesitated, wanting to go closer, yet afraid, too. Now that I was so awfully tired, I was clumsy, too. I could not manage my feet well, I stumbled often, and if I went closer, would be sure to alarm the camp. Moreover, the horses would smell me. Hesitantly I moved closer, pausing often. Somebody moved near the fire, throwing a shadow as he passed close to the fire; then I heard somebody say, "It is a waste of time! The man is dead! Who could survive out there without food or water? And without a horse? Juliano is sure to have caught and killed him."

"What difference does it make? Are we not paid for what we do? Sit down, rest yourself. It is for a few days only."

For a moment I swayed on my feet, sick with disappointment; then I turned away and walked on by. One step at a time, half-asleep, I stumbled on. Several times I staggered; once I fell to my knees. Saddlerock Spring must be ten . . . No, more. At least twelve miles.

There was another spring nearer, but it might be watched as well. On I went, walking, staggering, almost falling. My feet were tender, for the skin had often broken.

Again I fell to my knees. For a moment I stayed where I was, wanting nothing so much as to fall forward and to sleep. At last I got up and walked on.

Somehow I clung to my rifle. Time and again I used it to push me up from the sand where I had fallen. Now I was existing only for water, any kind of water, anywhere. There was Two Hole Spring . . . I had heard of it . . . somewhere nearer than Saddlerock. Without a drink I would never make it.

Suddenly the mountains were lifting up before me. I started on, smelled smoke again, and stopped. Peering through some scattered brush and the rocks, I caught a gleam of fire. Carefully I edged closer.

A fire . . . one man. A big rawboned Anglo with a straggly beard. A hawk face and long, sparse hair. He added fuel to a fire. I could smell coffee. My stomach growled ominously. Edging closer, I thought of that coffee, of food, of water, of . . .

He saw me.

He had picked up the coffeepot to fill his cup. His eyes held mine. Slowly, carefully, his eyes never leaving mine, he put down the coffeepot. He held the stub of a cigar in his yellow teeth and he rolled it to the corner of his mouth.

He had a straggly mustache that fell on either corner of his mouth. His shirt was stained and dirty. He slowly straightened up, rolling the cigar again.

When he was straightened to his full height, he smiled past the cigar; then coolly he reached for his gun. Dumbly I stared at him. I was stupid with exhaustion. I saw his hand clasp the gun, saw it start to lift as it came free of the holster, saw the yellow teeth, the wolfish smile, and his gun came up. Then I shot him.

My rifle, held in my right hand, fired from the hip. The bullet struck him, and, shocked, he stared at me. Then his gun went off, the bullet going into the ground. Stepping forward, I swung the barrel of my rifle against his arm and the gun went flying.

He fell back in a sitting position, staring at me as blood spilled over his belt and stained his pants. Picking up his cup, I filled it with coffee. Holding the cup in my left hand, I made a gesture of salute. "*Gracias,*" I said, and drank.

He made a gesture of indifference, as much as to say: Help yourself. I drank again.

One of his hands rested on the ground; the other held his belly where the bullet had gone.

"It was for fifty dollars," he explained.

"It is a lot of money, sometimes," I agreed; then I added, "You make a good cup of coffee."

"*Por nada,*" he said.

I finished the coffee and refilled my cup. There was no pain in him yet, only shock. "They will come," he said. "The shot . . ."

"Of course," I agreed.

He pointed toward his pack. "There is bacon," he said, "but you have no time."

"I can take it? And the coffee?"

"Of course," he said, and then he added, "They are at the Old Woman. They will run you down, I think."

"Who knows?" I shrugged. "There was a pair of saddlebags."

"The bacon is there," he said, "and the coffee."

"I'll take them, and the pot." I emptied the last of the coffee.

"It was for fifty dollars," he said. "Fifty dollars to be here, a hundred if I killed you."

"Ah? You have bad luck," I said. Taking my time, for my hands were unsteady, I reloaded my rifle. I would need every shot. There was a canteen. Taking that and the saddlebags, I slung them over my shoulder and took the cup and the coffeepot.

"There is the horse," he said. "It is saddled. Take it."

"*Gracias,*" I said again, and then, as I started toward the horse, I turned back to him. "Another time, I might have bought you a drink."

"Of course," he said, "and I, you."

He was sitting in a pool of blood now. I lifted a hand. "*Adiós!*" I said, and he tried to lift a hand to me but could not.

At the rim of the firelight I untied the horse. "Fifty dollars?" I said. "It was not enough."

"Who knows?" he said, and he rolled over with his cheek against the rocks, his eyes staring toward the fire.

"*Adiós,*" I said again, but he did not answer.

The horse was a tired horse, but not so tired as I. I rode him down Rattlesnake Canyon and then cut back into the hills toward Saddlerock. The canteen, when I hefted it, was only half-full. At Saddlerock I could fill it if it was not watched.

It was not. Dismounting, I emptied out the water, rinsed the canteen, and refilled it with the fresh, clear water from Saddlerock. I lay down and drank, and drank again. The horse was in no such shape as I and drank but little.

They would be coming soon, and there would be many of them, nor was I in any shape for a fight. Yet they would find the other man and be cautious.

Morongo Valley. Was it ten miles? Or further?

Mounting up, I turned the horse into a canyon that sloped toward the desert. I walked the horse, saving it for runs yet to come.

The shot would have been heard. On such a night, clear and cool, it would be heard far. . . . Two shots.

By the time I had gone a mile, the coffee had brought me alive enough to think.

They would be coming fast down the Burns Canyon Trail, and they would cut me off from Morongo. They would know about the Indians and me, as they had known about the Indians and my father.

They would cut me off, they would drive me into the desert.

Not that, not again. Please . . . not that again.

Turning my horse, I sought a way over the low ridges and found it. There was open ground beyond, with some Joshua trees. I wove a way among them, ran into a clump of boulders, and had to swing wide around them. And then I heard them.

They were coming fast down the Burns Canyon Trail, and there were a lot of them, judging by the sound. I ran my horse toward the gap near Chaparrosa Spring, hoping to pass them and ride into Morongo ahead of them.

Suddenly a yell and a shot. There had been riders at Chaparrosa, heading me off. There were five or six of them. I fired then, and fired again. The horse jumped sharply and faltered.

What . . . ? Riding hard, I rode into the desert, and under me the horse's gait became unsteady. They had fired, my horse had been hit.

Please, I whispered, just a little further! *Please!*

Gamely, desperately, the horse ran on. Then he tumbled and pitched forward and I left the saddle over his head but landed on my feet, running.

My rifle was gone with the fall; the saddlebags flapped over my shoulder, and the canteen. Desperately I clung to them, saw some boulders and went into them, ran down a slope and wove my way between other boulders and the Joshuas.

Pausing to listen, I heard them passing off to the south. They would ride on, find the fallen horse, and begin to search.

Only minutes . . . just minutes. . . .

They were coming.

52

Meghan sat close to the fire, her arms around her knees. She stared into the fire and was frightened. She had been a fool, a complete fool, and now she was trapped.

Tomás was across the fire from her, preparing food, and he was also trapped, and it was her fault. Such a kind old man! He had tried, very gently, to dissuade her. He had tried to tell her how impossible it was to find one man in all that vast world beyond the mountains. She had not believed him, and now it was too late.

By the third day she had begun to realize the impossibility of it, but her stubbornness refused to let her turn back, and she could not believe she would not find him. She must find him.

There were two other men with them, and one of them, named Iglesias, had not worked with Tomás but had volunteered to come along. From the first, he made her uncomfortable. He insisted on trying to ride beside her, and kept throwing meaningful glances at her, taunting, contemptuous glances.

Once, riding near her he had said, "He is an old man. He can do nothing for you."

On the night of the third day two other men had ridden down from the hills and joined them. They did not say anything, but they rode along. And they knew Iglesias.

Obviously the meeting had been arranged. They looked boldly at her, letting their eyes go over her body and smiling at each other.

One of them had looked at her and said, "Soon."

She wanted to turn back now but was afraid that would only precipitate matters. Perhaps if she waited, something might happen.

She was desperately afraid, but she must not let them know. She also had the small pistol her father had given her, but it was hidden and they had not seen it.

There were three of them. She had never shot a man and had never believed she could; now she believed. Now she knew it would come to that.

Now she could not think of Johannes. All her wits must be upon this situation. Tomás glanced at her. He knew she understood and he knew she was ready for whatever could be done.

If anything could be done.

"Johannes should be near," she said suddenly. "He would not have come further than this."

She said it, and hoped they would believe it, even though she knew it was not true. Johannes was nowhere near.

Tomás straightened from the fire. "Of course," he said. "He should be riding in at any moment."

The other men ignored their talk. Except the boy who had worked with Tomás. He was quiet; he was frightened, too.

"You are young," one of them said suddenly, "but you can be in it, too. The old one is too old. He does not matter."

That one, the one whom they called Biscal, he looked contemptuously at Meghan. "We know where he is. He is in the desert, he is on foot, and they are following him. By now he is for the buzzards.

"He will not come," Biscal smiled. "No one will come. We are alone."

"Captain Laurel is a man," Tomás said suddenly. "He fears no one. He has much power, in Mexico as well as here."

"Bah! He is far at sea. And when he comes back? She went into the mountains, so who knows what bear killed her?"

It was said now, it was declared, it was in the open. "You do not know my people," she said, "or the friends I have among your people. If I am harmed in any way, they will never stop until they find you and hang you."

Biscal chuckled. "You are not the first, and I am not hung. Although," he added, "you are the most beautiful. Had I not promised them, I would keep you for myself."

She was still frightened, but now there was something inside of her that was very still, very ready. When the moment came, she would let him get close and she would kill him first.

The boy would help her, she was sure of that, and Tomás as well, but there were three men against them. She must kill one, quickly, surely.

"She is under my protection," Tomás said quietly. "She will not be harmed."

"Don't be a fool, old man. Stay out of this and you may live. Of that I have not decided, but if you are wise . . . who knows?"

Tomás knelt beside the fire. He stirred the coals under the coffee, seemed to touch the pot, and jerked his hand away, his eyes meeting hers. He was telling her something.

The coffee, the hot coffee. That was a weapon, too. She remembered her father once saying that anything could be a weapon, that men had been killing each other for a million years before a gun was invented, and if one did not have a gun, there was always something.

To be alert, to watch her chances. That was the thing. Not to run, for she could not run as fast as any one of them in her heavy skirts, and running away left her vulnerable to attack.

She was thinking now. The coffee had been one thought, but there were others. There was a long stick near the fire. She took it up and poked it into the fire as if feeding the flames. There was that stick . . .

"Let us eat, Tomás. Let a man's pleasures come later." Biscal turned his head and gave her a sidelong glance. "I have seen you about the town and wondered how I could get you." He jerked his head toward his silent companion. "We talked of it. And then you decided to go into the hills . . . perfect! We could not have planned it better!"

Should she shoot him now? Unexpectedly? He had stated his intentions, and if she shot him without warning, when he had not moved toward her, she would take them by surprise. She might have to shoot but one.

To kill in cold blood? But to defend herself? The riding dress she wore had a slit inside the pocket to allow her to reach her pistol. That had been her father's idea, and she had scoffed, doubting she would ever need a gun.

Yet she must not put her hand in her pocket without reason or they might leap upon her and find the gun. She would, when the time came, make believe to sneeze. She would seem to reach for a handkerchief and then shoot him.

She need not even take the gun out. She could shoot through the material.

Iglesias was looking at her. "You are not afraid?" He seemed surprised and puzzled.

"Afraid? Why?" She leaned forward a little. "Have you ever seen Johannes with a gun? He is very good, you know, as his father was. Do you not remember what happened when they tried to steal his horses? There were many of them and he was alone."

"Come!" Tomás said suddenly. "It is time for eat. Bring yourselves to the fire." He indicated a stack of tortillas. "Help yourselves."

It was a cool, starlit night. The smell of the fire was good. Meghan Laurel looked to the stars, and then to the fire. In her mind she whispered: *Johannes, where are you?*

She had been such a fool, but knowing that did not help now.

Where was he? Was it true that they were pursuing him into the desert? Even now he might be out there, suffering, dying, alone.

There was nothing she could do, nor was there anything he could do to help. What must be done, she must do. I will not wait, she told herself. I shall shoot him at once.

Before he is ready. Before he makes a move. Shoot him suddenly and the others will be frightened.

She had never killed a man, never dreamed that she might, yet her father had warned her she might someday have to defend herself when he was not near.

Suddenly one of the horses lifted his head, nostrils flaring. She seized upon the thought. "Look at him!" she exclaimed suddenly. "There is somebody out there!"

Startled, they looked. Iglesias, who had been crouching by the fire, stood up and peered into the night.

"Coyote," he said at last.

"Was it?" she asked.

Biscal looked around uneasily. He spoke low-voiced in Spanish to Iglesias, who shook his head impatiently. Biscal took another tortilla and scooped beans and meat from the pot, yet occasionally he stopped to listen, too.

She arose and went to the fire. She took her own tortilla and scooped something from the pot, and ate. "It tastes good, Tomás. You are a good cook. May I have some coffee now?"

"Of course, señorita!" He filled a cup and handed it to her. She sipped a little, then placed the cup on a rock near where she sat. She was ready now. Had they noticed that she took the cup with her left hand? She thought not, but Iglesias was looking at her, puzzled by something.

The horse's head was up again, ears pricked. So were the others'. All were looking off into the night; then one turned and looked across the fire at something.

Biscal swore and stood up, peering into the dark. "Sit down," Iglesias said impatiently. "You are jumpy as a girl!"

"Something is here," Biscal muttered. "I don't like it."

An old man, a boy, and a girl against three grown men, all strong men, vaqueros at least a part of the time. She must shoot one, throw hot coffee on another, if she could. She must be ready, and she must not give herself away, and when the moment came, she must move fast.

"What was *that?*" she asked suddenly.

Biscal looked up. "What? What did you hear?"

"Something . . . I don't know. There was a sound. I—"

"There was nothing!" Iglesias said irritably. "Nothing at all!"

Biscal looked around uneasily. Tomás stooped over the pot, then half-straightened, listening. Biscal wet his lips, watching.

The third man, who had remained still, looked from one to the other. "*Estúpido!*" he said contemptuously. He got up. "I do not wait. I am ready."

One of the horses shied suddenly, and they all turned to look.

Meghan took the opportunity to get to her feet, cup in her left hand. She glanced at Tomás, nodding slightly. Her right hand slipped into her pocket, through the slit, grasping the small pistol.

The boy, at some signal from Tomás, was on his feet also. He was watching Iglesias, waiting.

Now they all heard it, something stirring out there. They heard a footfall, then another, then silence.

"Who is there?" Biscal challenged.

A slight breeze stirred the leaves. There was no other sound. Meghan had shifted her attention to the third man, who was not listening. He was looking at her. "Now," he said, "you come to me, little one, and if you beg a little, I may not hurt you so much!"

"Don't be a fool!" she said sharply.

Iglesias threw his coffee to the ground. "Now! Now it will be!" he said. "I, first, then . . ."

53

For a moment after the soft rap on the door, Miss Nesselrode sat very still. It was late, scarcely the hour for visitors, and since the appearance of Alexis Murchison she had been careful about opening the door to anyone. Rising, she crossed the room to the door, listened for a moment, and when the rap came again, she asked, "Who is there?"

"It's me, ma'am. Kelso."

She opened the door and he stepped in quickly, removing his hat as he closed the door behind him. "Sorry to come around so late, ma'am, but I saw your light and figured you'd want to know."

"Is it about Meghan Laurel? Or Johannes?"

"No, ma'am. A long time ago you asked me to sort of look into what happened to that Spanish boy who arrived on the ship with Tía Elena."

"Oh, yes. I had forgotten."

"Found something kinda peculiar. That woman we heard about? The one who took the boy and rode off with him in the night? She was Felipe's sister."

"Felipe?"

"That vaquero who sort of fell off a cliff out on Don Isidro's ranch?"

She remembered now: she had been interested, although just why, she did not recall. So much was happening, with Johannes disappearing into the desert, and Meghan going after him.

"She loved that boy like he was her own. Taken him away, cared for him." Kelso took out his pipe. "Mind if I smoke, ma'am? This here's quite a story."

It was late, and she was impatient for news of Johannes and Meghan. Jacob Finney had gone back to the wild country looking for them. Now, however, she was tired, and she needed the rest. Nonetheless,

Kelso was a good man, a sincere, hardworking man, and she would hear him out.

"Will you have some coffee? It's hot, but not very fresh, I'm afraid."

"Been drinkin' that kind of coffee since I was a youngster." He struck a match on the hearth and lighted his pipe. "That boy's name was Alfredo. That woman was paid to take him away, and she done it. Only thing was, she was a childless woman and she came to love that lad. She took him into the mountains down near Pala . . . Injun country. She wanted to keep him away from folks, keep him to herself.

"Then she picked up with a man. Taken to livin' with him from time to time. He was an Anglo, quiet sort of feller, prospectin', trappin', tradin' a mite . . . that sort of thing. He took to the boy, too. Used to take him picture books he found—some of them had been left behind at one of the missions when the padres left."

Miss Nesselrode refilled his cup. She half-started to rise. Kelso must think this was important or he would not have come around at this hour, so she sat back down, trying not to show her impatience.

"Old books, they were. Had to do with building over in Rome an' Greece, things like that. Pictures from Spain, too, pictures of an old mosque in Córdoba and such.

"That boy, he growed up with those books. There weren't many white folks around where he was, and not many of the Injuns could read. I reckon it was a lonely life, especially after she died."

"Died?"

"Yes, ma'am, an' when she died, that boy disappeared. Of course, he wasn't just a kid. He was somewhere in his teens, I reckon, might have been older.

"Folks thought him odd, those few who met him, and he went somewhere off by himself."

"That's too bad, Mr. Kelso, but I fail to see—"

"That man? The one who lived with the Spanish woman? He kept in touch with the boy. He was the only one knew where he lived, although he told nobody, nobody at all."

She was very tired. She arose and began putting things away, hoping Kelso would leave. He held his cup, staring into the fire; then he looked up suddenly.

"Ma'am? That feller? The one who lived for a time with that Spanish woman? He was kind of a loner. Made mighty few friends, although a lot of his kind knew him by name, drifters, prospectors, and the like. But there was one man he considered a friend."

"Mr. Kelso, it is very late, and I—"

He got to his feet. "Sorry, ma'am, but I figured you should know. The one friend that man claimed was Zachary Verne."

For a moment she just stood there, but curiosity overcame her weariness. "Sit down, Mr. Kelso. Please have some more coffee."

"Like I say, that man was a loner. Had some good qualities, though, and the best one was loyalty. He never forgot a friend or a favor, so when he heard Zack was coming back to California, he met him down in the desert. Met him at that place where the hot spring is and all them palm trees? You were there, I think maybe you might have seen this man. He came to meet Zachary Verne and to get him off the stage. His name was Peter Burkin."

Of course she remembered! He had seemed a roughhewn sort of man —friendly and honest had been her impression.

"If you will recall, he came to warn Verne that if he went on into Los Angeles he'd be killed. Nobody would think too much of it, as folks were gettin' killed all the time, and Verne would only be remembered by a few.

Burkin warned Verne, then took him to a place he knew, and that was where Verne and the boy lived until Verne was killed, and the boy lived there for some time after, until you sent for him."

Long after Mr. Kelso had gone, she lay awake thinking. Alfredo . . . that had been the boy's name, and he had come over on the same ship with Elena. Don Federico, only a boy then himself, had supposedly tried to kill Alfredo.

Why had Alfredo been suddenly spirited away and hidden for all those years? And where was he now? If he was still alive?

Peter Burkin would know, and somehow she must find Peter and talk to him. Yet, what business was it of hers? That Burkin had also known Zachary Verne was pure coincidence, no doubt, but the woman who cared for Alfredo had been a sister to the mysteriously murdered Felipe. She supposed it all tied together somehow, and she was still thinking about it when she fell asleep.

When morning came, she awakened disturbed by Kelso's information, yet uncertain as to why it should bother her. Of course, anything that even remotely concerned Johannes was of interest. He was the only "family" she possessed, and from the beginning he had been the son she had always wanted.

Los Angeles had changed, and she had seen and was seeing it change. In the passing of years it had grown from scarcely two thousand to a busy city of almost sixteen thousand people. From the beginning she had gone out to the limits of the town and bought land; now much of that land had increased several times in value.

Down at the end of Spring Street there was an amusement park, the Washington Gardens, a place of about thirty-five acres of fruit trees and vineyards where a few wild animals were kept, and there was a place for dancing and a bandstand. Further along there was the Agricultural Park and its racetrack.

Houses were beginning to appear on the hills back of the town. There were three principal streets. Main was the busiest, followed by Spring and San Pedro, the latter a dusty thoroughfare with many orange groves. One of these was Wolfskill's orchard of well over one hundred acres.

Every day now there was change, and every day she found herself looking to the hills. The air was clear and beautiful, the town a place of gardens and vineyards.

Elena! Try as she would, she could not keep her thoughts from returning to Johannes. She must see Elena. Who was Alfredo? What did she know of Peter Burkin?

She walked to the door, glanced at the street, then turned and walked back behind the railing that separated her desk from the reading room.

Where was Johannes? And Meghan?

There had been no word. Jacob Finney had ridden away with Monte McCalla, Owen Hardin, and two other men. They were heavily armed and had packhorses, ready for a prolonged stay.

She must get word to Elena. She must do that now, at once.

Johannes, if he was alive, would try to reach his Indian friends, but his enemies would know that and be prepared for it. Yet she could do nothing. Unless . . .

Maybe, even at this late date, she could stop it.

Don Isidro, who rarely came to town these days, had come in that day. She would go to see him. Hesitating only an instant as she reviewed the situation, she sent her girl for Kelso, who would be sleeping in the small cabin on the back of the place. Both Finney and Kelso had become minor partners in her ventures while still on salary. Finney had been prepared for it; Kelso was more reluctant.

"The town is growing, Mr. Kelso," she had said impatiently. "We must grow with it. The Californios are doing it. You must also."

"I've no head for business," he grumbled.

She had smiled at him. "But I have, Mr. Kelso. Leave it to me."

He followed the maid back into the house, shrugging into his coat, for the night was cool. She noticed he was wearing a gun.

"We're going to see Don Isidro," she said. "I am going to end this, once and for all."

"He won't listen, ma'am."

"He'll listen. Doña Elena is there, too. Together we shall make him listen."

Only a few lights showed, but there were several horses in the corrals, and from the men's quarters there was loud talk and laughter. Kelso stared that way, then said, "That's a bad lot, ma'am. You sure you want to go through with this? They tell me the old man's gotten meaner with years."

"They are drinking. They will not even know we are here, and we shall not be. Not for long."

Reluctantly he walked up to the door and knocked. There was a long silence, and he was lifting his hand to knock again when a hard-featured woman opened the door.

"*Sí?* What is it?"

"We wish to see Don Isidro."

"He wishes to see nobody. Especially he wishes to see no gringos."

Miss Nesselrode's tone was sharp. "Then we will see Doña Elena. We will see her *now!*"

The woman hesitated a moment; then, turning, she walked away from them and they followed. She passed through an arch, there was muttered talk, and then Doña Elena appeared.

She came to them. "My good friend! You come *here?* It is danger-ous! What is it you wish?"

"To speak to Don Isidro. Don Federico has followed Johannes into the desert. We hear he is watching all the water holes to kill him when he appears. I want it stopped, and I want it stopped now."

"He will not listen, señora. It is dangerous here. You must go."

"I must see him."

She hesitated. "Please? Come this way."

He was slumped in a great hide chair, a cigar in his fingers, and he looked up, then straightened when he recognized Miss Nesselrode.

"What is this woman doing here?" he demanded harshly. "Get her out of here! How dare you permit her to come into my house!"

"Don Federico is in the desert. He is pursuing your grandson and is trying to kill him. I want it stopped."

"*You* want it stopped? And who are you? Get out of here!"

"I wish her to stay, and I wish you to listen."

Don Isidro turned sharply as Elena spoke. For a moment he was speechless; then he said, "*You* wish? Who are you to wish anything? Go to your room!"

"No, my brother, I shall stay. If anyone leaves, it shall be you."

He stared, the veins in his forehead swelled, and his face turned white. "*Elena!*" he shouted. "You . . . !" Words failed him.

In the moment of silence as he struggled for words, she spoke quietly but firmly. "No, my brother, you will not order me from this room, which is mine, nor this house, which is also mine."

Don Isidro struggled to rise, then fell back. "Woman!" he shouted. "How dare you speak to me in such a manner? *Your* house?"

"My house," Elena replied firmly. "You ignored the taxes, I paid them. You ignored the loans that came due, I bought them up. This house is my house. The ranch is my ranch. You may live on here if you behave yourself."

He started to his feet and reached for his cane. He grasped it and started as if to strike her, and then her words seemed to have reached him for the first time.

"What have you done? Where would you get such money?"

Doña Elena seemed no longer frail. "I had money from our mother," she replied quietly, "and I have invested it. All the while you sat about, eaten by hatred and pride, I was doing as many Californios were doing. This land is mine, this house is mine.

"You will send a rider to Don Federico. You will tell him to return. You will tell him he is not to harm Johannes Verne."

"I will kill you!" He stared at her, his features twisted from the violence of his emotions.

She smiled. At that moment, Miss Nesselrode thought, Doña Elena was magnificent. "If you do"—her voice was clear—"Johannes Verne will inherit. Then you will be living in *his* house! Eating *his* food! I have left it all to him. My will has been filed in the manner of this country. My lawyer has been instructed."

"You cannot do this," Don Isidro muttered. "It is a trick! You are insane! I shall tell them you are insane."

"And will they believe you or me?"

There was a stir in the doorway behind them. The woman stood there, and beside her were three men. Two of them held guns.

Miss Nesselrode started to speak, then stopped. "Ma'am," Kelso spoke quietly, "I told you we should not have come. You surely meant well, but . . ."

Don Isidro sat down again, his cane across his knees. He took up his cigar, brushed away the ash, and held it to the candle. He puffed, then puffed again. The hand that held the cigar trembled.

"So now," he said, "all is not the same. If what you say, my sister, is true, and if you own this place and Johannes Verne is your heir, then who is his heir?

"Does he have a son?" The old man smiled. "So I shall win, after all.

"Don Federico will kill Johannes. You will be killed, and *I* shall inherit it all!"

He waved a hand at the men and the woman in the doorway. "And these I shall pay, richly, as they deserve."

He looked up at Elena. "You see, my sister, I shall win it all. I shall go to them, these people who sit in their offices, and I shall be greatly worried. I shall tell them you two have ridden into the desert after Johannes, and they will believe me.

"Especially after your bodies are found. They will have no doubts. They will say, 'Oh, those foolish ones! Why did they go?'

"And I shall smile, and be content, at last."

54

Into the night, into the desert, back to the long days when the heat drained the strength from my body, back into the silences, alone.

They would be coming after me when dawn broke; until then they could find no trail, although a sound might bring them.

Pausing, I could hear the sound of running horses, then silence as they, too, listened. If they found me, I would die within minutes, and I did not wish to die. In Los Angeles was Meghan.

Stepping carefully to a flat ledge of rock, I walked along, careful not to kick a pebble that might alert them.

By now they knew I was without a horse and that I had lost my rifle, with which I might kill at a distance. Also, they must have some idea of my physical condition. With the coming of daylight, catching me should be easy, and once I was located, they had only to close in to rifle range and kill me, with no danger to themselves.

There was a large flat rock near where I had stopped, so I sat down. They would waste no time now, not wishing to trample out any footprints, but would wait for daylight.

Now I must think. They would know of my Indian friends and would patrol the edge of the desert to keep me from them. My guess was that Don Federico, probably through Chato, had made contact with one of the gangs of bandits who infested the area and hired additional men.

As I sat, I chewed on a stick of jerked beef, then drank a few swallows of water. No doubt they would scatter themselves in a long skirmish line as they rode into the desert, and he who sighted me would signal the others, who would then close in. When all had gathered, they would kill me.

To outdistance them in my present condition would be almost impossible. My alternative was to hide.

Where? How?

Rising, I walked into the desert, and finding a dry wash, followed it for some distance. Heavy sand dragged at my feet, yet in the sand my feet would leave no discernible impression. Off to the east were the Bullion Mountains, of which I could remember nothing, although in the long days and nights among the Indians we had talked much of the desert. They were north and east, and I wished to work my way to the south, closer to the San Jacintos.

Slowly, steadily, I walked. Exhaustion left my muscles heavy and my brain dull. I slogged on, step after step, like a man walking in his sleep or drugged. Several times I stumbled. At least twice I fell. At last, able to go no further, I fell on the ground near several ancient Joshua trees. Rolling over on my back, I looked up at the stars. I was through, finished; I could go no further.

My eyes opened to a gray sky. Clouds. . . . I could not hope for rain, but they might stay. Even an hour or two would help. Slowly, and with difficulty, I sat up.

Sometime during the night I had lost the rags of one moccasin. With my knife I cut off part of the leg of my pants and wrapped it about my foot, tying it with a strip of rawhide left from my buckskin shirt.

For a moment I sat still, gathering my strength; then I rolled over and pushed myself up. By now they would be looking for me.

How far had I come? Three miles? Five? Perhaps even ten. I had walked steadily, although not making much time, but if I had made only two miles an hour, I could be ten miles away now, and they would have to find my trail.

South of me now was a wide, rough stretch of country, a place of great sandstone boulders, heaps of them, and many Joshua trees. It was a place where a man might hide. Somewhere in that vast sweep of country was where Peg-Leg used to hide his stolen horses. I broke into a stumbling run and held it for what must have been a half-mile; then I fell. Pushing myself up, I saw horse tracks.

Several horses had come through here, most of them unshod. They had come through on the run several days back. Pursued by something, man or animal. Yet they might lead me to water.

My canteen was still more than half-full, so I held to my course, following the wash, which led generally east.

The mountains were on my right, but my enemies would be there also. Suddenly on my right I saw an ancient cairn. Just three rocks, one atop the other, slick with desert varnish and almost pushed over by the Joshua tree growing up beside it.

Pausing, I stared at it, my eyes blinking slowly as my fogged brain tried to make sense of it. Old . . . old it was, older by far than the Joshua, perhaps as old as some of the people who left chipped blades along Pinto wash, made so long ago that rivers had run in the desert.

Yet I was starting on when I saw the other, smaller rock on the side of the cairn. A rock that indicated direction, but direction for what? To what?

Direction . . . I had no direction. Only a desire to escape, only a longing for the mountains, the cool, cool mountains. I took the direction the rock showed.

A dozen steps, maybe two dozen, and then a dim trail, such a trail as only the desert-skilled could recognize, and only a few feet of it, but a direction. I followed it, found more of the trail, and stupidly happy to have found something familiar, I staggered on.

Pausing near a giant Joshua, I peered around me, blinking. Nothing, nothing yet. But somewhere they were coming, they were looking for me.

Taking a brief swallow of water, I shook my head, trying through the fog of weariness to order some thoughts. Keep to low ground, don't let even my head show. My pursuers would have the advantage of being on horseback and could see further.

There was a chance that, feeling sure of me, they would not start at once but would breakfast first. I might have an hour, perhaps a little more.

The ancient trail lay before me, no more than six inches wide, often less, but an Indian trail walked by those who put one foot down ahead of the other. Where the trail led, I had no idea, except that the direction was right. I started on, trotting now.

The morning clouds were gone, the sun was hot. Distantly I heard a shot. Had they found my trail, then? It could be, but I had left them little. Slowing to a walk, I turned down through a stand of Joshua trees and boulders, then across a small, shallow valley; then I sat down and rested again, but the rock was almost too hot for sitting, so I got up and went on. Now the old trail was more definite, and looking back, I could see no tracks or evidence of my passing.

A place to hide . . . *anything!*

I stumbled on. My improvised moccasin had worn through and the other was falling apart. My mind was hazy with exhaustion. I staggered, fell again, got up again, standing on my feet, staring through the shimmering heat waves.

Who was that?

Somebody . . . something . . . in the heat waves. I blinked my eyes and squinted against the glare. Somebody . . . an Indian?

An old Indian . . . or was I seeing things? I had stopped. He was an old Indian, very old. He wore a faded red shirt, open to the waist. On his head a sort of cloth band or turban. "Who . . . ?"

There was a flat piece of turquoise on a string around his neck.

He lifted a hand and pointed to the rocks on my right. I looked, then looked back.

He was gone.

Starting forward, I called out, looking around. No one . . . and no tracks.

Of course, on this ancient trail, so worn, so hard-packed, such tracks would hardly be seen.

Suddenly I heard a distant call, then a shot. The old Indian had pointed. . . . I turned and ran where he had pointed, fell, got up again, and saw a crack between the boulders and went through it, worming my way into the cool darkness of a place heavily shadowed by the rocks.

There was a small tank where rainwater had collected; a few gallons remained. There was a place where ancient fires had burned, blackening the rocks. I crawled back, deeper into the shadows. From my holster I took my gun, and there I lay, waiting for them to come.

There was a rush of horses' hooves, horses that charged by, scattered among the rocks, some riding on. After a while several riders came back.

One of them said, "Now, where the hell . . . ?"

"Back yonder somewheres," another said.

"Tonio," another said, "he loco. Hears nothing! He always hearin' something! He always claimin' to hear something, see something! I t'ink he hears *nothing!*"

"I don't think he ever got this far," the first voice said. "I ain't seen a track in miles, an' he can't be that good!"

"Seen some horse tracks back yonder," another commented.

"Wild stuff. I seen tracks a dozen times. Must be some of that bunch Ventura an' his crowd was chasin'. He said he ran 'em into the desert."

"Ain't more'n five or six head."

The voices grew fainter and passed out of hearing. I waited, clutching my gun. The place where I lay was hardly wide enough to turn around in, although right where the old fire had been there was room for two or three. It was no kind of a hideout, just a place where some Indians at some time had come to get out of the wind. The entrance crack being narrow, it was an unlikely spot, and there were a thousand like it not too far away in this vast jumble of boulders stacked into amazing piles.

Pillowing my head on my arm, I went to sleep, and it was the cold that awakened me. My arm was stiff and asleep. I shook it, pounded it to get the circulation going again, and sat up, listening.

There was no sound; all was very still. Lying back down, I went to sleep again, and when I awakened it was morning. Drinking a little water, I leaned back against the rock wall and rested, dozing.

They would be out there, waiting and watching. Maybe not within miles of where I was, but watching. This was not very far, I judged, from Stubby Spring . . . or Lost Horse Wells. At least, somewhere around. When night came, I would crawl out of here and start on my trek to the mountains.

There was a deep canyon west of where I lay, and if there was a trail into it—and there might be a way down from the spring—I could follow the canyon down, cut through the hills beyond by the canyon where the palms were, and then cross the valley to my friends.

Thinking of it made it sound easy; doing it would be something else. It would be a long, tough trip, and they might know about Stubby Spring and have it staked out. By that time I would need water with which to cross the country ahead of me, and I was going to get it.

If one or two men waited at Stubby Spring, we were all in trouble. I had a loaded six-shooter and twenty-four rounds in my cartridge belt, and I was in no mood for playing games. I'd been run over some of the driest, roughest country around. My feet were sore, I was worn down to a frazzle, and I was mad. If they were waiting there, it was because they intended to kill me, so they had bought cards in a rough game.

When the shadows started to fall, I edged out of my corner in the rocks and listened before coming clear out. I heard never a sound, but came out and started to walk. Stubby Spring was not far off.

Reaching back, I slipped the loop off my six-shooter and hitched it into position.

My canteen was full from the tank and I took a swallow just as I started. My mouth was dry as the inside of an old packrat's nest, and my temper was running on mad.

A moment before they saw me, I saw their horses. There were two of them, and they saw me as I saw them, and I shot the one with the rifle.

I staggered but fired as I did so. The man who shot at me swore in Spanish, although he was an Anglo, and then cut loose at me again, but he missed, his shots going wild because he had taken three of mine.

He was settling down to the ground, and their horses were running wild off down the trail. Sitting on the sand, I was thumbing cartridges into my six-shooter, and when I was ready to start shooting, I looked over to where their fire was, and they were both down.

Holding my gun ready, I got to my knees and managed to lunge up to a standing position. Then I walked up to their camp, and there was a coffeepot on the fire and some bacon frying.

One of them had fallen so his pants were beginning to smolder, so I nudged his leg over with my toe and ate the bacon. Then I drank some coffee and went to where the rifle had fallen. My bullet had ruined the action, and the smashed-out-of-shape bullet had ripped off it into that man. He was torn up pretty bad.

55

Lying near the fire where the two men had taken them from one of the horses was a pair of saddlebags and an old canvas rucksack. Dumping out the contents, which consisted of odds and ends a drifting man carries, I found a needle and thread, both of heavy stuff for mending coarse cloth or other gear, and filling the empty loops of my cartridge belt from theirs, I headed into the broken country near the canyon's edge.

That canyon looked to be all of two thousand feet deep, but where the runoff from Stubby Spring fell into the canyon it looked like a man might make it. If I could get down there, any pursuers would have to ride a long way around.

Right now I wanted to get away from the spring, so I refilled my canteen, drank from the spring, and carrying the empty saddlebags and the rucksack, I found my way into the broken country near the canyon's rim.

Sitting down in a hidden spot where I could watch the trail from the spring, I started to build myself a pair of moccasins. It was not a difficult job, and every Indian and most mountain men were doing it constantly, as moccasins had a way of wearing out.

Taking my time and using the material from the saddlebags, I cut out the moccasins and stitched them together, a better pair than I'd had since starting. I put the rest of the leather into the old rucksack and started hunting a way down into the canyon.

Nobody had ever told me climbing down into a canyon like that was going to be easy, so I took my time, easing from ledge to ledge, walking along here, using hands and feet against the rock wall at other places, until I got down.

There might have been easier places, but I'd no time for looking. On the bottom I rested in the shade of the cliff and then started down the canyon.

Maybe I'd walked three miles when I saw the buzzards. There were several of them and they were circling above something down below. Checking my gun to see if it was there, I climbed around some boulders, stepped along on some rocks, and went around a dead Joshua washed down by some flash flood.

Suddenly several buzzards started up from the ground, but they did not fly away. What was down there was dying, not dead.

Now I moved with greater care. My ears told me nothing beyond an occasional squawk from the buzzards. A couple of them had stopped flying and had perched themselves on rocks close above something they were watching. I could see their ugly necks crane to peer closer.

Then I came around a corner of rock and saw three horses. Two of them were down, one struggling to rise. The third horse was standing, legs spraddled, head hanging, obviously all in. Yet when one of the buzzards started down, his head came up and he moved at it.

They heard me scrambling down the rocks. The horse lifted his head and stared.

It was my black stallion.

For a moment I stopped dead still. I never saw a horse that looked worse and was still on his feet. He had fallen or been attacked by something. One shoulder was all torn and bloody, and there was a nasty laceration on one hip.

His head was up and he was staring at me, but he moved a little closer to protect the mare that was down.

"It's all right, boy," I said, "I'm coming!"

His ears pricked a little. I think he knew my voice, and he should have. I'd talked to him enough, from time to time.

Then I remembered the tracks I'd seen now and then and the conversation I'd overheard when somebody named Ventura was spoken of as chasing a small bunch of horses—"not more than five or six head." Well, there were only three of them now, and one was dead. Coming closer, I saw the horse that was down had a shattered leg, one of the worst breaks I ever saw. That down horse was suffering a good bit and needed killing, but I dared not do it until I'd done something for the stallion. A shot now might frighten the stallion into running, and in the desert like this, he would surely die.

Speaking softly, I walked nearer, trying not to frighten him. He was in no shape to run, as whoever had chased them had simply run them ragged, and tough as he was, that big stallion was only hours away from going down himself, and then the buzzards would move in.

Edging closer, I took off my hat, and unstopping my canteen, I poured about half of the water into my hat and held it for the stallion to drink. He shied a mite but was too bad off to run, and when he smelled that water, he moved closer.

He dipped his nose into my hat and drank. He drank it all and wanted more, but what I had must be kept. We had a long way to go. However, in that canyon there was water, the canyon where the palm trees were. Getting there was another thing. It would be tough for me, tougher for that black horse.

With the straps from the rucksack, I made a makeshift bridle. From the beginning I'd had a hunch that horse had been ridden at some time or at least handled by some man or woman. He stood quiet while I slipped the bridle on, and let me lead him off down the canyon a ways. Leaving him standing there, I walked back and put that down horse out of its misery.

Leading the black stallion, I started down the canyon. There was water aplenty at Thousand Palms, but getting there would be a trick. No longer did I have just myself to worry about, but a mighty big horse that would need a lot of water.

The canyon down which we were walking, with the desert opening before us, collected runoff from several intermittent creeks, so when I saw a hollow near a boulder with cracked mud in the bottom, I decided to take a chance. Horses, wild horses at least, were good at finding water and sometimes pawing the dirt out to get at it.

Using my bowie knife, I started digging at the ground to see if there was water. When I'd worked maybe a half-hour I began finding damp earth, and down deeper, water began to come in. Scooping out more dirt, I let the water seep in. It was slow, but it came. That stallion needed no urging. He just put his head down and sucked it all up.

We stayed right there until sundown, and whenever there was water enough seeped in, I let the big black drink. Meanwhile I scouted around and found some jimsonweed growing. That was no great wonder, because it can be found growing most everywhere along roads and up canyons, even sometimes on the bald desert. Crushing up some of the leaves with water, I plastered them on the sores. Then I washed my hands with fresh sand, not trusting the weed too much.

When shadows started to gather, I got up. "All right, boy," I said, "let's you and me go home."

He came right along after me, and I did not even have to lead him. He knew when he'd found a friend. I would have dearly liked to ride him, but he was in no shape for that.

We started, taking our time, because he was a very tired horse. The water had done wonders for him, and I'd managed a drink for myself before we started out. Most of the way was downhill, a long, gentle slope. It would be that way until we were fairly close to the palm canyon; then we'd have to climb a bit. By that time the stallion would smell the water and would be eager to get to it.

We plodded along past smoke trees and occasional palo verde that grew along the wash, until we found the wide valley scattered with palms—singles, twos, and groves. Some were ragged with thick skirts of palm leaves that had served their time and folded over at the bottoms of the trees, with the leaves of successive years thickening the skirts as the trees grew tall. Some had been burned, leaving the trunks blackened but alive, but here and there the fires had proved too much and the palms had died.

It was a wild, desolate scene of fallen trees and scattered palm leaves, long dead. From among the palms a lonely coyote trotted away with only occasional backward glances at us who disturbed him.

From along the base of one grove there was a trickle of water rimmed with the white of alkali. Bad-tasting though it was, both the stallion and I drank and drank, then drank again.

Climbing a bench away from the small stream, we found a place under some palms where I searched for sidewinders or rattlers and found none. Lying down on some palm fronds, I promptly fell asleep and awakened hours later with the stallion nudging me with his nose. I put my hand on his neck, and he shied unconvincingly. Rising, I checked the sores on his back. They looked better, but I found no jimsonweed to renew the dressing, although the locality was a likely spot for it to grow.

"Come on, boy, we're going home."

Ten miles or so to the mountains across the valley, but ten miles in a wide-open valley with no place to hide.

It was early evening before I walked up the dusty lane to where the store stood.

The small ramshackle house was empty. The door hung on leather-strap hinges; the chimney had fallen, breaking through a part of the roof; wind whined under the eaves and whispered sand across the porch. I looked within. Dust, a broken box, a couple of empty bottles, and a sad-looking dented bucket. Well, he had not been a settler, only a squatter, moved on to fresher fields.

Walking beside the black stallion, I went along the road toward home. Rounding the last dune, I saw the ocotillo that fenced the place, but the house was gone.

The walls had toppled; the chimney was a dark, questioning finger; a charred beam lay across where the living room had been. Leaving the horse, I walked up to the ruins. The spine and part of the charred cover of a book . . .

Walking on past, and calling the stallion, I went to the water trough. It sat there on its sturdy forked legs, unshaken by earthquake, unharmed by fire, clear cold water running from the rusted pipe into it. The stable roof had collapsed, but the corners still stood.

In the gathering dusk I stood and looked around. Gone . . . all gone, this last place where I had lived with my father and where, despite his illness, we had been briefly happy.

While the stallion drank his fill, I sat on one of the fallen stones. What now of my lonely giant? What of the strange one from the mountains who came to my house for books and brought the smell of pines?

At the pipe I emptied and refilled my canteen. I could not remain here. My enemies would come here first of all, and they could not be far behind me. By now they would have found the bodies by Stubby Spring and my destination would be obvious. They would not take the time to track but would come directly here.

Tired though I was, I must find another place, a place to go, to hide. And then I must return to Los Angeles and to Meghan.

But where now? To Palm Canyon? There were nearly always some of the Indians there, but why take them trouble?

Yet I might be able to borrow a bridle and saddle, and the sores on the stallion's back were not where they would be chafed by a saddle or a girth.

Yet as I turned away, something stopped me. Turning, I walked back to the chimney, counted the bricks in the fireplace, and then worried one of them loose.

My father's gold, my gold. I had forgotten about it until now. It was still there. I pocketed the gold and replaced the brick.

All I wanted now was to rest, to stay in one place, to relax if even for a day.

There was a place I knew, a place where I had gone sometimes with

Francisco; it was a hollow surrounded by mesquite and a few palms where grass had grown, and no doubt had one dug, he might have found water there, a seep from the mountain that rose sharply up for almost two miles right behind the place.

It was a place to hide, a place to rest, a place where they might not find me.

When I reached the place, nothing had changed. I picketed the black horse, using a length of rope found at the stable, and then I stretched out on the soft ground, looked up at the stars and the black wall of the mountain, and then I closed my eyes and slept.

In the night the mountain stirred, rumbles came from deep within it, and I awakened, listening, suddenly alert. Another quake? We who live with them become accustomed, at least to the small ones. A few stones rattled down the dark flanks of the mountain.

Tahquitz again, trying to escape from his walled-up cavern.

I thought of that, thought of our own Tahquitz, the mysterious visitor from the mountain, and then I thought of Don Federico.

Suddenly I sat up, and just as suddenly I was mad; a deep, fierce anger stirred in me. I had been chased and shot at, my life made miserable by the harassment of one man . . . or two men. Yet my grandfather had bothered me less, of late.

All right, they wanted a fight. I would give it to them. Tomorrow I would become the hunter, and no longer the hunted.

Again I slept, and when I opened my eyes a man in a pink shirt, a blue neckerchief, and a wide hat was sitting on the bank watching me.

"You sleep well," he said, "for a hunted man."

It was Francisco.

"Today I become the hunter," I said. "Now begins a war."

"I think so. It is time."

56

Tomás was near the fire, his dark eyes alert. The boy had dropped back toward the shadows, nearer the horses. "Leave her alone," Tomás said.

Iglesias did not turn his eyes from her. "Do not be an old fool! Who will know? Who comes here?"

"Johannes Verne will know. He reads sign like an Apache. He will come. He will find you."

"Bah! He is dead. They are killing him in the desert! She is a pigeon to be plucked. She is the little dove and we are the hawks."

Biscal was on his feet, and so was the third man, who was edging closer. Meghan's heart was beating slowly, heavily. Her small pistol was gripped in her right hand concealed by the folds of her dress. She had but two bullets, two shots to be fired. The barrel was short, and they must be close. She must not miss.

Yet she was not frightened. She had been, but not now. Her father, who had had many a brush with Chinese and Malay pirates, often talked of such things. "Think," he had said, "and act with coolness. Do what must be done."

Tomás looked across the fire at her and said in a casual tone, "Johannes will be with his friends, the Cahuillas. Tell them you are his and they will be your friends also."

The Cahuillas? Her friends? Was he suggesting that she escape? That she go to the Indians? But how . . . ?

They were edging closer.

"Stop!" Tomás ordered. He reached for his rifle on the rock near him, and Biscal shot him.

She saw him stagger, and the unnamed man lunged for her. She lifted her pistol and shot him in the stomach. As the gun lifted she saw the sudden flash of terror in the man's eyes. He was already within four feet of her, his hands outstretched. The pistol was unexpected, but he could not stop or even try to evade. He was too close.

His mouth gaped with a cry that never came. She was close enough so she heard the heavy, sodden thud of the .44 bullet as it hit him.

She stepped back quickly and turned the gun on Biscal and Iglesias.

"*Señorita!*" The boy shouted. "Señorita, *please!*"

It was her horse, saddled. . . . She fired another shot that missed, then grabbed the pommel and swung into the saddle. Her skirt caught on the cantle as her other leg swung across the saddle, but the horse was off, plunging into the night.

Behind her she heard another shot, a cry . . . silence.

Who had been shot? The boy? Tomás again?

She had no memory of using her spurs, but she must have, for her horse was running wildly into the night, leaping rocks and weaving through the brush and cacti.

South. She must go south, into the wilderness Johannes loved so well; she must try to find him, try to find those Indians who were his friends. Tomás had not suggested she ride back toward Los Angeles. . . . Why? Did he fear there would be too many bandits there? One had less to fear from the wilderness than from men.

She drew up, listening. There was no sound of pursuit. What of Tomás? What of the boy? Yet, to return now would make all their sacrifice for nothing, and make their situation no better and hers worse.

She glanced at the stars. She had been often at sea with her father, and the stars were familiar. She knew no trails, but the North Star was there. She looked for the Pointers in the end of the Big Dipper, and found the North Star; then she turned south.

The San Bernardino Mountains were on her right, low against the sky. She would be safer if she were closer to them. There would be better grazing for her horse, more chances of water.

Far behind her the boy lay in the brush, biting his fist to keep from crying. The old man was hurt, maybe he was dying. He had done what the old man told him. Prepare the horse, have it ready, then get away. There was no reason he should die.

"What of you?" the boy asked.

"I am an old man. I will do what needs to be done and trust in the Good God for what comes. These are evil men, and she is a fine young woman."

At the last moment he had not been foolish. He fled, but with a good horse under him. Now he waited, wishing they would go away so he could go to Tomás. He was a boy without a family whom Tomás had befriended. Tomás had given him work, made a place for him where he was not really needed, but where he must find work that needed to be done.

The old man was down there, and he was hurting from the bullet, if he was not dead. The boy hoped he was not dead.

The young woman had shot one of them. She had shot that dark, ugly man whom he did not know. He was someone who rode with Biscal, someone who might be one of the men of Vásquez.

Beside the fire Tomás had his eyes almost shut. The hurt was very bad, and he, too, wished they would go. He lay very still, guarding himself against a sound, hoping they would think him dead.

There was much blood. He could feel it, and he could feel the hurt, but the little one was gone, she had gotten away, and the boy was gone, too. So be it. He was an old man, not new to suffering and hurt. He could accept it.

He wished his rifle was nearer. He might kill one of them or both, and so let the boy come back, and then they might help the señorita.

Hah! The small pistol! Who would have thought she had such a thing or would use it?

Iglesias walked over to him. Tomás heard his boots on the gravel. Suddenly he was kicked viciously in the ribs. He made no sound. To moan was to die.

"It was a little gun," Biscal said, "two barrels. I have seen such a one called a derringer, and she has shot twice."

"She is unarmed, then?"

"Of course. Let us go. It is very wild land. She will be lost and wandering. Let her be without water and she will welcome us."

"The small pistol," Iglesias said. "Who would have believed?" He looked down at Tomás. "He was an old fool. He need not be dead. Who is he to interfere with me?"

Biscal looked sourly at the fallen man, then at the other one. "She shot true, the little one," he said. "That one is dead, too."

He took up his rifle and walked toward the brush where the remaining horses had been picketed, away from the flies. "She will not go far," Biscal commented. "Our horses will find her horse. Let us go."

Iglesias looked around. "You get the horses," he suggested.

When Biscal had gone, he walked to the fallen man and went through his pockets. "Fifty pesos," he muttered. "You had fifty pesos."

When he had it, he stood up and walked toward Tomás. "Bah," he spoke aloud, "you had nothing. Not for even one drink. It is better you are dead."

Not until the last sound of their horses had died out did Tomás move, and when he moved, it hurt. The bullet, he believed, had gone through him, for there was blood under him, too.

The coffeepot was on the fire. It was his coffeepot, and neither Biscal nor Iglesias had bothered with it. Their drink was tequila. Well, he could use a little himself. He could use it now.

The boy came slowly down, watchful, leading his horse. "What can I do?" he asked.

"For the señorita there is nothing. Now it is in the hands of God." He looked up at the boy. "For me, also, it is in the hands of God, and you."

"I have not the experience."

"We will drink the coffee, some for you, some for me. Then you will put water in the pot, get it hot, and bathe around the wounds. I do not know what good it will do, but I shall feel better."

"Does it hurt much?"

"A little. I have been hurt before." His face was gray and his eyes showed the hurt his lips would not reveal. "In my saddlebags there is tequila, a little only. I shall have a drink. Then, when you have bathed the wounds, you will put some on the wounds. Again, I do not know what it will do, but we shall see."

He leaned back and closed his eyes, and the boy became busy.

"There are plants. My good mother knew them all. I shall have to think. I shall have to remember."

The boy came with a blanket and put it about his shoulders, and they drank the coffee.

"Now," Tomás said, "the washing."

A stick dropped in the fire, and sparks went up. The boy filled the empty coffeepot and turned; then he stopped, frightened.

A man was standing at the edge of the firelight, a man like he had not seen before.

He walked on into the camp, a horse following him. He glanced around, at Tomás, then at the boy. "Yes," he said, "make hot. I look at him. While I am looking, you tell me what has happened."

Yacub Khan knelt beside Tomás and drew back the coat; then with a knife, razor sharp, he cut away the bloody shirt.

"Tell all. Leave nothing out. Where is she who rode with you?"

As the boy talked, Yacub Khan went to his saddlebags. Working as he listened, he took the hot water when it was ready and bathed the wounds, front and back.

Tomás' eyes flickered and opened. He peered at Yacub Khan, wrinkling his brow. "Do not worry," Yacub said. "I have experience with this. From long ago I have seen men gun-shot, saber-cut, and stabbed. Stab is often the worst. I do what can be done."

When day was breaking, Tomás was resting. "Let him rest. When he is awake, make broth of the dried beef. I come this way again." He paused a moment. "If I do not, wait five days and then take him home."

Tired as she had been, Meghan had slept but fitfully. Dawn was breaking now, and the strangeness of the place awakened her. She had slept among trees at the mountain's foot, and now she sat up. Her horse grazed placidly on a patch of grass nearby.

She was thirsty and hungry, but there was no time to think of that. Johannes was somewhere to the south, and fortunately Tomás had been leading them that way before the trouble began. She saddled her horse, watered him at a trickle of runoff water, and started south.

Tomás was dead—of this she was sure. If not dead, then so badly hurt he could not help. The boy, if he escaped those others, would not know what to do. He would, if he could, ride home.

Iglesias and Biscal would follow her. They would be good trackers and they would come on fast. There were ways of hiding a trail, she supposed, but even had she known how, she had not the time. What she needed was a weapon. She had the pistol but no ammunition . . . yet, might there not be another cartridge or two in her saddlebags?

She was not in the desert, but at its edge, following a dim trail left, she expected, by Indians. Down lower she might find an easier trail, but also one more exposed. She was riding through foothills that were wooded or partly wooded.

The trail was suddenly open for some distance, so she rode faster. At the crest of a rise, she drew up among some piñons and glanced back. Was that *dust?*

She glanced ahead; the trail dipped down among the trees, then went up the slope opposite, winding higher along the slope. She would be visible while climbing, but there was no help for it. She rode on, glancing back from time to time. She had reached the bottom and was about to start up the far slope when her horse shied violently, almost unseating her.

She fought the animal for a moment, getting him under control, then started up the slope. What had it been? A mountain lion? A wolf? A bear?

Suddenly off to her left she saw another trail coming up from the desert, apparently to merge with her trail. Frowning, she stood in the stirrups, looking ahead.

Nothing. . . . Glancing back, she saw a rider come from the trees. . . . Iglesias.

Touching her spurs to her horse, she plunged ahead; then a rope shot from the brush and fell neatly around her horse's neck. The horse reared, and she fell. Grabbing at the pommel, she failed to get a grip and hit the ground hard. Her skull rapped on a rock.

She felt the blow, felt a wave of fear and horror, then nothing . . . nothing at all.

Biscal came from the trees, coiling his rope. He glanced at the unconscious girl, then tied his horse and hers.

"You'd better hurry, Iglesias," he said, "I think . . ."

He had squatted beside her, but suddenly his eyes were riveted upon a foot, a foot in a moccasin, and it was the biggest foot he had ever seen.

Awed, he tilted his head back as he came to his feet. His jaw dropped, and he gaped; his eyes went up and up . . . he screamed.

He started to step back, and a gigantic hand swept down and he was knocked from the path. He fell, hitting a rock ten feet below. His body slipped clear and fell again, bringing up on the rocks fifty feet below.

His eyes opened to the sky and he whimpered, tried to draw his knees up and turn. He could not. His back was broken.

Iglesias . . . where was Iglesias? A shadow crossed his face, and Biscal opened his eyes.

A buzzard. . . .

57

Her eyes opened to darkness and flickering shadows. She lay watching the weird lights dancing on the low ceiling without being consciously aware of them. They were just something that was there, like the dull ache in her head. After a while she closed her eyes, but when she opened them the flickering shadows were still there, doing a strange ballet on the ceiling of the cave.

That was ridiculous, of course, yet it did look like a cave. But what would she be doing in a cave? She closed her eyes, living with the dull ache, a result of the fall, no doubt.

Fall? What fall? Oh . . . yes, of course. She had fallen from her horse, or been jerked from it. But who would . . . ? Her mind, still foggy, fumbled with the idea.

Now she was remembering. Somebody had thrown a lasso from the brush and jerked her from her horse.

Biscal, that was the name. He had come from the brush coiling his rope as he walked toward her. That was the last thing she remembered.

Panic-stricken, she opened her eyes wide. Her fingers groped. She was lying on an animal skin, on a fur or hide, and she *was* in a cave and somebody had covered her with a blanket.

She was clothed except for her boots, which lay beside her. She started to sit up, but was hit by a wave of pain, so she lay back down. Something slipped across her eyes, and when she put up her hand, she found a damp cloth. It had been folded and placed across her brow. Slowly her mind fumbled its way back to awareness.

She listened for explanatory sounds. Beyond the crackling from the fire there was nothing. She turned her eyes toward the inner blackness of the cave, for this was a cave. Against the black wall she made out a rifle rack holding two rifles, and standing nearby, a pair of the largest snowshoes she had ever seen. On a rock shelf near them was a row of books.

Books? In a *cave?* She turned her head toward the fire.

The fireplace had been built against the wall, and judging by the flames, had a good draft. Nearby, other shelves were lined with cooking utensils. There was a wood box as well as an ax and a cross-cut saw. Obviously this was no temporary shelter but a place where somebody actually lived, at least from time to time.

Who had brought her here? What kind of person would live in such a place? There was a solid, tight-fitting door with hinges, one of the largest doors she had ever seen other than on a stable. Looking around again, she realized the cave was a permanent habitation prepared by a neat, careful person who enjoyed reading. That could be neither Biscal nor Iglesias, who were vaqueros turned outlaw.

Suddenly the latch lifted and the door opened outward, grasped by a hand as large as a dinner plate. She sat up quickly as the door was filled with the most tremendous human being she had ever seen. A huge head with beetling brows, bulging cheekbones, and a massive jaw. He came into the cave, closing the door behind him.

"Do not be frightened. I am your friend."

He placed her saddlebags on the floor near her. "Your horse is cared for. All is well. You may rest."

There was an amazing resonance to his voice, as though he spoke from a deep well. "The *banditos?* Do not fear them. They are gone."

"What happened?"

He sat upon the floor. Sitting down, he was almost as tall as she. "One caught you with his rope. He was surprised when I stepped down from the rocks, but he reached for his gun." The giant was embarrassed. "I slapped him over the cliff. He fell on rocks, far below."

"And the other one?"

"His horse was frightened." There was a shadow of amusement in the big man's eyes. "I have that effect on horses that do not know me. The horse ran away with him."

He turned to the fire. "Will you have coffee? You must pardon the poor things I have here. This is just a place where I stay sometimes when I am in these mountains." He paused, glancing at her. "Sometimes I am not well. I have headaches and must be prepared for that." He pointed off to the south. "My home is in the San Jacintos."

"You are Tahquitz!"

He chuckled. It was an amazing, rather marvelous sound. "Tahquitz! He used to capture maidens and take them to his cave and eat them." He gave her a sidelong glance. "But I am not hungry!"

"I'm certainly glad you're not, but I am! Dreadfully hungry!"

He handed her the coffee. "I have little here, but I will see what can be done." He glanced around at her. "You are Meghan Laurel. I am Alfredo."

He took down a frying pan and a slab of bacon. He began slicing bacon into the pan with an amazingly sharp knife. "Do you know who Alfredo is? Alfredo is the disgrace. Alfredo is the shame. Alfredo was born large and grew larger, and my father was embarrassed. He hid me away and then brought me to California, but on a different ship. Then he gave me to a servant and gave her money to take me away. Anywhere away from him. He could not stand it that he had sired a monster." He added sticks to the fire. "She was a rare woman, that servant, a rare, rare woman.

"She had come from Spain with him, and she loved my mother and loved me, too, if you can believe that."

"I can believe it."

"She was a wild one, that woman. She said she was a witch. She had come from the desert, and was a Berber.

"Do you know of them? They were a white nomadic people who ruled all the Sahara and what lay north of it, from as long as could be remembered.

"He expected me to be killed or abandoned, but she carried me off at night to a remote village of the Indians, and at night when I had the headaches she would rock me to sleep and sing to me the songs of her people. I remember them yet.

"The following year she took me into Mexico to a priest who was a wise man. His blood was as hers, and it was he who taught me to read, write, and work with numbers. Much else besides. He was a good, good man, educated far beyond his time.

"He explained to me that I would be very large and that there was within people a fear of anything different than themselves. It was a deep-seated, primitive fear found among many wild creatures. A white wolf to exist among gray wolves must become a fierce fighter or be killed. It is a fear, perhaps, of attracting attention and therefore danger.

"He told me that if I was to survive I must understand this, that I must be tolerant even when others were intolerant, that I must be wary of man."

"You knew my name," Meghan said, remembering.

"Johannes is my nephew. His mother, Consuelo, was my sister.

"We brought double disgrace to my father. I by being born a giant, and she by marrying a poor seaman."

He dished up several slices of bacon, adding a handful of piñon nuts and several cold tortillas to the plate.

"It is very little. Had I expected a visitor, I would have prepared for it."

"Where is Johannes? I must find him! Is he all right?"

"He lives, but he suffered much. I think he plans to move against them. It would be like him, and like his father."

"You are sure he is all right? Alfredo, I must find him! I love him very, very much and I am afraid he will not come back to Los Angeles."

"Of course he will come back."

"You do not understand. Don Federico came to see me. He was charming. I suppose I was flattered by it. He was an older man, and so handsome! I told Johannes, and I never thought . . ."

"You should have been wiser, but who of us is? Johannes wants to be nowhere where that man has been. Don Federico is an evil man, as he was an evil boy. He thinks only of himself." Alfredo smiled suddenly, amusement dancing in his eyes. "He believes me dead, and wishes to believe it. Perhaps it is time to give him a hint."

"Can you take me to Johannes? I must see him!"

"I can take you to where he is, or at least to where he was, or I can see you in safety to Los Angeles."

"Take me to him! I must see him! I must see him before he goes off again!"

"When the sun rises. Stay here . . . you will be safe." He gestured toward the forest. "I have another place."

"Why don't you come to Los Angeles with me? There's no need for you to stay here!"

He chuckled. "Los Angeles has never been surprised by anything, I think. It began with the Spanish and the Indians, and it began with a flair. It has always loved the flamboyant, the graceful dons riding their splendid horses, their saddles plated with silver, but it is not for me. Can you imagine me down there?

"A man of six feet is considered unusually tall. Most men are five-feet-eight or less." He smiled gently. "I am seven feet and eight inches and I usually weigh four hundred pounds.

"They would gasp, they would stare, they would ask how tall I am and be disappointed it is not taller. The doors will be too narrow, the ceilings too low, and the chairs are made for dwarfs.

"Out here it is different. I am made small by mountains. I am a midget among the trees. Down there is fear, hatred, and jealousy. Here there is pure air, simple food, and I have my books.

"You see, I have become a night person. I see as well by night as any bat or owl. The trails I walk are walked by me alone, and I have places where I can sit and look down upon the desert or even that hot spring where the palms grow. I can look down there where Johannes is—Johannes, my friend."

"You have talked to him?"

"Oh, no! Perhaps that is why he is my friend. We have shared books, and some thoughts, I expect. He knows of me, knows what I am. Perhaps he even knows *who* I am. I wished him to know me, so I left my signature, knowing it would explain more than words.

"To live in a city, one must be larger than one's environment or enjoy belonging to the crowd. Out here a person can become a part of it all. He can walk the heights with the eagles and the clouds, but it needs a special kind of person.

"For me there is no other way. Down there I would be viewed as a monstrosity. My own father saw me that way, so what could I expect from others?"

"Does no one ever see you here?"

"Perhaps an Indian now and again, but they are polite. I do not intrude upon them, and they avoid me."

"They believe you are Tahquitz."

"Nonsense! They call me that because I live on his mountain alone, but they know better. It is a joke among them."

"They are a simple people, I think."

"Simple in their needs, perhaps, but a very complex people."

"You are complex."

"No. Within this giant house of flesh lives a quiet man who would prefer working at a trade. Or perhaps he is a poet whose dreams are too large for his words.

"My home is among the mountains. Men destroy what they do not understand, as they destroyed the son of God when he chose to walk among them. I do not wish to be understood. I wish to be left alone. Your Johannes has done this. He is a kind man, a thoughtful man."

"Are you never lonely?"

"When would I not be lonely? When a man is one of a kind, he will be lonely wherever he is. I am a man apart but have become adjusted to it. I have the mountains, and I have my books. I also have the friendship of Johannes."

He got to his feet, towering over her. Instinctively she shrank. "You see? Sleep well, then. I shall return in the morning. But please . . . rise early. I would like you to see sunrise on the desert from my mountains. Until you have seen sunrise from here, or from over there in the San Jacintos, you have seen nothing."

He went out, ducking his head through the door, closing it softly behind him.

In the night that followed, she wondered if he was out on the dark trails of night where owls cruised on silent wings among the dark ranks of the soldier pines, and only the wind for company.

58

When Don Isidro finished speaking, there was a moment of silence. If Miss Nesselrode was alarmed or frightened, she offered no evidence of it.

"Señor, I am afraid you live in the past. Forty, perhaps even twenty years ago you might have gotten away with such a thing, but no more.

"You have deliberately isolated yourself from the community to such an extent that you are not aware of the changes that have taken place.

"The story of your pursuit of Zachary Verne and your daughter are well known, but that was long ago. If anything were to happen either to me or to your sister Elena, there would be an immediate investigation, and I have been careful to record all the facts and leave them in safe hands.

"If anything happens to Johannes Verne, I shall see you hanged. If anything were to happen to your sister or to me, you would certainly be hanged, and these"—she waved a hand at the group in the doorway— "as well. What then of your pride in your family and your name? It would be disgraced forever, and by you."

She turned on the group in the door. "Put your guns away. Are you afraid of a woman, that you draw guns? Have you thought who will pay for what you do? He has no money. He can pay you nothing, nothing at all. You are fools to follow so blindly where a blind man leads!

"Get out of here! At *once!*" She gestured imperiously. "Mr. Kelso, if they do not leave, shoot them!"

The guns lowered. Confused, the men looked from one to the other, then at Don Isidro. Kelso had drawn his gun. It was a colossal bluff, and nobody knew it better than he, but he stood quietly, waiting.

A man at the back of the group silently turned away, then another. The woman was the last to leave.

"Don Isidro." Miss Nesselrode spoke quietly but her tone was cold and level. "If I were you, I would send a man to recall your Don Federico. I would suggest, also, that you tell him he is not your heir, and never will be. Until he knows that, your own life is not secure. He has shown himself to be a man who will stop at nothing."

"What she says is true, my brother. Even as a boy, he tried to kill Alfredo. A few days ago he threatened me. He only pursues Johannes because he is a possible heir who might dispute his claims to your estate."

Don Isidro stared at her with sullen eyes. "If what you say is true, I have no estate. I have nothing."

"That is true," Elena replied, her voice low. "You have not managed well, my brother, so I have done what was needed, with Miss Nesselrode's help, but Don Federico does not know this. You must recall him. You must recall him at once, before more damage is done."

"According to our laws, you would be an accessory, Don Isidro," Miss Nesselrode added. "It is your own safety you must consider."

"I have no messenger. You have sent them away."

"Write the order," Miss Nesselrode replied. "I will see it delivered by one of those who used to work for you."

Elena went to a desk and brought paper, ink, and a quill to him.

For a moment he stared at the paper; then slowly, reluctantly, he wrote the order.

He looked up at her, his eyes ugly. "You have destroyed me."

"No, my brother. I have tried to save you. You have been destroying yourself. From the first, this foolish pride and your hatred destroyed everything you were or could have been.

"You were harsh and cruel, but how much of it was due to Don Federico? A good deal, I believe. It is he who has been your evil genius, always at your elbow, advising or suggesting. I think you would have relented long ago had it not been for Federico."

The old man shifted in his chair. "The little one," he muttered. "He called me grandpa!"

Kelso holstered his gun. "Ma'am, it's late. I don't know about you, but I was a tired man when the evening began."

"Yes, yes, we must go." Miss Nesselrode turned. "Elena? Will you come with us?"

"I shall stay. He will need me now."

Peter Burkin stripped the gear from his horse at the pole corral among the pines. Through the trees he could see the gleam of water from Hidden Lake. He was later than he had planned to be and would spend the night, something he rarely did.

Hoisting a heavy burlap sack to his shoulder and gripping another sack in his hand, he started over the trail.

It was late afternoon and the sky was clear, the air cool. Twice he paused to rest. "Ain't as young as y'used to be," he said aloud, "or else this here trail is gittin' steeper!"

Alfredo was sitting outside, holding his head in his huge hands.

"You all right, boy?"

Alfredo looked up. His features seemed to have grown heavier, his flesh thicker, but that was probably the way the light fell.

"No, Peter, I do not feel well. It is harder to walk now. I . . . I think my muscles grow weak."

"Brought you some extry grub, some books, an' such. I ain't so spry on these trails, m'self. Gittin' old, I reckon."

Burkin looked around. "Got you a place here, boy. You surely have! Ain't a purtier or more peaceful place anywhere."

"I found Meghan Laurel," he said.

"She is safe?"

"She is with the Indians. With Francisco's woman."

"Was there trouble?"

"Two men. One ran away. The other I . . . I slapped him."

"*You* slapped him?"

They were silent, watching the sun's face grow red as it slipped beyond the mountains where the ocean was. "You all right, boy? Anything I can do for you?"

"You have done too much, Peter. Without you . . . without you I could do nothing."

"Don't worry yourself, Al." Peter took up a stick and poked at the pine needles. "Never had nobody m'self until I met her. An' you.

"I had a lot of dreams, one time, but they come to nothin'. Never had eddication enough, an' I wasn't much of a hand for readin' like you an' them Vernes. I missed out on a lot until I met your ma."

"She wasn't my mother, not really."

"I know that, boy. I know that. But she thought of herself as such, an' so did I. When she was dyin', she told me you was different an' that I should sort of look after you."

"And you did. You've been the father I never experienced, Peter. You've been kind."

"I'm gittin' along, boy. That trail seems to git steeper all the while. If anything should happen to me—"

"Don't worry about it, Peter. I don't believe I shall be around long."
As Peter started to speak, he lifted a hand. "No, Peter, I feel it. And
just as well. I am tired, you know? I've loved these mountains, loved
them so much. And Johannes? He's meant a lot to me.

"We talked, you know? With the books, I mean. If there was one he
liked especially, he'd sort of pull it out from the rest.

"I never wanted him to see me. I just wanted to be a person, a
friend, like. If he saw me, he might think different of me. When I left a
book for him, I could think of him reading it, and I could wonder what
he thought of it. He could do the same with me."

"He's a nice boy. Got a good feelin' for country."

"When they burned the house, I thought it was the worst thing
could happen to me."

"I know how it is, how you worked on that floor."

"I wanted to build something, something that would last. In some of
those old books you found in the mission, it showed some mosaics.
That was what I wanted to do."

"Gittin' late, boy. Maybe you better go in an' lie down. Take a rest,
like."

Peter Burkin sat alone after Alfredo had gone inside. Be a blessing,
he told himself. Not that he wished harm to the boy, for he was all he
had left. Only, that trail was getting steeper and he was getting kind of
stiff in the joints and long in the tooth for the long rides.

Folks were beginning to notice, too. They'd seen him come and go,
and they were asking themselves why. Someday one of them would take
a notion to follow.

When he went inside, Alfredo was lying on his huge bed. He was
staring up at the ceiling of the cave.

"Fix you some grub," Peter said. "You just take it easy." He began
slicing potatoes into a pan, and got out the slab of bacon he had
brought with him. "Anything I can do for you, boy?"

"If you are in the San Bernardinos sometime, you can pack the best
of that stuff over here. I doubt if I shall go back."

Peter glanced at him. "That bad, eh?"

"Yes, Peter. It is an effort now. Once everything was so easy."

"But you're a young man!"

"Once, before we left Spain, my sister got an old woman she knew to
take us to a Moorish man. As he was a Moslem, nobody went to him,
but my sister heard that he knew more about medicine than anyone.

"She told him about me and he said he had known such cases, but they were rare. He told her what I could expect, so I have been ready for this." He smiled suddenly. "And I am only a young man to you, Peter. I have not been a young man for a long time."

"You ain't as old as me. My pappy was one o' them Kentucky riflemen who f't with Jackson in the Battle of New Orleans. I was born whilst he was away at war."

Alfredo closed his eyes and rested. It felt good just to lie quiet in the half-darkness. After all, he had had a good life. All this mountain country had been his for a time, and he had learned to live as the Cahuillas did. When occasionally he encroached on their groves he had always left something in payment to acknowledge their ownership and his trespass.

Often he would lie in some secure place above them and watch where they gathered their food and what plants they used. Peter Burkin and his mother—he thought of her so—had taught him even more.

Peter had told him that Zachary Verne and his son were returning, and they had agreed he must be stopped from going to Los Angeles.

He avoided Indian trails but moved through the woods or mountains parallel to them, trying not to use the same exact route twice. In his earlier years, when he had been very strong, he could travel incredible distances, and he had ventured far into the desert. Peter had taught him about gold and precious or semiprecious stones he might find. Over the years he had made several small finds of gold and several fine opals.

While still in his early years, and living in the Indian village, he had learned about Telmekesh, the place where the spirits of the dead lived, which was reached through a gate between two moving mountains; the good were permitted to pass, but the evil were crushed as the mountains slammed together, closing the gate.

He had become a skillful hunter, but knowing the sound of a rifle could be heard for some distance, he preferred more silent means. He used a bow and arrow occasionally but had come to prefer the sling. Due to his length of arm and extraordinary muscular power, it had become a formidable weapon in his hands, and one with which he could kill at a considerable distance.

"Come, boy. Set up an' eat. Cookin' for you is like cookin' for an army. Takes time." They sat opposite each other across the flat top of a chunk cut from a great stump.

"Meghan went to Francisco's woman? She will be all right, then."

"And you, Peter? What will you do?"

Peter looked into the fire; then he looked around at Alfredo. "I don't

know, boy. Get me an outfit an' hit the trail, I guess, but I won't be far
from you—"

"Peter?" Alfredo placed a great rubbery hand on Peter's. "I mean, af-
terwards? After that?"

There was a long silence. "Well, son, I hope there won't be no after-
wards. You an' that woman"—his voice grew husky—"well, I never had
nobody before. Not rightly, I didn't, although Zack Verne was always a
friend. You been part o' my thinkin' for so long—"

"Peter? Go to Johannes. Go and see him. I don't want you to be
alone, if it comes to that. Johannes will do big things, I believe, and he
will need a good man, and he likes you."

The big voice rumbled off into silence, and the two men sat quietly,
watching the fire.

Before the day broke and while Peter Burkin slept, Alfredo slipped
into his moccasins and a blanket coat and left the cave. He stood outside, stretching and looking carefully around. This cave was not unlike
his temporary home in the San Bernardinos, except that the cave was
larger and there were several inner rooms. It had two other entrances,
both of them some distance away. One was natural; the other he had
created himself when he discovered how close the cave came to the
outer wall of the mountain. Both entrances were carefully hidden.

Standing still, he looked around before moving. The chance that
someone might have approached the place was always a possibility, although he had never seen a white man atop the mountain, and the
Cahuilla avoided his area. Often there were deer feeding on a small
meadow nearby, and once he had seen a bear.

It was a grizzly, a huge beast that when standing on its hind legs tow-
ered even above him. The bear took a couple of steps toward him, and
he stood his ground, unworried. He knew the beast was nearsighted and
curious. When it found out what he was, it stood staring at him and he
at it; then it dropped to all fours, and apparently satisfied, walked away.
Yet, when some fifty yards off, it raised up on its hind legs again to look
back, shaking its big head as if mystified.

Now, on this morning, he walked back into the pines and followed a
vague trail, his own, to the edge of the mountain and to what he called
his chair. Actually, it was a ledge of rock, a quarter-circle of it, that
offered a convenient seat.

It was a place to which he often came, some eight thousand feet
above the valley below, looking down upon the canyons and the palms
that gathered near the hot springs and wound in a green, lovely ribbon

up a canyon to the southeast. The widest of the canyons was below him.

Here he could watch the sunrise and sunset over the valley and look far up the pass through which Romero, Williamson, and Ben Wilson had traveled. He also could look eastward into the desert, a vast expanse of white and pink that was constantly changing color under the rising or setting sun. By day, cloud shadows paraded majestically across that vast emptiness.

This was the place. When the end came, if he could make it, this was where he would come. He would sit here, as he sat now, and wait for the long silence.

He started to rise, but his muscles seemed without strength. He tried again and half-fell back to his seat. For a long time he sat still, staring out over the desert. He tried again, but there was no strength left in him. His head ached. . . . The headaches had been worse lately. He sat still, his eyes closed. Slowly, then, he opened them and watched an eagle riding the hot air rising from the desert, soaring out there on magic wings, soaring, soaring. . . . For a moment he lost the eagle, his vision misting over.

He lifted a huge hand and stared at it, slowly closing the fingers. It fell back to his lap. He looked again, trying to find the eagle. It was there, tilting its marvelous wings against the sky.

He tried again to rise, but this time there was no response whatever. He relaxed slowly, sitting very still, his big hands resting on his massive knees.

"Now?" he whispered. "Is it *now*?" And then, more softly still, "Why not now?"

59

Francisco sat on the sandbank watching me. "It was spoken that you had come. Your house is gone, so I knew you would be here, in our old place." He glanced around. "Nothing has changed."

"Not here," I agreed. Then I looked at him, smiling a little. "You eat well, Francisco. There is more behind your belt than when we met."

He shrugged. "I have a woman. She is a good woman and she fears that I shall eat too little. Yet I can still run, and wrestle."

"You were always good. Sometimes you beat me."

He studied the breadth of my shoulders and shook his head. "No more, I think. You have grown strong."

"I have enemies," I agreed.

"You have a woman?" he asked mildly, flicking a stick at the sand.

"No," I said, "but there is one of whom I think."

He got to his feet and stretched, whipping the sand from his hat, which he had lying beside him. "She waits for you," he said, "and talks to my woman."

Surprised, I got to my feet and went for the black stallion. *"Meghan?* Here?"

"She looks for you. She fears you will not come back to her." Then he added as we walked along, "She has had much trouble, amigo. She speaks of this to my woman, and she to me." He glanced at me. "She killed one man. Shot him."

"Meghan? I can't believe it."

Francisco shrugged. "Who knows what iron is in the heart of a woman? She escaped and they followed." He paused, looking across at the clustering palms. "The big one, He Who Walks the Night . . . he found her and left her close to us. She rode on in alone."

"The big one? Tahquitz?"

He shrugged. "It is a name. No doubt he has another. Your woman says he is Alfredo."

So . . . Alfredo. It all was falling together at last.

Meghan came quickly to her feet as I came up to the fire. For a moment she simply stared; then she ran to me, and it was natural that I should take her in my arms.

"I think we should go home, honey," I said. It was the first time I had called anyone such a name, and I was astonished at myself, but she accepted the term without question. Who knows about women?

We talked, and we ate the food Francisco's woman brought to us, but when I went to my horse again, it was saddled and Francisco was there. He told me then what had happened with Meghan, and when he had finished he said, "So she killed one, and the Big One, he killed another. One is left, and he is the worst. He is Iglesias."

"So?"

"He has come far, amigo, to ride back for nothing. Do you ride carefully, then."

Meghan emerged, her clothing brushed and her hair rearranged. She was the girl I'd dreamed of, and more.

Francisco went for her horse. "You go too soon," he said. "It is long since we have talked."

"Remember the wild plums we used to find at that place on Snow Creek Trail?" I said. "It would be good to go there again."

He nodded, putting his hands on his hips. "You come back. You and your woman. We build a *kish* for you. You stay."

Meghan, when we were riding away, asked what a *kish* was. "A shelter . . . a house. Often around here it is built of palm fronds."

We rode on, talking only a little, happy to be together. Yet I remembered what Francisco had said about Iglesias and turned often to look back.

"There is an Indian village ahead," I said. "We will stop there. I know them. It is a place where Peter Burkin often stopped when he rode through."

"He will be an old man now?" she asked.

"I suppose so. I do not think much of ages. People are people. What does it matter how old or young they are? It is a category, and I do not like categories. It is a sort of pigeonhole or a label. But it would be good to see Peter."

*　　*　　*

Iglesias was a frightened man. It was not only his horse that had been scared. He had seen the huge man loom up before him and he had seen the casual whip of the great hand that flipped Biscal off into the gorge. When he finally got his horse stopped, he was far up Burns Canyon, so he kept going, camping that night in Round Valley under the looming peak of Tip Top Mountain.

When morning came, he fixed a small breakfast and considered. Maybe he had been dreaming. It was fantastic. There could be no such creature as he believed he had seen.

But that girl! She was real, vital, beautiful. In all his life he had seen nothing like her hair of red-gold, her slim, lovely body. He wet his lips with his tongue and swore. To have such a one and let her get away? He had to be stupid.

Yet . . . her home was in Los Angeles, and she would be going back. To go back meant she had to go through San Gorgonio Pass. If he were to take the Ciénaga Seca Trail to Big Meadows, he could go up South Fork and cross over to the Falls Creek Trail. He had done it once, with several others, to escape some ranchers who were pursuing them.

He might get down into the pass and by discreet questioning discover whether the girl had gone past. It would not be easy, but he planned to ride into Los Angeles anyway.

He allowed his horse to graze a bit longer while he thought out the way. He camped that night in Ciénaga Seca. Once, on the following morning as he was riding into Big Meadows, he looked back and thought he caught some movement. Deer, probably. There were a lot of them around. Yet before turning up South Fork, he looked back again.

Nothing. . . .

A mile up the canyon, he camped. The wind off the peak was cold. Perhaps he was a fool. What did one woman matter? But such a woman!

He drew his serape around him and thought about her as he stared into the fire. Somebody would be with her. One man, no doubt. Wait for the right moment and shoot him down.

Stopping for a drink near Dollar Lake, he was getting into the saddle again when his horse's head jerked up, ears pricked. Although Iglesias watched his back trail for the next few miles, he saw nothing.

Tomorrow he would be in the pass. Tonight he would rest well. He checked his rifle. Tomorrow, one shot for him, one for the horse.

Of course, there might be more than one man with her, and that would complicate matters. Yet . . . he had done it before.

*   *   *

Before his eyes opened he heard the fire crackle and was immediately alert. His fire should be down to mere coals, and a fire does not crackle unless with fresh fuel. . . . He opened his eyes.

A man was squatting on his haunches beside the fire, roasting a strip of meat over the flames.

He was not a tall man, but was enormously thick and strong. Iglesias could see the powerful muscles in his shoulders and arms, and the thick thighs that bulged the material of his pants.

Slowly, warily, Iglesias turned over and sat up. The man smiled at him. "You sleep soundly," the man said. An accent, but not Spanish, not German . . .

"In your business it does not be good to sleep too soundly."

Iglesias was wary, but his pistol was under his jacket on the ground near him. His knife was there also. "And what is my business?" Iglesias asked.

"You are a thief," the stranger said. "Occasionally a murderer. And you attack women," he added.

"I could kill you for that," Iglesias said.

"You mean you would like to kill me for that." The man looked into Iglesias' eyes and smiled. "But you could not kill me, you could not kill me at all."

The man took the piece of meat in his fingers, and Iglesias knew it was hot, but the man did not wince. If it burned, he showed no sign of pain.

Casually Iglesias let his hand drop to the jacket, and the stranger smiled again, tearing off a small bit of the meat with his teeth. "Do not look for the pistol. It is gone.

"So is the knife. I took it away while you slept." The man smiled again. "My rifle is on my horse, but I shall not need it, either."

"What is all this talk? Who are you?"

"If you had gone back where you came from, you might have lived," the stranger said, "but you decided to try to find the young lady again. That was when I knew you must die."

"What are you talking about? Are you loco?"

"You do not learn. She escaped from you, and you followed. You left one of your friends—"

"I have no friends!"

"Naturally not. One of your companions, then. You left him dead and unburied. Then you almost came up to her, when your other companion was killed."

"Who are you?"

"Who? It does not matter, really, but I am Yacub Khan. A friend of the young lady and her father. A friend, also, I believe, of the young man—Johannes Verne." He smiled again. "But no friend of yours."

Iglesias was thinking. This man did not seem to be armed, yet he was obviously very strong. To fight him was out of the question. Yet, a stick, a stone . . . What would the man do if he simply got up and walked to his horse?

He got up, and the man continued to eat. Iglesias stared at him, uncertain what to expect. "You talk too much!" he said. "I shall leave."

"Look around you. Take a good, careful look. I want you to see this place. Really *see* it. Lovely, is it not? The sunshine on the water? The leaves rustling, the—"

Iglesias stooped suddenly and picked up a thick stick. The man simply looked at him, finished what he was eating, and stood up.

"Look around you," he said again. "Even one so evil as you can appreciate beauty. I want you to look, because it is the last thing you will ever see."

"You're crazy!" Iglesias began to back toward his horse.

He sensed rather than saw movement. He lifted his stick and felt the stranger's hand grasp his shirtfront. Iglesias struck down with the stick, but his hand was at an awkward angle and he could not use it with force. Yacub Khan was right against his body. A hand moved up; he felt the shock of the blow, and something within him burst.

Yacub Khan held his grip, looking into the panic-stricken eyes. "If you had gone the other way, you might have lived," he said, and dropped him.

Walking across to Iglesias' horse, he stripped off its gear and turned it loose. Then he went to his own horse and mounted.

A valley opened to the westward, a widening valley with a creek in the bottom. Turning his horse, he followed it. No doubt it would emerge in the pass or just beyond it. Anyway, the direction was right.

Iglesias lay on the grass, trying to catch his breath. It would not come, but blood did. It came up from his mouth and ran down the side of his face and neck and to the pine needles.

60

It was quiet in the large room. Don Isidro sat in his cowhide chair, staring out across the patio. Elena, working with her needle, glanced at him. He rarely talked to her, but now he did not talk to anyone.

"I shall return to Spain," he said suddenly.

"Why not?"

"And you?"

"I shall stay. I have friends here. I like it."

A woman appeared in the doorway and stood waiting. Elena looked up. "Yes?"

"There is word. The Señorita Laurel is with Señor Verne. They are coming home."

"That is good news indeed." Elena never asked how they knew, for the word came by devious means, one person to another, and often with such swiftness it was hard to believe.

The woman still stood there, and Elena asked, "There is more?"

"*Sí, señora.* The Big One is dead."

She disappeared from the door, and for a long time there was silence in the room. At last Don Isidro spoke. "Did she mean Alfredo?"

"Yes."

"I wonder how they know? How could they know? I thought . . . I believed him dead long ago."

"The woman loved him." And then she added, raising her eyes to him, "They know everything, Isidro. They always know. There are no secrets in the great houses. We delude ourselves in believing otherwise."

He stared blindly out across the patio. All so useless! So foolish! Back there in the desert, when the boy said so bravely, "Good-bye, Grandpa!" I should have gathered him in my arms and taken him home. The thought faded and he leaned his head back against the chair.

After a few moments Elena arose, crossed the room, and covered him with a blanket.

She must send word to Miss Nesselrode, for she would be worried.

At the reading room Miss Nesselrode looked at the boxes of books newly arrived by ship. There were three, two from New York and one from London. Now was the time she needed Johannes. He had always enjoyed opening the boxes and putting the books on the shelves.

So much was happening. Ben Wilson and some others were putting in a power plant to light the city with gas. It would stand, she believed, opposite the Pico House. New streets were being laid out and some of the roads leading into the town were being improved, and they needed it.

The door opened and she looked up. It was Alexis Murchison. He hesitated just inside the door. He was, she thought absently, a remarkably handsome man.

"May I come in?" He spoke hesitantly.

"It seems you are already in. What can I do for you?"

"I just wanted to tell you that I have decided to remain. I mean, I am going to stay in California."

She put down her pen. "And what will you do here?"

"I shall work for a firm of commission and forwarding merchants. In fact," he added, "I shall be managing the business."

"You should do well. You speak Russian, and no doubt French as well. You will be dealing with a variety of shipmasters as well as local businessmen. Do you speak Spanish?"

"A little."

"You will find it an asset. Much of your business will always be done in Spanish." She took up her pen. "Well, this is news, indeed. Congratulations. I believe you have made a wise decision."

"Miss Nesselrode? I was wondering if I might call upon you?"

Her eyes were cool and appraising. "You are calling, Mr. Murchison. Please come again."

He hesitated, then turned and went out, closing the door behind him.

She stared at the door, frowning a little, then took up her pen again. After a moment, unable to coordinate her thoughts, she put down the pen. She got up and walked to the back to look in the mirror.

"You do need a new dress," she told herself irritably. "It has been months since you've done any shopping." She paused, thinking of it.

She would recruit Elena to go with her. Elena would be pleased. She got out too rarely.

Yet it was not Alexis Murchison of whom she was thinking, although he had been, oddly enough, responsible for her train of thought. There were others, and one who would be returning from the sea. And there would be, she was sure, Meghan's wedding to Johannes. She had made *her* mind up, whether they had or not.

The Flores Cantina, near Spanish Town on the trail from San Bernardino, was a place frequented by travelers. After the flood which had destroyed many houses and part of the town, this place had been built and had done a modest business. Who Flores had been, no one remembered. He had the idea and had started the work, and then disappeared into limbo, which in this case was probably Sonora.

It was a place shadowed by trees, with a hitching rail. There was an inner room where drinks were served, and meals also if the chef was in the mood. Outside there was a small patio with a few tables.

To one of these tables, seeking shade because the sun was high, came Don Federico. In his pocket was a letter from Don Isidro, recalling him from the hunt, but disowning him also. The letter was in his pocket; a burning anger was in his brain.

Seated in the shade, he ordered a bottle of tequila and a glass. There he was joined by Chato, so he ordered another glass. A few hours ago he would have not considered sitting with Chato; now his anger had made him less particular. And they shared a hatred.

At a nearby table sat two Anglos, both of them vaguely familiar. Fletcher had grown older and a bit heavier. He was known as a businessman who gambled. The business to which he devoted his time was buying horses, cattle, and other things, and he asked no questions as to their origin or previous owners.

Glancing at the two who had just entered, he asked his companion, "Know them?"

"Uh-huh. The one with the flat nose, that's Chato. Thief, murderer. He'll do whatever it takes, and they say he's a mean fighter."

"And the other?"

"Don Federico. You should know him."

"I do, but it has been some time, and I wished to be sure. By their looks I'd say things had gone wrong for them, very wrong."

Fletcher refilled his glass. Don Federico, it was said, had money, and no sooner did Fletcher come by such information than he began to try to discover ways in which he could get some of it. Preferably, all of it.

"Last I heard," Fletcher commented, "he was hiring men to guard water holes against Johannes Verne and offering big money to anybody who killed him."

"If I'd known there was money in it, I'd have killed him myself. I never did like him." He glanced over at Fletcher. "We went to school together. He used the name of Vickery then. He'd just come around the Horn from the East."

"He never came around the Horn," Fletcher said. "He and his pa were in the same wagon with me. Them an' that Nesselrode woman."

"She's one of the wealthiest women anywhere, or that's what I hear."

"She's done all right," Fletcher admitted grudgingly. "She's a smart woman, and tough." He told his companion about her killing the Indian on the way west.

"So he never come around the Horn after all! I figured him for a liar. I wonder if ol' Fraser ever knew?"

"He knew. He was in the wagon with us."

"What about that?" Rad Huber was angry. "That double-dealin' pen-pusher knew all the time!"

They sat silent, waiting for their food. There was silence at the other table, too. Fletcher glanced at Don Federico and then said, "He got away from you, did he?"

Don Federico's head snapped around, his eyes angry. "I do not know of what you speak," he said. "Nor do I know you, or wish to."

Fletcher was amused. "No reason why you should have known me before," he said, "but there is now. I want him dead as much as you do. Almost as much," he amended.

Actually, it was not true. Fletcher had never liked Johannes or his father; neither did he have any great animosity against them, but always alert for an idea that meant money, he had just the glimmerings of an idea.

"Come over an' join us," he invited. "I think we should talk. Might be to mutual advantage, if you get what I mean."

Federico hesitated, then shrugged and moved across to the other table, Chato following.

"Heard it said you were his heir," Fletcher suggested.

"I was. I am not so now." He took out the letter from Don Isidro and passed it over to Fletcher.

Fletcher studied it, then turned to Huber. "Rad? See if you can borrow a sheet of paper in there, will you? I want to show these gents something."

When he had the paper, he studied Don Isidro's note for a moment, and then wrote in a quick, flowing hand, an exact imitation of Don Isidro's writing:

> *I, Don Isidro, being of sound mind, do give and bequeath all my goods and chattels, as well as all lands and properties to my beloved heir, Don Federico.*

Then he signed an exact duplicate of Don Isidro's signature.

Federico stared, looked up at Fletcher, then stared again. The note and the signature were flawless. He, who had seen as much of Don Isidro's handwriting as anyone, could detect no difference.

"What do you want?" he demanded.

"Half," Fletcher replied.

"*Half!* You are insane!"

"Half is better than nothing. You get half, I get half. We are both rich men. Otherwise, you get nothing."

"There are two heirs closer than I."

"With this last will and testament, nobody is closer than you."

"Nevertheless, there are Tía Elena and Johannes."

"Two only? That is nothing."

"He comes up the trail now," Chato said. "He should be along within the hour. The good Johannes Verne and his bride-to-be, Meghan Laurel."

"Who?" Rad interrupted. "What do you mean, his *bride?*"

"It was a rumor I heard. There are no secrets. Everybody talks."

"They are coming up the trail now?" Fletcher asked. "Just two of them? Then there it is. The old woman, we can get anytime. Johannes is coming. It is a trail not much traveled at this hour. What are we waiting for?"

Don Federico stared at the paper in his hand. Here it was, all so easy, so simply done! He had thought all was lost. All he had wanted and worked for through the years . . . gone.

And now it was here. He thought quickly. Who knew Don Isidro's signature? Not over three or four people. Elena, of course, but she would be gone.

"You see," Fletcher said gently, "everybody knows Don Isidro has wanted his grandson dead, so why shouldn't the grandson want *him* dead?

"There'll be some shootin', and when folks come to investigate, they'll find the old boy dead, his sister dead, and Johannes Verne with a gun in his hand."

Don Federico studied the paper in his hand, but he was seeing Madrid, Paris, Rome, even London. As for fifty percent, half was better than nothing, but suppose, after the will was written, and after . . .

After all, Johannes had gone to school with Rad Huber, and he had come across the plains with Fletcher, so why should they not join him in an attack on Don Isidro?

Fletcher needed him, but he himself needed nobody. Once that will was drawn . . . And even with this one, written only as a demonstration . . . ?

"All right," he said, "they will be coming. We had best get out there."

"Meghan, too?" Rad objected. "Now, see here, I—"

"Of course. She must be killed, Rad. We can't have witnesses. Besides, she turned you down, didn't she?"

Don Federico folded the paper and put it in his pocket along with the letter from Don Isidro. Then he followed them out to their horses.

The patio tables were empty, and a girl from inside came to gather the glasses and the remains of their meal. When she had gathered the dishes, she wiped the table quickly and stooped for a couple of fragments of food that had dropped to the floor.

The girl came quickly through the darkened inner room, where a woman sat alone at a table in a corner. "Did you notice that heavyset man? In the dark suit? Whenever he comes here, if I'm not around, you be sure you get your money, do you hear? I know him, and I don't trust him."

"*Sí*, Señora Weber. I shall be careful."

"I came over the trail with him, María, and knew him for what he was."

"*Sí, señora.*"

"You're a good girl, María. When I sell this place and move to Los Angeles, I want you to come with me. I want to open up a place there. I think it's a coming town."

"*Sí, señora.* I would like to go."

Mrs. Weber walked to the door and looked down the road. It was almost time for the stage.

Odd that those four had left together and gone back down the trail.

Well, it was none of her business. And that was what she thought until she heard the shooting.

61

It was a warm, lazy afternoon. Our destination for the night was only a bit further along, and we were both tired.

"There's a place called Politana. I believe it's on what they call the Bandini Donation, a strip of land Juan Bandini, Lugo, and probably others had donated to some New Mexicans, good fighting men, to create a buffer between their ranches and raiding Indians." It had been rumored that some of those Indians might have been led by Peg-Leg Smith or old Bill Williams.

I turned in my saddle and glanced back, but the trail was empty. Yet, far back, I believed I saw dust hanging in the air. I removed the thong from my pistol.

"There are people there whom I know, and there's a cantina. I've heard it is kept by an Anglo, but I couldn't say for sure."

"I just want to rest, and I am hungry," Meghan said. "Besides, I want to get back before Father returns, and his ship is due in almost any day. If I am gone, he will be worried."

"We can get some fresh horses there and move along faster." I glanced back again. Yes, that was dust, and it was closer. More than one rider, and probably three or four.

Leading the way, I rode into a small stream, then drew up as our horses needed to drink. "Let them drink," I said. "They've earned it."

There was dust in front of us, too. "Meghan," I decided on the instant, "let's get off the trail. Somebody is coming!"

"But—" she protested.

"There!" A small bypass trail led into the trees. "That way! Quick!"

She spurred her horse and went up the bank and into a small copse, where she drew up. The bypass trail led on through the trees, to rejoin the main trail a hundred yards further on. Evidently it was used when the main was impassable for one reason or another.

"If anything happens, take that trail and ride hard for the cantina. It can't be more than a mile or two. Don't worry about me."

"I have a rifle now."

"Meghan . . . please! Don't argue. If trouble begins, walk your horse a short distance so they will not hear you, and then *go!*"

"Johannes, *I love you!*"

"And I love you, but let's live to enjoy it. Please! If I am worried about protecting you, I cannot protect myself nearly so well."

Reluctantly she rode along the bypass, and I rode back to where we had forded the stream. If Meghan could reach the cantina . . .

Riders were coming into view not fifty yards away. Standing back among the trees, they could not immediately see me, but I recognized each of them.

Don Federico, Chato, Rad Huber, and Fletcher . . .

"I'll be damned!" I said softly.

To try to turn away now would only reveal my presence. I could only hope they would miss seeing me. Careful to make no whisper of sound, I drew my rifle from its scabbard. My left side was toward them, my rifle across my saddle.

The black stallion stood very still, ears pricked, sensing trouble as a wild horse will.

Fletcher pulled up. "Why not wait here? They'll have to come this way, and they can't see us until they're right atop of us."

It was Chato who saw me. He was looking all around, and our eyes met and held. We both knew it was to be today. "I am not a boy now, Chato," I said, and I fired.

It was point-blank with a rifle at less than twenty yards, and I missed.

At the instant I spoke, Chato, the most experienced fighting man of the lot, instinctively jumped his horse, and the bullet intended for him hit Rad Huber and knocked him sidewise in the saddle, almost unseating him. His horse jumped, and Huber, wounded, fought for control.

Chato fired, as did Fletcher and Federico. A bullet burned my hand, and I dropped my rifle just as I got off a second shot.

Palming my six-shooter, I put two bullets into Federico.

Then suddenly the afternoon exploded with roaring guns and charging horses. Flashes stabbed the air, and there was a smell of gunpowder. The black stallion swung away, and I fired into Huber as he turned toward me, blood staining his shirt.

Fletcher was down, but other riders had come in, and all were shooting. Wheeling the stallion, I was in time to see Monte McCalla put a finishing shot into Fletcher as he tried to rise. As quickly as it had begun, it was over.

Besides McCalla I recognized Jacob Finney, Owen Hardin, and Yacub Khan. Two others were strangers; by their style, they were El Monte boys.

Thumbing cartridges into my pistol, I holstered it.

Hardin swung down, picked up my rifle, and handed it to me. "What's the matter?" he said, smiling. "Can't you keep out of trouble?"

"Where'd you come from?"

"Miss Nesselrode sent us to round up Meghan Laurel, and we were just tryin' to catch up when we ran into Khan here. He come down Mills Creek an' ran right into us.

"We were ridin' along enjoyin' the afternoon when we saw your dust up ahead, and when you topped a rise, we recognized you. Just about that time we saw four riders headin' into the creek bottom, so we used our spurs, an' all hell busted loose."

"Where is she?" Jacob looked around. "Where's the girl?"

"Gone along to the cantina," I said, and for the first time I looked down at the bodies.

There were but three: Rad Huber, Fletcher, and the don.

Chato? Chato was gone!

"*Meghan!*" I shouted, and I slapped spurs to that black stallion and took off with a lunge.

That cantina was only a little way ahead, and Chato . . . !

The others were behind me, running their horses. The clump of trees, the hitching rail, the patio with its tables . . .

I hit the ground running.

Chato was standing in the shade of a big oak on the edge of the patio. His gun was in his hand.

"Meghan?" I shouted.

"I do not fight women," he said. "I fight only men."

"I am a man," I said. I was fairly certain now that he had not harmed Meghan, so I could concentrate fully on the job I had to do.

Shadows fell on the cruel face, the flat nose, the old scars. "I should have killed you then, in spite of the old man. You were trouble. I could see it in your eyes, and you were but a baby."

"I am a man now," I said, and I shot above the stabbing flame from his gun.

He took a slow step back, and I shot again. The gun fell from his hand, and he grabbed for it, falling to his knees. He tried to get up then, and fell headlong, his hat rolling free.

"You should have died in the desert," he said.

"I am Johannes Verne," I said, "and I was not afraid."

ABOUT THE AUTHOR

Louis L'Amour, born Louis Dearborn L'Amour, is of French-Irish descent. Although Mr. L'Amour claims his writing began as a "spur-of-the-moment thing," prompted by friends who relished his verbal tales of the West, he comes by his talent honestly. A frontiersman by heritage (his grandfather was scalped by the Sioux), and a universal man by experience, Louis L'Amour lives the life of his fictional heroes. Since leaving his native Jamestown, North Dakota, at the age of fifteen, he's been a longshoreman, lumberjack, elephant handler, hay shocker, flume builder, fruit picker, and an officer on tank destroyers during World War II. And he's written four hundred short stories and over eighty books (including a volume of poetry).

Mr. L'Amour has lectured widely, traveled the West thoroughly, studied archaeology, compiled biographies of over one thousand Western gunfighters, and read prodigiously (his library holds more than two thousand volumes). And he's watched thirty-one of his westerns as movies. He's circled the world on a freighter, mined in the West, sailed a dhow on the Red Sea, been shipwrecked in the West Indies, and has been stranded in the Mojave Desert. He's won fifty-one of fifty-nine fights as a professional boxer and pinch-hit for Dorothy Kilgallen when she was on vacation from her column. Since 1816, thirty-three members of his family have been writers. And, he says, "I could sit in the middle of Sunset Boulevard and write with my typewriter on my knees; temperamental I am not."

Mr. L'Amour is re-creating an 1865 Western town, christened Shalaka, where the borders of Utah, Arizona, New Mexico, and Colorado meet. Historically authentic from whistle to well, when it is constructed, it will be a live, operating town, as well as a movie location and tourist attraction.

Mr. L'Amour now lives in Los Angeles with his wife Kathy and their two children, Beau and Angelique.

8 9 10 11 27 45 31